Praise for Hugo Charteris

Such is the wit and robust originality of Mr Charteris's style, not only in his descriptions of the local dignitaries and functions but in the Rabelaisian sophistry sizzling through his hero's mind, that one is tempted to overlook the savage Russian mood behind the story. As in his other books, Mr Charteris is a skilful conjuror who knows how to keep us guessing, and *The Lifeline* poses enough riddles to occupy intelligent readers for several happy hours.

Times Literary Supplement

Most successful comedies of the past decade have been featherweights. *The Lifeline* is one of a tiny minority that not only attempts true heavyweight comedy, but gets away with it magnificently. Everything about this book is big. Its leading character is colossal, the dialogue is twice life-size, there is enough detail to ornament a baroque cathedral…

Tulloch Traquhair is the start of the trouble, a vast bull of man recently sacked from a Robin Hood TV serial after a scandal involving Maid Marian. He settles in a tiny Highland town, takes over a derelict hotel and is determined to make money. The town waits on tenterhooks to find out what his game is, and so does the reader. I would hate to spoil one line of this glorious book.

Eastern Daily Press

How I enjoyed this book! It is written with rare skill and originality and it is full of situations of high comedy and a shrewd observation of human nature, set out with a mordant wit…I have read this book several times with delight and amusement and I shall always keep it by me, to go back to it when I want a little light relief!

Derbyshire Evening Telegraph

It explodes with gusto and zest. I enjoyed it vastly.

Books of the Month

Mr Charteris is a writer of assured skills [with] a sharp eye for character and situation, and a pretty sense of the ridiculous, so that he never fails to entertain…

John O'London's Weekly

"What Nelson's Column is to Trafalgar Square, the Distillery chimney is to Fluach, and there it was now like a big gun pointing straight at God...." Words [which] give some idea of the writer's wit and pungency. He has a splendid gift for characterisation and (for an Englishman) an unusually penetrating knowledge of Scotland and the Scots.

Edinburgh Evening Dispatch

The Lifeline is concerned with the predicament of the exuberant romantic, the cavalier of another age, stranded in an increasingly tame and conformist world. It is a good theme, fundamentally important yet rich in comic possibilities, and Mr Charteris, a witty, observant and imaginative writer, exploits it well. The narrative has pace, colour and tension...[providing] a wealth of material for the writer's very real comic talents. He captures quite brilliantly not only the glowering Scottish landscape but also the narrow, self-absorbed parochialism of small-town life. His characters, even the minor ones, are creatures of flesh and blood, superbly drawn in an astounding diversity of mood and temperament. He has, moreover, the rare ability to create genuinely comic characters without once toppling over into caricature. This talent is enough to distinguish him from the general run of British novelists.

Frank McGuinness, New Statesman

Providing many chuckles and several belly-laughs, this story of very free enterprise in a Highland hotel is a refreshingly mischievous satire on that tartan rural round which reaches its apogee at the local Games or the Unionist garden fete. Mr Charteris casts a disillusioned eye on many cherished myths and delights, too, in the absurd. But he sees his characters clear and true, and his rich comedy never slips into farce.

Glasgow Herald

This is a genuinely funny book, and [...] Tulloch's engaging ways and highly developed sense of fantasy, not to mention Hugo Charteris's refreshingly unhackneyed humorous writing, [...] undoubtedly carry the day.

The Tablet

The Lifeline is written with a consistently brilliant flow from the first page to the last. [Mr Charteris] has one glorious gift: he is like nobody else, he is *sui generis*. The remote Highland township of Fluach is his own demesne and we glory in his baronial rights. A Falstaffian fake has never been taken so elaborately to pieces. The fantastic false persona of Tulloch Traquhair may not have demanded such a concentration of ironic analysis but it is all so grotesquely funny that one does not mind.

Observer

In Tulloch Traquhair Mr Charteris has drawn a most splendidly outsize figure, and amiable fraud in the best Falstaffian tradition, a cross (if you can imagine such a thing) between Mr James Robertson Justice and Mr Burl Ives, either of whom ought to jump at the chance to portray such a juicy character on the widest screen available. But what no screenplay could ever convey is the rich fertility of Mr Charteris's language, his deep vein of serio-comic inventiveness, the rich, semi-lunar landscape of his inimitable fantasy.

The Bookman

The Lifeline is an exhilarating, comic, rough-and-tumble of a novel which stands quite on its own, exuberantly idiosyncratic. It eludes classification by mercurial changes in shape and substance so that it is, equally, satire, high comedy, farce, adventure story, novel of character and tract for the times. Its most consistent qualities are those of Rabelaisian caricature and romantic poetry. An attempt to define it intellectually is like trying to take a photograph of the sea. You achieve a likeness but the essential quality of movement and change cannot be caught.

... The story bowls along with an apparent inconsequence which covers a carefully developed interplay of character and events. It is full of brilliance in its style, in its understanding of personality, in its use of comedy and in its exploration of ideas.

World of Books, BBC

Nicely poised between uproarious farce and pure comedy with more serious matters intervening, this novel is also remarkable for its supporting cast of villagers, humble and proud, and for its overhauling of the novelistic vocabulary.

Daily Telegraph

In *The Lifeline*, Hugo Charteris has written a racy, hugely amusing, slyly unmoral novel about low life in the Highlands.

Manchester Evening News

A vastly entertaining novel.

Scotsman

The Lifeline is good clean fun of the very highest order.

Northern Times, Golspie

The Lifeline shows Mr Hugo Charteris giving a performance of brilliant virtuosity. It is all great fun but it is not simple fun. Apart from his joyous indulgence in his hero's "grandiloquence and circuitous speech" the author is out to discover what is behind the public persona of a man who might have written high poetry and looted continents but is now a shadow on a very small screen. Those who follow him will be rewarded by the added dimension; those who do not want to sound depth charges can just take the book as it is and enjoy the sardonic portraits of local worthies and the continuous flow of riotous incident, all superbly described.

Derbyshire Echo and *Doncaster Gazette*

Uses words in an adventurous, utterly original way.

Francis Wyndham, London Magazine

Mr Charteris does write extraordinarily well […] he achieves a remarkable combination of glitter and accuracy. This is a highly entertaining novel.

Bernard Bergonzi, The Spectator

THE LIFELINE

by the same author

A Share of the World (1953)
Marching with April (1956)
The Tide is Right (abandoned 1957, published 1991)
Picnic at Porokorro (1958)
The Lifeline (1961)
Pictures on the Wall (1963)
The River-Watcher (1965)
The Coat (1966)
The Indian Summer of Gabriel Murray (1968)

THE LIFELINE

by

HUGO CHARTERIS

introduced by

DAVID BENEDICTUS

SANDNESS
MICHAEL WALMER
2021

The Lifeline first published 1961
© The Estate of Hugo Charteris

Introduction first published in this edition
© David Benedictus 2021

Published by

Michael Walmer
North House
Melby
Sandness
Shetland, ZE2 9PL

ISBN 978-0-6489204-6-5 paperback

INTRODUCTION

To get the boring stuff out of the way first: Hugo Charteris (1922-1970) is not to be confused with Leslie Charteris, the author of the 'Saint' books. Hugo published nine novels, and sold some seventeen TV screenplays. Indeed, he is not to be confused with anyone, being a writer of unique talents and blessed with such striking good looks that it is usually the first thing that people remember about him. His family were Scottish aristocrats, and he was the third grandson of the 11th Earl of Wemyss. He had two distinguished brothers-in-law: the Earl of Rothermere, who owned the *Daily Mail* and who employed Hugo as his correspondent in Paris, and Ian Fleming. Hugo was educated at Eton and Trinity College, Oxford, and served in the Scots Guards during the second world war, winning the MC. He lived most of his life in Scotland but is buried in Skipworth, Yorkshire, where his wife, Virginia, survived him by 42 years. The couple had five children, the eldest boy dying in a drowning accident.

The English-speaking world is tripartite, those who have heard of Hugo Charteris, those who have not, and those who confuse him with Leslie. Those who have not heard of him could do a good deal worse than introduce themselves to his talents by reading this fourth of his novels which (as soon as you are done with this tiresome introduction) awaits you on the next 300 and something delightful pages, not as compelling perhaps as the James Bond thrillers, but a good deal more sophisticated.

The three great qualities of Hugo's fiction are the strength of the characterisation (plenty of whimsical humour at the expense of the Scots), the elaborate set pieces (a hunt ball, a highland games, and a fair quota of naughtiness in and around two hotels in Fluach), and a literary style as unique as it is mischievous.

The principal character is Tulloch Traquhair, a giant of a man with a ginger beard, recently retired from playing character roles (always the same character) on television. Should "they" ever decide to film *The Lifeline* there will be few problems for the casting agency, now that James Robertson Justice and Eddie Kulukundis, 20-stone philanthropist, have sadly left the way clear for Brian Blessed, remembered by just a diminishing minority as Fancy Smith in *Z-Cars,* and more recently as the only man to walk to the magnetic north pole, and the only man almost to climb to the top of Mount Everest three times – without oxygen.

Tulloch, whose bank balance is more than a little stretched, determines to renovate and reopen the Strathire Arms in Fluach, with the aid of his administrator, Meldrum, known to Tulloch as Reoraidgh, posing another problem for the type-setters. Tulloch has sentimental feelings for Meldrum, as well as for the Teddy Boy whom he selects as his final choice to be Fluach's beauty queen. The authorial comment here runs thus:

> Indeed the fact that he enjoyed warm feelings for people of the same sex, for Communists and people in prison directly underlined him as the fine contemporary ideal of the modern British citizen and helped him to become the object of a certain snobbery.

Hugo's literary style incorporates an astonishing gift for vivid and improbable gymnastics with metaphors and similes, along with the elegant funambulism of his adverbs and adjectives, and the pyrotechnics suitable to a writer with Eton and Oxford in his CV (I should know), plus the vocabulary of a lexicographer. A couple of examples: at a funeral Tulloch – never one to conceal his emotions – folds his hands in front of his sporran and weeps until his face looks "like a lettuce after a thunderstorm"; a bicycle race (an event in the Cullan Games) will be ruined if the Canadian Prime Minister (don't ask!) fails to show – if so, the unfortunate spectators are in for "three heats of the ten-mile bicycle race round the 400-yard perimeter of the arena, 96 minutes of eleven youths going round and round and round with cheese-coloured thighs pumping slowly like something in the window of a watchmakers".

Relish for language of this calibre is not easily found in today's gloomy best-seller lists. They give prizes for all sorts of things nowadays but chuckleworthiness goes by unnoticed. Read Hugo Charteris and see if you would award his fiction the Chuckle Brothers Trophy. I am sure I would. All this and Brian Blessed too. Bring it on!

DAVID BENEDICTUS

Hove, February 2021.

To my father

"Blessed are the forgetful, for they get the better even of their blunders."

"One must separate from anything that forces one to repeat 'no' again and again."

Nietzsche

I

WHENEVER THE TRAIN stopped a voice could be heard by all the passengers. Being short and Highland the train stopped often, and because the January day was unseasonably mild and many carriage windows open the few travellers got a clear impression of this quite unusual voice. Was it a wireless? A portable? There were no crackles but it did keep on like a programme, providing a steady background to the occasional bleat of a ram, the familiar creaking crump of mail baskets going on to trolleys, and to the valedictions and uneasy platform platitudes of other much smaller voices. Indeed, the latter sometimes broke off as though diverted if not actually quenched by that one monopolising, resonant male bass.

At Upper Kintullochy in particular the cutting provided an amplifier and the breeze a vehicle for the booming monologue. When the porter-stationmaster called " Are ye right, Tam ? " holding up his green flag, he was smiling as though conscious of interrupting and the engine itself seemed to reply with a competitive " toot." Then the train wheezed forward again.

Two children were the first to give in. After a careful approach-march through the van they reached the carriage that was first class at one end. Here the boy went ahead and soon beckoned his sister forward, at the same time waving her in to the side as though the alternative would be an arrow through the collar bone. By then he was inching an eye round the edge of woodwork. Suddenly he paused, paralysed, and urged her on quicker, as though she were missing something that couldn't last.

The voice was quite close now—louder than any voice the

The Lifeline

children had ever heard, and there was its owner, with his back turned fetching something from the rack—a man built in proportion to the noise he had been making. For not only was the rack about level with his mouth, but his body seemed to fill the whole compartment. Whether he had something inside his kilt as well as himself they could not tell but his legs were nothing but himself for you could see what the flesh was like at the bare knee—a natural preliminary to the girth of the calf at its fullest point. The boy's heart missed a beat while he imagined a football hissing parallel to the ground, not a foot high, into the far corner or perhaps simply exploding when kicked or knocking the goalkeeper's head off. Space cartoons of torsos that would hardly fit into armour and advertisements for muscle-building became real before the young male's astonished eyes, and the sister looked suddenly dreamy because the man had turned and now she knew who he was by his beard and bright eye: God.

Adults, farther away, in neighbouring carriages, could hear the voice even when the train was on the move; sometimes they lost the deep and rich timbre when it merged with the vibration of the carriage bodywork. And once they heard a laugh like that of a villain in melodrama, *heugh heugh heugh* . . . a sort of *spoken* laugh.

In time one or two made spurious journeys down the corridor. One saw a jolly giant in a kilt and beard holding forth with his hands out, another a grave, unconvivial, colossal official fingering and discussing the pages of a report, face pinched up in hair-splitting concentration, and a third, during a mysterious lull, saw an old woman with a beard and her belly and bosom stuffed five times larger than life with cushions fit for a pantomime, shamelessly asleep, displaying stockings, a nervous tic, and a hole in one sole. But it was all the same person.

At Buie Halt a prize ram appeared on the platform steered rather erratically by a young girl. At once the rich bass voice broke out with particular gusto as though touched on the very

The Lifeline

quick of interest by each, if not the combination, of the two creatures.

People exchanged glances. Old weathered shepherds with faces like Punch, hollowed cheeks and pinched lips that scorned dentures eased their sere mouths into ironic smiles. " By God ! " said one. Yet many of them suffered curiosity against their will. After all, what could there be to say at Buie Halt at such length if it wasn't a speech he was making ?

The vague but compelling lure which attracts knots and finally crowds to lonely lunatics in Hyde Park, here and now obliged people to put down newspapers they had already read and stare out of the window at the ram and the girl as though there must be an explanation, which escaped them. Was the man drunk ? When you caught a word by itself he sounded like a minister, but the overall drone was of a drunk.

Normally a journey on that line is too slow even for people who enjoy sitting still and doing nothing in fine scenery. There is something dreamlike in the long pauses neither in nor out of a station, about motionless incarceration, behind glass, half-way up a mountain, on a lovely day. Destinations come into sight, across strips of sea, and then recede before appearing again, an hour later, while seagulls took short-cuts. No wonder the train is nearly always empty except for a few railwaymen, school-children and civil servants.

At first the voice had made a difference, redeemed the long unwinding familiarity of the trail. But after seventy miles at an average speed of fifteen miles per hour it got mixed up with the noise of the wheels, was disregarded.

Upper Kintullochy, Rossiemurchat, Gardale, Farg, Balblair, and now Fluach—a little seaside town of two thousand inhabitants containing the County Offices, the Secondary Modern School, the Distillery, four or five hotels for " the Season," a harbour for a hundred boats, (containing one,) and the office of the *Northern Trumpet*.

What Nelson's column is to Trafalgar Square, the Distillery chimney is to Fluach, and there it was now like a big gun

9

The Lifeline

pointing straight at God and, behind it in the distance, like an illustration to a fairytale, the turrets and spires of Strathire Castle peeping through a breach in rock and forest.

Long rows of eyes, dazed by the slowness and familiarity of the passing scene, were gazing phlegmatically at the deserted platform—when suddenly it became occupied by the owner of the Voice—hailing a porter.

His dress at that date in the 1950s was the uniform of such rare individuals as lairds, officials of the Scottish Tourist Board or Community Drama, of Scottish Nationalists and of Lallans poets. The combination of ginger beard and worn, bulging brief-case suggested the further possibility that he was an M.P., a Liberal politician and Highland "character" just beginning a two-day tour of his constituency—islands and isolated hamlets, some historical backwater, where Liberals were different, got in and threw stones to accelerate the passing of the Reform Bill. But even this possibility was not the reason for the stares which the big man drew. The stares were for his size and imperial face, and for the literary, concerned way in which he held his book, with one fat finger still inserted where he had left off.

And then for some people there was something vaguely familiar about him. Hadn't they seen him before?

Surely. . . . Yes, no, yes, surely that was, wasn't it, the man who played Little John in Robin Hood ? When he looked at the starers their eyes pretended to read the poster behind him saying, " Come to Nottingham for your holidays," with a picture, strangely enough of Robin Hood himself on it, and then the posters for Bwylth and Southend and a manifesto on the increase of fares. But all eyes soon came back to him, for if it wasn't himself it was his twin, though the idea of two such men, the one identical with the other, was laughable.

On the other hand, if it *was* the actor—Tulloch Traquhair (several people had got it now)—what on earth was he doing up here ? And why did he look as though he were dressed for a film of the '45 ?

Of course . . . a few now remembered what it had said in

The Lifeline

the *Express* and *Mirror* yesterday: " From £5000 to the dole."
But why . . .?

Why this, why that? Was it muscle, was it fat? Why here, why not there? Why a Red MacPherson tartan? Where was Zoë Prin, Maid Maryon with whom his name had been linked? . . .

All these questions hovered about the isolated figure on the platform.

Occasionally a furtive, helpless unco-ordinated movement of the victim's small eyes—away from the long gallery of starers—suggested he was conscious of this insistence, this huge ocular hunger just as he might have been conscious of midges, or confetti.

2

CRAIGLEA FARMHOUSE stands four miles north of Fluach in a clump of wind-warped fir and sycamore which huddle round it like a band of heroes round a standard in ancient battle. To-night fairy lanterns dangled unexpectedly among the frosted, stunted, shattered branches and the cheerless eastern prospect of three flooded fields, a railway embankment and the derelict O.P. in the dunes, was hinted by a full moon.

Westwards, inland, the dark straight outline of byres and barns rose against the night sky and behind them, darker still, the baleful edge of that deserted, towering interior, home of grouse, deer, sheep, salmon and an occasional shepherd—the ten-shillings-an-acre country which makes up seven-eighths of Strathireshire.

The Wotherspoon windows shone warmly like scarfed lamps and from behind them came the steady garrulity of a drink party.

There are still a few ceilidhs in the hills and on the west coast but in the population centres of the east, congregational leisure, in remote Strathireshire, is organised in the form of clubs—bridge, drama, W.R.I., country dancing. Should people—particularly the more prosperous or professional classes—come together without organisation, a sort of twilight sleep has to be induced by means of alcohol before inter-communication, let alone pleasure, becomes remotely possible.

In fact, only one or two families, apart from the usually absent landowners and lodge-folk, have the money, space or inclination to take this sort of risk. The Wotherspoons took it with a sort of symbolic extremism, as though the only answer

The Lifeline

to life, particularly resident, Puritan middle-bracket Strathireshire life, was to get everyone drunk.

To this end, it was said, they doctored the drinks, which was why the Chief Constable, the Lord Lieutenant and the Adjutant of the Seaforth T.A. had given up attending their parties.

The Wotherspoon " bar " was indistinguishable from several commercial " private " ones in Chelsea. Every detail of the decoration was inspired by a marine motif. The very counter was a sort of jetty with bosses at regular intervals for securing boats. Fishes swam overhead and the murals, executed by Nadia Wotherspoon, showed the thwarted relationships of octopuses, mermaids, crabs and divers.

Although other rooms had been got ready for the party and equipped with drink, everyone had congregated in the bar as though a good general jostle of flesh against flesh might help the drink do its job and limit conversation to its only value—a friendly noise. To-night's party was a little bit different from usual because everyone, while pretending to concentrate on each other, was in fact half-absorbed by the extraordinary booming which like an organ's diapason, gave the general chatter a sort of regular groundwork and base. Eyes kept compassing round to the voice's face which was not only new in Strathireshire—an event in itself—but also familiar, yes, on television, in newsprint and now in yesterday's *Express* headline: *Little John Traquhair—from £5000 to the dole.*

In mid-sentence, looking away from him, people whispered " Tulloch Traquhair " and smiled as though he were partly in their power. Only when they had resumed conversation did they steal a glance, back, straight in the big man's direction as though they had just taken something out of his pocket, without his knowing.

Royalty and celebrities, familiar in photographs, often amaze in the flesh by being quite unnaturally small. Traquhair astounded people for an opposite reason: having imagined his size to be a trick of camera angles, they found him bigger in fact than on the screen. Perhaps, after all, the horse he had

The Lifeline

carried in the serial last year had been a real one? This and many other secrets seemed to lie concealed under the dense beard and tiny mercurial eyes, eyes which were not so much like those of a celebrated giant as of a mouse looking for cheese, hungering for cheese while actually living inside a cheese factory. Could such eyes really be colleagues of that confident, resonant brass voice, with its full melodious range, of that stature which very properly remained stationary, letting others always come to it rather than displacing itself in the direction of others, and of that laugh which, though spoken, yet seemed genially acquainted with the quite unmentionable inclinations of everyone present so that Mrs. J. S. Mackay, the contractor's wife, after staring at him sideways, actually blushed when she heard it. "For goodness' sake!" She turned, giggled and looked with a touch of challenge at her work-obsessed husband as though this provocative sound were some kind of stick with which she would beat him if he didn't take a bit more notice of her.

"He's talking about bulls again," said Mrs. MacFarlane, the banker's wife.

At first there had been no apparent reason for Traquhair to talk so much about bulls to the Marxist Director of Education even though the man was wearing a Regency waistcoat with chased buttons and might conceivably have been a "hobby-farmer" or even some agricultural expert from "the Tech."; still less reason to discuss bulls with Miss Purdy, a squat woman with a flushed face, tartan deerstalker and a voice as loud as his own who had met every remark he made about bulls with information about her nephew who was going to Rugby next term. But now that Traquhair was talking to Henry Wotherspoon, a farmer, it was not so surprising, particularly as Wotherspoon had found a bull on the buckle of Traquhair's belt.

"With Highland cattle," Henry said, peering at it. "It's often quite difficult to tell the difference between a bull and a cow."

Traquhair leaned over to look at the ironwork on his navel,

The Lifeline

a movement which precipitated an obscuring crease just above where he wanted to see.

"It's his belt," people whispered, "there's a bull on his belt."

"My dear Henry..." came the great voice like Paul Robeson imitating a duke. "My dear Henry, you can take it from me that that is a bull."

People noticed that he had affected a tone of indifference, but it was not a success. He sounded piqued.

But why should he be piqued? Did he regard himself as some sort of bull? Did he wish people to believe that *everything* about him was in proportion? The proof, if required, seemed handy. His kilt came to his knee-caps which, given his girth, made it look short as a skater's skirt, and it was safe to assume that anyone so aggressively Highland would wear nothing underneath. Mrs. J. S. Mackay blushed again: his name, his conversation, his laugh and now the idea of him being in proportion all over. "For goodness' sake," she said, raised a hand to one of her scorching cheeks and turned away as though from a furnace.

Traquhair's buckle was scarcely lower than the level of Henry Wotherspoon's chin. But Henry was shortsighted as well as small. In the present emergency he was standing, as so often, unnaturally straight, in fact leaning over backwards slightly as though to gain a vantage point for his eyes. In one hand he held a bottle with which he had been filling people's glasses. When he spoke his voice had the peculiarly formal, dried-up quality of an unconfident schoolmaster addressing a class of C. stream lags. Perhaps this dignity was the more conspicuous, to those who knew his family, since he alone of nine brothers and sisters spoke without a trace of Scottish accent. He had won scholarships, gone on for a bit, and then finally come back—with an heiress, Nadia—formerly de la Joséph. He had come back from the big world to Fluach, to inherit an aunt's farm.

Although he had only met Tulloch Traquhair twice, each time at Scotch Corner, in 1952 and 1954, he addressed him with

The Lifeline

familiarity and now, turning to introduce him to the wife of the water engineer said, "Tulloch—do you know Mrs. Hailes?—Mr. Traquhair."

"I have not had that pleasure," said Traquhair, taking the hand of the stranger who had in fact more or less accosted him, having taken up a conversational position at his elbow.

Wotherspoon took this opportunity of resuming his duties as host. Spout poised, he moved from group to group, receiving whispered inquiries with a noncommittal smile and answering in a tone suited to discussion of the weather.

"I know, jolly bad luck, wasn't it? They didn't give a reason, did they? Yes—he's going to live up here."

"Farm?"

"Actually, I don't know." Henry moved on, spout proffered, averting his eyes, admitting the lie with a smile. "Better ask him."

"It can't be his real name."

"Better ask him."

Rumour, unsourced, got round that the big newcomer had been on the Everest expedition, played Macbeth at Stratford, been twice married; that he had been an all-in wrestler, a politician, an Aldermaston marcher; that he had bred much and been a Jap P.O.W.

Tulloch Traquhair's hidden lips, were now, for the second time, bent over Nadia's hand and his voice murmuring like a bumble-bee in a drum.

"Dear neighbour."

"Are you in yet?" Nadia said dryly.

"Fractionally. Fractionally. My other, my much worse half, is at work as we speak."

"Why didn't you bring him?"

"You don't know what you're saying, dear Nadia!"

Nadia Wotherspoon never made up. Her pale, changeless face surmounted her black cotton dress with the chilling indifference of a ghost concerned with a previous century. She had several children who lived elsewhere, with the cattleman's

The Lifeline

wife, cousins, schools and on the loose. She was happiest here under the dartboard, in the bar, in front of a Dewars glass mat and a Capstan ashtray. It was somehow public without The Public—gave the best of both worlds. Here where Henry's father had kept guns, roll-top desk, black iron boxes, deeds and an etching of Moses, she sat on a steel stool and absorbed liquor as though a secret tube conveyed it straight from the glass to some gutter outside where the rain washed it away. Sometimes about two a.m. she would commit herself to an opinion which suggested that, unknown to all, she had been making progress in the direction of anarchy. But did she ever leave it? Rumour had it she dragged Henry down the stairs by the hair and made him give her practice with a revolver in the garden at night. He had to shout and then she tried to get him.

How was anyone to know if all the revolver nonsense was true? She was half-French and an heiress, so people in Fluach thought it might be. After all, they said, "What is there for her to do up here?"

Officially she made table mats and bred Boxers.

Henry moved through the steadily drinking throng as though things were shaping well. In the war he had been adjutant of a Cameronian battalion and outwardly ever since, had seemed to cling to that identity, as though it at least had been unambiguous.

"Brian—your glass is empty."

The proprietor of the Seaforth Arms, Brian Creevie had the sloe-black soft eyes of some Highland girls. His mouth, too, had a disturbingly sensitive line. His rather beautiful face suggested a Dominican novice by El Greco—or an image in a slightly asymmetrical teaspoon. He always spoke with breathy urgency as though every subject in the world was a sort of loose snake which might bite if he didn't lock it up immediately, once and for all, where it belonged, in his own point of view. When others spoke he turned away while his lips parted in a smile of tolerance and his eyes became more alert.

The Lifeline

For the last twelve months he had been under a considerable strain which was all the worse for being public. Everyone knew he wanted to buy the Strathire Arms; everyone knew that both he and his aged mother with whom he lived had made every effort to find out to whom the hotel belonged since its last " proprietor " had been led away, one quiet Fluach morning, into a waiting police car—as close to a plain-clothes policeman as a Siamese twin to its colleague. Everyone knew Brian had failed. Finally everyone had heard his compulsive speech, his eternal gramophone record on the possibilities of dirty work; of collusion between a member of the council, the sheriff and some obscure company in Glasgow. The plot was complex as the back of a wireless. The convener's nephew wanted a hotel but was still training in Switzerland. Creevie wouldn't mind if he thought the convener's nephew was fit to have charge of a flea-circus. Seeing he wasn't, the place should be put up for auction. Of course it should be, anyhow. Instead it was lying empty and the Highlands were losing dollars. Further: there was the moral question. Did the county wish to linger in the suspicion that one of its hotels was still owned by a gaol-bird? He could well believe it of a council dominated by Wee Free ministers who charged their gardeners on the rates while they nattered till they got their name in the *Trumpet*; ministers who, when they granted the Strathire Arms a licence (it had been a temperance hotel since 1880) made sure the first holder of that licence was an experienced crook with a wartime line in hooch. He himself could run the county with one teenage typist and a telephone, etc. He supposed the fact that John Stephenson (the previous owner) had published his wartime experiences as financial adviser to the Pay Corps shortly after his arrest, made everything all right. Where nowadays, he should like to know, did anyone draw the line?

" No auction yet ? " Henry Wotherspoon had said.

Creevie smiled, looking away. " My dear Henry " (he spoke fast—fast almost as an auctioneer, for instance), " I'm not interested any more. The place is falling down by now." His assumption of indifference survived two seconds only and he

The Lifeline

whipped round on the questioner with a passionate gesture. " Anyone would have to spend *five thousand pounds* . . . *five thousand* . . ."—one or two little bubbles accumulated on his lips—" before a *dog* could stay in it now." His hand was way out, stiff.

" Perhaps John Stephenson's coming back."

Was his host teasing him ? Creevie's expression was always alive to such a possibility.

" You mean in nine years, given full remission."

" You knew him, didn't you, Brian ? "

Suspicion as to why Wotherspoon had mentioned the subject and now kept pursuing it, for a moment stayed Creevie's tongue. Was he being led on to a limb ?

Too tempted, he said, " Did I know him ! " and smiled. Ignorance had seldom been one of his admissions except occasionally as a boast. His smile shone. " I could tell you one or two things about Johnny Stephenson, thank you very much." He said it with a certain talent, rammed it home with a look over everyone's head, continuing to smile as though he was lucky to be still alive knowing as much as he did about Johnny Stephenson. And of course it could be true : he did often know the most surprising things.

" But, my dear Henry," he added conclusively, and more quietly. " If I did tell you what I knew I'd be looking over my shoulder all the time, thank you *very* much."

At this moment a voice, one might say *the* voice, broke in :

" And for what, sir, if I may ask, would you be looking over your shoulder ? "

Strangely enough, to communicate over ten yards, Traquhair had spoken not louder but quieter than hitherto. Other conversation which had survived till now, died out. People had only been waiting, if not for an introduction, then at least an opportunity of giving the man their whole and undisguised, as opposed to their partial attention. The resulting silence was widespread.

Brian Creevie flushed. But his extraordinary clear eyes met Traquhair's with cool and slightly aggressive mockery as

The Lifeline

though he knew him well; as though he and everyone in that room had something *on* him.

" Well, Mr. Traquhair, since you ask, I'd be looking out for one of his pals."

" Sneaking up behind you, one presumes, with murrrderous intent ? "

" By the way, do you two know each other ? " Wotherspoon interposed.

Deafly Traquhair continued : " But supposing you saw one of Johnny's pals *in front* of you—armed with nothing, sir, but *esteem and affection* for Johnny Stephenson . . . ? "

3

TRAQUHAIR'S grandiloquent and circuitous speech might suit his stature, beard and dress but it perplexed his hearers who were accustomed to very simple sentences indeed. Creevie, however, was one of five or six who understood him at once. Indeed, his voluble eyes and girlish mouth seemed to rejoice as they caught the meaning even before speech was finished. " Well," he said, " I'm awfully sorry if I said anything which might offend a friend of Mr. Stephenson. I didn't know there was one present. Not—NOT that I would suggest for a single MOMENT many good men don't go to prison for ten years, while worse ones stay out for far longer. Good heavens, no, Mr. Traquhair. I'm extremely sorry . . ." and saying this, his smile vanished and he met the big man's face as though he really were sorry.

Very, very quietly and staring at Creevie with eyes like rifle beads, Traquhair said, " Sir, I . . . accept . . . your apology."

The fact Traquhair had boasted of being a friend of J. Stephenson now soaked in all round. The silence was complex, and, considering how much had already been drunk, tense.

Henry Wotherspoon, ex-adjutant though he was, also had something of a Third Secretary if not the Third Programme about him. He persevered, " I still don't think you have been introduced—Tulloch Traquhair—Brian Creevie."

Traquhair stooped and said, " Did you say Creevie ? " And while he asked the question he looked slyly up, level, under his shaggy brows like a poacher peeping over a brae, refusing to believe the worst. He certainly was an actor.

The Lifeline

" Then you've met before ? " said Wotherspoon.

Disregarding his host Traquhair took Brian Creevie's hand and staring into his face as though they had met in another life he said, " *Creevie!* Mr. Creevie, how *do* you do ! "

What on earth did the actor mean ? Everyone stared and listened.

The enormous physical disparity which existed between the two men was thrown into ludicrous relief by the bear-like greeting which Traquhair lavished with both hands on Creevie's one, and which perhaps for that very reason, he prolonged.

" Very well indeed, Mr. Traquhair, and how do you do ? I'm sure we all feel we have met *you.*" This attempt to reverse the act made no difference to Traquhair who continued shaking Creevie's slim hand with a sort of solemn surmise.

" Did you meet in the war ? " said Nadia dryly, and when no one answered, she went on : " Tulloch was in Combined Ops with Johnny Stephenson. I didn't know you went abroad Brian. . . ."

" Only for three years," Creevie said with confidence, but no amusement.

" Perhaps you were all in Spain together," Nadia said. " You never told me, Brian."

" To my knowledge Johnny Stephenson was not in the International Brigade," Tulloch said, releasing Creevie's hand and taking out a snuff box. " I think he was too busy in those days—*heugh heugh*—in the West End—perfecting those skills for which his country subsequently awarded him the M.B.E."

" For book-keeping?" said Creevie. He had read Stephensons memoirs and marvelled that a man previously convicted of fraud could ever have won an M.B.E. in His Majesty's Pay Corps.

" In times of national emergency," said Traquhair, " ability, pure ability, irrespective of how you hold your knife and fork —is at a premium. Johnny's system of regimental accounting released thousands for cannon-fodder."

The Lifeline

Having completed this statement Traquhair bowed very slightly in the direction of Creevie. A moment later everyone was startled by a harsh double intake of air as the big man snorted up snuff from the back of a hand which he angled first this way and then that and finally waggled to one side.

"So you were in the International Brigade, Mr. Traquhair?" Creevie said, not without insinuation.

"I was. . . . Are you preparing a dossier, Mr. Creevie. Let me save you trouble. I am a devoted admirer of the Russian character. I was in church there recently. So nice to be with people who really do believe in God."

The big man's eyelids lulled low: Comrade—Archimandrite Traquhair was this? Swathed in incense, festooned in purple silk, crowned in gold, whose words like winds moved multitudes on the seas that lay inside themselves: God, Communism, *Vox populi, vox dei*. Amen. He snapped shut his snuff box. Momentarily his eyes had completely closed. A slight tic disturbed one side of his ginger beard. With eyes open he again bowed slightly towards Creevie.

"Show your wound," said Wotherspoon and gave a rather high-pitched laugh.

Traquhair feigned modesty. "Which one? Estremadura? While Johnny Stephenson, unlike Mr. Baldwin, was preparing for the war with Fascism, Mr. Creevie, I got this—at Estremadura." With these words Traquhair pulled up his kilt far enough to elicit a prudish gasp from one or two of the ladies. There, for all to see, was a shrivelled gash in his thigh, so deep that at one smooth point it must have lain against the bone. "Estremadura," he said.

Creevie's face was that of a man recognising the result of a motor smash before Triplex. He turned away with a smile as delicately poised on his lips as a nervous fish in shallows. Exhibitionists bored and embarrassed him. A moment later his smile was gone as though it had never been; but, while it lasted the party membership of Tulloch Traquhair, his association with the late Mr. J. Stephenson and his motor accidents were bracketed, floodlit, for the community to see. While he

The Lifeline

held no brief for the excesses of the Presbyterian Church on the moral plane, nor for the exaggeration of Mrs. Gunter-Sykes and Sir Duncan Fidge, M.P., on the political, it would nevertheless be as well for everyone to remember that the apathy called tolerance in high places which had led to Burgess and Maclean going to Moscow ... had its roots in just this sort of pseudo-intellectual chi-chi. Trust Nadia to import Chelsea!

He walked away.

People caught his eye as much as to say, "Tulloch Traquhair," and he gave the smile back to them, doubled, and passed on till he coupled up with John Mackay, the contractor.

"John."

"Brian."

"How're things?"

Traquhair was booming in the distance. Creevie smiled as though he could imagine Mackay's thoughts.

"Not so bad. How's yerself?"

And Mackay's smile answered Creevie's—eloquently. Then Mackay said, "No auction yet?"

"Believe me, John, they can let the place fall to the ground for all I care."

Mrs. MacFarlane, the banker's wife, had threaded her way through the crowd in Creevie's wake. Now she too earned a smile from Brian who began to feel the centre of an alternative meeting. He prepared for the usual competitive sally about this or that share or property of hers which had appreciated and his that hadn't and got ready to cap whatever boast she might make. Instead she pushed him roughly in the arm.

"What's this?" she hissed in her usual conspiratorial voice.

"Ogersdorp," he teased. "On the floor, Mrs. MacFarlane, where I said they'd be."

"Ogersdorp!" she said contemptuously. "It's not stocks I'm thinking of, Brian. It's hotels."

"What about them?"

"Well, listen to that. He doesn't know: *there's lights in the Strathire Arms.*"

The Lifeline

" Johnny Stephenson's ghost, I suppose."

" And a car outside."

" People have been up before."

" With luggage to the roof? And milk and papers ordered till further notice ? "

Creevie did not like to be informed. It undermined his whole sense of identity. He disguised his concern by looking dubious, looking as though he were merely comparing her statements with a more comprehensive report already at his disposal.

" You've lost it," she hissed intimately, making it plain that she was not prepared, like others, to listen to his excuses about not caring. " You've plain lost it."

" It " of course was not merely the hotel.

She knew and she knew that Brian knew that with every day that passed more and more workers were assembling in camps beside the projected site for the vast Cullan dam, not six miles away. Fluach would be their home town. Fluach at the end of each week would receive these orphans of labour into her arms, thirsty men all, fat-walleted with overtime and longing for the only recreation available—intoxication. While the W.R.I. got a lecture on baking and the bridge club met at Mrs. MacFarlane's and the drama rehearsed Rattigan, they, the hydro workers, would be temporary gods to the tune of about £1000, tinkling into the tills of Fluach bars every Friday and Saturday night. It was a killing to dream of.

Brian already had one hotel and bar, well placed. But the Strathire Arms had better parking space for buses, bigger bar accommodation, and was the first bar you came to on the main road from Cullan.

There was another thing—and of this also Mrs. MacFarlane and Brian Creevie were well aware: the visit, this coming summer, of the Canadian Prime Minister, Mr. Hilldersley.

If, as forecast, the Prime Minister were to visit his grandpaternal croft as well as the Glen Cullan Games, the peak event of Fluach's season, then he would almost certainly stay at a Fluach hotel—unless of course the marquess were in residence at the castle.

The Lifeline

If properly opened up the Strathire Arms was the biggest hotel in Fluach—a place for a Prime Minister to stay in.

Hence the stakes were large. They involved both status and big money, in other words—what did they not involve?

Mrs. MacFarlane, staring, felt as though she would like to shake Brian till he dropped his silly affectation of indifference.

"Brian!" she hissed as though waking him when the house was on fire. "D'you hear what I say?"

Coolly he said, "Who does the luggage belong to?"

"Well, who d'you think?"

"I never speculate."

"Mr. Traquhair, isn't it? Who else?"

Creevie turned slowly. Traquhair was talking about savage ceremonies now.

Creevie's shock gaped in his eyes, although the smile had returned precariously to his mouth.

"You're suggesting he's come here to run the Strathire Arms..."

"No. Brian, I'm knowing it. That's what. Isn't he out of a job?"

"Actors are often laid off. They don't become hotel managers."

"Actor! He's no actor: he's himself. That's why he got the sack. What'll you take?"

Living as they did for capital gain they had many bets still outstanding. Some would take years to be won or lost: elections, marriages, council house allocations, fish, girls, survivals. For a moment Brian toyed with taking on another but something about Mrs. MacFarlane's expression put him off.

It was two hours later. Intoxication had provided Traquhair with many competitors. The room was by now full of Traquhairs, all holding meetings, some with themselves.

Traquhair himself was looking down at the wife of the Director of Education with a fixed smile which published what it cost him to listen.

The Lifeline

" A song, a song . . ." someone shouted.

" Tulloch, perform," said Nadia.

Careful not to hear first time, Traquhair now lent the director's wife an ear which was more generously low than before. Rescue was at hand.

" No," shouted a transformed Wotherspoon. " Tulloch's got to practise. Let's see if he can pour." He came out from behind the stockade. " Come on, Tulloch."

Traquhair went in. The place afforded a certain prominence like a pulpit or the dock. No one could get behind him. Not even Creevie or a knife blade.

He poured. The bottle had a spherical measuring attachment which after a merely insulting dribble ceased to yield. He shook the bottle and steeply increased the angle of delivery. Now it did not even drip.

No one gave his guests more liberal measures of drink than Henry Wotherspoon who frequently tilted bottles three or four times when pouring someone a whisky. But just as the little tables had proprietary ashtrays so the bottles had these spouts.

Nadia said: " Well ! You'd better start advertising for a barman."

" I can understand corking something or uncorking something but this . . . stingy commercial compromise, disobedient to the laws of gravity . . ." Traquhair shook the thing into a foam, held it up to the light and then tried to disguise his amazement as it now yielded another limited trickle. His face reflected a certain fascination.

Henry Wotherspoon said : " I think you ought to make an announcement, Tulloch, or else I shall have to."

" *Le Patron*—*heugh heugh*. Very well. My friends . . ." Traquhair bumped the bottle on the counter for silence which he only partially obtained, some voices being now autonomous. " My friends—from—shall we say May first—a good date— a date after my own heart—the Strathire Arms will once again open its doors, need I say also, its arms to all in search of a bed, board "—he raised what he was holding—" and bottle."

Brian stepped forward out of the crowd.

The Lifeline

Even the autonomous voices petered out in deference to the general hush.

Brian Creevie said: "Mr. Traquhair, I'd like to know *how* you managed to buy that hotel. You know I tried several times."

Traquhair bowed ironically in the direction of his questioner.

"You shall know: the hotel has not been bought; I was appointed manager in Brixton Prison. In the presence, should you doubt it, of two rozzers, myself divided from Johnny by a slab and grill, he in prison garb, head shaved and his voice full of that concern which one would expect in the voice of any conscientious but unavoidably absentee landlord. . . . Satisfied?"

Creevie looked as if he certainly was.

But what about everyone else? Were they to believe a single word? And if they were . . .

The laughter was awkward, the clapping thin, sporadic and soon died out.

Creevie said: "Then are you giving up acting, Mr. Traquhair?"

"Mr. Creevie! . . ." Traquhair began in a warning tone.

"He's leaving the stage," Nadia said placatingly.

"But I thought you were a jolly good actor, Mr. Traquhair."

The last thing anyone had expected was that Creevie should pay Traquhair a compliment. Yet how else could such a statement be taken?

"There now. Blush," said Nadia. "Aren't you pleased?"

On the contrary, Traquhair's little eyes seemed to have become smaller, smaller even than when he had defended Stephenson. They fixed on Creevie with sudden sobriety, as though Creevie had at last taken a shot at him with a rifle, as expected.

"Actor . . . ?" he whispered.

"Yes, I thought you were jolly good."

There was again silence round the two men. At last Traquhair whispered:

"Bow, though I perhaps ought, to the opinion of a regular

The Lifeline

viewer of Robin Hood, on the matter of acting, I must yet protest, my dear Creevie, that *I am not an actor.*"

"Well... I hardly know what to say." (It was obvious from Brian's smile that he had known exactly what to say.) "I'm sorry. What are you then, Mr. Traquhair?"

"What am I?... What am I...? What did you say? What am I...?" (Traquhair's face worked.) "I am myself. *I'm Tulloch Traquhair.*"

"Yes, yes, of course but... I meant profession. Is that your profession?"

Someone laughed. Traquhair frowned.

"Haven't you changed the question somewhat, Mr. Creevie?" There was then a fractional pause before Traquhair added: "I'm a military historian."

He must be drunker than he looked, people thought.

"A military historian!" said Creevie, taking care not to conceal his surprise entirely.

Traquhair gazed at Creevie some seconds before saying: "But does it matter so much what a man '*does*'?"

"Well, I should say it did."

"Then the whole nation is pitifully implicated."

"Not at all," said Creevie brightly, and looked Traquhair in the eyes.

Was Creevie smiling? Was he saying, "Actor" again?

Traquhair's little eyes seemed to climb out of range of that hypothetical smile and look down on its wearer from immense anonymous heights—with Olympian antipathy.

But his lips and tongue had apparently gone numb and blunt. Perhaps there were two Creevies by now, side by side and this when one was already one too many.

"And you, Mr. Creevie," he said. "Apart from being a hotelkeeper, which is probably the least important thing about you—what are you? I beg to submit that you may be . . ."

His eyes drifted out of focus and a gaseous disturbance suddenly knitted his lips into a compressed purse as though something rather like Creevie had attacked him from inside just at the very moment when Creevie was attacking from outside.

The Lifeline

As though in double defence, he poured himself another drink from the spouted bottle and suddenly muttered the single word, " Meldrum " as though it were a charm against Creevie, the wife of the Director of Education and against the chromium contraceptive which frustrated the natural functions of the now vertical bottle; a charm against everything, perhaps against life itself.

4

TRAQUHAIR opened his eyes. He seemed to be at the theatre for in front of him stood a well-lit backdrop of an old-fashioned building, the White Horse Inn. He waited expectantly for a fat German tenor in shorts and Tyrolean hat but instead someone shook his knee and said, "Mr. Traquhair—your hotel." He could smell new car leather. Silhouettes became strange faces, when an inside light came on.

"*Your hotel*, Mr. Traquhair."

He got out with difficulty and saw he had been travelling in a new Consul. As it drove off he heard laughter inside. He waved after it calling out:

"Good-bye, Ian. Good-bye, Helen. Good-bye, Mrs. Mac-Farlane. Good-bye, Kenny. Good-bye, Jean. Good-bye, Donald. Good-bye. Night-night, Jack. Cheeri-oh, Brian. See you Saturday then, Margaret . . ." *Diminuendo*, his voice tailed off into sad silence. It was not as though he had spoken satirically and now repented it, but as though he had suddenly recognised in his voice the tentative repetition of a parrot whose speech is superficially identical but intrinsically different, recognised perhaps even a raucousness that had its roots in envy.

"MELDRUM!" he suddenly bawled, and turned towards his new dwelling heavily and wearily as though it had just then whispered something in his ear, calling him from the Wotherspoon party to the future.

The Strathire Arms, built in about 1800, has the thick walls and broad simple windows with stone margins which charac-

The Lifeline

terise many of the first permanent dwellings—fortresses apart—to be set up in the Highlands. Some hundred and twenty years older than the " lodge style " of the Spotes house at Rossiemurchat, with its innumerable white-painted corrugated iron excrescences, larders, privies, sculleries, and a hundred years older than the cherry tinged neo-Gothic of the MacFarlane's bank-house, the hotel was probably built only a little later than the Bishop's Palace in which Creevie lives with his mother. (The minister, Mr. Megginch, has a council house, one of a block copied from and suitable to Greenock. We have a Socialist council.)

Since Mr. Stephenson's departure the Strathire Arms had deteriorated rapidly, partly on account of the proximity of the War Memorial Hall just across the road. On dance nights boys drained their half-bottles with a long vertical pause and popped them over the garden wall, or if it was raining made use of the broken window at the back and drank in comfort inside. Couples sometimes lay together on sofas, and one or two tramps had come to depend on the place. Questions had been asked at County Council Hygiene Committee meetings and an inspector had looked into the matter. But reform was delayed perhaps because the place had come to combine the facilities of a rubbish dump, much treasured in the Highlands, and, rarer, more treasured still, privacy for winter fornication. Certainly months had passed and the premises had gone from bad to worse.

J. S. Mackay and Sons had had word from agents in Glasgow to go in and do something to the pipes during the frost. Plumbers had gone in and came out with vivid descriptions. Cockroaches swarmed in gleaming black profusion between the flags and linoleum, and spiders of almost tropical dimensions had set up skeins so thickly that some windows were opaque as phlegm and any unpremeditated step into the dark could earn a flimsy suffocating veil which came with you, trapping even the eyelashes and horrifying the lips as though alive.

Although various strangers from the south had visited the hotel in the past months, parked their cars outside, gone in

The Lifeline

with their own keys, and in one case stayed a night, none of them had given local gossips the smallest handle to catch hold of. Like the man they presumably represented, Stephenson, they had come and gone, without revealing more of themselves than a face, a number plate, a make of car, and a suit of clothes. Fluach had come to regard the place as a write-off, a building which like a charred wreck on the edge of a prosperous port, bore witness month after month to the fatal and now monumental mistake of its vanished owner. Thus and thus only are the wages of sin.

On Sundays the people of Fluach are about equally divided between the brick-built Church of Scotland and the corrugated iron Wee Free. In both it is difficult to get a seat. Presbyterianism, though yielding by inches, is still strong, quite strong enough to prevent golf or even gardening on Sundays. The Reverend Abigail Skene (Halpick) still maintains his high majority at Council elections by Gaelic instructions to his flock which are as little likely to reach the columns of the *Northern Trumpet* as anything uttered in the Germany of Goebbels. All this may well be doubted by people from the south and, in fact, is doubted but there it is. Liberal influences of the last hundred years stopped at Taylor's Garage from which the narrow road branches off towards the low duneland to Fluach and the village of Halpick. There, cut off, live inbred descendants of seafarers whose fathers no more went to sea after seeing a minister than to-day their sons would vote for the free-thinking grocer who on one occasion stood against Skene for the Council and got two per cent of the votes cast in spite of being previously implored by ninety per cent of the voters to stand.

Fluach, it is true, is more liberal than Halpick, but even so it may well be imagined how the Strathire Arms had stood in the eyes of our inhabitants ever since the proprietor went south in handcuffs. The blind windows, the rank garden, the jackdaw settlement in the chimneys all added up to the kind of stare Skene gave his congregation: yes, the place was an illustration of the wages of sin. Indeed, who knows but what Skene may not have used his dominating influence in the

The Lifeline

council to preserve its gruesome dereliction in the same way as once long ago, gibbets were made as prominent as possible and never cleared of their ghastly, decomposing loads. To Skene a stranger was almost the same thing as a criminal. An opportunity to illustrate the fate of both with one permanent, prominent mass of decay, might well have appealed to his censorious disposition as well, of course, as providing him with rumours of, " luxury and licentiousness by candlelight," on which could be based whole sermons—and long stares from the pulpit at one or other adolescent member of his flock, too happy by half.

Traquhair was seeing his new home for the second time in his life. The first had been two years ago when he had stayed a week with Johnny Stephenson.

The place looked different then. Everything had looked different.

" Meldrum ! " he roared again. Anger and distress accentuated his voice's natural power. But the empty street merely echoed the anguish of the sacked actor. A poster on the War Memorial Hall " Are you good enough for the Army ? " caught his eyes and drew from him a huge gesture which mysteriously provoked a cat from a near hedge so fast that it blended with the moonlight. Only its shadow seemed to cross the white road fast as a projectile.

Traquhair moved now towards the porch where the Rolls was parked. Just when he was about to shout again there came a glimmer of light and a rattling of chains and the front door opened showing a man dressed in a pouchy kind of nylon overalls such as is favoured by explorers and the S.A.S. He was carrying a candle which cut up his lean, bearded, hungry face into dramatic planes of contrast.

" *Ecce Homo!* Trust our Reoraidgh to find a candle when there are a million volts on his doorstep."

" There are no bulbs," the man said in a factual tone. " Although the place has been used as a public lavatory and a brothel."

The Lifeline

In the man's free hand was a broom. Yet it must have been near morning.

Several other candles were burning at various heights in the passages and by their light, after a few steps, Traquhair could make out that evocative pattern of life interrupted which divers find in wrecks at the bottom of the sea.

"His last breakfast," Meldrum said, pushing open a door and seeming to derive satisfaction from Traquhair's subsequent silence.

Indeed there stood a table laid for one, confronting a marmalade pot which looked as though it were full of black smoke.

Traquhair said: "They didn't even let him finish his breakfast, the swine."

"He stuck his neck out," Meldrum said.

"A free spirit," said Traquhair.

Resting his hands one on either side the buckle of his belt he began to move through the lower regions of the once prosperous hotel. Some slight provisions had been made against damp—newspapers stuffed up chimneys. Certain things had been covered. But it was all makeshift, partial. On the whole, the place had not been touched for a year—till this evening. Meldrum had made a noticeable start. Traquhair saw little piles of debris everywhere—the piles being in a sort of pattern. He wished Meldrum wouldn't do things in patterns. He kicked one of the patterns . . . just a little.

Coming to a halt before an assembled pile of glass fragments, dust, dud bulbs, a contraceptive, assorted dried excrement and newspaper, inevitable ubiquitous newspaper, Traquhair remained silent for a long minute. At last he said: "Well—did you look?"

"Yes—I looked."

Meldrum came closer, close as a shadow, and stared straight at Traquhair.

Two spies meeting in a foreign country at the bottom of a disused coal mine could scarcely have seemed more secretive.

"Well . . ." boomed Traquhair suddenly with a show of

The Lifeline

indifference. "Why are you tongue-tied. It has a certain relevance. Does it exist—or doesn't it? Sometimes you choose the strangest moments to go broody on the simplest information. Is it ..."—he flung out a hand—" or isn't it? And if it *is* ... then *does* it?"

"It is. And it does." Meldrum held out a key.

A little snort escaped Traquhair as though he had been dug in the ribs. He turned away from the key.

"*Heugh heugh*," he laughed in his meatiest voice. He felt sober suddenly. "Superb! I'm so glad ..." And he went on walking round as though in a spotlit pool at the Palladium. But the eyes of Meldrum followed him closely.

"You didn't lose much time, did you?" Traquhair said in a suggestive tone. "*Heugh heugh!* Good man!"

"What d'you mean?" Meldrum said; and lowered the key.

"What I say."

"But you asked me to find out ... before I did anything else."

"A joke, Reoraidgh. ... Well? Can't you raise a smile? There's a little saying which few people understand as they should: *honi soit qui mal y pense*. It means people are suspicious because they themselves are nasty. Whoever said I intended to make use of this ... coincidence."

"Then why did we ever come here?"

Traquhair dragged a kitchen chair under his rump, sat and sighed wearily as though with a child that refused to learn its lesson. "We've come home, haven't we? Besides beggars can't be choosers. I got the offer."

Meldrum stood still and his dark, passionate unyielding eyes slipped lower on Traquhair's person. "Was that it? ..." he muttered, and he added, "You didn't try very hard to get another job. ..."

"Listen to that!" said Traquhair as though addressing many people. "No one would believe it! From you!"

After a moment of victorious silence he went on: "Please, Reoraidgh. It's three o'clock!"

Meldrum turned away towards the back. Traquhair called

The Lifeline

after him, " Is Olivia settled in ? Is she liking it ? And the children—are they liking it ? . . . Are you happy, Reoraidgh ? The return of the native, eh ? Have you had some food ? Did you have a good journey up in my Rolls ? Why weren't you at the station ? Were you delayed ? . . ."

His enormous voice boomed down the echoing empty passages—now empty even of Meldrum's thin speechless back. A door crashed.

Traquhair's eyes closed as though the echo of his own voice were winging back at him like a sharp wind which he couldn't stand.

" Oh, how dreary," he said. " One comes away only to find one is still there."

After a moment he lowered his head into his hands.

A huge tear seeped from his lids. No prize cabbage after an August storm ever wobbled out a bigger, more liquescent, diamond-fired tear. It blazed in the candlelight and then started a long journey downwards leaving always a little more of itself behind on Traquhair's ageing cheek. At last it touched his collar and became nothing but a fast-fading smear.

" Oh, so dreary, so dreary. . . . Don't leave me, Meldrum," he muttered.

A few minutes passed. Suddenly he heaved himself up—and started looking for whisky in the Rolls and among packing-cases, without success.

The blundering of this immense man in the twilit chaos suggested the invasion of some Congo post office by a gorilla. No civilised object, cutlery, books, or lamps appeared to be entirely without significance to him ; he picked many of them up as though they suggested some purpose either forgotten or impossible to guess, a purpose which always eluded him for he put them down only after consideration and then went on looking for whisky, finding none.

At last in an old suitcase covered with foreign labels and airline tickets he found a bottle—but it was empty and, anyhow, the wrong kind. Camp Coffee. He revolved it close to his eyes. The label showed an officer of some Highland regiment

The Lifeline

receiving a cup of steaming coffee from the hands of a coloured, apparently an Indian, servant. The officer's position suggested imperial ease, a godlike second-nature sense of superiority, an at-home-ness even on the Equator. Traquhair stared at this simple object with almost superstitious attention and finally let fall the lid of the case and went away as though he had in fact found what he had been looking for—whisky. And he took it upstairs and into several rooms before finding one with luggage in it. There he put it on the mantelpiece in a film of dust, centrally, where he could see it. Then he fell rather than lay down on a bed which had been roughly prepared for him—among suitcases, parcels and dust.

5

HE HAD NOT OFTEN seen the dawn. Even on campaigns, safari and on ship-board as a deckhand—even for a short time as a milkman he had still seldom seen the dawn. Only very occasionally had the world, to his knowledge, developed shafts of greasy pallor which might have come from under the very door of death, but which he had assured himself were the early symptoms of another day. Then had he answered punctual cocks or church clocks or stray guns with a groan and turned his face still deeper into sheets, blankets, coats, quilts, burnouses and greatcoats and sought that easier realm where events moved unimpeded by the dreary demands of his eternal creditor—Reality.

To-day he was brought to his senses by a man leaving the room. It was a small man but, like himself and Meldrum, bearded and past youth. He carried a sack and his boots had mouths and even a few spiny teeth the better to clutch large sandwiches of newspaper. He first appeared seated in a pool of light where after various noises preparatory to movement as the clearings, explosions and sharp expostulations of an ancient car, he fixed up his dentures and got to his feet. Coming close he considered the supine Tulloch with a stare in which recognition and resentment were finally superseded by doubt; then he moved with a sure step towards the window which he negotiated with the few movements and style of an expert. It was while watching this departure with the acceptance of a dreamer that Traquhair saw the dawn.

Later he worked out where he was and for half an hour lay staring at the ceiling as though stunned. His own decisions

The Lifeline

often took him this way. All his life he seemed to have been falling out by the roadside, as it were, of time and taking stock, dazed, before getting another lift.

At nine he came down in his kilt, grey shirt open at the neck and feet in buckled slippers. His unstockinged legs were covered with thick black hair beneath which the flesh showed strangely white and delicately veined. There was a smell of cooking and he suddenly burst into a few snatches of confident song, as he often did when about to meet Meldrum.

Avoiding the nails of packing-cases and the more noisome piles of debris he went into what had once been Johnny Stephenson's living-room in the private side of the house and there sure enough, on the same table where last night he had seen the mouldy remains of Johnny's last breakfast, stood the fresh promise of his own first. The room had been tidied and was made cheerful by a noisy friendly fire, fluttering away like flags in the wind and striking lights from surfaces which must have been dusted that morning, or perhaps in the small hours.

The thought that Meldrum might not have stopped working all night did not dismay him.

" That's the boy," he said approvingly as though his secretary were in earshot. " Ring out the old, ring in the new. For what we are about to receive . . ." Hearing a movement behind him he went on: " Well, Reoraidgh. What's the annexe like ? Good kip ? Children settled in ? "

The other's silence was more descriptive than words.

" Two eggs in future, please," Traquhair went on cheerfully. " I never agreed with the old saying *un œuf* is as good as a feast."

Standing behind him, Meldrum said : " What was the party like ? . . . Congenial people ? "

" A new breed," said Traquhair. " A different stamp. Wit, fancy, warmth ; interesting people interested in their lives. None of your jaded commuters, rush-hour faces moving under the bright ads. like a tier of question marks after. ' Is it worth it ? ' *Heugh heugh* one exception : Creevie—a fellow called Creevie, an assassin out of a trouser-press, a cuff-shooter with

The Lifeline

soap-conditioned hands and airy-fairy gestures, a milk-curd Rizzio, a disgrace to our sex, Reoraidgh. I tied him up. But him apart: a different story. We've struck lucky."

Traquhair bunched up over his breakfast never looked over his shoulder at the man who seemed to take pleasure in remaining out of sight, and in using silence as a form of speech.

"I propose to get mussels for a bouillabaisse before we have been here much longer. You can see them from upstairs. Can't you imagine the Creevies of this world living year in year out on a gastronomic gold mine and never doing anything about it. *Moules marinières* or *à la Normande*...."

"For the hotel guests," came Meldrum's voice from behind.

"And then the blessed silence, the sound of the waves, the faint tang of seaweed, Ben Cullan like a badly-iced ginger cake, the last snows. Enough but not too many people. Ah, this morning, first thing; the lonely heron in the shallows with the sun like a blood-orange beyond. Austere, divine reflections. The harmonious stiltedness of that lanky movement which stirs no ripple. Chinese beauty, Reoraidgh. Just your cup. Doesn't your heart quiver?"

Meldrum said nothing.

In early February the sun at Fluach seldom gets off its knees. If you have a low window then sometimes a great ball of red fire seems to have bounced briefly on to the horizon and looks in at you as it rolls along with blinding brilliance. But if it is cloudy and or if the window faces north, east or west then nine o'clock can be very dark. This window did face north so it was therefore by the light of flames that Meldrum again appeared now, coming round Traquhair's elbow still holding a broom, as though he had never let go of it all night but had kept sweeping during the hours that his employer's organs had struggled to assimilate pints of Wotherspoon "cup," Benzedrine, meringues and lobster.

After such a night Traquhair felt tunnelled enough by dreams. Yet here beside his chair stood a man who might have stepped out of one.

"Say something, Reoraidgh. Smile.... Be with us."

The Lifeline

Like Traquhair, Meldrum had a beard and was tall. But after that all similarity ceased. Whereas Traquhair's face had a womanish softness, a eunuch blandness and his eyes a babyish innocence, Meldrum's was rough and deeply cut and his black eyes heavy with more experience and pain than was likely to have come the way of one man in one life except through adventures within himself. He suggested an ill-shaven soldier from a Calvary—but a soldier whose weapon hung slack, almost dropped from his hand, a soldier who looked on with an almost crucified stare. It might have been a talented, even a sympathetic face had not this stare of his been tainted with a gleam that was altogether too private, and which fired up sometimes into an exalted, sardonic bitterness and set a clinical question mark to the whole man. At times Meldrum in mid-room, mid-speech seemed to forget where he was, and therefore to justify Traquhair's feeling invitation: " Be with us. . . ."

What right had the man to look like this? He had an attractive, cheerful wife (Traquhair would ask no one to believe it till he had seen her). He also had six children in spite (Traquhair suspected) of knowing about birth control. Poor, yes. But why should he walk about looking bereaved?

"You should get another dog, Reoraidgh," he said deflectingly.

" Shouldn't I first consider the life it'll have to live."

" No," said Traquhair without hesitation and then rocked his head a bit like a French porter making no comment. Some people really stuck their necks out too far. The consideration which Meldrum advocated for a dog had surely never been allowed to the six little Meldrums.

Traquhair derived a certain satisfaction from these thoughts. He finally gave them modified utterance thus : " We do wrong, Reoraidgh, to take you too seriously, don't we ? "

A moment ago he had been prepared to feel guilty about the man's wolfhound Loki being run over in London; had been about to offer a new dog out of his own pocket simply because, if it hadn't been for Tulloch Traquhair Ltd., Meldrum

The Lifeline

would never have gone to London (except possibly for observation at some later date). Now, because of Meldrum's accusing tone, he felt less inclined to give him a dog.

He squashed a bit of toast into his egg, withdrew it, salted the tip slightly, and put the yolky sog agreeably into his mouth. People underestimated boiled eggs. Besides, if Meldrum had really loved Loki would he have finished him off with a meat axe in the mews, in full view of the neighbours? That the answer to this question might simply be " Yes " put an end to the pleasure of thought.

" You still have your bird, don't you? " Traquhair said astringently.

Meldrum answered disinterestedly in the affirmative.

Traquhair, briskly cracking open his second egg, smiled.

Meldrum's blackbird had come with them from Bath, survived London and now presumably was hanging in the annexe. Unlike most blackbirds it was snow-white. Its song was typical of its wild cousins. The endless improvisations seemed self-creating for one gave rise to the next and, as with African drumming, fatigue seemed in inverse proportion to intensity.

Meldrum made extraordinary allowance for his pets. Indeed, there was no limit to his consideration, witness his behaviour with Loki and the meat axe. He spent hours looking for worms. Stray cats dreaded him on sight. Sometimes he gave his shoulder as a perpetual perch while he worked and at others would fall into a sort of trance watching the bird's unconsidered movements, its preening, fluffing up of feathers, washing, eating —the speculative angling of its head and the strange dead gleam of the eye as sleep deprived it of focus, the little drama of the lower lid rising up slowly and obscuring the eye gone dusty with sleep like an horizon covering the sun.

" I went for petrol. They wanted cash," Meldrum said.

" Did you have any? "

" Isn't it going to be a bit difficult if that's the way they all see it? "

It. How typical of Meldrum was this sudden creation of a

The Lifeline

whole " It " out of a complex and, anyhow, vague, indefinable situation.

The noise of Traquhair eating was the only reply.

Meldrum continued: "Just tell someone—anyone—you knew him and you'll be lucky if you get a bottle of milk."

Traquhair shaped bread and butter delicately into a convenient thickness for insertion.

Meldrum moved: "But don't take offence. I'm not suggesting the man has been born who'd be fool enough to blab that out—in a place like this."

Traquhair continued to eat.

"And what sort of place is this?" he at last said. "I find places and people have much in common all the world over. Merely because you were in Ack-Ack in Wick for six months during the war I hope you aren't going to pontificate about what you do 'up here.'"

Meldrum was silent until he said: "Some places are still a bit different."

Traquhair heard the noise of Meldrum's broom beginning to sweep and had already closed his eyes in relief when the flat, tired voice of Meldrum added from the distance.

"Who's going to get it ready? The beds, the heating, the catering . . . I mean . . ."

Traquhair said: "I think it would do us both a lot of good if this afternoon we got out on the hills."

Meldrum simply said: "Hills!"

"We need some meat," Traquhair went on briskly. "A little reconnaissance, a little practice. . . . February. We could still take a hind."

"There's deer all right. How much ground goes with this place?"

"We'll take the map with us and work it out. Meanwhile on with the job."

Meldrum muttered something. It sounded like: "What with?"

Suddenly Traquhair began to boom:

"Reoraidgh, a word in your ear! It's very important to

The Lifeline

be rich if only for income tax purposes. When you are rich it naturally costs a lot to keep everything up, not least your own standard of living, so you are entitled to claim a great many allowances 'off tax' to pay for servants, farms, gardeners, foresters, cars, chauffeurs, secretaries as well as ten per cent depreciation per annum on everything you possess. . . . I'm particularly anxious we should be rich *quick*. Because once we are rich, we can stay rich. I mean—if we had a thousand sheep on the hill we could live off the subsidy alone in a lean year, and if the sheep died we'd profit by the loss, provided a little was coming in. Of course you have to have a little coming in —that I grant—but the bar should provide that without any difficulty. Once we have a reliable minimum then the more numerous our additional activities—pony trekking, archery club, angling association, rock climbing group, archæological research, if only building extensions—the easier it will be to show loss and yet even while showing loss—still, magically, expand, appreciate. D'you follow ? I don't wish to pose as an economist, Reoraidgh, but I've kept my eyes open. Already I see you ogling the weak point in my argument even though I've dealt with it conclusively: the initial hard-standing; well, we have the bar : we will take eight hundred pounds our first night."

" I wasn't thinking of that," Meldrum said.

Traquhair made an affected gesture with one hand as though he were a beau in *Love for Love* waving a lace handkerchief, and a moment later he took snuff like a sea mammal.

" Well, what were you thinking ? As though you knew ! Anyhow, do you follow ? I don't want to hear the old complaint on behalf of dear Olivia that she doesn't know whether she's coming or going. Believe me. She always knew—even though her apparent point of arrival makes prescience seem incredible."

Meldrum muttered something.

" Come again ? "

" Nothing, nothing."

Traquhair went on coolly : " Once things are shipshape you

The Lifeline

can start a holiday line in pony trekking. Get back to horses. Your appearance and manner will help."

Meldrum stopped sweeping and looked up at his employer. " I've never looked after a horse . . ." he said blankly.

For answer Traquhair got to his feet. Last night he had dreamed of Meldrum on a horse.

" Well, it's high time you did," he said confidently.

Meldrum remained standing, staring. Reproach was on the tip of Traquhair's tongue: " I thought you would have liked it up here . . ." etc. After all, he might have found another job in London and never come north had it not been for Meldrum. People dying sometimes left their money to a pet cat or in old age bought a house which would suit their dog. The close pet —with its devotion to food or mousing is often presumably the last creature to revive, vicariously, a spontaneous feeling for life. Yes, possibly in a sense he had come north to suit Meldrum, though of course Meldrum's presence, in his London flat, already indicated a certain predisposition on his part for the wilds.

" You aren't going to disappoint me, are you, Reoraidgh ? " he said with an edge to his voice.

And with this he left the room, leaving Meldrum in the all-encompassing wasteland of work, looking much as Columbus's seamen must have looked at their captain when the rations changed from furry green biscuit to leather, hemp and rats.

But this sort of thing had happened before. It was merely typical that the secretary should be working in a practical way to make feasible one of Traquhair's fantastic ideas, while Traquhair, the progenitor of the idea, should already seem a little frustrated, if not frightened, by the surprising degree of realisation it had already achieved.

Meldrum moved to a window and looked up at the surrounding country. His expression showed familiarity, tempered with surmise, and a few minutes later when Traquhair came down in kilt, tweed jacket, silk stock, deerstalker and shepherd's crook he examined him with unusual attention.

" I've got some calls to make," said Traquhair.

The Lifeline

Meldrum watched him go as far as the door then he said in a cold, hard penetrating tone which stopped Traquhair dead.

" What shall I do with that ? " And he pointed to a key on the window-sill quite close to where the big man was standing.

Traquhair looked down at it uneasily as though it were alive. He recognised it from last night.

" I'll put it here," said Meldrum walking over and picking it up, as though relishing its visible tangible existence. And he put it up on top of the edge of a picture frame. The picture was a Victorian painting, on glass, of a dying stag. Faith, Hope and Charity were on the other walls, Stephenson having left them there on arrival—and departure.

" Then you'll know where it is," Meldrum said.

6

APART FROM the castle, with its hundred and eighty rooms, most of them furnished and covered with dust-sheets, there is no big house in or around Fluach except for the Bishop's Palace beside the old kirk.

The palace is really older than the castle and was even once, more of a stronghold, for it was here that Bishop Enulphus held off the Earl of Moray and with his own hands dispatched three hostages, young kinswomen of the earl, by flinging them down from a high tower in sight of the besieging forces. Only a few old stones of the original fortress remain and in one of them, hollowed out by weather, Mrs. Creevie, the present owner, keeps some tidy rock plants guarded by terracotta dwarfs. In fact, the palace has long since been a manse, a large simple house with generous windows in which the glass has archaic irregularities, flaws which distort vision. It stands beside the old kirk.

For hundreds of years the minister had only to walk down fifty yards of well-tended drive to reach the graveyard where Fluach's old bones lie under rude lettering, Celtic crosses, barbaric in-woven patterns like carpet-beaters and animist motifs of salmon and dogs worn smooth by time. In the middle of this archaic meeting place of Christianity and Paganism stands the white, house-like kirk with its little bell visible on a beam under a canopy something like a bucket in a covered well. There, for centuries, congregations waited the appearance of the minister and measured his sermons (by the sun, clocks and lately by pan drops, four being the limit), facing him submissively as sheep waiting for a gate to open. Some ministers

The Lifeline

had been feared as witch doctors are feared; few had been loved. In either case, given the absence of the marquess, the manse had contained the embodiment of intimate parental authority. The drive and garden were kept up voluntarily by men of the parish, a privilege now enjoyed by the weekly cinema. Beside the manse lies the kitchen garden with wall high enough for a prison. After the second war it became impenetrable with weeds of tropical dimensions; recently, too, the interior of the manse began to crumble because the ten high-ceilinged rooms had been heated for too many cold winters by nothing but two one-bar electric stoves, a small cooker and the often tepid bodies of an overworked minister's wife and her large family. Thunderous and comminatory were the sermons sometimes on the grasping spirit of distant Unions, pale as a one-bar electric fire the plea for a different national atmosphere. Then, defeated, the minister went to a council house and the palace was bought by Mrs. Creevie, who left the precincts of her hotel just as Victorian industrialists left their factories. And inside the tall, light, well-proportioned rooms of the palace grew up an interior which might have appeared on some stand at Olympia as the Ideal Managerial Home; and outside it a rockery with mauve rocks imported from Surrey to thicken up the remains of the fortress, crazy paving, begonias and in summer an unused *chaise-longue*, bore more witness to the birth of a new world, even here, in Fluach.

As though in final, total repudiation of the past, old Mrs. Creevie had exiled the portrait of her husband the locally celebrated Ian Creevie to a cloakroom where monogrammed hairbrushes consorted with waders, groups of officers, public school " Houses," isolated putters and an arquebus. The minister's parlour was now a drawing-room with a grand piano. Mrs. Creevie's tabouret with threaded needle parked between stitches, lay beside *Tatlers*, *Fields*, *Country Life* on a low stool in front of the "Adams" fireplace, which had been installed instead of the old plain hearth.

Brian's bedroom was more of a " bed-sitter " than is normally discovered in a private house. The teapot and cups

The Lifeline

and the miniature electric cooker stood out with the defiance of rebellion, as did the locks on the inside of the door, sufficient for a prude's lavatory or much jewellery. Sometimes a notice " ENGAGED " hung on the outside of the door. The periodicals close to his bed, technical, electrical, managerial were almost always surmounted by the *Financial Times*.

He was forty-two.

Old Mrs. Creevie had a voice like honey in which she distilled remarks that left an aftertaste of arsenic. She had as many friends as she appeared to want: none. The loss that most mothers incur—children growing up and giving their devotion to others—she had avoided, and now at eighty-two she was fighting death with one hand and her son with the other over the supposedly settled question as to whether or not you can take it with you. As far as Brian was concerned she was right in knowing that if you take it with you as far as the last moment then that is as good as taking it with you since there is, anyhow, nowhere to go; but what worried him—gnawed him—was that to do this, under the present system of taxation, was equivalent to removing it from those who came after. When she had pneumonia last year and the daily help had to go away to her sister, she had been dependent on him for basic necessities. To drive the point home he had got the doctor to say she shouldn't have the telephone in her room. Consequently for ten days or so she had lain in the palm of his hand.

Before she rose from her bed she had transferred ten thousand pounds of stock.

But a week later it appeared there had been some irregularity. Her signature had in every case differed fundamentally from the usual. She had written left-handed. When the bank requested fresh signatures she scrapped the whole transaction declaring she had changed her mind. With tonics and careful economy of energy she went back to her tabouret and accounts as coolly as ever. Brian never mentioned his defeat. Neither of them ever did. A veneer of invulnerability, of total independence was the commonest weapon used by each; Brian

The Lifeline

put up the engaged sign rather more often than usual. She paid no attention. She had soon completely recovered and, when it came to the matter of the new tenants at the Strathire Arms, he listened in amazement to a voice that seemed to have a keen, confident, personal interest in events ten years hence.

"I somehow don't think it will last very long," she purred, pulling wool from the tabouret as though it were Traquhair's long gut. "You see, dear, everyone *knows* he was a friend of Stephenson and that will speak for itself. I'm sheur *I* shouldn't like to stay in a hotel of that sort."

Her Edinburgh accent with its off-Scottish burlesque of refinement always added a peculiarly penetrating thrust to her insinuations. Her pauses could be terrific . . . the wool coming slowly out of a design till tension was solid. "You see, dear, I have a feeling that you've only got to keep your ear" (*pull*) "to the ground" (*pull*) "to hear something *most* interesting" (*tension complete*) "about both Mr. Traquhair and Mr. Meldrum. Isn't it rather odd he himself" (*new stitch*) "never gave a reason for ending his contract with the B.B.C.?" (*Pull.*) "Don't tell me a man like that couldn't get a part." (*Pull.*) "I saw him in the chemist. . . . They'll be doing *Samson* for the children soon, and after that *Goliath*. Then *The Tempest* . . ." she added rather surprisingly with a tightening of her lips. "Caliban." (*Tension complete.*) "Besides" (*new stitch*), "why on earth should two people like that have come to a place like this except to be where no one knows them. . . . They aren't the first. Goodness me, no!"

Brian, who had been on his feet pacing as though about to leave the room (his normal occupation in his mother's presence) began to speak with his usual impetuosity.

"As though I cared two hoots what happens to the Strathire Arms. I've got quite enough on my hands as it is, Mother. But it's the principle I object to. If I hadn't spoken out the other night I don't think anyone would have said a word. I mean, where do you draw the line? I'm jolly sure I wouldn't last long if my employer was in Brixton. . . ." (Here he looked at his mother.) "I said what I thought: that one had to draw

The Lifeline

the line somewhere even in Strathireshire . . . and one might as well draw it this side of fraud, and those who sided with criminals. Good heavens: rivalry!" He spat the word out with such contempt that a smile came to his lips. "Mrs. MacFarlane called him my 'rival.' Rival, I said. He couldn't run a flea-circus. If that hotel keeps going, then more frauds were perpetrated by J. Stephenson, Esq., than he was ever charged with."

"Did you speak to Johnny Mackay, dear?"

"Yes. Mister Tulloch Traquhair has written to him, thank you very much. He wants the place done up inside, done up, I said, rebuilt is probably more like it."

"I suppose Johnny will ask for an advance."

"He said he didn't like to. Something about the man, he said. Something about him! . . . There's plenty about him, I said. But I doubt if it'll be money!"

"Flesh," said Mrs. Creevie, sewing. "And overweeningness."

"They'll never get girls," she added softly. "Never!"

Brian scarcely seemed to hear for he suddenly said: "Kilts, if you please!"

"And bows and arrows in the back, the coalman said," Mrs. Creevie mused. Finally, as though from her stomach, she said: "Someone told me people are saying he's like Mr. Creevie to look at."

Brian had never been in a position to discuss his father. He had always taken his opinions in that direction from his mother. What else could he do, having scarcely known the man? Besides, the subject had always made him uncomfortable. He picked up the *Express* which usually meant he would be gone in thirty seconds.

"I don't know, I'm sure," his mother whispered cavernously and her flecky pouched eyes peered searchingly over the tabouret. "We shall have to see . . ."

This made Brian move to the door. She caught him half-through it.

"And that woman! The barman's wife!"

The Lifeline

"What about her?"

Mrs. Creevie did not reply.

Brian came back. "You mean Mrs. Meldrum?" he said. "The blonde. What about her?"

"She's no better than she ought to be," said Mildred Creevie and then, although her lips did not move, a voice which sounded exactly like hers said: "Just a trollop!"

7

OLIVIA MELDRUM was a *cendré* blonde whose long locks fell naturally to the shoulders in the timeless hair style of the early Garbo. She had wide blue eyes but surveyed you with a sort of perpetually stupefied penetration as though—yes, she could love you too, whatever you might be, as well as life, poverty, dirt, drudgery, Meldrum and six little Meldrums even at a moment when most citizens were opting for a small car instead of a third child. She sponged—pilfered almost, but only trifles. Traquhair didn't mind. If a woman couldn't sponge on her husband then she had to sponge on someone else, that is if she was to be in a position to let six children sponge on her, which they naturally had to for a few years at least—so he had no objection to things missing from the kitchen (besides, pay day for Reoraidgh was flexible and if some butter was missing it invalidated protest). All the same, he drew the line at his shirts which he had sometimes seen his secretary wearing. Disappearance of bread, fats, left-overs of meat and fish was different, perhaps even flattering.

A tendency on the part of Olivia to dramatise what needed no dramatisation—in particular the life she had chosen—sometimes gave Traquhair apprehensions about what she might not one day do if ever she felt life with Reoraidgh lacking in drama. At present, even stowed away in the annexe, she was safe in this respect. Meldrum was a quiet embodiment of drama, day in, day out, and she herself, immured as she was with such a seemingly unworthy mate, shone out with all the more lustre and had attracted much attention both in Bath and London. And then every year she marched to Aldermaston.

The Lifeline

Was she in fact self-sufficient ? Something androgynous about her face suggested she might perhaps be her own husband and her own wife, too, and therefore marvellously well married, Meldrum being merely her cross and her publicity.

Somehow the picture of Olivia married to an effective man simply didn't come. Her first husband, for instance, was said to be now a " poor white " in Calcutta.

Once or twice she had vanished leaving all her children in the care of a woman, so old she could scarcely stand, who would arrive a few minutes before or after her departure. Traquhair had met a film producer who had known Olivia Meldrum, also a waiter in Soho, a rich politician and well-known educationalist Dame—and a left-wing TV commentator. They knew her, but they did not know Meldrum. Therefore, Traquhair concluded that when Olivia went off on one of her sudden flits she either revived various acquaintances in a world she had known before marriage—or else acquired more curious, often prominent—acquaintances in a series of brief encounters in a world to which she aspired. Sometimes Traquhair thought it must have been she who had made Reoraidgh give up his job in Bath to become secretary to Tulloch Traquhair Ltd. Why ? He suspected she had an eye for weakness—for instance, for himself. Her blue eyes were full of womanly compassion ; her low urgent voice might, perpetually, have been that of a nun in the middle of an earthquake emergency ; but behind the murmurous sympathy her stupefied blue stare contained tenacity, the mad lucidity of a fanatic. She was tall and the slow, speechless movement with which she cleared hair from her lowered eyes, after contradiction or obstruction to her will, seemed to indicate the essence of resistance—and the futility of all words. Her skin was tinged naturally browny gold, and even after the long tugging of six voracious Meldrums, her breasts still lifted her dress, still fitted her for the role she could so profitably have filled, failing stardom—modelling. So, too, did her face. With a certain imaginative adjustment she could have figured in the never-never land of Sulamidt Wülfing's heavenly infants, as one of

The Lifeline

Augustus John's pastel gipsies, or with another subtler but perhaps even smaller change, as one of Fuseli's beautiful but insidious apparitions.

This was the mysterious Olivia Meldrum, wife of Meldrum, a troubling presence whom Traquhair would often gladly pay a vanished pound of butter not to meet.

Was it surprising that he did not wish to know her reactions to the filthy annexe of the Strathire Arms?

For a week he only saw her in the distance—or going out of the hotel with provisions. Then they waved to each other like distant friends.

Or like accomplices?

He knew that Reoraidgh must have told her about the key. He knew, too, that if she had not wanted to come north Reoraidgh would not have come, and they might all have been still in London.

Naturally, therefore, the wave he gave her was a little uncertain, reluctant, dependent; perhaps even a little ritualistic and propitiatory like throwing salt over the shoulder.

But he calmed his fears by thinking: " It's her young. The preservation of the species. Involved with Meldrum, she has every right to make ends meet in whatever way possible. It is her sacred biological role."

After thinking this he felt better, for he believed nature to be basically constructive.

8

ALL SMALL PLACES thrive on gossip but in Fluach Presbyterianism gives it a special succulence. The new tenants of the Strathire Arms would have enjoyed celebrity even if they had merely been new inhabitants. But that Traquhair should have taken the hotel direct from the ex-convict Stephenson (and boast as much), and that he should be a semi-celebrity in his own right, and also look like a twenty-stone Robinson Crusoe disguised as Lochiel, and have a secretary who made mothers call their children in close, and a secretary's wife who might have been a film star, a model, an artist or perhaps even worse (for she had that street-walker's look sometimes, something hard and indefinable), all added up to the biggest local news since the previous marchioness was forcibly removed from the castle by a coloured butler acting under the marquess's orders.

In public the matter was never talked of openly any more than would have been a murder during the night. Direct reference to an event of magnitude is always eschewed in Fluach as though it would bring bad luck to the person mentioning it. For instance, to-day Mr. MacFarlane, the banker, who always remained in his inner room until he spied, through the unfrosted M of MANAGER on his glass door a customer worth his attention, came out and standing as usual so straight as to make his paunch seem a sort of credential, a certificate of trustworthiness and immense backing as well as a badge of equality with his wife, he said to several different clients: " Well, well, Mr. So-and-So. What's new in the big world ? " and fiddling with his fob, hooking his thumbs in his waistcoat pocket he accompanied even clients without capital

The Lifeline

—this was unusual—to the door. There on the scrubbed threshold of the Caledonian Tea Bank, after the usual veiled probes into their latest activities, probes which were presumptuous in proportion to their overdraft, he said things like, " The place'll be filling up with tourists soon, won't it ? Ai—ai—new facilities, new faces . . ." The lack of ending to the sentence, the reference to the tourist trade when speaking to a client not engaged in it, the "new faces, new facilities" was all typical of Fluach reference to the thing everyone had in mind.

In the same way the butcher, Harry Skene, who went in for quite a bit of small talk over the scales, both to lubricate business and, it was alleged, to distract attention from the scales pointer, aired several subjects including the weather, but with five customers in succession got as far as dropping change into their palms before permitting himself the comment, " Big changes out east." (The Strathire Arms is in fact on the northern edge of Fluach, but for years that sector has been known as " Out East," presumably since the days when it constituted the West of Old Fluach of which some humps and a few big stones still remain.)

And the customers said: " Is that right ? " which might have been about the small change, the scrag-end or the big change out east.

Such delicacy may be compared by some to the reluctance found among certain savage tribes to refer directly by name to the beast which has ravaged their crops or the storm which is threatening their roofs. But for others a more solid and simple explanation could be found in that basis of all morality : do as you would be done by. In other words, the people of Fluach did not talk with familiarity of a neighbour's business—even if it was murder—in case he should talk with familiarity of theirs. Polite Highland eyes were oblique and this was the case with no one so much as with the policeman, Sergeant Murray, who was related to many of us.

Of course in private, in the backs of shops where, say, Major Murray, the Excise Officer, uncorked a flask and took

The Lifeline

a dram of official "sample" with the cobbler, their two faces suffused with violent autumnal flush of rowan, bilberry and maple did, after a mere grace, as it were, of indirect reference to changes out East, to cover the identity of the whisky, assault the subject frontally, referring to Tulloch Traquhair by name and making comments about his size, his kilt, his henchman, his henchman's beautiful wife, and his origins. The man, they said, evoked the memory of big Ian Creevie who used to toss the caber at the Cullan Games before the war. In those days the games were still local, not monopolised by the bicycle race between Polish students over to help with the harvest. Ai, they said, big Ian was no bigger. Finally, they shook their heads deferring judgment on all but Traquhair's capacity to make the Strathire Arms pay. Indeed, they reverenced him a bit for the amount of capital he must have behind him even to make the attempt. Their estimates of what he would have to spend on the place varied between three and seven thousand.

" Creevie was wanting it, wasn't he ? " said the major, offering the flask again, as though it were medicine.

He, and everyone else, knew perfectly well Creevie " was wanting it," but it was a nice way of bringing the fact up so they could enjoy it communally with noncommittal "aies" and stares into spaces, stares which took comfort for their now obscure lives, small incomes and old age from the spectacle of Creevie's frustration. Sympathy might have been forthcoming to someone less rich, less apparently successful and above all, less "stand-offish." (Poor Creevie with his seventeen golf balls putting alone on an empty green Saturday evenings in April—stand-offish !)

Such whispered confabulations in the backs of shops, over family teas, in the safety of the open air was all the direct discussion the subject got till the Tuesday after Traquhair's arrival, the publication day of our weekly *Trumpet*—usually referred to as "the Raggie."

The *Trumpet* is devoted to local events. Its small circulation depends on offending no one and this necessity results in very bare reporting indeed, even of W.R.I. cake competitions. It

The Lifeline

has something in common with those *Ocean News* mimeographs circulated on big liners : it lists, so to speak, the times for housey-housey and the names of people on board—and council meetings (expurgated), little else.

Trumpet photographs usually suggest London pea-soupers where people get lost when they go out to post a letter. But it does own one or two permanent blocks, particularly of the M.P., Sir Duncan Fidge and Mrs. Spote, our biggest landowner, which produce clearly recognisable images, though of course by now we know them so well we do not examine them any more than we read the standing ad. for DRUMS, kilts, bagpipes, or the request for GAME with which certain southern butchers exhort local deer gangs.

Imagine our surprise, then, when on the inside or council-meeting page we saw a new photo, in clear, so to speak, of the new proprietor of the Strathire Arms and " Mr. Reoraidgh Meldrum, his secretary," one in a kilt the other in a space suit and both, believe it or not, armed with long-bows and quivers.

The caption read thus : " Our picture shows Mr. Tulloch Traquhair, the television star, and new proprietor of the Strathire Arms and Mr. Reoraidgh Meldrum, his secretary, enjoying a little relaxation on the moors. Both Mr. Traquhair and Mr. Meldrum are keen amateurs of the bow-and-arrow. They hope to do some shooting in their spare time."

Bow and arrow ?

Not for years, not since a certain royal personage stayed at the castle and begot our present water engineer at the weekend, had there been such surmise. Readers must remember that it is only sixty years, not a lifetime since the last outlaw in Great Britain inhabited the hills behind Fluach. We still have unexplained fires and that kind of thing which are done, not, as in the big cities, by people whom " no one knows," but by people we all know well, by the people next door.

People who had seen Meldrum in the flesh and now saw this picture of him with a bow immediately remembered where Stephenson had gone ; and Traquhair struck them as a Little John of real life, a fellow to reckon with. They could see him

The Lifeline

crawling over sharp stones in his bare knees and letting the stag—or the policeman—have it, right behind the shoulder. . . . He must despise rifles and modern ease—relish difficulty, hardship, physical prowess.

Most of us, at one time or another, have had cause to visit the office of McWilliam, our solicitor, and have therefore seen some of his father's early sporting groups in the waiting-room —pictures of Ian Creevie, Brian's father, old McWilliam and the previous marquess, iron-shod, bearded giants all, staring out over enormous space (one imagined), with the eyes of eagles, the muscles of gorillas and the hearts of poets. An evocative chord was therefore struck in nearly all of us when we saw this picture of Tulloch Traquhair and Reoraidgh Meldrum in the *Trumpet* staring out over enormous space, etc.

When Traquhair saw the picture he at once accepted it as the pair, if not a copy, of one that already existed in his own mind. That huge, bearded head turned from the dead beast and staring out over the shadowed hill with an expression that was half warlike, half Messianic, accorded exactly with a sensation which dwelt in his breast. What could the League for the Abolition of Bloodsports have done against such men ? Given up. For here was no cruelty only the fulfilment of a timeless harmony between hunter and hunted, meat-eater and meat. Here were eyes which could scarcely have looked on at the lone bullock in a truck, crazed with the stink of slaughter-house blood, dragged by seven laughing men. . . . Ah ! . . . They have hitched a rope round its neck, dragged it inch by inch till its leg catches in a strut ; now they have levered the leg loose with iron, and the beast is hauled slithering down a ramp where it sprawls with splayed front legs before seven aprons slimy with blood and eyes a vista of flayed carcasses strung up on tackle from iron girders. Fear makes it dumb, dribble and shit. Fear kindles in its eyeballs a microcosm of life, cornered and penultimate but so concentrated as to spread and involve everyone in unwilling affinity so that the laughter has to increase a bit above the aprons and a man comes forward,

The Lifeline

in spite of the extra work it'll mean, and turns it to a dead weight there, instead of farther in. It had a name; was one of seven. On a small croft.

Such meat was for the plates of logical positivists, men who disapproved or had no feeling for blood sports—or anything else—but who yet ate blood; not for this bearded and equable giant on the front page of the *Trumpet*. . . . His killing instinct was ventilated and related to digestion.

As he put the paper down Traquhair had a twinge, a familiar twinge, the sort which took the place of memory. . . .

In fact Meldrum had taken him up an easy slope but every hundred yards Traquhair had to sit down and watch his own flesh pour as though he were literally dissolving. The drops tickled his ears and neck and the top of his paunch, his crutch was a moist oven, the insides of his stockings sodden and his dark chest-hair showed like a huge shadow through clamped, almost transparent nylon. The sweat had even come through to the outside of his kilt. After a time he had not been able to carry his bow and quiver. He had laboured in the wake of the nimble Meldrum like a pregnant sow chasing a terrier. "Mercy," he had gasped.

But Meldrum had had no time for him; had simply left him weeping sweat from every little eye in his body, groaning that he was done. Meldrum had gone forward with his bow, disappeared and after a time came in sight, moving up a far slope like a snake. Traquhair watched his progress through glasses for half an hour before he finally caught sight of the deer, a group of pale-brown smears on the browner face of the hill. Meldrum seemed to be in full sight of them yet they remained still and unsuspecting. A queer thrill seized the fluttering heart of Traquhair. He thought, Shall I now . . . now . . . or shall I get a little closer ? Just a little . . . How high that clump of heather ? High enough, for the hinds' eyes are not in the tops of those thrilling pointed ears but lower, even lower than the brow. Beautiful eyes, boys' eyes, eyes of legend . . . on . . . another squelch, black moist peat, the very shit of time, against the cheek; harebells, bilberry and a beetle

The Lifeline

fugitive under the nose. Wild thyme and bog-myrtle in the pale sog between the heather. Another yard. Then lay the bow flat. I can smell the rankness of the tired male. Draw it out full. Two score. Rise slowly, by millimetres so the eyes of the sentinel see only heather following the wind's rhythm, a horizon heave merely in a breeze . . . pricked out now at last with two vigilant stars of death that hypnotise . . . and aim. . . .

He could see Meldrum rise to his knees. Suddenly the deer scrambled to their feet and were joined instantly by others till now unseen; the stationary smudges turned into a formal ballet which seemed to rock as though on air, down away into the glen. Only one remained. It stood looking round and then up, took two or three paces as though dragging an impossible weight, then wheeled its head sleepily and pitched sideways out of sight. Meldrum stood up.

By the time Traquhair reached him, he was gloved to the elbows with blood and the hind's entrails lay like a colossal, variegated jellyfish billowing beside its hollowed loins. Meldrum's knife gleamed as he cleaned it on moss. His face was tranquil.

Together they examined the arrow's point of entry, an inch behind the shoulder, six inches deep.

Four hours later, after a drag which had reduced Traquhair to the edge of physical collapse, their home coming had coincided with a visit from the editor/reporter of the *Trumpet*, and at his request they had taken up the pose on the low ground (above the henhouse) which later, as one of the *Trumpet's* permanent blocks became familiar to the inhabitants of Fluach continually arousing vague memories not only of Victorian Balmoral and Landseer pictures, but also of local personalities who died between the wars.

The hind was left out of the picture, at Traquhair's request, because it was not a stag. But that a beast had been shot with an arrow soon became generally known, and no one supposed for a moment that anyone but Traquhair had shot it.

The picture in the *Trumpet* and the rumour of the whole

The Lifeline

episode added to speculation, already rife. And then the following day, Sunday, the nine people in Fluach who took the *Sunday Times*, among them the Creevies, noted the following letter:

Dear Sir,—

In assessing the merits of Mr. Hargreaves' *Horn in the Forest* I was surprised to see your reviewer fall into the old error of supposing Robin Hood to have been a man of peasant stock. His true name was Robert Fitz-Ooth which was perhaps corrupted (later ?) to Robert o' the Wood, having first passed through the stage of Robert Ooth, on the tongues of the motley, and even perhaps Robert Oot or Ood.

Dr. Stukely's *Palæographia Britanniæ* leaves little room for doubt that John Scot, tenth Earl of Huntington, died *anno* 1237 without issue and therefore Robert Fitz-Ooth was by the female line next heir to that title as descended from Gilbert de Gaunt, Earl of Kyme and Lindsay.

Nor can I allow the suggestion that archery flourished in Scotland in the thirteenth century. It was James I in the early fifteenth, who, anxious to end the English superiority in this arm, decreed (1424), " That all men might bush themselves to be Archares fra tha be twelve yeres of age and that ilk tenne pounds of land there be made bow markes . . ."

Before that our Caledonians' skill in toxophily had been summed up in the following lines, from a royal, Scottish pen:
    With that a freynd of his cried Fy
    And up an arrow drew
    He forgit it sae furiously
    The bow in flenderis flew.

Finally, I must insist the popinjay was used just as much in Scotland as in England. Nay, more.

              We remain, sir,
                Yours sincerely,
                    TULLOCH TRAQUHAIR,
                    REORAIDGH MELDRUM, *Archer*.
                            Fluach

The Lifeline

The newcomers began to take all kinds of shape in our eyes. Who and what were they? Never before had two such questions remained so long unanswered in Fluach. Perhaps the man was, after all, a " military historian."

Even the two "daily helps" who had been engaged by Mrs. Wotherspoon on behalf of Mr. Traquhair were largely defeated. After a week they could only say that two of "his own" stockings ended abruptly at the instep "so as to save mending the toes"; though it's true that when a Pickford's van came, bringing the remains of his possessions, their inventory spared us the kind of curiosity, about furniture at least, which would otherwise have gnawed us slowly over the months.

Was the place to be a museum? In Traquhair's rooms we heard of stuffed birds, old weapons, ancestral portraits, targets, fetishes, Battersea china, silver grouse, coach horns, barometers, sporting prints and warming-pans—surely all inessential beginnings for a modern hotel. The few people who had caught a glimpse of Meldrum were less surprised to learn that he had none of this. He just had a bare table, chairs, a live cage bird, some linen and pots and pans; and she " hardly a stitch "—some batik skirts, brilliant blouses, and various sizes of curtain rings for her ears—or were they for her ankles?

There was no end to speculation. Some people, in despair, said Traquhair was a half-brother of the water engineer; others that his beard was false.

Old Mrs. Creevie announced firmly that he had tuberculosis. But Brian Creevie said nothing. He merely pointed out that Traquhair himself had said all there was to be said at the Wotherspoons. As to the man's general resemblance to his father, Ian Creevie. Well, he didn't remember his father. Anyhow—so what! From a distance Lionel Spote looked like Mr Ferhat Abbas, the Algerian leader.

9

THE NAME of Ian Creevie is still a force in Fluach and Rossiemurchat. He was one of those huge patriarchal Highlanders who gave substance to the legend which grew up round the person of Queen Victoria's manservant Tom Brown, that legend of the Highlander as " Nature's gentleman " which emerged so strangely from a history bespattered more even than that of Corsica, with bloody, unforgiving feuds, treachery, cruelty, piracy, dissension and murder.

In the heyday of highland sport and books about sportsmen, Ian was a sporting legend : no one had shot quite so straight, walked quite so far, caught so many salmon, stalked so many deer or endured such weather as Ian Creevie. The marquess had given him the freedom of his remoter moors. Foreign princes had been sent out with him after game. And in the Great War he had served with the Seaforths and become a major whose influence on his company had depended very little on his rank. After the war he inherited his father's inn, the old ramshackle Seaforth Arms. It seemed to jolly along regardless whether he was there or not. Guests came and went. He was rooked with moderation by a manager from the south. Most days he shot or fished, most evenings he drank and yarned with doctors, younger sons of younger aristocratic sons, lawyers, sheep farmers and various poor relations of the Strathire family who shared his tastes. Then—in the middle of his stories about tummy-dancers, sheikhs and bloodletting, he suddenly got married to the trim, minxish daughter of a regular client, a forceful golfing distiller from Edinburgh.

Miss Mildred Caley was everything in the world that Ian was

The Lifeline

not. In a way the match was symbolic of a historical development; the colonisation, by new rich from the south, of the Highlands. While other Creevies, who had got to hell out, were making good in America and Canada—and even in London, this one, remaining as a sort of super gamekeeper to an absentee, anglified marquess, seemed to have "held out," remained true to type. Yet suddenly he went and succumbed to a woman he could have put in his game bag but who, mysteriously, put him in hers.

"Oh," she purred archly. "Ian Hamish—I see I've got to seevilize you."

McWilliam, our solicitor, who used to drink and shoot with Creevie says that in spite of all the talk about tummy-dancers and Cairo night-clubs Creevie was really very innocent and had to be taken somewhere by friends a fortnight before the wedding to be initiated into the mysteries of sex. As a result, says McWilliam, he gave the rich and refined Miss Caley " a right shock " on their wedding night.

Whatever McWilliam may have meant, it's certain that something went wrong early. For from then on Miss Caley seemed to surround herself with an expanding *cordon sanitaire* which gradually pushed her husband and everything to do with him, out of the hotel.

Within a month of marriage the manager had been sacked and a parlourmaid in frills, like a mutton chop, appeared in the dark, ferny lounge. Brass became burnished, floors smelt of polish and the refinement with which visitors were questioned about their comfort made them feel beholden to Mrs. Creevie for some kind of uncommercial, real old Scots hospitality. They paid their bills with a sense almost of shame, were tempted "to ask her back" and booked a year ahead. The Seaforth Arms was transformed inside and out. She began calling it "a Family Hotel" (pronouncing it "Femily") and a sign went up to that effect.

She took over the books entirely.

In the past Ian Creevie had always seemed to sweat out his excess whisky on the moors and in the rivers. Now he became

The Lifeline

heavier in speech and movement. The old people say they used to wonder what he did with his feet when he went indoors. And of course it wasn't only his feet she found dirty. It was his whole self. He was seldom at home in the evenings and his cronies became more than ever essential to him; by day he took to the moors with the forlorn resolution of a tinker, a man who has no choice but to live under the naked sky. He had one child quickly and then that sort of thing seemed to stop like everything else.

Brian Creevie was brought up by a nanny from the lowlands who was always keeping him clean—clean enough for his mother's floors. In time two or three companions were selected for him. But even from them there was a danger of "catching" —or worse "learning something." Cousins, on his father's side of course, were forbidden to approach him. He acquiesced, because the alternative was to be left for long periods of darkness and isolation in his room.

Mrs. Creevie had been fond of darkness, isolation, sickness, ferns, insinuation; had hoarded mementoes, grievances, preserves and her own life. On Sundays her husband used to inspect the turf of the golf course since he couldn't play. Weekdays, while Brian sat with bib and nanny upstairs, he munched his piece on the moors, eyes gone blind with lack of thought, focusing a buzzard, a pair of antlers.... It was as though some extraordinary weakness had reduced the man to living, as had his farthest forebears, deep in the hills, where he was content to look down, in all senses, on agricultural land, permanent dwellings, and kitchen smoke; look down and patiently avoid battle.

Brian had gone to private and public schools. On parents' day the sight of Ian Creevie with his beard and kilt in an egg-and-spoon race would doubtless have made up for many of Brian's shortcomings at cricket and football. But never once did his father visit his school. In the holidays, catching sight of the child for the first time, he had a habit of closing one eye as though instinctively correcting the sight afforded, stereoscopically, by both. Sometimes he fumbled for contact,

The Lifeline

suggested doing one of the things he liked doing and then became aware of a gulf which he had let grow under his eyes.

Embarrassment clogged his tongue. The child, like everything else in the house, did not seem to him to be his any more.

For by then Mrs. Creevie had taken over—" rescued," she called it—almost everything her husband possessed. " The last straw," according to her was when " dear sweet Ian Hamish— I'm sheur you won't believe me," had a chance of buying the Strathire Arms for five hundred pounds. " And," said Mrs. Creevie to Mrs. Harrison, the then minister's wife, " he led me to understand that he had in fect burt it. Imagine my hörror when I urpened the *Trumpet* and sur it had been burt by the St. Giles Temperance Trust. Now everyone knows my feelings for strong liquor except in möderation but to tell you the truth, I smelt a rat—yes, I smelt a rat. And then—what d'you think ? —only two years later, the place was visited by the police for reasons I hesitate to mention. (Girls," she muttered ventriloquially.) " I said, There, Mildred, what did I tell you ? You should have hed the courage of your convictions and taken the metter out of the hands of poor dear Ian Hamish, öriginnally."

After that Mildred had the courage of her convictions, and Ian Creevie began to drink seriously. He lost his friends—the marquess among them. And more and more he began to frequent people whom his wife considered socially beneath her.

One occasion in particular Brian would never forget. It was during the summer holidays, at the Cullan Games. He had been walking round the arena between the back of the crowd and the side shows and canteens and had stopped for a moment to stare at a pipe-major putting down beer. Sweat was pouring through the man's saturated eyebrows into his eyes. . . . In one hand he was holding his fur shako by the chain chin strap, like a huge bucket. A drummer was pissing behind the tent like a burst pipe. There was sawdust on the ground and vomit. Suddenly his father had staggered out of the tent hailing the pipe-major by his Christian name. Then he had seen his son.

He stopped as though struck in the face. Perplexity clouded

The Lifeline

his beery eyes. Then going up to the pipe-major and putting his arms round the massive shoulders, he whispered loudly: " John . . . is that you, John ? Well, listen—she brought him up to be ashamed of me, is that right ? Well, man, who d'you think's ashamed—him or me ? Look at him . . ."

Blood drained from Brian's cheeks leaving him the colour of a newly emptied milk bottle.

He was ten.

By then already the spectre of whisky had linked its arm in Ian Creevie's, and was finishing the slow taxidermy, complete to the glassing of eyes, which many of us in Fluach know well and the wives of our poor still fear worse than death.

In fact, the Ian Creevie whom people had once known had already " passed over," as Mildred would say ; the rest of his days were expected to be just a long familiar formality.

But this was not the case.

That very week, which enshrined the incident Brian could never forget, his father surprised everyone, came to life, as it were, vocationally.

The annual circus had camped as usual at the end of the golf links with all the side shows clustered round the big tent. It was called McCann's circus, but the real name of McCann, the proprietor and his wife, was Gruber, German Jews. The wife, Betsy, was a spirited little woman, agile as a marmoset and a deadly shot with a pistol. She used to gallop round the ring on a horse exploding balloons with some kind of low-velocity dart. The balloons went bang but no holes appeared in the canvas, and none of the audience ever let out a yell of pain. In fact, no one really knew quite how it was done. Cynics, who said the balloons were detonated by remote control, were quite unable to prove their point. Most people, were, anyhow, only too glad to believe in the extraordinary skill of the tiny galloping Amazon and cheering broke out as soon as the arena blossomed out in readiness for the event without which no day would have been complete. Imagine the general astonishment one evening, after the appearance of the balloons, when

The Lifeline

instead of Mrs. McCann, the German Jewess, there appeared Ian Creevie, the Highlander, on his hill pony, Morag, armed with a Colt .45 automatic. His flaming face and gleaming eye made mothers draw their children in closer, and he, as though relishing the general dread, went several times round the ring, always threatening to start picking off the balloons. Suddenly a thickish voice in the background invited him to have a go. The next instant there was a deafening explosion and some people thought they had been hit. The children were delighted and looked round to see which of the balloons had become a limp shred falling to earth. None! At the fourth shot there was a tremendous answering crack outside the tent where one of the guy-ropes had parted. But at the fifth a balloon did simply vanish and a hole appeared clearly in the canvas above it. By then people were using each other for cover.

After emptying his pistol he continued to career round the ring quite delighted with the effect he was having on the community. Round and round he went until at last, conscious perhaps of certain obligations and a growing monotony, he began to slip one foot over the saddle to join its mate in the approved circus style. It was then, as he attempted this fairly simple manœuvre that everyone realised he was almost sleepily drunk. Had he gone on and tried to stand up on the cantering horse he would certainly have come heavily to harm. But at this moment Mrs. McCann appeared at the ring entrance with the weight-lifter. Greatly excited, she spoke to the strong man in a foreign language. The next moment the weight-lifter was coasting alongside the cantering Morag and at a certain moment he removed Creevie as neatly as though they had been rehearsing for months. Only a weight-lifter could have done it for Creevie weighed fifteen stone. The movement must by then have stirred up the alcohol in his blood for he went out in the strong man's arms like a light—or perhaps one should say, like a concussed general—with his Colt dangling heroically from one hand. He didn't come round for hours. There was an awful fuss. The police were called in, but our police are something special. Not only are they usually related, if not to the

The Lifeline

culprit, then to one of his friends, but they have to live amongst us usually alone, afterwards, and as often as not retire amongst us; so to say " the police were called in " means nothing. They are in, all the time. Sober truth were those words of a man recently up before the sheriff who when asked whether he knew that what he had done was against the law, replied: " Since when, Your Honour, has the law crossed Kintail Bridge ? " (Some twenty miles south of Fluach.)

Mrs. McCann had to make some sort of statement that Creevie had been hired to do the act, but had taken the wrong gun. She produced a licence for a .45 automatic which apparently she had been granted in case one of the lions went mad. The lions were in Aberdeen but, luckily, she was meeting them in Oban. For two Sundays Mrs. Creevie stayed away from church, having taken to her bed. The good name of her family hotel which she had built up over the years was smirched and she herself personally humiliated—perhaps as she had been on her wedding night. Creevie himself went over to the west coast where he had a friend with a hotel in Ullapool— to "rest." This was odd as McCann's circus was due at Ullapool that same week. Some wits said he had been signed on, but there was no word of a repeat performance and in a week or two he came back, literally to die, of some obscure disease, probably assisted by apathy.

Before he took this step tongues wagged freely. What had he been doing in the circus tent ? Mr. McCann hadn't come up that year. What was Ian's relationship with Mrs. McCann ? Why had he gone to Ullapool ? It was whispered Ian Creevie had been " friendly " with her for several seasons.

There was a huge wreath from the circus, very gay, with explosions of roses as big as balloons all round it and this, with its associations, consorted oddly with the sermon preached by Creevie's old uncle, a Wee Free minister, who used the occasion to do what he had never managed to in the past— lecture his nephew to his face and point the wages of sin. The desolate and yet stricken exultation of the old man's improvised prayers, his intimate and fearful asides to merciless divinity

The Lifeline

whose very finger seemed present pinning down the corpse of Creevie just in case a dangerous spark still remained, produced such a sad effect that not even the customary libations of whisky could wash the taste of death out of the black mourners' mouths. And the subsequent sight of Mrs. Creevie, for eight months, dressed like a black artificial flower, with a face white as an unbaked scone, did no one any good at all and confirmed an impression of something vivid and indigenous defeated by something alien and sick.

10

WHEN TRAQUHAIR and the Meldrums had been in Fluach a month the gossips led by Mildred Creevie began to say, " I told you so." For despite the ceaseless activity of the "barman," as Meldrum was called, and the dailies, no serious progress towards making the place fit to receive guests had yet been made. John Mackay, the contractor, and Brian Creevie's only friend, received a letter written apparently with a broad paintbrush and blood in which he had been invited to *"togail an teine* (kindle the fire) in yet another Highland hearth." Ignorant of Gaelic and obsessed with competition for the Cullan dam sub-contracts, Mackay had not answered until he received another more explicit letter asking him to kindly send round a representative and quote an estimate for a new public bar and renovations both inside and out. This Mackay had done, pricing himself, he hoped, out of Traquhair's market since at present he wanted to concentrate on the Cullan dam, and the five or even six-figure sub-contracts soon to be allotted. Of course he could not entirely neglect local custom—the day would come when he would again need it—but Traquhair was not only a stranger he was also frivolous, judging by his correspondence, unemployed, judging from the newspapers and a friend of a criminal, according to his own words. Weeks passed and Mackay was scarcely surprised to hear no more from the new hotelier. Strathireshire is rich in lunatics, cranks and bankrupt enterprises. Refugees from society, some with good mostly with bad reasons, tend to congregate there and no one expects them to prosper or answer letters. Alfred Stiggins who invented a combustion engine which ran on water, wrote

The Lifeline

countless letters to Fluach tradesmen about supplying them even with free samples of his special fuel. In time people disregarded him. John Mackay began to do the same to Tulloch Traquhair.

One mild morning, it might have been any mild morning, the laird, toxophilist, actor was sitting in the backyard on a kitchen chair. Most people would have imagined him prey to anxiety and it is true : he was. He was taut as a harp.

For above him dawn is breaking, breaking above Ben Cullan. (The time in fact is 11.30 a.m.). As light increases the summit seems to be missing, because the snow-covered slopes recede till they lose all definition and blend where the summit should be, with white sky. Lower down, big scattered boulders show up particularly black in the partial thaw and a single grouse looks the size of a turkey. Dark patches are appearing everywhere lower down but the eye moves naturally up again, intrigued, and fixes on two lines of black dots which are conspicuous for their regularity.

A shimmering red rim of sun now tops the grey sea beyond the icefloes of the Inverurie Firth. Formations of gulls in jet silhouette pass soundlessly overhead towards the cheerless water. Oyster catchers bleat and in the hills a wolf howls. The two lines of dots have begun to move—towards each other.

The lines of dots are in fact mounted men. The hairy facial shagginess of both men and ponies is something seldom seen in primitive tribes to-day nor in the pictures of ancient civilisations : it leaves little freedom to eyes and mouth. It is almost a form of clothing. Much of the ponies' shagginess is pale brown, and of the men's—pale red. No saddles intervene between the wiry bodies of the two kinds of animal ; and the humans are only dressed in rough cloth, bound criss-cross at the legs. They carry claymores and round leather shields, and their eyes, unlike those of the ponies, are injected with a glittering mixture of fear and aggression which soon affects their tongues. Howls break out in one line and are answered

The Lifeline

from afar by similar howls from the other. Then there is speech, half-mingled with the howls, and gradually the emerging repetition of one word, one shout which soon becomes concerted and rhythmic, affecting the moments that heels are hacked against the ponies' sides and the waving of the swords. One man in particular seems to give order to this chorus. It is he, the one who is big, almost as big as the pony beneath him and a little in front, who has a red beard in proportion to the rest of him.

As the lines close towards each other an unexpected similarity between them becomes apparent. Each line is made up of exactly twenty units. Immediately some principle of prior arrangement and even " order " seems to characterise a scene which till now has discounted the possibility of either.

The horses are trotting, sometimes swerving to avoid obstacles. The howls become delirious. . . .

When the horsemen are only twenty feet apart the far line suddenly halts and from the back of every pony an armed man leaps down—still leaving an armed man in the saddle. Magically, one force has doubled!

Borne on by their impetus the first line cannot turn back. In a few seconds, outnumbered two to one, they are fighting for their lives. Clangs and grunts, howls and groans, thuds of pony against pony, wild neighings and the rattle of scree as hoofs or feet stumble, turn gradually to terrible scuffling silence punctuated by the sounds of final falls. Hot blood cuts brilliant rivulets in the dazzling snow. . . . The huge leader of the outnumbered swipes the hands from a man holding his horse's tail so that for a moment the two severed relics remain clinging intelligently while the wrists spout blood; at the same instant he has kicked down an attacker from the side with a backward thrust of one foot, while parrying the blow from a third full on the angled plane of his shield. The striker has no time to recover his balance for the big man's sword has already turned from amputating slash to impaling thrust—through muscular throat. Satisfaction rings a cry from his lips, his pony rears . . . he seems to turn it in midair, shouts a

The Lifeline

command and a moment later he is free and has drawn away, is joined by one other—sole survivor.

This other now appeared. Traquhair after one glazed, hypnotised instant, closed his eyes, a little resentfully.

"You ought to be more careful, Reoraidgh," he muttered.

"What is it?"

"There's this," said Meldrum. "Shall I give it to you or put it in your room?"

Traquhair's eyes focused apprehensively and saw a bit of paper held not far from his face.

"What is it?" he said irritably, and took it.

Meldrum's handwriting must have told a thing or two to an expert.

Traquhair saw a list of brooms, dusters, food, petrol, nails, detergent, buckets, bins . . . every item priced down to the last halfpenny.

"And what has that got to do," said Traquhair, indifferently handing back the bit of paper, "for God's sake, with anything?"

Meldrum said: "There are still such contemptible questions as where the next nail is coming from, the next packet of Buzz, the next chop . . ."

Traquhair's little eyes flitted up and in a trice took in the severe but dogged expression of a man who had worked hard with his hands, many days and much of many nights, but who had been rewarded little better than a convict, with food, shelter and humiliating instalments of pocket money. Possibly no one had worked harder in the whole of Great Britain in the last weeks than that sad, educated man standing there.

"Did you speak to Mackay?" Meldrum said.

The name Mackay with its powerful associations coming as it did hard on the heels of gripping hallucination made Traquhair veil his eyes with lowered lids as might a schoolboy screen his paper from a sharp-sighted rival. He even turned while saying, "Mackay . . .?" doubtfully and resisted an impulse to let his eyes stray back, up on to the slopes of Ben Cullan.

The Lifeline

" J. S. Mackay."

" Just seventeen times, that's all," said Traquhair.

" And what was the result ? "

His secretary's tone irritated him. For a moment he was tempted to ask Meldrum whether it was true that he had described him, Traquhair, to one of the helps as " a phoney old lay-about " for this was what had eventually reached the ears of the Wotherspoons' cattleman's wife and finally, via Nadia, his own.

" Ah, Reoraidgh, Reoraidgh," he sighed, "when will you have a little faith ? " And he closed his eyes. It worked. He heard receding steps, finally the sound of Meldrum at work again in the distance, toiling " by the sweat of his brow," possibly even " worshipping God with every move he made," something like that, something " whole " and so full of faith that Traquhair became disgruntled simply from thinking about it.

" Supposing I told them what I know about you," Traquhair muttered, " would you still address me in that tone ? "

An unspoken but clearly imagined "Yes" brought a frown to Traquhair's face. Minutes passed. Finally Meldrum won and Traquhair found himself trying, as he did each morning on waking, to prepare himself for an interview with J. S. Mackay, the thing that hadn't yet happened even once.

II

THE SMOOTH PALE GLOBE which was to be seen in Fluach Main Street one floor up, motionless, all day and much of many nights and after 2 p.m. on Sundays, through the window above the showroom full of Frigidaires, was the pate of John S. Mackay. At night you could see it in the distance when you turned into the straight, by the chemist's, and from there on it was clear as a full moon till you passed the ironmonger's; then—if you were in an interesting or powerful make of car, it tilted briefly and took you in.

Small and incapable of decentralising, partly because he imputed his own pride to others (and hence doubted every man's co-operation), and partly because he wished to maintain the strong personal relationship which his father had enjoyed with all his employees, the life of John S. Mackay was a nonstop feat of physical and mental agility. His father had had twenty men and a few hundred pounds' worth of equipment; he had four hundred men and a million pounds' worth of machinery alone. The £100,000 sub-contract for the Government and the tap and plug lost by an apprentice at Upper Kintullochy could be paired in his attention in the same five minutes. He all but ran down passages and when reading his eyes went flat like racing dogs. Subordinates took messages from between his shoulder blades so as to leave his eyes free for other work. Half Sundays he spent on trunk calls, the other half in an Aston-Martin which answered his need to dispose and get ahead with only minimal problems of decentralisation. At lunch his wife knew him as a *Daily Express* from the waist up, with a telephone cable disappearing underneath his elbow as

The Lifeline

though having come in and put down a whisky, he had then plugged himself in to some sort of dynamo.

After the buzz in the inter-com announcing Traquhair's imminence, Mackay stole a look out of the window and looked at his visitor's car—1926 Rolls. He briefly shook his head like a district nurse finding a nappy that should have been changed last month. He had no time for the vintage car boys.

When the door opened and he saw Traquhair close up (for the second time), the impression he had got at the Wotherspoons' party and from the man's correspondence was confirmed.

"Good morning, sir!" said Traquhair.

"Good morning, Mr. Traquhair," said Mackay in an objective tone.

Mackay refused snuff and was not interested in Traquhair taking it. His eyes fell to the two immense legs. The man was a freak, for goodness' sake. He ordered two cups of office tea, gave Traquhair a seat and then faced him sitting half-round from his desk in his swivel chair. At such moments Mackay's shaggy brows seemed to shoot up in two points like the ears of an inquiring owl and he stared hard with his soft eyes full of obstinate apprehension. A man of few words, he always saved them up for what he imagined to be the whites of a client's eyes. "Frankly" was one of his favourite words and he believed there was no man in Fluach more entitled (by virtue of his sincerity not by virtue of his power) to use it. Certainly there were occasions when he gave displays of frankness such as had not been witnessed since the death of the factor of the previous duke, who had treated Mackay's father like dirt.

"Well sir . . ." said John Mackay briskly, and it was as though he had pressed the handle of a stop-watch and the long red arm was from now on eating its way round the first circuit. Traquhair's front wheels were still on the starting line.

"There are many Mackays in these parts," said Traquhair, stirring his tea and looking at his host in a human and broaching fashion. "At what date did they make their home in the land of the treacherous southerner?"

The Lifeline

Mackay's face underwent a momentary blankness.

"They belong farther north," said Traquhair.

Mackay gave a brief swift denial of any knowledge or interest in such questions. Frankly, he said, he knew little of Scottish history and cared less.

"All stock of Ochonocar all . . ." Traquhair murmured sonorously. "*Bratach Bhan Chlann Aoidh!*"

Mackay blinked but said nothing, did nothing; simply stared and touched the cuff of his left wrist.

Traquhair took a noisy sip and then ceremoniously put the cup down, flipped a clean coloured handkerchief and mopped his nostrils with a stylish two-way movement.

"With Sunday overtime booming," Traquhair's eyes lit far away, immaterially, on the sea's horizon, "and never a squeak from our noble Lord's Day Observers and Councillors, the Cullan dam will no doubt bring a cloudburst of cash to Fluach."

Mackay said he was sure he didn't know, but it was certainly possible.

"I should have thought the Cullan dam must concern you fairly intimately," went on Traquhair in a stimulating tone, his little eyes flitting back to the contractor with a fleeting invitation, as it were, to waltz.

"Yes . . . we're doing some of the work for them. We hope to do more."

Traquhair said: "The dam is of great interest to us . . . to the Strathire Arms."

"I'm sure it will be, Mr. Traquhair."

Every syllable that left Mackay's mouth invited Traquhair to get down to brass tacks.

"Hence—as it were—I was wondering how soon we could put the place on its legs again. Pipes, window-panes and a new spacious bar, seem to be the priorities. As in my last, as in my ult. Above all, the bar. The man you sent round was most helpful. Most. Though short sighted. At one moment I thought we had lost him!"

"Well, Mr. Traquhair, I'll be frank with you: we're up to

The Lifeline

the eyes. But I don't want to see you stuck and I don't want to discourage the kind of custom we'll need again when the dam's finished. You got our provisional estimate?"

"Indeed, I did. I just wanted to know how *soon*. . . . April seemed a bit . . ."

Mackay suddenly stared at Traquhair almost emotionally as though the big man had said something quite different, something pathetic.

"Well, Mr. Traquhair," he burst out in a fast, low and reckless tone as though confessing some crime to a judge and jury he slightly despised, "I'll be frank with you, and I hope you won't take offence, because I've nothing against you. In fact, frankly I sometimes enjoyed watching you with the kids. But look! See it my way. There's plenty about this Strathire Arms which is none of my business but which needs a bit light shedding on it before folks round here are going to give a thousand pounds' credit. I never had a bad debt from Johnny Stephenson. Frankly, I found the man pleasant enough for all the dealings I ever had with him. But facts are facts. He's in gaol," (Mackay flushed), "and the place is gone to wrack and ruin. Frankly, Mr. Traquhair, I quite appreciate your being used to saying 'do this and do that' and the things being done, but on this occasion I'll have to ask you for an advance of fifty per cent of the estimate submitted." Here Mackay's eyes shone, swam almost with tears and he flushed more, staring at the possibility, no doubt, of being faced with someone as touchy as himself. Galled by bland silence, he went on faster than ever. "I'll not deceive you. Compared to what you may be accustomed, to this is a funny part of the world. It's not a case of once bitten twice shy; I've been bitten *a hundred* times. So that's it, then. Fifty per cent. Take it or leave it. I'm sorry . . ."

"And what part of the world . . . do you suppose *I've* been accustomed to?" said Traquhair, smiling.

Mackay's eyes dropped briefly to the kilt. "Well, I gather you've been working in the south . . ."

"For my sins!"

Mackay stirred impatiently and his eyes went blank as

The Lifeline

though time were limited and here they were again off at a tangent. Eleven forty-two.

"But, Mr. Mackay . . ." Traquhair purred, "whoever suggested there would be any difficulty about an advance of . . . of . . ."—he waved a big hand with extraordinary delicacy as though at a bad smell—"fifty per cent?"

Mackay stared glassily at the big man's face and particularly at below the lips where it began to disappear into beard. What went on in there?

Traquhair took out a cheque-book and for a second held it up as though it were a bone and Mackay a dog on its hind legs.

"Now . . .?" said Traquhair. "May I? Otherwise I may forget. I'd pay you the whole sum in advance were I not confident you might then despise me as a fool for not appreciating what a 'funny part of the world' this is. Though candidly, Mr. Mackay, after fifty years' experience, off and on, of the land in which I was born and bred, I have found Highlanders as honest as people elsewhere."

While talking, Traquhair had started writing scratchily. His expression suggested he was starting a Foundation for the treatment of people with persecution mania.

Suddenly Mackay said: "Put it away, put it away—I'll not take it. People don't quite appreciate . . ." There was a brief buzz. Mackay turned and said:

"Well?"

"Is Andy to come out west with the van this forenoon, Mr. Mackay?"

"Yes," he said. "For God's sake," and switched the man out and turned—to find a cheque for five hundred pounds on his blotter.

And Traquhair had risen.

So then, reluctantly, did Mackay, the top of his head reaching to the level of Traquhair's nipples.

"Frankly, Mr. Traquhair, I'm embarrassed . . ." He looked near tears.

"I know the feeling," Traquhair said gravely but unsympathetically.

The Lifeline

Mackay saw him downstairs and praised the durability of Rolls-Royce engines with a face still wrought up, eyes still glistening.

On the following day work started on the hotel.

And the same week no one was surprised to see an advertisement in the *Trumpet*:

MAIDS wanted. All purposes. One to help in bar. Happy disposition, good appearance essential. Good home. Apply T. Traquhair, Strathire Arms, Fluach.

It lay between Mrs. Gunter-Sykes's standing advertisements for a housemaid and a shepherd, but coming from a hotel, situated in Fluach, it stood a dog's chance.

12

THERE WERE only two girls of outstandingly "good appearance" in Fluach. One worked in the MacFarlane's bank and the other in the Highland Dairies where she fed bottles still bleary with milk into a great clashing machine which cleaned them with steam. This was Helen MacDonald. During lulls she came to the front in a gleaming wet rubber pinafore and on a sunny day dressed thus, auburn hair to her shoulders, and bosom full as the eyes of every young man who saw it, she was as conspicuous as the distillery chimney and much more beautiful. If she hadn't been virtually an orphan it's likely her parents wouldn't have let her work "at the Milk" as the place was notorious. Psychologists could have a high old time theorising upon the cause of what went on in there and comparing statistics of illegitimacy, say, with those of the Coal Board. They might accuse the milk or the rubber aprons or the low I.Qs. of employees, or simply lay all at the door of the overseer, Fadgeon, himself, but the people of Fluach themselves were not given to analysis. They were content with stating the Highland Dairies was no place for a nice girl, and leave it at that. Of course we all know you can't make sweeping insinuations even about milk or rubber aprons or Fadgeon, they don't mean anything at all: but by April, after three months with the Milk, Helen was expecting. Fifty years ago the elders would have grilled her till she divulged the name of the man concerned, but nowadays not much happened except the people with whom she lodged said she couldn't have it there, and the Milk manager, Fadgeon, wouldn't promise to hold her job open. No one mentioned the matter much really.

The Lifeline

There was a general assumption that that sort of thing and person was taken care of nowadays, and certainly the hospital was going to take her when it came, and after that people said something would probably turn up, or there were these societies for adopting children whose mothers couldn't keep them.

It was strange how everyone knew the father and probably less strange how the father always looked as though he knew everyone knew. He had " side-boards " and delivered groceries for P. J. McConnachie. He dressed as a Teddy at dances and was a great whistler behind the big basket on his bicycle, but after Helen's condition became known he whistled so much and said " Good morning " to so many relative strangers that he must have been dry lipped by twelve noon. No one did more than he to prove Fadgeon's innocence. He really seemed to work at it.

But he got his books when McConnachie heard. McConnachie's daughter is in the choir and he thought people wouldn't wish to have the boy delivering things any more, an opinion which was reinforced when the Rev. Megginch transferred his custom elsewhere.

Helen's friend, Cathy, did all she could to help. Cathy had survived two years with the Milk and knew from the girls there was a woman in Rossiemurchat who helped girls " slim." But for some reason Helen always changed the subject. She just went on singing those daft songs she made up and dancing, sometimes, with an armful of pints ; or she'd pretend she was the manager and Cathy the secretary, get her into a corner mumbling, " There's no harm in it " and catch her through the skirt by the back of her suspender belt.

One morning they had cleared the cages and the bottles were all going round like people in a queue and they were standing on the wet floor with faces flushed from exertion, Helen said :
" Did you see where it said in the Raggie ' Wanted ' for a maid."
" I never saw when it didn't."
" T. Traquhair. Good appearance. I've applied."

The Lifeline

" And how'll that help ? "

" It said ' Good Home.' "

" You're not a lost dog."

" Perhaps I am, Cathy."

" That hotel's still wanting a roof. I'd wait for the roof," Cathy said.

Helen said, " Will they let me take my rubber apron ? It would be handy, wouldn't it ? . . ." She raised its ends in a gesture suggesting ballet-like reception of a baby for bathing and changing.

Cathy turned her head away. " You're daft."

" If it's a girl I'll be half-talking to myself. Where did you come from ? It's the size that frightens me, Cathy. Where's a thing like that to come out ? "

" You should know."

" Be quiet. It couldn't."

" And it could if it had two heads."

" That's enough from you, Cathie Mackay." Then a moment later : " Are you going to the dance first week ? "

" I might be. But you're not . . ."

" I think I will, won't I ? I think I'll be queen again."

Cathy looked at her friend to see if she were serious.

" Thon big feller in the kilt's to be judge. T. Traquhair. He won't know I'm a Fallen Woman. It might be my last chance. Afterwards my hair and teeth will fall out. . . . It's the calcium ; I read it."

The girl's carefree, exhilarated, bantering tone seemed to have an increasingly depressing effect on her ill-favoured friend, who at last came close to her, and said : " Helen, where are you going when it's born ? . . . You might come to us for a bit. . . . I might ask Ma. For a bit, just."

Helen said : " I'll just be seeing what they say where it said ' Wanted,' and ' Good Home.' Perhaps Mr. Traquhair will let me work there a month or two and keep my job open."

Cathy looked sceptical. At last she said : " What about your father ? "

The Lifeline

" He's in one room now. Mrs. Henderson, Galbraith Street."

" Couldn't he get two rooms ? "

" D'you think I'd want it ? "

" What's he doing now ? "

" Major Murray took him back for outside work where he can't lick the empty barrels. That's what they say, isn't it ? Don't worry, Cathy. Sure I'll be queen again first week. I'll give you a feel of my sash and a loan of the stockings. And I'll get a kiss from that great tickly beard if I'll let him."

" You'll get some funny looks. Helen ... what about Major Murray ? Isn't he ... related ? He's got a big house. Empty too." Cathy's voice had tailed off in embarrassment. But she need not have worried.

" My real dad you mean ? " Helen said brightly and drew herself up in an official, military fashion. " G'morning, Helen," she said. And she went off jiggling her bottles as though they were medals, responsibilities and tin knee caps. Major Murray was a distant cousin of her father's but, like everyone else she had heard the rumours that in fact *he* was her father. She believed it.

Something pendulous about the lower lip; something amber about the big eyes. . . . The mirror had told her more than any rumour.

" G'morning, Helen," she repeated, averting her eyes in a responsible fashion from some imaginary version of her expectant self, suddenly encountered. " A bit cauld."

13

MOST PEOPLE in Fluach grew accustomed to the daily spectacle of Traquhair going down Main Street in kilt, jacket, tam-o-shanter, brogues, dirk and shepherd's crook, like the Marquess of Strathire himself at a bull show; but Brian Creevie did not. He was fond of saying: " Who does he think he is ? "

Animosity between two people, or even between two families, sometimes seems to be a sort of hobby in our part of the world. Hatreds get watered and tended like hothouse plants; preserved from any influence which might bring them to an end. But once they have acquired a certain stature they usually remain static until, years later perhaps, one party dies and the other records his adamant mood by abstention from the funeral even though the deceased probably gave him as much daily pleasure, say, as his portable wireless on winter nights.

In the eyes of the ignorant or partly informed some such uneventful cold war might have dragged on for years between Traquhair and Creevie.

After all, Brian Creevie's susceptibility is no secret in the village, or even in the whole county. If it wasn't written on his face then it was still plain in his history. Ten years since the baker had told him he couldn't play the piano for toffee after a golf social; ten years since Brian had addressed a word to the baker or gone to a golf social. And then, people said meaningfully: " There's his mother." She was a great one for keeping hatreds on ice, and everyone knew she had always wanted to own the Strathire Arms. Now with the Hydro

The Lifeline

workers flocking in at the week-end and Mr. Hilldersley coming to stay for the games her feelings could be imagined.

Then suddenly something happened which lifted the whole matter out of the normal range of Fluach feuds.

Our football ground is called Creevie Park. It adjoins the Seaforth Arms, and owes its name to a gift of land from Brian's father. For years between the wars it was just a shaggy field where youths played in any old clothes at all times of day and night. Now it has a corrugated iron wall eight feet high, white netted goals, sawdust markings, a latrine with a slightly sloping corrugated roof and a concrete arch entrance painted in alternate green and apricot bands, flanked by oil drums painted pink and joined by an ornamental chain. One quarter of the *Trumpet's* total weekly space is devoted to what goes on there and every year a Football Queen Dance is held to pay for transport to away matches and improvements. Normally Brian, as the reigning Creevie, had always been invited to choose the queen, although lately a generation had grown up which saw less connection between Brian Creevie and football than between any two things imaginable, and said so. Referees and managers, on the other hand, shook their grey heads and said it was only right the queen should always be chosen by a Creevie. Now this year (Fluach's second of television) when the matter came up, the younger members seized on the presence of a TV star as an opportunity to break with dead custom, painlessly and profitably. Creevie, they said, if he really had the good of the club at heart, could not but agree that the name of Traquhair on the posters would increase the takings at the door.

The innovators may have thought they were sincere in advancing Traquhair's TV. celebrity as the reason why they finally invited him, but it's possible that the daily spectacle of that immense Highlander in the main street had, even when they ceased to notice him, worked on them like subliminal advertisement, so that when they pictured a dais, a crowning jovial sporting Highland moment, they saw up there not the Highlander Creevie but Tulloch Traquhair, the stranger.

The Lifeline

Perhaps they had another motive too. They had heard by then, as everyone had, of Traquhair's friendship with Johnny Stephenson the ex-convict and probably warmed to such an association seeing in Traquhair a vague symbol at least of drink and golf—if not of soccer—on Sundays and of all those other Sabbath liberties which only fear of each other prevented them from taking. They probably heard the man's ebullient voice in the shops and felt that in some way he was the dose of salts for the general constipation propagated for so long by the Rev. Abigail Skene and his predecessors, from the pulpit.

At any rate, they plumped for Traquhair and their elders gave way.

The first Brian knew of it was when he picked up the *Trumpet* and saw Traquhair's name in even bigger characters than that immediately beneath of the famous Scottish broadcast band which was to be brought up from Glasgow for the occasion.

Brian made a breathy speech of indifference to his mother who at once considered taking legal action to close the footpath (to the football-field entrance), which crossed fifty feet of land still held by the Creevies. Brian said he wouldn't hear of it. He would simply go to the dance and take much pleasure in seeing that old windbag choose what he, Brian, thought Traquhair had little interest in—a pretty girl. Meanwhile, he would look forward to the arrival of a member of the Football Committee coming as usual to his hotel door and asking for a bottle of whisky to raffle. He would take the greatest pleasure in giving him two. "What they don't quite understand," he added darkly, "is that within twelve months they'll be begging me—or someone—on their knees to come and choose their queen. Because Mr. Traquhair *won't be here*." With a delighted, fastidious smile playing about his thin lips he left the room where his mother started a new row of knitting very, very slowly and neatly as though she were peeling skin off Traquhair's rump.

In fact that very morning when Brian got to his hotel he found a member of the Football Committee waiting. Brian duly gave him two bottles of Scotch to raffle and told him he

The Lifeline

hoped the dance would be particularly successful. The player, who had never associated the name of Creevie Park with Brian Creevie, any more than he associated that of the Seaforth Arms with the Seaforth Highlanders, took the usual bottle and the extra bottle, cocked his head briefly sideways, said, " Thunks varra much, Mr. Creevie," and retired without any idea of the emotional turmoil which lay behind the thin pale face of the donor.

Brian could not resist calling after him :

" I see you've got Tulloch Traquhair this year, Macpherson."

The man paused, mystified. " Ai..." he said. " Tha's right, Mr. Creevie."

" I'm sure he'll draw a big crowd."

" He's quite guid," the man said.

" Quite " means " very " in Fluach. " Guid " means anything you like. Brian winced slightly although he knew the man was not consciously drawing comparisons.

Later, however, as he went through the bar takings he smiled —to himself.

Patience !

Anyhow—as though he cared.

14

THE CHEERFUL SLAPPING SOUND of an oscillating cement mixer, the purposeful knocking of hammers and methodic crump of workmen's feet on bare boards had now for several days surrounded the Strathire Arms with an atmosphere of authentic constructive resurgence—reflected nowhere more clearly than in the face of its proprietor. He walked about with a sheaf of papers in one hand surveying progress or sat at his desk and wrote letters to brewers and distillers. Afternoons he could be seen driving away in his Rolls and people supposed he went to Inverurie on business though it soon became known that he was already a familiar figure in pubs, many miles away, on the west coast.

Still, it was possible these expeditions did have some bearing on business. Even when the daily helps reported that he did a lot of cooking himself, out of books, and brought in " half the beach " cockles, mussels and sand-eels, and played on the guitar and told endless stories to the children out in the back —people still thought such activities might have a real bearing on hotel-keeping, as practised by the French, say, among whom Traquhair was reputed to have lived when making films of Sherwood Forest.

In most Highland hotels the brunt of work falls on the wife and more often than not the husband is neither on one side of the bar or the other, but right across it with the weight of his elbow and head. Creevie and Traquhair were both exceptional in having no wives though, of course, until recently Creevie had his mother and Traquhair, as gossips were quick to point out, had Meldrum who slaved away like a wife even though he had one himself, slaving away for him in the back.

The Lifeline

Traquhair was quite aware of being the object of rumour, aware, too, that by now everyone (including Meldrum) knew that he had openly boasted of being a friend of Johnny Stephenson. (Traquhair could tell by the way Meldrum looked at him that he had heard of his indiscretions at the Wotherspoons'.)

But in spite of all, things were going well and now out of the blue came this invitation from Fluach Rangers to choose their Football Queen. "A small matter, Roeraidgh," Traquhair said, showing him the letter; "but indicative, I think, you'll agree."

He could not help then reminding his secretary of his recent pessimism. "Some places are still a bit different," Meldrum had said, and, "When you've been here ten years you'll still be a stranger," and so on. Instead, what had happened? The people of Fluach had taken him to their bosom. And not only him: Olivia, he pointed out, was already on Christian-name terms with a grocer and a sweet-merchant, and had been to tea with the vicar; her children, too, had many contacts.

Traquhair could not resist a dig or two at his secretary. "Dance Reoraidgh, life is on your side after all. You won't lose face if you abandon your heroic despair. Or would you sooner go to South Africa or to Tibet, where it might have some objective justification? . . ."

These and similar prods were really references to Meldrum's "secret." Framed in badinage and trotted out at the strangest moments, they had not the slightest effect. Meldrum continued to work hard at simple tasks and could sometimes be seen getting advice from the workmen who talked to him as though he were one of themselves. Lately he had assembled pyres of stuff to be burnt in the backyard, and in these Olivia and even Traquhair would poke about, occasionally extracting an object which could still be put to use. "You betray yourself," said Traquhair, exposing a still-serviceable towel-horse; "you would really like to put the whole building on the bonfire."

Meldrum said nothing.

The last snows had gone from Ben Cullan and the days were

The Lifeline

mild. One morning Traquhair was walking round "Meldrum's auto-da-fey" in his slippers when he saw the striped material of a sun blind showing between the three legs of a mutilated straw-seated chair. He got hold of one end and had soon rescued a deck-chair corrugated with dried hen dung. Having given it a shake and brush up, he took it to a corner out of the cold breeze where he laid it out with more satisfaction than he would have got from a new one. Then he gave it his weight by stages, supporting himself for safety's sake with his hands on the ground. It held, cradling him at last in a long, shallow, restful curve. Then his beard was disturbed by a smile.

Yes, another mild, God-sent day. The bare birch on the lower slopes of Ben Cullan were giving a purplish promise of spring and some native blackbirds had joined Meldrum's in a garrulous series of vocal experiments. Warm wet after snow had taken the lid off a thousand smells and Traquhair's big nostrils swelled and tasted as though they were eating like huge sea-anemones.

There was no better way of living than simply sitting smelling and relishing every minute of life . . . which, after all, was so short, so dismally short—a fact which hit you in middle-age like a bus from behind.

He looked up at Olivia's window; she might have spotted the chair herself and had designs on it. But no competitive sally interrupted him, and he was able to settle and listen to the satisfactory sounds of men at work. Things were shifting now. Not long to wait before the tide turned. Olivia had promised to secure a cook, a good one. . . . His smile became sensual and succulent, and his eyes slowly closed, started wide and closed again.

Poor Meldrum! Where would he be, he thought, without Olivia and me. Burning himself.

The sun seemed to reward him, for his sensible salvage, with its warm perfumed caress and soon his eyes remained closed. Yes, the last week had seen a big difference. Creepy, feathery feelers of sleep ran down his limbs as though all the consciousness in his head were being pleasantly broken up, melted and

The Lifeline

sent through his limbs making them at first heavier and then lighter as though he were gradually beginning to float.

Now Traquhair slept—the kind of sleep that he often enjoyed by day : dream and half-dream wrestling for possession of various pictures all of which included himself, a shadowy being, a comparative stranger, as the one moderately involved spectator. Limp and vacant were his features until three women began to undress beneath a tree in blossom. A breeze—a Mediterranean breeze moved the shadows of flowers across their skin and on a log nearby sat a slender youth in the tartan regalia and feathered bonnet of Prince Charles as depicted by the makers of chocolate boxes. In his hand he held an apple.

His face is that of Meldrum, twenty years ago. . . .

Who are the three women ? One of them may be Traquhair's first wife, another Olivia, another last year's Maid Maryon, Zoë Prin, who went back to modelling after her breakdown. The slender tartaned youth, a younger, happier Meldrum, tosses the apple once or twice provocatively in the air while inviting the ladies to be quick and stand before him as naked as the day they were born because the prize was not to be awarded for artifice, and he hadn't got all day.

This happier Meldrum was a really conscientious judge. No skimping.

The word face suggests that part of the human being which has most to say, but the face of an attractive girl, bare as an unsaddled mare, is relatively dumb.

Fingers are neatly engaged at a button, there followed the thrilling liberty of emerging flesh—while the garment falls to the floor, creased and looking dead as a perished petal. No dolls here, no spindle shanks but lusty spanking woman-meat, breasts that loll with neat heaviness, buttocks that wobble a slow heaven, skin that crisped with the goose flesh of exposure and nervous anticipation. . . .

Alas . . .

Meldrum encourages them to hurry and in return feels the edge of their tongue. For a brief moment they are united against him even though their fate lies in his favour.

The Lifeline

Judgment! As though there could be any standard, in such a matter, but personal preference. Now Meldrum is looking at faces. . . .

Surely there had been only three Graces. Here was a fourth —still fully clothed.

"Well, my dear, let's have it off," he mumbled, closing his eyes again. "Don't worry. Well, I remember being scanned for crabs in the M.O.s nissen hut. First they cut our hair down to bristle then bathed us, then paraded us naked before a cold stove on scrubbed boards and we waited a long hour for an old drunk to come back from lunch, put on his specs and look under our arms and between our legs. In that time tramp and banker rubbed paunches, smelt humanity weakly laced with Lifebuoy, sang " God Save the King " in reverse and compared invisibles. Off with them, miss, I could never do with corsets. Talk of levelling down. Who's interested in a vertical platform fringed with ironmongery? A fishmonger's parcel. Two plaice. The poor cheeks get limp and starred with grog-blossom living in such an airless sandwich. Heugh heugh—modest, eh? What's your name?"

"Helen MacDonald, sir," said an accepting voice.

Traquhair's eyes skipped open with furtive speed but once having seen and taken in the girl standing before them, they lulled to again, as though waiting for help from dream, a counter-attack on intrusion.

Then he heard: "I came about the ad. in the *Trumpet*, sir. I was told to come through here and speak to the gentleman in the kilt."

His eyes remained open a crack, but there was still a film over them.

Yes, yes—it was another dream. The separation of her shirt from her throat and of her sleeves from her arms, of the hem of her skirt from the backs of her thighs, of her lip from her lip, of her hair from her cheek, all these separations were but tiny aspects of one all-encompassing separation that rooted immediately in his guts like nausea's opposite. A melting, sweet weakness as though his four limbs had given up activity and

The Lifeline

life so that the fifth which lived in anonymous unfeeling darkness, should for a time have life all to itself and make up for long boredom with brief bliss, for waste water with the liquid of creation.

He, even he, was prone to these visitors. How could he tell them from gate-crashers?

His lips moved and his nostrils dilated; his head rolled sideways and he muttered: " Come, Reoraidgh—what is it you do with her?"

But the bonny judge had vanished.

Sound of a sole moving briefly on gravel created havoc, like wind in smoke, with the shapes in his mind. Again his eyes flitted open and became cagey, almost insulted at the continuing spectacle of the same girl as before in the same place. Resentment made it difficult to be pleasant.

She said: " I came about the ad. in the *Trumpet*, sir. I was told to come through here and speak to the gentleman in the kilt."

His eyes floated over her face, her large amber eyes (a little haunted, hungry or just shy?), full lips (the lower one a shade pendulous, sluttish), shoulder-length hair; full figure, cheap smart clothes, the most made of colour. " How d' you do!" he said reluctantly. Her figure was so lovely it made him sad and happy at the same time. " And you want to work here?" he said with a touch of incredulity.

" I saw where it said 'Good Home' . . ."

It came back to him now, his wording.

" Home. But what about work? . . . Wages? . . ."

" Yes, sir."

" Yes, what?"

" I'd like the job."

" Without knowing what it entails?"

Helen said nothing; instead she blushed.

Perhaps she had heard him say something unsuitable. Traquhair averted his eyes and adopted a more official tone.

" Have you any references?"

" Yes, sir—from the Highland Dairies."

The Lifeline

" May one ask why you are changing employment ? "

She flushed again. At last she said : " I was needing something different." Then suddenly blurted out : " I'm going to have a baby," as though she had been sentenced to it by the sheriff.

All Traquhair's inside seemed to gather up slowly inside him in a confused, cornered emotion.

" Ah ! " he said. " And no husband ? . . ."

" That's right."

" Parents ? "

" My mother's dead. My father's in the distillery ; but I told them at the insurance that . . . he's not at home like."

" In the distillery ? " said Traquhair and he glanced curiously beyond her as though her father might be watching them over the wall. But there was only the big chimney up there. With difficulty he brought his eyes back from it.

" Where are you living ? "

" Shore Street. Mrs. Thomas says I can't keep it there."

" But you want to . . . keep it ? "

Helen's face showed signs of bewilderment. He said quickly :
" Well, well, of course. Then come here, come here. There's room for another small one. If you come here you will be doing Olivia Meldrum a good turn. She would prefer you to have triplets, a black eye and a man chasing you with a meat axe, but we mustn't spoil her : she already has Meldrum. And now she will have you." He glanced briefly at her lower stomach as though measuring the months of work she would give before having other interests.

" August the seventh," she said.

" Isn't that the day we are also to expect Mr. Hilldersley, Prime Minister of Canada ? "

" Don't know, sir "

" I think you'll find it is."

He showed her out as though she were a guest and fortified her on the way with a vision of what the Strathire Arms would soon be like : a bar here, a sun parlour there, new fittings, new furniture. She could hang her washing here and her child

The Lifeline

could play there. From this window here she could watch it play and still do some work. And it was arranged, only as a mere detail, that she herself should start work the following day.

At the door, she said: "Will you be judging the queen to-night?" and gave him the smile of an accomplice.

"Well, will you be there?" he said.

"I'll be there," she said, and smiled uncertainly as though wishing to smile more and say more too. Then suddenly she looked him full and provocatively in the face. "See you perhaps!" Then she left.

Traquhair bowed in her wake and after watching her for a bit went back to his deck-chair.

He was scarcely seated when Olivia appeared in the distance holding the youngest Meldrum as though grafted to her with one arm and a bucket with the other. As usual the baby was naked below the waist to save laundry, and her own head turbaned making her look like a pale gold negress. The squashed-up inception of the cleft between the boy's buttocks sent him half-way back to the judgment beneath the apple tree.

He waved conversationally, and Olivia, having both hands occupied and being too far away to say anything made some movement with her head and eyes, which not so much hailed him as noted his existence and position.

"May I call on you soon, Olivia?" he shouted.

She smiled with the greatest friendliness but that never meant anything. She always managed to give an impression, rather like the people of Fluach, of immense tact, as though, knowing as much as she did or as did anyone who kept their eyes open, the only means of avoiding enmity and distress was to smile with brilliant friendliness all round. Thus her smile became, whether she intended it or not, too easily a sanction, in certain circumstances an act of complicity.

Which was it now? If an act of complicity then . . . complicity in what?

Traquhair's eyes narrowed suspiciously on the departing woman, but having narrowed, even though alertly, the lids

The Lifeline

found themselves unable to resist a natural, mutual attraction —and closed.

A few moments later snores echoed out over the backyard and though at first Traquhair's immense brow seemed troubled —perhaps by a sudden reminder of the key, perhaps by the banging and hammering of Mackay's workmen in front— gradually the lines melted and by the time his head toppled sideways he was smiling very slightly, as though his blind eyes had sighted the endeavours of an earwig on the chair's woodwork.

In fact what he saw was the young happy Meldrum sitting now by himself without an apple and without women under the almond blossom. It was now he, Traquhair, who held the apple and who now gave it to Meldrum—Meldrum long ago a student.

A blackbird with eye cocked sideways, hopped three times sideways as Traquhair whimpered once pleasantly in his sleep.

But as the big man's sleep deepened, his brow became creased with a frown. Could fate sell any man a crueller dummy than to bring him into the world desiring not wombs but dead-ends? Without increase and without God either, such a one might be excused for trying to make, as it were, a beacon of himself—a spark.

15

THE JUDGING of the queen was billed for midnight. At eleven-thirty Traquhair still had not come. By then the War Memorial Hall was stiff with people and the parking space outside the Strathire Arms lined with cars and long-distance buses. Shadowy figures like weeds in a stream waved slowly in silhouette across lighted doors and windows, and the headlamps of late arrivals swung inwards illuminating pale youths in twos or threes, their hair draggled over their foreheads, shirts open at sweating throats and cigarettes sticking to upper lips like film gangsters. The sudden brilliance would harden faces, narrow eyes into a sort of bemused, aggressive hunger as though they had been surprised in mid-conference about mass rape. Late comers who intended to dance walked hastily past these loafers and bought their tickets quick like people coming in out of the rain. There was often a fight about now, and young Chisholm, the builder's apprentice, was already talking in an inflammatory tone and looking at strangers as though searching for the man who had murdered his mother.

Most of the young men were inside the hall in a big group under the band. They bulged right out more than half-way across the floor and over a third of the hall's length. Behind them was space and chairs, empty except for three or four men supporting their heads either by their hands or by chins tilted into breast bones. In some cases these had already been motionless for two hours.

Made bold by numbers, the great bulge of stationary men not only limited dancing space by half but also seemed anxious to inhibit what dancers there were, for they scrutinised each

The Lifeline

passing couple as though the women were for sale in a shop window in their underclothes and their partners either invisible or a bit absurd like tailors' dummies.

Now and again eyes would flit through the circling dancers and weigh up the unpartnered—a line of girls sitting along the far wall under Boer War Highland uniforms, outnumbering the chairs and therefore, in some cases on each other's knees, all conspicuously sober and never raising their almost defeated and yet none the less dully expectant eyes to the close bulge of men. Occasionally two girls did resolutely rise and push off, as it were, right into the deep end, and there clinging in desperation to each other's deprived flesh execute a cheerful one-step right under all those eyes which, even when they sank coarsely to below a girl's waist, seemed to prefer hopeless, bloodshot abstention to such a tepid compromise. Jive had not yet reached Fluach and wild native dancing was dead but somehow not yet buried.

Of course there were a few men who did dance quite happily, and there were some others who were content to sit and look on, but the mass which bulged out into the floor did represent the majority.

This sad and ugly sexual hiatus, this chasm which seemed to writhe with all the titillations of tabloids, the tight silhouetted curves of girls on bathing balls, throwing out breasts and bottoms and holding in stomachs in case anyone was put off by a reminder of the consequences of consummation, left no one with much spare interest for the choosing of the queen or for the man who was going to choose her. Besides there had been so many queens—queens chosen by Mr. Spote Rossiemurchat, Ian Creevie the Palace and Mrs. Smith Benghazi—Salmon Queens, Badminton Queens, Cricket Queens, Table-tennis Queens, Masonic Queens and Football Queens that the whole thing had lost the lyrical edge which the title implied. Only a few men and rather more women cast occasional glances at the door to get a sight of the face which, through being so often seen on a telly screen, had acquired a stepped-up value, as though simply by seeing it in the flesh they

The Lifeline

would enjoy vicariously a *frisson* of what it must be like to be him.

At the very opposite end of the hall stood two natives of Fluach who had not been seen at a War Memorial Hall dance for years. They stood near the exit to the lavatory in shadowy non-participating anonymity with eyes focused now on the dancers, now on the main door, quite obviously without any intention of dancing. Although no one looked at them everyone by now knew that Brian Creevie and Johnny Mackay of J. S. Mackay, Ltd., were present. Why? The presence of two plain-clothes men could not have caused more conjecture.

Earlier in the evening they had met for a drink and had started an argument in which Creevie tried to persuade Mackay that he "could kiss his hands to his fifteen hundred pounds" this being the value of work he had done on Traquhair's hotel in excess of the five hundred pounds' advance already received.

Mackay had looked dubiously at Creevie.

" Oh, I know what you're thinking, Johnny, I know what everyone's thinking : that I've got it in for Tulloch Traquhair because he got the Strathire Arms. But people think what they like, no matter *what* you do or say. So I'm not going to waste time trying to convince you. But if you're interested—just go along to the dance to-night and see for yourself what kind of man you're dealing with. That's all, that's all." (Creevie's hand was up as though taking an oath of freedom from bias.) " Just go and see for yourself—see for yourself, Johnny." (His voice had developed a lilt.) " That's all and if certain things happen as I think they'll happen then you'll agree with me : *you can kiss your hands to your fifteen hundred pounds.*"

Prone to believe the worst and bewildered by a past in which canniness had often resulted in financial setbacks, the suggestible eyes of J. S. Mackay rested with awful surmise on the intense face of his adviser. He might have been a young girl having her fortune told by a gipsy.

" Surely not, Brian," he murmured.

The Lifeline

" Well, Johnny, come with me then and take a look for yourself."

All this had taken place in Mackay's house. Here in the hall they were silent partly because whenever they spoke people round about seemed to be listening, not surprisingly, for their combined presence at a dance, when neither of them were choosing the queen, or even in the company of the person choosing the queen, was as exceptional as a boat in Fluach harbour. Dances in the War Memorial Hall are seldom if ever attended by the over thirties of Fluach's "middle class"—a sketchy category this providing the backbone of bridge, drama clubs and W.R.I., a category now only one generation old since up to the first war there was only the marquess and the assorted remains of a more or less classless and decadent clan system, the left-overs of two hundred years of emigration, rural poverty and the provision of mercenaries for lethal wars.

At eleven forty-five Traquhair appeared in full Highland evening-dress, sweeping through the boys and young men like a cock pheasant through a crowd of sparrows. He had everything : red-and-white-check stockings, black-and-white horsehair sporran, silver dirk, lace frills and cuffs, stock-and-stags' horn buttons. A path was made for him until he reached the thickest part of the male bulge. There, when the youths saw what like of man was trying to move them out of the way they simply stood their ground as though struggling with hallucination. Defeated, the club secretary took Traquhair back and along the outside and somehow reached the stage where he stationed him near the microphone.

Creevie, when choosing the queen in past years, had always worn a blue suit.

Creevie did possess a dress kilt but wore it only for the exclusively middle-class occasion, the County Ball, once a year at Inverurie Hydro. J. S. Mackay, whose ancestry on both sides of his family was rooted in this area and traceable on tombstones petering out at last into sculptural erosion and gloom, did not now even possess a kilt. When his wife last told him

The Lifeline

to get one, he said : " For goodness' sake, Margaret, I'm not daft. . . ."

Their emotions at seeing this newcomer dressed like the Marquess of Strathire himself, yet owner of nothing but a convict's relic, standing up in front of the biggest crowd seen in any one place since Sir Duncan Fidge, M.P., gave his first version of his disagreement with the Director of Education over the dumb child of Skelly Island, cannot easily be imagined.

And for Mackay, of course Traquhair's exaggerated get-up was not only bad taste, it was also a bad omen.

" Well, for goodness' sake . . ." he murmured, and his pinched face suggested the proximity of a bad but unanalysable smell. Part of him was going down the street, there and then, in the middle of the night, and drafting a personal letter requesting payment before the tenth instant. While this part of him was writing the letter, the other resident part of him continued to watch Traquhair with the closeness of a detective. Every little thing about the man—every gesture, inflection of voice, detail of clothing might give a clue to the eventual fate of his fifteen hundred pounds.

Or was Creevie wrong ?

Such a possibility was not envisaged by Brian's clear, soft eyes as they rested confidently on the person of Traquhair. As far as Brian was concerned every little thing about the man had *already* confirmed his suspicions. And now, " Watch this," he murmured with real delight, as though they were at a circus.

The mike crackled and Denis Mackay, the Football Secretary announced, " During the next dance Mr. Tulloch Traquhair will choose ten runners for the Football Queen. Everybody dance, please. Take your partners. . . ."

At first there was no great difference in the number of people on the floor. Then gradually a few of the boys who had been blocking the top end took partners from the long line of waiting girls. Former beauty queens and runners-up at the Masonic, Salmon, Golf, Cricket and Boys' Brigade dances were soon all in circulation. Any girl, in fact, who had a dog's chance and some who did literally have a dog's chance.

The Lifeline

Suddenly Creevie leant towards Mackay and murmured: "There's Helen MacDonald. . . . The girl he has taken on at the Strathire Arms."

"He's taken *her*?" said Mackay blankly.

"I thought you knew," Creevie said with mounting confidence. "Oh, yes, he's taken Helen MacDonald."

"Surely not . . ." Mackay murmured. "Surely not, Brian, for goodness' sake. And she's here to-night?" He knew of Helen's condition. Who didn't?

John Mackay was very much aware that no one's private life would comfortably bear the light of day. In fact, he usually grunted instead of criticised. But that a girl, having got a baby from nowhere and then having nowhere to put it, a girl who was "*just nothing*" (a financial category this, on his lips, with moral and educational undertones) should come and push it, here to-night, under everyone's nose. . . .

At last he spotted her.

"Well, for goodness' sake . . ." he whispered. "Does she want us all to know?" (He knew what he meant: there are two different kinds of "knowing" in Fluach.)

"Why not?" said Creevie. "She'll be the queen. You see."

Brian elaborated this prophecy in exactly the same breathy, exultant tone as, a moment ago, he had assured his friend he could "kiss his hand to his fifteen hundred pounds." Mackay therefore linked the two issues together: if one occurred, then the other would also.

Helen, in sleek satin, seemed small for a girl in her fifth month. Indeed, her condition might have escaped the notice of anyone who did not know of it. Her bosom, it is true, which always did her credit, no longer struck the golden mean between the voluptuous and the shapely, but had now abandoned itself frankly to a beautiful alimentary heaviness which, had it been unrestrained, must almost have touched the incipient dome beneath. Her lips, too, seemed redder and fuller and her eyes against all probability shone with nervous happiness.

The Lifeline

Mackay stared at her. The mere fact that Traquhair should have taken her on was somehow further evidence that his fifteen hundred pounds was on roller skates.

Helen paused quite close. Catching their eyes, she immediately turned her face away and said something to her partner.

Illegitimacy is accepted among our fishers as smoothly as dinner-time but Helen MacDonald was not a fisher. Indeed, what was she? There was something to be said for John Mackay's opinion that she was "just nothing"—for not only did she have no family but she belonged neither to the fishers, the crofters, labourers, nor the middle-class—not even to the tinkers. She belonged to no group and was virtually an orphan. Her mother was in Fluach churchyard and her legal father an alcoholic who had been taken back at the distillery on sufferance, could scarcely be said to exist.

"Quite a family party," said Brian. "There's the little stranger's father."

"P. J. McConnachie's boy" indicated by Creevie was the only Teddy in the hall. His tie, like a strangled iridescent adder, seemed to cling to his Adam's apple by one tiny tooth, his coat shoulders shot out sheer well beyond his flesh and from this broadest point he tapered sharply till from the knees down to his bare ankles his shanks were only a few inches thick. Here at the bottom he again swelled suddenly and finally into a pair of huge ginger and white shoes cushioned on two inches of crêpe. These were oscillating violently from the knees in mid-jive and earning his whole attention as though down there a living part of his own self were giving him enormous, and all-exclusive pleasure. His partner co-operated sketchily, blank faced, while her eyes roved, and her body went and came back in regular repetition, like a component in a machine.

Never once did Helen look at her child's father or he at her, even when the movement of the dance brought them close together. He was good-looking, with sandy hair, sandy skin and high cheekbones, full lips, and his eyes had a curious, untamed, mindless look which he seemed to cultivate as part

The Lifeline

of the dance. . . . People he knew he seemed not to know; but when briefly he caught the eye of a stranger, John Mackay, for instance, his eyes became briefly personal, familiar.

"For goodness' sake . . ." whispered Mackay again and he turned towards the door, took two steps but came back again involuntarily, raising his eyes to the figure of Traquhair—to business—and Brian's prognostications.

Suddenly the music stopped and the dancers, bewildered, came to a halt, staring up at the stage where Traquhair had lifted the mike to his lips.

Speaking extremely low and with the full, buzzing timbre of his deep voice, he said: "Honoured as I am, ladies and gentlemen, to be asked to judge your queen, I shall be unable to do so if the nonparticipating gentlemen immediately below me insist on occupying my field of vision. I humbly suggest they equip themselves with partners from the still-unexplored seam of beauty which I see sitting idle on my right."

The effect of this speech on the people addressed was one of merely increased stupefaction. One unpartnered man, nearer to Traquhair's feet than any other, and more conspicuously trespassing on the dance floor being three-quarters the way across to the women, said: "Ugh?" as though Traquhair had so far spoken in Swahili, and had better repeat himself in English.

"You . . ." said Traquhair, pointing at him. "Please step back."

The man then looked first to his right and then to his left as though near him stood someone who was doing something wrong. But he discovered he was more or less by himself so he again looked up at Traquhair in doubt.

"Ur?" he said darkly.

"Step back," said the big man quietly, but ominously.

Some fifty variously intoxicated eyes, all bereaved of violent outlet, were by now fixed on the gaudy foreign body by the mike.

Someone growled. Someone else said something unintelligible.

The Lifeline

Football secretary Mackay whispered to Traquhair but the big man merely continued to level his index finger the size of the big Scunthorpe sausage which had often preceded him on TV; then, when that had no effect he began to slip back his kilt-coat from a shoulder that emerged like half a horse's rump under nylon. Suddenly prevented, either by the size of it or a hole in his shirt, or temperance, Traquhair became still, swaddled or lassoed, by his own size in mid-threat. And he repeated, " Get back ! "

No one can have expected what happened. The man below, who must have weighed less than one of Traquhair's legs, raised a horny fist and shook it very slowly in the big man's face. At the same moment somebody shouted : " Give us a song, Tulloch," a cry which of course would never have been raised to Brian Creevie, still less to L. Spote, Esq., or any of the other normal choosers of beauty queens.

There was a ripple of irreverent laughter.

By now the football secretary had reached the floor and muttering to right and left with arms outspread, he gave an impression of moving everyone back, a manœuvre which Traquhair then seemed to supervise, while regaining the cover of his garment.

In fact no one moved. The man he had singled out remained looking up at him with a look of defiance from which all trace of apprehension had vanished. But Traquhair nodded as though satisfied.

The music struck up again and the couples by queueing, squeezed round the bottleneck space in front of the stage. From time to time Traquhair pointed and a card was handed to a girl who thereby became a finalist. One of the first to be selected was Helen MacDonald.

" What did I say ? " said Creevie. He and Mackay were by now both standing on chairs.

Mackay was speechless.

When only one card was left, Traquhair seemed to have difficulty in making up his mind. He even raised his hands in a gesture of hopeless defeat which the remaining ladies cannot

The Lifeline

have taken as a compliment. Then suddenly he grinned. It was a vast public grin; they saw him say something to the usher and point, and continue pointing insistently.

People could see the usher's face of hopeless doubt as he tried to catch the eye of the club secretary; they could see him at last spur himself into whispering something back up at Traquhair and Traquhair by way of reply simply stick out his index finger more firmly like an emperor indicating . . . yes, at the handsome Teddy boy whose jive had carried him temporarily so far from his partner that the usher had not even the chance of making the feasible mistake of giving it to the female. He had no choice. He had to give it to the Teddy boy. And people close enough heard Traquhair say with vibrant pleasure: " That's right. The Ted! Isn't he beautiful."

Chi-chi is alien to Fluach life. There was little laughter, much astonishment and a good deal of supposition that the Teddy boy had merely been given the card to hold on behalf of his partner.

But the usher told someone. That person told others. Soon everyone was talking about it. Was it an act of derision or genuine admiration? No one knew.

By now it had also got around that Traquhair, far from being ignorant of Helen MacDonald's identity or condition, in fact knew both, in fact had taken her on as barmaid with full knowledge of her "case" only that very morning.

Brian Creevie was ecstatic. The selection of a *man* was a bonus. " What did I say," he hissed, and he hit one hand into the palm of the other. " Wait another five minutes and you'll see Miss Helen MacDonald get the crown, thank you very much. Or the man."

John Mackay made his way from the hall.

He is the biggest employer of labour in the town and pretty well liked. People noticed his going.

It was as well for him that he went because a few minutes later Creevie's prediction was fulfilled: Traquhair slipped the silk-emblazoned sash over Helen's head and gave her a formal kiss, bent to the microphone and said something in Gaelic.

The Lifeline

A flash-bulb exploded, a rare event in Fluach, for it is our *Trumpet* editor himself who takes photographs.

Then from out of resonant knocking and crackling came Traquhair's voice:

". . . for the other ladies and for you, sir, there will also be a prize." His voice dropped suddenly and struck a different tone which by some extraordinary *tour de force* did touch people's emotions. " Indeed, I would like to give everyone of you here all that he or she wants. *Gu robh math agad.*"[1]

[1] Thank you.

16

TRAQUHAIR, with his feet snared in flex from the electric accordion, was seemingly unconscious of the emotions he had stirred up. He beamed down from his eminence and paid no attention to the football secretary, Denis Mackay, who kept plucking his elbow. At any moment it seemed likely he would launch into a whole speech in Gaelic or perhaps dance by himself on the stage.

Mackay, an energetic official who was also a member of Fluach Amenities Committee and science teacher at the Tech., had just heard from the door that the takings in five shilling tickets were already over ninety pounds—twice as much as usual. Nevertheless, he saw no reason why this should entitle Traquhair to promise prizes to the runners-up. Runners-up never get prizes. When at last he got the big man's attention two eyes squinted back at him narrowly while he said he felt sure Mr. Traquhair must have "made the arrangements" to justify his recent announcement as there were no prizes for runners-up, any more than there ever had been.

"Prior arrangements..." murmured Traquhair. "Through normal channels...."

His little eyes seemed to become smaller and smaller in his head while the man went on and on making the same point against the din of the band. Then, looking him straight in the eyes, Traquhair shouted sarcastically: "You may send the bill to me," and then turned his back.

Someone plucked the secretary by the sleeve and said something about the takings. Mackay simmered down, asked for a list to be made of all the runners-up including the Teddy boy.

The Lifeline

At mention of the Teddy boy Traquhair turned round and said: "Something gay and fashionable costing about a pound for each of them..." Which put people in even deeper doubt as to the big man's true attitude to his last choice, the male.

More dances followed. Imperceptibly Traquhair had taken over the role of master of ceremonies. Soon his face was lit by a seraphic smile which owed much to the occasional half-bottle handed up to him for autograph.

People close to him (on the War Memorial Hall stage), had noticed that as the evening wore on he had become increasingly "Highland" in speech and manner. When he came to congratulate the winner and two runners-up he inquired their names and then repeated them like a character from a Scottish novel—saying "Chean" instead of Jean Murray and then Pelinda Prannen instead of Belinda Brannen. He then addressed each of them in Gaelic and familiar as are all dwellers in Fluach with at least the sound of Gaelic (from a few of the older fishers and performers at the annual mod), there was not one who had any idea what he was saying. Yet this merely had the effect of making him more Gaelic than ever and soon, even when he was talking English over the microphone, announcing "Strip the Willow," his voice was subject to the lilt of one whose normal speech is Gaelic. There were prolonged calls for a speech, interrupted by a voice calling him by his Christian name for a song and when he paused, in a mildly affronted manner in mid-sentence there were cat calls and loud requests for him to continue. After some demur which he mimed most successfully while the uproar thickened, he went on where he left off.

By now the bulge of men across the floor had thinned out. Only the man he had told to step back was still standing triumphantly, even hopefully, in exactly the same spot as one hour before.

Traquhair said: "Where was I?... Litter..."

"Ai!" said the stationary trespasser. "Litter!"

Many people supposed, quite wrongly, that Traquhair was

The Lifeline

now making a veiled protest against the state in which he had found his hotel on taking it over. Some of the youths who were fresh from dropping their empties over the Strathire Arms' wall, took it as a reflection on themselves and one of them invited Traquhair to come down and say it to his face. But Traquhair seemed grateful for interruptions. Like a tiger in the zoo looking in the direction of a poodle's sharp bark, he surveyed the group where the invitation had come with a calm omnivorous, almost affectionate stare. Then he went on where he left off: " Litter ! "

" Ye big . . ." shouted someone.

" Well ? " he said. " Go on . . ."

And when the voice and all voices fell silent he pursued this new track.

Few, if any, of his audience had ever frequented royalty and so could not be amazed that Traquhair should share royalty's obsession with litter, but they did find such a passion odd, in a big shaggy man, who looked as if he might have cigarette ends in his beard.

He went on for a bit interrupting himself now and then to write an autograph on someone's shirt, half-bottle or scrap of paper. Sometimes he introduced one of the autograph hunters to the audience. But he had a word in private with each one, putting his lips to girls' ears, flattering or making inquiries about her job, life, family, all in " Highland " English, and stooping to be on a level with her mouth when she replied. None of his fans could resist an impression of great sincerity and highly individual concern. Indeed, one girl, alternately blushing and paling, began to "unbosom" herself to such an extent that she ended by whispering at length in his ear. The big man's face melted into an amused and understanding smile, and there was laughter from the body of the hall.

Was it possible that this atmosphere stemmed from the fact many adults were familiar with the Robin Hood programmes ? Creevie watched in amazement, for by now even he could not blind himself to the fact that despite the almost aggressive familiarity of some of the interjections Traquhair was having

The Lifeline

not only a success but a liberating effect on the gathering. A kind of generous euphoria was spreading, such as happens in a good music hall when the audience mysteriously begins to contribute to its own entertainment, and even to affect what the artistes will do next. " What's that fat man's name ? " said Traquhair, pointing. " Traquhair," said several voices. " MacGregor," said another. " Gregor," exclaimed Traquhair ominously. " *Is Rioghal mo dhream!* Royal outlaws, prawlers. Victims too." No one showed any sign of knowing what he was talking about, but the personal convivial way in which he delivered the words as though impressed if not awed into rhetoric by seeing before him the living scion of so much bloody history, made the person addressed feel suddenly more important than hitherto though none could have given a single good reason why. And so it went on—and on, for Traquhair, as Creevie of course noted, was reluctant to bring his conspicuous moments on the stage to an end. He spun out each autograph and started conversations on every topic under the sun, so that often people went up just to hear what he was saying. Then to justify their presence, they had to buy an autograph.

The profits were beginning to be impressive.

Finally it would have taken only the preliminary drone of a bagpipe and whooping would have broken out. The crowd would have begun to swirl vaguely at first, almost as though trying to remember something, and then taken shape as definite circles made up of alternate men and women. There would have been reels danced orgiastically, heels high as a colt's in spring and violence alternating with grace, neatness with abandon—the spectacle which was common in Fluach before the first war.

But there were no bagpipes. The pipe-major was doing the teas by the cloakroom. And at the very moment when the pale ghost of local patriotism seemed to be taking on the hues of warm flesh, Traquhair, its medium, took himself off to bed, followed insistently by a few last autograph hunters, and by Creevie himself whose prophecies had by now been so over-

The Lifeline

fulfilled that they had ceased to have much resemblance to what he had prophesied.

Brian felt confused. Something about Traquhair was vaguely familiar so that he began to feel, like everyone else, that he had seen the man before though in his case he doubted if this were possible. When Traquhair came down from the stage Brian moved towards him feeling sure the man would cut him, as he had so often in the street, even though their hands had been clasped wedded for half a minute at the Wotherspoons, ... As though challenging "final proof" Brian halted by the door and sure enough Traquhair swept by without recognising him, even though Brian looked him in the face.

Then Brian felt contempt for every one, particularly Traquhair. If his father had not given Creevie Park to the footballers there might have been no football, and no dance either.

He followed Traquhair closely and felt tempted, given a chance, to "say something "—he didn't know what but he did feel pregnant with a desire to make contact. Perhaps he would have if something hadn't happened which seemed to him the most extraordinary event of the whole evening.

The man at the door was Henry Walker from the National Health, a keen supporter of football even though middle years now confine him to the touchline where he runs up and down in shorts, all weathers, with a flag.

As Traquhair passed the tall towers of silver and bundles of notes, Walker rose to his feet and said seriously: " Py Cod, Misterr Traquhair, ah great night thart you gafe us, it was that. Why, man, I can't remember a petter," and he warmly shook Traquhair's hand.

Walker was born and bred in Birmingham where he stayed until he came to Fluach two years ago as secretary to the National Health. For 270 odd days a year he sits in a Nissen hut office, hot enough for a humming bird or python, co-ordinating doctors' prescriptions against chemists', real charges and Government subsidies; evenings he plays badminton or

The Lifeline

bridge. Before coming to us he had had no contact with Scotland.

"Why, man," he went on, looking down at the money collected, "you'll have given Fluach a covered stand the night, ye will and all . . ."

Creevie was familiar with the crofter's daughter in the Fluach telephone exchange who speaks with a pure "southern" (U.S.A.) accent but this struck him as odder still, particularly as the girl concerned never spoke in any other way, whereas Walker normally spoke B.B.C. English. Walker had had a few drinks of course, but nowhere near enough to account for this transfiguration.

With difficulty Traquhair disengaged his hand from that of his admirer. Like some lovers whose physical ardour decreases the more it is reciprocated, he showed signs of apathy when confronted by such urgent response. "*Oidche mhath leibh! Oidche mhath leibh!*" he muttered, and moved on.

Creevie paused beside Walker to see if he would sustain his new identity even with those who knew his origins. But Traquhair had apparently left such a vacuum that Walker was sucked out after him, to the door and even into the road in his wake calling something festive and complimentary.

For a moment Creevie stood outside in the fresh air watching the big man move towards the still-lighted door of the Strathire Arms, perhaps to be greeted in Gaelic by a Lithuanian cook. At last an almost peaceful look came into his eyes, a look such as may be seen in the eyes of a toddler who comes round a corner and sees what his mother has built for him . . . a high, high, perilous structure of bricks, one on top of the other, supporting on the swaying summit something noisy and breakable.

17

So that was that and reality, as seldom happened, had provided Traquhair with the same gratifying sensations as alcohol. He had looked out over the heads of the crowd with a sense of buoyancy such as might be experienced by the prow of a ship responding to the rhythm of gay, jostling waves. He had given point, definition to the shapeless sea while from the sea he had drawn a *raison d' être*, an exhilaration. To be bigger than everyone else was an everyday matter for every day he had a barber's view of heads, saw scurf and the bridges of noses and the pallor of skin beneath thinning hair, dust in men's hat brims, eyes turned up to him and in general moved through life like a knight through populace—but usually such regal sensations, when unaccompanied by drink, had to be sustained by an exhausting effort from within, an effort which facts, personal circumstances (such as wearing the uniform of a commissionaire or the make-up of an actor) had often tended to undermine. This intractability on the part of facts distressed him; he repudiated them as boring if not positively deathly, aimed as they were at joy without which he preferred not to live. Yet they were for ever catching up with him, necessitating ever more prodigious avoidance, deeper, faster gulps of whisky, quicker ever more promiscuous search for the inebriating effect of other people's company, of stories, sensations, dramatisations. Because what were facts by themselves—nothing, if not actually poison. They needed value, pattern.

Sometimes he seemed to be an exile suffering from loss of memory, always looking for someone who could tell him the few facts he would have valued: his name and his home, the

The Lifeline

point of life.... But other people always had work to do, lives to live. They all knew their names and homes, or seemed to. Consequently he had to force himself upon their notice, perhaps even share their homes, and origins... hence Meldrum, whose sense of origin, of identity seemed to survive everything, the century, the babel of viewpoints, the revolutions, and that mirage of a wife, Olivia.

But last night he had been able to dispense with Meldrum —able even to dispense with alcohol. A thousand eyes had underlined him, *located* him.

Next day, still lulled with a healing sense of being himself and applauded, he opened his eyes.

The print of the Highland chieftain over the mantelpiece, the head of a stuffed lion, an untidy disarray of books, a bottle of White Horse and dirty glass standing on an unopened copy of the *Caterers' and Publicans' Almanac*, and the bottle of Camp Coffee on the mantelpiece dawned on his consciousness like the eyes of wolves round a tiring traveller lost in snow. For some minutes he watched, then with a dull grunt he kicked off the white encompassing bedclothes, stood and frizzed up the hair of his chest. Then the hotel shuddered to his purposeful movements.

Suddenly he noticed a curious silence. But why "curious"? In trying to find the answer his mind fogged out of focus and he found himself thinking of something else. With a sense of frustration and impotence he groaned as though he had sighted the face of a familiar and treacherous bore. A sort of fear that he could not have described clutched his heart and he poured himself half a tumbler of whisky and drank it in gulps.

Then he went downstairs.

Meldrum had left his breakfast ready. It was ten o'clock

Two or three times Traquhair tried to focus his attention on the curious silence. Why should he expect noise? After all, it wasn't as though he had come up from London yesterday. He didn't still wake up and expect a road drill under his window, buses like heavy surf, lifts choiring and humming.

The Lifeline

Meldrum came in with a lot of letters.

" I didn't see you last night, Reoraidgh."

" I had some things to do."

" We were quite merry. . . . You should have been there. . . . Girls . . ."

Whenever he talked sex, Meldrum always looked embarrassed. Aware of this Traquhair sometimes took pleasure in spinning the subject out, but this morning he fell silent waiting for his secretary's inquiries, the interest which anyone might have expected him to take in an occasion on which his friend and employer had for once been successful. But nothing came.

" Yes, I looked for you when things were warming up . . ." said Traquhair in a broaching tone of voice. " *Heugh heugh!* I had them in my hand, I sent them, Reoraidgh ! "

" What's happened to Mackay's men ? "

" So that's it," said Traquhair. He looked speculatively out of the window. He had known there was something wrong.

" Yesterday the men thought they were coming back here this morning ; they told me so."

" What are you suggesting ? " To discourage an answer Traquhair turned to his mail singing, " Oh dear what can the matter be," and at the very moment when Meldrum was about to reply he began to talk.

" What's all this, circulars, bills ? Why didn't you bring Olivia to the dance ? Air, light, laughter, exercise, a nip or two, a teaspoonful of oblivion. A little fun, Reoraidgh. A sensation of hope—forgive me for mentioning the word. She'd have been queen. What's this ? . . ."

He held a letter at arm's length. " Is this from you ? " The handwriting was atrocious.

" There were two by hand," Meldrum said. " That was one."

" Sir ! " read Traquhair aloud, but then for some reason fell silent, reading on to himself:

" Lost orphan of the Cullan Seer where hast thou hidden from thy berieved people, wrestled with destiny and delayed by a twelvemonth the words of the fathering prophet to whom

The Lifeline

in the end thou hadst to yield? Was it not in the back end of the year that has passed thou shouldest have come? They said you would never but I walking homeward *chunnaic mi giulan a'dol a null air an abhainn*[1]—so I was ready, and now declayre thee for what thou art—the long-awaited, giant child of Nan Og, red-beard who, said the Brachan Seer, would lead his people again when 'the burns shall be dry in Glen Cullan while sheep on the top of Ben Chialla drown, when foreigners camp on Loch Drhu and a King comes out of the West. Hail."

It was signed: " The Recogniser."

Traquhair read it again. By the time he reached the end for the second time he began to look sleepy. Meldrum said, " Well? " Traquhair folded the letter away, tucked it right away into his kilt.

" Rizzio was there. He turned up at the end like the old maid at the bottom of the pack."

" You mean Brian Creevie? . . ."

" I mean Brian Creevie. Have you met? "

" In the post office. And here and there . . ."

" Dark horse that you are, Reoraidgh! And did you speak to him, did you fraternise? "

" You seem to bear him some sort of grudge. I found him . . ."

" Well? "

" What one would expect."

" And what, pray, would *one expect*? "

" Well, he's obsessed by himself."

" On the contrary, I heard he was still dressed by his mother."

" I said '*obsessed*'—by himself."

" She loves me, she loves me not, she loves me . . ." Traquhair muttered as he ripped through a number of long trade envelopes. After brief glances at their contents he began to speak, mainly to offset the silence of Meldrum and the cement mixer which, more and more, somehow, seemed to be linked. " The possession of a bar and the proximity of several thousand hydro workers you might think were two out of three condi-

[1] I saw a phantom funeral crossing the river.

The Lifeline

tions necessary for vast profit. The third condition, the one thing lacking is something to put in the bar. Accordingly, I contact distillers, assuring them of a market simply slavering to consume their products. What happens? I get pages of forms asking me to supply bank references, trade references and pro forma invoices asking for advance payment. . . . Further, they remind me that my quota is that of 1939 when this place was a temperance hotel. No one is ever joking, that is the important thing to remember."

Meldrum watched his employer unfold sheafs of printed matter which all said the same thing.

" Bank references . . ." muttered Traquhair.

" You're not known," Meldrum said.

" You ought to be on the Brains Trust."

Traquhair continued ripping open large envelopes. Now a smaller one . . . from his bank.

They were favoured with his letter, but in fact no mistake had been made. The quarterly payment of eight hundred and fifty pounds from International Aviaries had been taken into account and this still left an overdraft of £562 3s. 4d. In the circumstances they had no option but to refuse to cash any further cheques and they would be glad to know what steps he intended to take to balance his accounts.

Traquhair grunted.

" What? " said Meldrum.

"Farmers are supported by the Government, get grants for combines, subsidies for every bestial accouchement, miscarriage or otherwise, and beasts that don't exist, and they can pay their bills in ten years, but when I want to start a pub I'm asked "— he began reading—" to fill in pages one, two and five in block letters, and give bank references."

Meldrum said : " So this is it ! "

" Sometimes you make me think I'm in the middle of a take of Robin Hood. There's only one reference needed : a glimpse at Creevie's bar on a week-end night. An Indian god with a hundred arms couldn't pull beer, take cash, clink till, shove change fast enough. There's your reference."

The Lifeline

He came to a smaller envelope. Meldrum said: "That came by hand."

Dear Mr. Traquhair,—You will recall we agreed work on the Strathire Arms should be paid on completion of stages. In the circumstances I should be obliged if you would pay our account dated 7/4/58. This covers work to date on the bar, outhouses, two bedrooms and the lounge—£1,547 2s. 10d. as per attached accounts.

Yours faithfully (*scribble*),

J. S. MACKAY

Traquhair felt Meldrum's eyes on him. He folded the letter away and put it with the other in his kilt.

He went back to eating and the clink of his knife and fork now added a delicate filigree frame to the silence.

Meldrum said: " Nothing . . . funny . . . happened last night, did it ? "

" Funny ? "

" Unusual."

" Why ? "

" The postman gave me an odd look."

" And you were surprised ! Reoraidgh ? *Heugh heugh.*"

" So nothing did happen. I mean apart from your choosing . . . the queen." Meldrum looked grudgingly at the cloth as though visualising the whole dreary business against his will.

Traquhair scooped out some porridge.

" Are you trying to account for why work has stopped ? . . ."

" Well . . . the bar isn't finished. The rooms aren't ready. Why should Mackay's men suddenly stop ? "

" And I brought you here—you and your six children. Is that it ? "

Meldrum said nothing.

Suddenly Traquhair leaned over towards his secretary and pointing one finger inwards at his own big body, said:

" Supposing that really it was *you* brought *me* here." His face was a picture of censure. " Just supposing ! Eh ? "

The Lifeline

" We know what brought you here," Meldrum said quietly.

There was a pause. Then Traquhair said : " My dear Reoraidgh—we know nothing."

Meldrum did not answer.

Traquhair gathered his mail together and went on in his previous flippant tone. " It's a pity you didn't come last night —you and Olivia. You ought to be seen about more. Make a better impression. People only see you doing the dustbins. They put two and two together. . . ."

Such was the censorious indifference of his secretary's face Traquhair was tempted to tell him what he had heard from Nadia over the telephone, that the school children had a name for him : " Muck'n Meldrum "—and an obscene rhyme that went with it. " Muck'n Meldrum " How d'you like that ? he thought. Out of the mouths of babes and sucklings !

Meldrum said : " You've had offers of parts since we came here, haven't you ? "

" Yes, Reoraidgh," said Traquhair without hesitation, " I've had offers of parts. How did you guess ? By the backs of my envelopes ? I've been offered a part as a minor pirate in *Treasure Island.* Puffins the new cigarette is launching an advertising campaign on the TV. They want a big game hunter looking over his shoulder saying, ' Puffins last longer, taste better and help concentration by means of their polarising particles.' A lion charges. I fade out briefly for a close-up of the particles polarising then I fade in again taking a shot. *Bang.* The lion rolls over. Switch to me, one foot on the dead lion, then fortissimo : ' Puffins are Worthit.' So you're right, Reoraidgh, I've had offers of parts—several."

Meldrum looked out of the window. The surrounding all-pervading silence spoke for him. And if that were not enough there was the eloquent heap of mail round Traquhair's elbow.

Traquhair stared resentfully at his secretary as though he had said something. Then he said : " Supposing—just supposing —that however awful that sort of work, when I got it, was, I might still be doing it but for you. Could you then still sit there like that ? . . ."

The Lifeline

" I've never said anything," Meldrum said.

" I know. But, believe me, you've been around ! "

Meldrum said : " There's all kinds of work in London."

" You don't say. One might think you spoke from experience ! Can't you see me strap-hanging with the *Daily Telegraph*, an eight-to-five man crushed in like a sow on the way to market, to and fro, the kind of work that makes life a long bereavement of oneself and no benefit to anyone else ; three weeks' holiday a year and a struggle out at week-ends through traffic where you can talk sideways for half an hour to a man in a fast car going the other way ; where you breathe a cocktail of diesel and petrol fumes and look forward to a slow march of days to an appointed end, all in a crowd of people dying of loneliness even though there are so many of them that they have to be packed like plates in a dishwasher according to shape. Advice comes well from you ! If it's a crime not to be adjusted to that, then give me crime. Life was meant to be enjoyed. . . ." He here looked out of the window and seemed at once to forget what he had been saying.

" Fun—is that it ? " said Meldrum.

" Yes," said Traquhair, and he walked out.

Once outside he surveyed the façade of the Strathire Arms. His mouth started to move again.

Although the new bar, like a section of concrete train, was largely completed, the sun parlour still looked like the interior of a house that had been bombed. Debris and junk lay about in piles and ladders the colour of birds' mess were propped against the walls.

In the parking space under the newly-painted sign, great heaps of cement and sand stood among planks and piles of brick. To a passing motorist the whole scene must have suggested closure for a year at least. A bus load of hydro workers would not have given the place a second glance.

There came a clinking of crockery from the house which seemed to be directed at himself. Meldrum was clearing. Each time it came Traquhair took a few steps.

Yes, making bows and fishing-rods by hand, he thought,

The Lifeline

varnishing, polishing, binding and preparing the cane with scarcely the use of a metal instrument or of that early discovery the wheel, making three hundred difficult pounds a year, a sum you could have multiplied by three with any carpenter or furniture maker, and then devoting your leisure, if such a word could ever be associated with such an internal Sisyphus, to reading T. S. Eliot and secretaryship of the Bath Archers in which office, your sole contact with society, you were maintained by local respect for your father's memory and your own brief career as a sanctioned killer. Why did I have to pick you up? Years since I met you—on a students' trip to Heligoland in the 'thirties. We shared a pair of binoculars to watch Godwit. Ah, Meldrum, it was like electricity. I got a sort of shock just touching what you touched and whenever I looked through the binoculars after you I think I saw dinosaurs, wild horsemen with streaming manes and taut bows, hermits by chasms, legionaries and the trim shape of a viking sail like a new moon on the sea's rim. I saw strange gods and Christ crucified and the old world parted from to-morrow like a body lopped from an all-too-brainy head. Others passed you off as daft or in need of attention, and so did I . . . except when I was with you. Then—then I packed your kit for you, lent you my socks and money, and took your indifference and rebuffs as favour. Traquhair thought it was all he was worth. The war came and your childhood on the North-West Frontier stood you in good stead. You sniped, really killed real Germans. Alone—I need hardly add. After years of comparative peace we ran into each other in Bath where I was doing a course in archery.

It was about the time of my second divorce. Nature abhors vacuums. I took you on—you, Olivia, six children and Loki, a dog which ate as much as me but could wear a wedding-ring round its groin. And then one night shall I ever forget it?— we got down to tin tacks. We got down to the prune: your "secret," Meldrum's Law: *The environment is master and must be destroyed.* You told me nuclear weapons would be used because nature is for ever trying to balance itself and succeeding, but now man had made such an adjustment synonymous with

The Lifeline

atomic war. Contemporary man will blame this and that according to his own political and psychological complexion, but future man, if any, will have no doubts. He will know that for atomic man psychological acclimatisation, in the time available, was not possible, *even if desirable*. Osmosis with the machine ... etc. That was our first Poor-Rory.

In spite of all this I signed you on as a hungry man takes his dinner, worse, as a blind man acquires an Alsatian. And where am I ? Under a bus !

A rhythmic hammering from within made Traquhair snort indifferently. He became conscious of the wad of communications in his hand, of the cement mixer like some primitive siege implement and the stacked tools—all idle, transfixed into one single social and financial comment.

Across the road stood the War Memorial Hall where only a few hours ago, aided by drink, he had experienced a feeling of omnipotence, of love and humility; he had been at one with many. Via drink—and himself.

Just as his face was softening under the embrace of such a memory he caught sight of a figure coming up the road leaning over to one side to balance the weight of a big suitcase on the other. And where, he thought, did she think she was going like that? No bus stop beckoned, no traffic suggested the likelihood of a lift and beyond the Strathire Arms the road mounted the first of many hills and wound northwards along the sea's edge without a house for miles. Poor girl, he thought.

All the same, he began to loiter towards the safety of his porch in case, after all, it was somebody collecting old clothes for the Guides like yesterday.

He lifted the hem of his burnous dressing-gown so as not to step on it and as he moved back towards the door, he had forgotten he was again addressing Muldrum : What about a minimum politeness to your benefactor, a merely normal human interest in how he got on last night, how he finally had drunks eat out of his hand like the wild birds of St. Francis, and spread a sense of identity like a fiery cross from his own heart, touching off God knows what forgotten chord in some

The Lifeline

sublime lunatic, some Recogniser. . . . Lost orphan of the Cullan seer, hail! Indeed. J. S. Mackay and Sons might take a leaf out of somebody's book.

Then he heard a voice behind him call: "Mr. Traquhair!"

To turn and see Helen MacDonald standing beside a suitcase which no girl in her condition should have carried, was in the circumstances a cold shock. Yesterday morning he had promised her a job, a roof, security. Later, on the stage, he had felt as though he were enacting some sort of Annunciation as he put the sash over her head; felt as if he was putting his hotel at her disposal. Then morning came . . . as it always did.

What happened? He left her standing beside a paralysed cement mixer carrying her own luggage.

The long silence and dressing-gown of the big man made Helen blush and toss the hair from her eyes as though he could take it all back what he said, yesterday, for all she cared.

"Meldrum!" he shouted, and then to her: "Wait. There's someone coming."

She said: "There's the pram to come from my cousins, first week."

"For God's sake!" he murmured reverently and shouted louder. "MELDRUM."

18

THERE HAD BEEN NO CHILD from either of Traquhair's marriages. Why should there have been? Why shouldn't there have been? Speculation in either direction was a cul de sac down which memory never took him. For of all the dreams he had realised marriage had perhaps been the most unlikely. As some party-goers wake up in the morning to find themselves wearing a policeman's hat, or mysteriously between the wall and the sofa of some house they have never seen before, so Traquhair had twice come to his senses and found himself married. Tarts were different, practicable. He had even settled down for as long as a week on several occasions with tarts. But wives! No. They gave him claustrophobia. The very part of them which should have cheered him up most made him frantic to escape. And yet, technically, it had always been they who had left him.

In Strathire at this date it was a common sound to hear the great rolling waves of Traquhair's voice inveighing against marriage. " *Heugh heugh*, my dear sir—an anachronism. Let's be honest with ourselves. The Sikhs have the last word on the subject: A boy for romance, a woman for children, a melon for pleasure."

But perhaps he attacked marriage a little too often, too loudly and emotionally. A suggestion of bitterness lingered in the echoes of his voice. Did he despair of ever achieving such a common badge of conformity? It was getting late in the day: he was on the far slope of life without a child's hand in his, without any promise that is of immortality, even by proxy, in this world or the next.

The Lifeline

And then children were the one section of society he could rely on. They gave him a big hand, at any time and any place. He supposed it almost followed that he should have no child !

The remedy which chance had now provided, a penniless pregnant teenager with a pram in the post, was in the best tradition of his hallucinations. But he went upstairs and verified her through a window : she was there again. And Meldrum had picked up her case.

Traquhair groaned and turned inward to the chamber-cupboard. This, though smelling faintly of its ertswhile tenant, now contained a bottle of whisky and a glass. He gave himself a straight draught for effect. No nonsense about tasting. He went into it as film-stars go into a kiss, mouth wide as a begging bear and his Adam's apple making a noise in his ears like a bath going out.

Then he banged down the glass. Bankruptcy and a birth !

When the glass was empty a second time and the heat of the whisky spreading through him like a compromise with sleep if not death, and the very opposite of pain or tension, furring his blood with innumerable little waves of pleasure and making him feel paradoxically both winged and yet more solid, a mocking smile came to his lips and he listened.

The noises of his hotel, in the absence of drilling and hammering, stood out like creaks at a funeral. He could hear Meldrum's voice and footsteps ; and he could imagine the feelings of the child-mother as she looked round her new home.

He made a flatulent noise with his lips, poured himself another drink and leaving the bottle on the dressing-table, walked to the window. There he stood for some time while steps and the two voices sounded remotely below.

Then his eye came back and flitted round his room. A Dutch hoe lay against the arm-chair still rusty from the salty wet sand in which he had scraped for cockles. A signed photograph of one well-known film star stood on one table and on another a photograph of himself drawing a long bow for a shot at maximum range. Books on archery and ancient

The Lifeline

battles, natural history and the Highlanders sprawled about untidily among sadistic thrillers and primers of Gaelic; and on the mantelpiece, under the reproduction of a Chinese duck painted on silk, stood the old bottle of Camp Coffee with the Highland officer being served by his Indian servant.

He found he was still holding his mail, the very chart of this present moment, big sheets, printed, small sheets handwritten, business letters, personal letters and the one anonymous letter. Morning had come and brought practical discouragement from the treacherous majority, theoretical acclaim from a single lunatic fan. He put it all down and after another stare out of the front window he went to the end of his bed and had a look out at the back, the henrun and the Meldrums' annexe. As usual the younger Meldrum children were playing about their door and Meldrum's bird was perched in its cage. All over the world Traquhair had seen birds hung thus at the mouth of grim, grey tenements and huts like imprisoned messengers, brilliant hostages from another world. And now he thought "Caged Bird Societies" were becoming as popular as motor shows.

Behind and overtopping the whole scene stood the distillery chimney.

A qualm assailed his mind, and he heard the words Meldrum had spoken to him not many minutes ago : " We know what brought you here."

Was *that* . . . chimney what had brought him to Fluach ? He didn't know. But he did know from a strange thrill below his navel, that it was what had brought him to this window for a look.

He had first heard of Johnny Stephenson, M.B.E., at a Hampstead dinner party from a journalist who had written an article in a highbrow periodical on the underworld of Soho. " King Johnny," said this man, was worth meeting. . . .

Traquhair had read *Combined Ops* (Stephenson's memoirs) and enjoyed it. The idea of the Crown employing a notorious swindler in the Pay Corps and promoting him to an advisory post in Britain's hour of need appealed to him. Not for a

The Lifeline

moment did he believe that the authorities had been deceived by Stephenson's *alias*.

Yes, he wanted to meet Mr. Stephenson.

This was a period when intellectuals were expressing something more than mere sympathy or interest in criminals, seeming to draw some sort of emotional nourishment from them, and the whole thing was easily arranged through an editor, a personal friend of Stephenson. He was a smart, small man, Stephenson, with a face like an anagram of the ten commandments, a low voice, half-cockney, half-genteel accent, charming smile, and muddy noncommittal eyes. His hands were particularly small and neat. Traquhair was struck by his calm. The kindly welcome which he extended to the simplest anecdote was worthy of a fellow-adventurer—or a psychiatrist. They got on well. Traquhair saw him several times in fairly respectable surroundings. With the proceeds of *Combined Ops* Stephenson said he intended to go straight, retire to a hotel in the north of Scotland. And he invited Traquhair to stay as soon as he was settled in. And this was what had happened. Traquhair had stayed a week in the Strathire Arms and it was there one evening that Stephenson had joked about running a pipeline through into the distillery. Traquhair had said, " Superb," and taken a walk round the room elaborating. As the memory of that walk came he closed his eyes.

Against his closed lids he had a vision of Stephenson's face, the restrained smile—a smile, one might have thought, of social responsibility, the smile above all of a professional. The subject had been dropped and Traquhair never gave it another thought, till a year later, when for old times' sake, he visited Stephenson in Brixton after he had been picked up on a charge that dated back several years.

This last meeting had made a deep impression on him. Earlier he had always been expecting Stephenson to do or say something which would show him to be a villain, a swine. But this never happened. Stephenson paid for more than his fair share of the drinks and was attentive and modest in conversation. That he did not ring up when he said he would and was

The Lifeline

seldom at the address forecast merely made him like a lot of Traquhair's other Soho acquaintances. Now, seeing him in prison clothes, guarded and with an ugly crew cut of grey hair, Traquhair felt a naïve identification with the culprit, a strong inversion of conventional values so that at one moment he went so far as to feel a failure and a hypocrite for not being beside him, in jug. Just when the prisoner began to develop a halo, Stephenson said: " Remember the old Strathire Arms. Empty nah, you know. Belongs to a company. Friends of mine. Why don't you rent it, Tulloch? Remember the plumbin' we discussed? *Well, it's finished, see?* Lovely job. Talk to Fred about it. Nice place. Situation . . . Modern faculties . . ."

A siren's smile had spread over Stephenson's face.

" Why not? " Traquhair had murmured, smiling too. All the same, he said, perhaps he had better think about it—the one thing of course which he had never done, any more than he had " talked to Fred "—Stephenson's "agent."

Months had passed. His second divorce had gone through with difficulty. Shabby months. It was then he had been sent by the B.B.C. on a "course" of archery, met Meldrum and brought him up to London where they had all shared a house in Putney. That summer, to escape from Putney, he had gone to Positano with Zoé Prin—Maid Maryon—and the papers had been full of Little John getting off with Maid Maryon. The sky had been blue, the scampi excellent, but the company heartbreaking. There was no common language in which to communicate except about superficialities. It was as though everyone were like himself—people without pasts or with pasts which were left out in case they got in the way of the present. No one could stop acting even though it was the one thing they could none of them do. He quarrelled with Zoé and accepted a lift home on the yacht of a Belgian millionaire who, off Trafalgar, disclosed the roots of his generosity. If this was his fate Traquhair could not love it. He asked to be put ashore and then flew home. At first Meldrum, with his pets and window-boxes, was a relief. Then more telephone calls from his ex-wife. He had begun drinking heavily and hating

The Lifeline

more and more (Meldrum's influence?)—his work. One day he told his producer he would sooner figure in "spots" advertising dud contraceptives to starving Asiatics than in all this fancy-dress boloney. He was sacked. Then between boozing, and bows and arrows . . . he considered joining the Church, until one day he had found himself, literally found himself visiting Fred, making inquiries about the hotel. . . .

Of course he wanted to rent it *as a hotel*, that was all. People with 'names,' quite small names, boxers, hangmen, cricketers, often turned publican. The name brought in the trade.

Fred understood. All the same, he handed him a diagram with the words, " S'lovely job, Tulloch. . . . For a riney die."

At home the temptation to tell was too much for him. Who could keep quiet about a magic wand if they possessed one? Not he. Olivia seemed not to hear but Meldrum listened with a dawning frown which finally became fixed, incredulous. Then: " Put it out of your mind, dear Reoraidgh," he had said. " We are going north to run an ordinary hotel."

It would be an exaggeration to say that Traquhair remembered all these events in detail. They came to him, as it were all at once, in a single chord, out of that huge great organ pipe of a chimney. Disturbing music! He turned away and went back to his room, and poured himself another drink. The qualm passed, the vision passed, and his eyes focused on the mass of letters lying where he had thrown them down. Facts! . . .

He went and rang J. S. Mackay. " Who's it calling?" said a low demure female Fluach voice, straight from the Senior Secondary.

" Mr. Tulloch Traquhair."

The subsequent silence was at first only to be expected; then as it dragged on Traquhair explained it away in terms of Mr. Mackay being at large somewhere in the office or even speaking on another phone. But at last it became sinister, hostile, and when the demure voice came on to the wire again, more demure, more dispirited than ever and said, " He's out," dour and laconic as a child compelled to repeat a word in a foreign

The Lifeline

language, Traquhair knew that Mackay would continue to be out.

A few minutes later he found himself—and it is true he did again literally *discover* himself standing there beside the picture of the dying stag . . . holding in his hand the big heavy black key which Meldrum had shown him the first morning of their arrival.

It was just a key. The leaf was like one of those maze puzzles children do in annuals : you go down there with a wavy pencil line and you come to a dead end or you go down there and arrive. There was a flick of verdigris here and a patch of rust there. South of Kintail Bridge it would just about have done as a prop for Robin Hood and nothing else. Just an archaic key. . . .

He heard a door banging somewhere, sometimes hard, sometimes soft, never latching itself, in Fluach's perpetual wind

19

WHILE TRAQUHAIR was holding the key balanced, a body of Fluach citizens called the Amenities Committee were taking their seats in the residents' lounge of the Seaforth Arms, which Brian Creevie let them have free except during the season.

This committee numbers five people of whom three must be present before any measure may be passed. It meets once a year or "when occasion demands." This year, owing to the impending visit of Prime Minister Hilldersley of Canada, the committee had met twice, mainly to appoint a chieftain for the Cullan Games.

Up till the first war the office of chieftain had always been filled by the marquess, but ever since then the mantle had tended to fall more and more on anyone who had some significant territorial or financial connection with the county. But what about this exceptional year, when royalty might be present? Would Mackay Halpick and his big Austin do? Would Brian Creevie and his Bristol, or J. S. Mackay and his Aston-Martin? Would Lionel Spote in trousers with the *New Statesman* concealed under the programme in his Lagonda—would he fill the bill? Would Mrs. Spote, Lord Seaforth's heiress, with her halting speeches and almost pathological aversion to appearing in public, would she do?

Henry Walker, who had done the door at the dance, said No, he did not think any of them would do and he paused staring down at his notes—a good moment to interrupt him, as it were, and introduce the remaining members of the committee.

First there was the President, Major Murray, of the Excise, widely believed to be the father of Helen MacDonald. Ever

The Lifeline

since the First World War, when the same shell-fire that shocked him half out of his wits overnight had also promoted him from corporal to acting-major in the same period, an atmosphere of military, social and personal crisis always attached to his person. His watery old eyes were for ever darting here and there as though denying any suggestion that he or anyone connected with him might not be doing his duty. During the second war he had acted as second-in-command to the Strathireshire Home Guard which was the same as commanding it, since the C.O.—Strathire himself, was almost always in the south. Later, in Churchill's revived Home Guard during the Korean war, Major Murray had surprised the whole neighbourhood by living, every Saturday all the year round, in uniform and warning people "in a position" that the "balloon might go up any day"—a metaphor which modern weapons endowed with a startling realism, the balloon seeming to be nothing less than the whole globe, and "going up" the sudden departure of that globe from orbit, like a punted football. When the balloon didn't go up and the Home Guard stood down Major Murray hinted at "irresponsibility" in high quarters. "A" Company, he said, would remain at the ready even though denied official recognition, uniform and travel allowance. (In fact, six of them did continue to meet every other Thursday for beer and .22 practice.) Murray still thought the balloon could quite easily go up any day, and in making this assertion his voice would always drop to a confidential whisper as though such a truth was not for every Tom, Dick and Harry, but only for those few men of Strathireshire "in a position" and unlikely to panic, men on whose shoulders in peace and war the fair name of Fluach and Scotland depended. The well-known rumours about his private life probably added to the stern moral state of trust and shared public responsibility to which he treated people in the street and all colleagues on the several committees he patronised. He was sure that he gave the Amenities Committee an indefinable something. And, indeed, he did. As Miss Jimpson, for instance, at the A.G.M., always pointed out, Major Murray's support and enthusiasm

The Lifeline

was something they would only appreciate properly when it ceased to be available.

Miss Jimpson (music teacher and drama secretary) never missed an Amenities meeting. Every year she followed Major Murray's speech of final, irretractable resignation with "a few words" about what Major Murray had stood for on the Amenities Committee and what he must therefore continue to stand for. Tears would overflow her eyes and match the more permanent and less emotional ones in his and he would take back his resignation with a burdened mutter, and a gesture signifying impotence in the face of public need.

The remaining members were Æneas Mackay Skimbo, Denis Mackay (science teacher and secretary of Fluach Football Club), and a crofter called John Dallas who had never yet been present at a meeting.

Since the war the committee had declined, lost its powers, its cinema, and its original committee, that is, with the exception of Miss Jimpson, who stayed on perhaps only for two reasons.

For eleven years now she had been urging (*a*) the erection of a public convenience between the first tee, the football field and the beach; and (*b*) the formation of a Fluach pipe band. Both lacks, she said, were crippling. The Amenities Committee should change its name if it didn't provide them. So strongly did she feel on these two points that she had twice got them formally debated and rejected by the County Council. This year, in view of the influx of hydro workers and the P.M.'s visit, her colleagues expected her to return to the attack, perhaps even to proclaim a state of emergency on both counts. Mr. Walker, therefore, now proceeded to compliment Miss Jimpson openly and at length on her efforts in procuring a chieftain, hoping thereby to deflect her energies from enthusiasms which in the past had consumed so much of all their time to so little purpose.

"We may be sure," he said, looking at her, "that Miss Jimpson was not exaggerating at our last meeting when she said the spotlight of the world would be upon Fluach this

The Lifeline

August. She was not of course referring to her own production of *Hamlet*" (Major Murray rumbled his feet) " which is to coincide with the games, nor to any project which she may still have up her sleeve—but to the visit of a Canadian Prime Minister to the croft on which his grandparents were reared and to the Cullan Games when he will sit among his ain folk."

Here he fixed her with a look of respect calculated to drive all irrelevance from her mind.

" Feeling as she did, it was to be expected that Miss Jimpson as early as last March suggested the appointment of a really fitting chieftain this great year. A man worthy of the office ! "

Now everyone was looking at Miss Jimpson and her eyes filled with grateful tears while a smile was born on the tremulous lips of her open, round, rosy face.

Major Murray's feet again spoke briefly on the hollow boards.

" And she said something then which we would do well to remember to-day. She said: 'This year things must not merely go smoothly, *they must have panache.*' She had felt this so strongly, she said, that after the January meeting (which she was the only person to attend) she approached Major Murray and myself, and as a quorum we agreed to her writing to the Marquess of Strathire and asking him to consider accepting the committee's invitation to stand chieftain on August third. This she did in February."

Walker's voice dropped. " Unfortunately Miss Jimpson's hopes, which we all shared, came to nothing."

Eyes sank to the table. It was common knowledge in Fluach that the marquess normally came north on August ninth in time to take a walk on the tenth, rest on the eleventh and be both limbered and rested for the twelfth when he went up Ben Cullan after grouse in a half track full of Americans and Belgian millionaires, flossy pointers and engraved guns.

" First," said Walker, " let me read you the final paragraph of Miss Jimpson's letter to the marquess."

" ' The Committee feels,' " he read and momentarily looked up at them like a television news-caster, " ' that no one but

The Lifeline

Your Lordship should be offered the chieftainship of the Cullan Games when the guest is none other than the Prime Minister of Canada—a country which so many Strathire folk adopted as their homes in olden days.' "

From anyone else but Miss Jimpson such a statement might have been taken as a reminder of the Highland evictions and, as such, moral blackmail on any Highland grandee. But from her it was safe, warm-hearted, impulsive. Clearly she had not believed that the marquess would not be as moved as she at the idea of Mr. Hilldersley, fleeing the affairs of a twentieth-century state to gaze for one healing moment on the blackened hearth and grey shell, the ruin become windbreak for sheep, where his great-grandmother had dandled his grandfather on her knee.

But she had been misguided, as now in heavy tones Mr. Walker attested.

" Here is the answer."

Dear Miss Jimpson,—My wife and I were touched and honoured by your kind invitation, but this year, alas, we cannot reach Strathire before August the ninth.

In 1937, when I and my wife visited Government House, Ottawa, we were extremely impressed by the vigour and friendliness of this splendid young dominion. In the North and West there are extensive mineralogical deposits. The Zambesi falls are one of the great sights of the world.

Yours sincerely,

The signature that followed was like a huge spider's web photographed in the ten-thousandth of a second when it is sucked up by a vacuum cleaner. It occupied three-quarters of the large page.

STRATHIRE

Tea was served and with loyal regret Miss Jimpson commented on the dignified refusal. She confessed a weakness for pageantry and she knew that no one had quite such an astonishing regalia for public Highland occasions as the marquess.

The Lifeline

Six foot three himself, his crummock or shepherd's staff, stood seven feet high. His tartan plaid and silver clasp, his flowing sporran and buckled brogues all made her heart beat faster. And she was not alone in this emotion. A lawyer from Inverness who had stood as a socialist for Strathireshire in the last election, for some mysterious reason fainted when introduced to our marquess at the inauguration of the Cullan dam site. This was the more striking because at that time the marquess was figuring daily in the national press over some quarrel he was having with his second wife. He had forbidden her entrance to the castle and she had climbed in by a fire-escape and been carried out struggling by the butler and footman, as the photographs proved. Of course the *Trumpet* printed not a line about such proximities, and in the same way good people like Miss Jimpson, whose little spare time from teaching music was devoted to nothing but communal good, seemed to have erased from memory that and many other aspects of the marquess's life, retaining only that symbolic idea of him which made him half a god, and therefore completely suitable for the role under discussion.

After the tea break she expressed her disappointment. Her face, as she addressed her colleagues, at first suggested that perhaps at last she had been disappointed once too often. But, no. She was resilient, her euphoria inexhaustible. What alternative could such a pageant-loving single woman suggest? "Perhaps you have guessed," she said invitingly. (A defensive look had come into her face.) But they had not guessed. The Amenities Committee with the possible exception of Æneas Mackay Skimbo (about whom more later), foresaw nothing but an appeal either to Lionel Spote, Esq., of Rossiemurchat House, his wife or Lord Strathire, three people who were all in various ways ideologically or ideally unsuitable. And until the Government inquiry on the dumb child of Skelly Island was completed they could not safely invite Sir Duncan Fidge, M.P., without offending the Director of Education, and many others.

"You see, I've been thinking, Major Murray," she said, looking intimately and pregnantly as always at the ex-officer,

The Lifeline

" that perhaps we could not do better, after what I heard about the Football Dance than to invite Mr. Tulloch Traquhair."

There was an astonished silence broken at once by Henry Walker: " Hear hear."

There then followed a cliff of a silence. Mackay, Football Secretary, had been so impressed by the hundred and fifty pounds taken at the door, that in telling Miss Jimpson of all that took place he had omitted, as had all her other informants, any reference to the selection of a male in the last ten of the Beauty contest. He had merely emphasised Traquhair's "touch" with the crowd; the impact of his appearance; his command of Gaelic and his emotional concern with Fluach and the people of Fluach.

Confronted now with the results of his enthusiasm reborn tenfold in another, in a woman moreover whose eyes sometimes brimmed over with vague love and enthusiasm for which life had provided no consistently suitable object, he frowned and could only think of the Teddy boy and the stationary tools (he had just heard about them), outside the Strathire Arms' porch; and "thon Zombie" in a space suit amassing rubbish at the back; and the song the children sang about him, in his class: " Muck'n Meldrum, Number Nine. . ."

Memory congealed and Mackay frowned. As though all this were not enough, without even starting on the man's association with the late Mr. Johnny Stephenson.

He stole a glance at Major Murray, but found him looking down at the table. The situation was dangerous. Æneas Mackay Skimbo and Miss Jimpson both, for different reasons, belonged to that small group of people who often had no idea what was going on in their own neighbourhood. Possibly neither of them had ever heard of Stephenson.

Yes, Mackay frowned, a very picture of schoolmasterly concern, while Miss Jimpson looking at him said: " You see, I've heard from Mr. Mackay how popular Mr. Traquhair was with the young people—and *it's the young* we must have with us if the games are to go on as they have in the past."

Major Murray was, of course, well aware that Traquhair's

The Lifeline

name had been linked with that of Stephenson and that Traquhair had awarded Helen MacDonald the sash when knowing her to be his employee and pregnant out of wedlock. Had the girl concerned been anyone but Helen he would therefore have spoken out briskly, but—as it was—he sat rigid, blinking, powerless apparently to approach the subject.

Meanwhile, the fragile yet compelling silence which Miss Jimpson had laid over them seemed to be gradually imprisoning them in her own point of view.

" What d'you think, Major ? " Mackay said at last.

" A good man, a good man," Major Murray said in his usual brisk, executive tone, with his eyes darting about, " I'm sure. But " (his voice dropped as though about to broach the balloon) " a sick man, they say. Must have someone fit. Oh, by jove, I should think so ! Must be fit ! "

" Sick ? " said Miss Jimpson in dismay.

" T.B.," Major Murray whispered as though announcing the date of D-day to someone entitled to know it. Then he cocked his head ruefully and responsibly, at the same time glancing conclusively at Mackay.

There was silence.

" Well, he can always say No," said Miss Jimpson.

Major Murray pushed out his lips and took in air fast, and as noisily as if it were mixed with a little scalding soup.

" By jove, by jove ! Supposing he says Yes. Sense of duty. Thinks he must do it and says Yes. What then ? "

" I never heard he was sick," Walker said, with a note of suspicion in his voice.

" He could be," Mackay said in a scientific tone.

" Oh, you men ! " Miss Jimpson suddenly sang, closed her eyes and took her lower lip under the tips of her teeth. As though this were not eloquence enough she then screwed up one fist and ground it on the table before she mastered her feelings sufficiently to say, " Sometimes I think you spend half your life being jealous of each other. I do. I do ! "

As a result of this thrust no man seemed anxious to speak, a situation which Miss Jimpson exploited nimbly.

The Lifeline

"Gentlemen," she said sweetly, "I always feel that here I have a right, nay, a duty to express the point of view of my own sex..."

Major Murray drummed briefly with one foot.

"Mr. Traquhair is such *a fine figure of a man*. Oh, laugh at me, laugh at me if you will. You see, on an occasion like this there will be so much pictorial publicity, television, that I think appearances will count for more than many of we older ones would like to admit."

Clearly the matter would have to be put to the vote. Before this was done the chairman looked at the one member who so far had not spoken though, in fact, it was four or five meetings since he had done so.

"Æneas?" said Major Murray almost invitingly.

Æneas Mackay Skimbo was a Catholic, but unusual as that was in Strathireshire, it was not the most unusual thing about him. He was also not quite five feet high, had served as a piper in the Boer War and been removed forcibly from a troopship in 1914 having understated his age by perhaps ten years. No one really knew his age. The pale-brown pupils of his small incandescent eyes were scarcely darker than the whites and these, even while he remained silent, occasionally flitted from face to face with a visionary conviction that was usually enhanced by a toothless smile of pleased certainty. All three of his sons were pipers in Scottish regiments and unlike him, could read and write. The rumour that he was a hundred had many believers. He came from a croft in the hills where he had recently earned a paragraph in the *Trumpet* by digging his own grave—not near his house, but a mile or two uphill, in a rocky place where recently, guided by him, an archæologist had unearthed primitive Celtic crosses and skeletons. When he spoke he spoke low and fast in broken English while his eyes increased their apprehensive probing right and left as though he were doing something risky and bold if not presumptuous, but from which no man born should stop him. He had religiously attended Amenities Committee meetings ever since he was co-opted to advise on the revived mod of 1946. He

The Lifeline

always did the journey, ten miles there to Fluach and ten miles back, on foot, just as he had attended Major Murray's parades during the periods '40-'45 and '53-'56.

For many years now, when the committee came to a vote, he had always voted, after a few humble inaudible words, with his great-great-nephew Mackay the football secretary for whom he showed the same warm affinity as he had to all the Mackays on board the S.S. *Cameronia* in 1914.

To-day he had been different, though no one had noticed.

His broad smile had seemed several times a preliminary to speech, but even when there was silence nothing came, nothing but flitting looks which seemed to encourage all present to keep on the way they were going.

" Nothing to say, Æneas ? " Major Murray said loudly.

" Is it the vote ? " whispered the old man keenly, but with a suggestion of bewilderment which suggested he had not heard a single word so far.

" Yes, we'd better vote," shouted the major, and he made a short speech to the effect that in his opinion, Traquhair had not been long enough in the district to qualify as what he, Major Murray understood by the word "Chieftain." Add to that the possibility of sickness and he thought he himself was left with no choice but to vote for Mr. Spote Rossiemurchat.

Walker said, " Traquhair chooses himself."

Miss Jimpson raised her hand as though taking an oath and said quietly, " Mr. Tulloch Traquhair."

The younger Mackay looked worried. At last he said he thought they "had the right policy" in asking Mr. Spote. He then closed one eye and sniffed; closed both eyes and blew his nose.

Two against two.

All eyes looked askance at Mackay Skimbo. Did he know what they had been discussing ? The little man leaned forward avidly as though this was what he had been waiting for, what he had known it would come to : First, he placed his index finger delicately on the table as though pointing to the infinitesimal spoor of a magic animal, a unicorn, while his eyes

The Lifeline

flitted round, rejoicing; then in a little earnest sing-song whisper, pronouncing the words like a comedian imitating a Welshman he said:

"But you see Tulloch Traquhair *is* the Chieftain. He *is* him . . ." And he smiled round equally at all, telling them.

Silence.

His great-nephew's eyes narrowed astringently so Æneas looked only at him when he went on:

"It was foretold. . . . And I did write to him through one of my sons."

Would anyone ask him to explain? The silence was diffident. It ticked away.

Traquhair became Chieftain of the Cullan Games.

The Chairman mumbled the appointment, then a further silence followed as though all present were dimly conscious of having done more than they knew.

Major Murray seemed particularly uneasy. His lips (the nether one was as like Helen's as George V was like George VI) twitched a few times and he blinked, cleared his throat and in general cranked up to utterance. But he could not utter, could only cast a fleeting resentful glance at the sprightly, youthful face of Skimbo whose conviction seemed to have cast a spell over them all.

Suddenly Miss Jimpson rose to her feet. "And now, gentlemen," she said, "although it is not on the agenda there is a matter which in importance follows naturally after Mr. Traquhair. I refer . . ."

Mackay, the schoolmaster, closed his eyes for utter weariness, but his uncle Æneas was radiant. Skimbo had never heard of the thing Miss Jimpson was always talking about. He probably thought a convenience was some kind of light English horse-drawn vehicle. In fact he did not hear her. He was smiling through the window at Redbeard Nan-Og come down again from Ben Cullan to lead his people, at himself throwing a tree trunk over the new moon, as the Brachan seer had foretold. Recognition would spread like fire through the heather.

And he Skimbo had been the Recogniser!

20

BY THE TIME the Amenities Committee had decided on his appointment Traquhair had replaced the key on top of the picture just as though some invisible force, emanating from Miss Jimpson and Æneas Mackay Skimbo, had crossed space and prompted his hesitant hand back into the paths of legality. And having replaced the key, and even cleaned his fingers from the grime which came off it, what did he do? He thought of the Caledonian Tea Bank.

In one of Traquhair's drawers there was a cutting from a Chilean English language newspaper which showed him in tail-coat, white tie and with his beard trimmed to a short neat triangle. In his hand, poised well up and out, was a conductor's baton and his eyes were downcast as though at a score. Normally he allowed his personal past no voice in the present. But now for some reason, in the truly deathly silence of his hotel, the past again intruded and this picture came to mind as a sort of comfort. (A plane had crashed with the maestro inside. The concert was for that evening. Penniless and desperate, he had stepped forward as Tullio Garibaldi, whom only the bottle and bad luck had kept from fame.) He had often heard the symphony which he had to conduct, but as long as he lived he would never forget the orchestra's silence at the first two downward movements of his arm, nor how despair turned to amazed relief when they came in on his third motion, which was in fact a shrug of despair, defeat. Well, the moment had come, as it were, for that third motion —and response from the orchestra, i.e. a Bank.

The Caledonia Tea Bank is a squat prosperous white-

The Lifeline

haulmed building opposite the police station. A twenty yards' stretch of purple gravel flanks the porch, but there are no ramps to reach it from the road; cars must jolt over the five-inch cliff of the pavement edge, which means they mostly stay by the kerb and thus leave the drive-in tidy. There is something arresting about this initial virginal tidiness. And, inside the bank everything is tidier still; always *new* like a coffin. Indeed the place does somehow suggest a ticket office for death. People whisper in mortuary tones and two of the clerks who work there have been in the building thirty years and come to the guichets like faded ghosts.

The sight of the enormous hotelier, however, seemed to infuse in them a spark of life, unwelcome life.

"Good morning," said Traquhair with confidential quietness and he put out his great arms so they spanned five feet of the coffin-wood counter and thrust his face commandingly close to the bars of the chromium coffin-metal grill. But all this seemed to have the very opposite of a harmonious effect. The accountant, shocked already by the appearance of a gaol-bird's friend, seemed to be tongue-tied as though he had had orders, like a butler, to tell Traquhair when he came—as he certainly one day would—that everyone was out except the pistol which lived in the safe. "Good morning, Mr. Traquhair," he said almost inaudibly.

He was a tall, pale, bespectacled man, a real white-collar slave, Traquhair thought. He would reach £750 a year by increments of £25 before cremation. Meanwhile, he probably dealt with the farming accounts of Mackay Halpick who got ten pound subsidy for each of the thousands of sheep that existed and the same for those that didn't. The world was full of heroes.

Traquhair considered him lengthily, politically.

"You know my name!" he said at last caressingly, and shifted his gaze to the notes in the man's hand—intending a look of mere admiration and approval of so much cash. But he must have failed in performance for the man suddenly looked as though he himself had just found the money lying about

The Lifeline

somewhere, money belonging to anyone as much as to anyone else, for he quickly put it away in a drawer which he locked instantly with a small key which was attached to his navel, as an electric light to a plug.

" Is there anything we can do for you, Mr. Traquhair ? Or would you like to see Mr. MacFarlane, sir ? "

The suggestion that the smallest transaction with Traquhair must necessarily be a matter for the manager, did not escape the big man's notice.

" That was what I had in mind," said Traquhair, with a touch of sarcasm and turning as he spoke, sideways-on—he had seen the door marked " Manager " and suspected MacFarlane was already in earshot. " It's a matter of some importance."

" I'll see if he's in," said the teller, and disappeared.

Left to himself, Traquhair looked around.

Paper rustled over to the left somewhere out of sight and a rubber stamp began to go *bon-bonk, bon-bonk, bon-bonk*. Traquhair's eyes flitted over the high-grade linoleum, the polished objects, scales, ledgers, trays to where a pretty girl was sitting with her back to him writing something, probably very elementary, and occasionally looking out of the window like a child at school where a month ago she must have been.

" There's an unpleasant wind," he said as though to console her for being in prison.

Somewhere out of sight the rubber stamp paused. The girl touched her hair and went on with her work. Then the rubber stamp resumed : *Bon-bonk, bon-bonk* . . .

" At least you have a good view here of the sea. I never get tired of the sea . . ."

At this moment, just as the pretty girl was turning to reward Traquhair with the sight of her face, Mr. MacFarlane, who had spied his visitor through the unfrosted " M " of " Manager," came out of his office with his hand out.

Traquhair took it.

The eyes of Mr. MacFarlane, thought Traquhair, in their fat cheeks are like two currants in one of those russet varnished buns which taste of paper. His curly hair gives him a look of

The Lifeline

childishness which consorts ill with his pompous manner. And why does he look at me thus?

After the Wotherspoon cocktail party Mrs. MacFarlane had gone home and told her husband that the new proprietor of the Strathire Arms was a friend of the bank robber Stephenson, a Communist and a drunk. This morning, after the football dance, she had added a fourth charge: the man was a " homogenital." Four shots fired with a humane killer into Traquhair's heart, could not, as far as her husband was concerned have killed him deader.

Never before had Mr. MacFarlane received a corpse. It says much for his profession that he remained confidential.

" Still very parky," he said. " Yes, yes. And there's more coming."

They went through and Traquhair was given a chair in front of a big desk on which, amongst other things, stood a two-way intercom. set, disguised as a cigar box, connecting with the living-room. Originally Mrs. MacFarlane had had it put in to save her a walk when she wanted to tell her husband that a meal was ready, but it had soon deteriorated into a simple form of relief for her curiosity. Then, when his promotion was postponed she used it as a remedy. How could she help him get on in his job if she only had his account of what was going on? He had wept. It had been the last citadel of his masculinity. But she had been adamant.

" Snuff?" said Traquhair.

The chased gold box and the tone of confident social seemliness with which it was offered (reminding MacFarlane of the way in which Mr. Lionel Spote had suddenly shaken him with the word " Pee?" after dinner at Rossiemurchat), involved his right hand, at that moment half in and half out of one fob and feeling for dust, in a startled convulsion, an outward movement which was initiated and arrested all within the space of half a second. This frustration of an extremity was then converted into a larger general movement of his whole form forward, then of his lungs, taking in a deep breath, a sigh of

The Lifeline

grateful refusal. He wondered if Meldrum were waiting outside with a van.

"So the aphrodisiac of the nose ...." (*sniff*) " doesn't interest you ? " (*sniff*) said Traquhair. "*Heugh heugh!* "

The two sniffs induced a glazed stare in the eyes of Mr. MacFarlane. What would happen next? How would the nose respond ?

He dreaded, without knowing, what homo-genitals did ; he merely suspected it was they who went on doing, after forty, what had once been dimly broached to him in Crieff Senior Secondary, but never realised, when he was fourteen. A measuring mark for their conduct was missing in that he was also uncertain what normal people did. Father of one girl though he was, he viewed his family with the same secret astonishment as he viewed Mrs. MacFarlane's "increase" near Redditch. (A field : she had passed it several times while staying with her brother in 1954, bought it in 1955 for £100 and sold it after the law changed in 1957 for £10,000.) At certain moments he was thankful to say he had not been too proud to do what he was pushed into. What the eye didn't see, the heart didn't grieve over and his wife, in both respects had kept him in the dark. And now he had a Snipe and a child none of which would have occurred without the leadership of Mrs. MacFarlane. Soon, if the microphone worked, he might get Aberdeen.

" A nice little place you have here," said Traquhair, looking round at the calendars, files and inventory furniture. " Chubb —such a good solid name for a safe-maker, I always think. . . . What a pretty garden ! Now I come to think of it, Mrs. Wotherspoon was saying what a great gardener you were, Mr. MacFarlane."

" Oh, yes, yes. Was she now ? Time to be getting things in soon, now. Hard work, hard work. You'll be a great gardener yourself, I think, Mr. Traquhair." MacFarlane screwed up his eyes and pursed his lips with a touch of irony at his corpulent guest. " Excellent exercise for the sedentary professions ! " At this moment there was a sudden click from the cigar box.

The Lifeline

He blinked. He was on the air: more strain. Meanwhile Traquhair was again looking round in the same way as Hodge looked round the room on his annual tour (Hodge was the head of Personnel, who refused him promotion).

" Well, well, what can I do for you ? " said MacFarlane, and heard the intercom. creak—a corset most likely, or a Biro opening to take notes. Helpful, often, yes. But it made for strain ; she wouldn't understand how it made for strain. And Hodge would hear of it. Yes, he would.

Traquhair now looked at MacFarlane unwittingly as though he would keep him in Fluach till he was due to retire. MacFarlane's chin came up.

" Let me be brief. I've a little project, Mr. MacFarlane, which I think might be of interest to the Caledonian Tea Bank."

" Yes, yes. Yes, yes," said MacFarlane, blinking like a signal lamp.

Traquhair described the hotel, the work being done on it (MacFarlane suppressed a smile, this was better; he knew work had stopped), the prospects of the bar, the hydro workers. . . .

Fortunately, at that moment, Traquhair had his back to him having risen to his feet and begun walking about (like Hodge) in order to give himself space for gesture.

" I need hardly tell a man of your position and intelligence," he said while MacFarlane smiled, " that we are on the edge of a new era. Look at that gigantic sphere at Dounreay. A reactor, they tell us. For me it is a signpost, a warning that we had all better bustle our stumps unless we want to get left behind. Well, if you ask me, Mr. MacFarlane, the Highlands *are* being left behind. The possibilities for making money in this country hit you in the face. How ? By the tourist industry."

He went on for ten minutes about tourism, ending thus :

" When I start on my network of seventy motels to stretch from Durness to Ullapool, I shall have to approach the City. But to-day—when it's a question of getting on with one public bar in Fluach, I felt I need go no farther than down the road, to the Tea Bank, because I knew there at least I would find one man who could see farther than the end of his nose."

The Lifeline

There was silence, while Mr. MacFarlane struggled, without success, not to feel pleased, and in all ways bigger than Hodge if not quite as big as Traquhair.

"You're needing this money at once, I take it, Mr. Traquhair?"

Traquhair measured the rosy bun and its two currants. Was this a trap?

"'At once' sounds rather drastic. Your assurance now would be enough. Your word, your name, Mr. MacFarlane... A word from you to your head office..."

"Yes yes—quite so, quite so..."

MacFarlane frowned in an effort to resist the picture which Traquhair had conjured up before his eyes—of himself leaning over to the large, puce hairy ear of Hodge which on this occasion had been lowered deferentially; of himself whispering and finally of Hodge nodding in judicious acquiescence....

Mr. MacFarlane's eyes became quite blinkless and still and his fob-fingers coiled in cosily as the forefeet of a hermit-crab. Even the frown on his brows had begun to thin out. Traquhair was talking again now, very quietly, though MacFarlane didn't hear more than stray words—"a man of your perspicacity..." "... the other day I was talking to Crumm, chairman of Luxitels..."

Suddenly four dry clicks sounded from the cigar-box in front. MacFarlane looked up. For a moment his eyes seemed confronted with fog. Then his visitor emerged, larger, more precise than ever: homo-genital, Communist, drunk and friend of a convict, a man who armed himself with these qualifications before inviting the Tea Bank to take shares in a shebeen.

The dry clicks came again and for one resentful moment MacFarlane could see in his mind's eye the instrument with which they were produced: the spanner of his wife's knitting machine gently chipped against the edge of the microphone/transmitter upstairs. Hodge's ear had vanished.

MacFarlane cleared his throat. "Yes, yes..." he said with a sudden edge of anger. "Quite so."

"I would make the thing a company." Traquhair went on,

The Lifeline

" and offer friends the chance of taking shares in it, but the truth is, Mr. MacFarlane, I'm greedy. I wish to have all the shares myself. *Heugh heugh* . . ."

There was a creak from the intercom.

Mr. MacFarlane, still on the rebound from his recent hallucination, spoke now with increasing sarcasm. " Well, well," he said, " very interesting. But what I say to our clients who come with a proposition is—what can you show? Security? Now I take it you own the hotel . . ."

Traquhair said : " I manage it."

" But you don't own it ? "

" In a sense, I do . . ."

" Could you sell it to-morrow, Mr. Traquhair ? "

" No."

" Then can you offer us any other security ? "

" I offer you, generally speaking, the profit margin of every pub in Great Britain; in particular I offer you the profit margin of pubs near big public works—near Dounreay, for instance, where they take £1,000 at the Cat every Saturday."

" Yes, yes, but that's as one might say in the future—or at least at the Cat. We are more interested in what we can be sure of, Mr. Traquhair. To tell you the truth, we haven't a very high opinion of what we call 'castles in the clouds.' Is there any other security you can offer, Mr. Traquhair ? Would the B.B.C. guarantee you an overdraft ? "

" Mr. MacFarlane—I offer you my name ! "

In Traquhair's opinion there came, at this moment, a noise like a slow puncture from the box situated in front of Mr. MacFarlane. Or had it come from some part of MacFarlane's person ? Certainly the man was now laughing unforgettably as though suddenly decided. In fact, he had stood up quite genially as though ten minutes' entertainment were always acceptable provided they didn't get in the way of work. " Your name, Mr. Traquhair ! Well, well, that's a thing we certainly take into consideration. It is indeed. But I'll have to think it over. Make a few inquiries—no offence of course—down south, isn't that right ? . . . you'd be known."

The Lifeline

He managed to flavour the word "inquiries" with a suggestion of criminality. Traquhair fixed him with eyes like rifle sights. But he went on: " Yes, yes, references, referees, if you understand me, sir, Mr. Traquhair—or a statement from your own bank. You see, you haven't even an account with us, have you ? Naturally we wonder why you don't go to your own bank."

" My bank is in London. I should have thought a Fluach bank was in the best position to judge about a local venture, Mr. MacFarlane."

" Well, perhaps your bank could get in touch with us . . ."
" A reference," said Traquhair. " A guarantee, is that it ? "
" Well, that's about the size of it. Yes, yes. Lord Nuffield say . . ."

MacFarlane frivolous ! The implications sank in. Traquhair knew shame.

MacFarlane beamed and again Traquhair had the impression that a noise—a sort of snort—came from somewhere in front of MacFarlane and indeed the bank manager's smile increased as though his own amusement had suddenly been doubled by being shared and approved.

" Lord Beaverbrook, isn't that right ? " he added.

" How about Johnny Stephenson," said Traquhair, rising, and putting one hand swiftly into his sporran. " Would that do ? "

The grin vanished from MacFarlane's face and apprehension took its place.

Traquhair flicked out a huge red silk handkerchief. The deafening report which followed came from his nose, but it obliged the teller next door to recount ten pounds in singles after a pause so protracted that the client on the other side of the bars asked what was the matter.

21

TEN MINUTES after Traquhair left the Caledonian Tea Bank the telephone rang in the Bishop's Palace.

Brian had just got back from the hotel and was standing with his back to the fire sipping a whisky and soda and smiling to himself. Certain memories of the football dance seemed to be taking clearer and clearer shape, rather surprisingly, as they dropped farther and farther behind in time. Beside him his mother was holding up what seemed to be a British passport but was, as could be seen in the aperture on the cover, the account of her dealings with P. J. McConnachie (grocer) in the year 1952. By holding it in a certain spot, high up and left, she could see the figures through a thin part of her cataracts much as a motorist, with no means of preventing his windscreen icing up, can often continue quite a time by peering through one spot, unaccountably spared.

Brian paused for a moment as though unwilling to answer the telephone, as though wishing in fact to go on where he had left off that morning, and put his mother still farther in the picture of the dance. But the bell insisted and still smiling, he walked over and picked up the receiver.

"Hallo . . ." he said.

Here his mother put down the little blue book, marked "P. J. McConnachie" and looked at him as though she had a presentiment.

Brian's smile was increasing. "Yes . . . yes . . . all right then," he said agreeably. "You win, Mrs. MacFarlane. Ten bob. You can have it now. . . . And thanks for letting us know!"

The Lifeline

" What was that ? " said Mrs. Creevie.

Brian came away from the instrument gladder than ever. " He's just been down to the Tea Bank for a loan. He gave Stephenson's name as a guarantee."

" No ! " Mrs. Creevie looked truly offended. " Shirly not, dear ! *Shirly* not ! "

" And was turned down *flat*, thank you very much. What did I say ? "

He lit a cigarette from the remains of the last, and put his hands out like a conductor at a rehearsal miming the spirit in which a particularly slow, smooth and diminishing passage is to be played. " Just wait . . . just wait . . . that's all . . . a few weeks, a few months and like a soap bubble on the carpet . . . not even a bang. . . ." Brian was almost singing, and for the next words his voice went high, treble almost. " Just . . . a . . . little . . . faint . . . phut . . . thank you very much."

" Well, dear, you were just going to say something when the phone rang. . . ."

" That Johnny Mackay isn't going to put another *brick* into that hotel until his bill is paid."

There was silence while one inhaled and sipped and the other sewed. Not for a long time had mother and son enjoyed such smooth intercourse.

" Did you speak to him last night at the dance ? "

Brian paused before saying, " No. Good heavens, Mother. What should I want with him ? "

" But you were introduced, weren't you, at the Wotherspoons ? "

" We certainly were. I made my feelings quite plain to him."

" But did he strike you then, dear, as . . . What they are saying ? "

" What are they saying ? I never know what they're saying. I'm only interested in facts, Mother. . . ."

" Well, he selected a Teddy boy," said Mrs. Creevie crossly. Brian had had no right to make her even drop a hint about such a subject.

The Lifeline

"If you ask me, he was just showing off. He never stops. I keep on expecting him to undress and show us . . ."

"*What?*" cooed Mrs. Creevie incredulously.

Brian took a few moody steps and a sip. "He's always talking about bulls. Whenever I heard him in the distance at the Wotherspoons he was talking about bulls."

"I don't follow, dear. . . ."

Nor apparently did Brian for he took another moody sip. His smile had gone. "That man gets my goat. He makes me a Socialist."

"But you said he was Communist."

"He tries to make you feel so small," Brian went on intensely. "Dressing up like the Marquess of Strathire, and having people introduced to him as though he were the Duke of Edinburgh at Wembley or something. I'd just like to know who he thinks he is."

The question—who did Traquhair "think he was"—in its literal simplicity seemed to engage both their thoughts for there was a long silence.

"I tell you, Mother—I'll take it from Lionel, I'll take it from the marquess—that tone and manner—but I will *not* take it from Mr. Tulloch Traquhair. I've got no sympathy with him."

"Sympathy!" murmured Mrs. Creevie. "Ai should think not."

"Well, it takes all types and there's room for everyone. But you know me. There's one thing I won't stand and that's people giving themselves airs. He reminds me of . . ."

Brian couldn't say all or even one of their names. He could only compress his lips at the great number of them there had been. Such a catalogue of slights starting at his Scottish public school in the thirties, carrying right on till last month when Spote, the Liberal, had told him over the port that with "his background" there were certain things he could never be expected to understand "except by rote." They had been alone with cigars beside the finger-bowls. He, Brian, had managed just to smile underneath one of the candle-lit oil paintings, of

The Lifeline

Holbein or something, of a man like Traquhair in a ruff, a man with a huge ring on his finger and a fat smile of almost mystical complacency, a great baby in its bath of privilege looking down at him with tolerant pity just as Spote had been doing at that very moment.

" You're lookin' feverish, dear."

" I'm not feverish, Mother. Believe me. I'm just fine. I've seldom been better. Nor do I care tuppence about the Strathire Arms. I'm just pleased for once that someone is getting their due. It so seldom happens . . ."

Mildred Creevie's silence sounded like a rare concession—agreement.

22

MELDRUM'S CAGED BIRD had a habit of heralding these cold March mornings as though spring had come. In fact, spring scarcely comes at all to Fluach where sand, hill, conifer and the occasional deciduous tree often wait till the middle of May and then declare the arrival of two seasons, spring and summer, all in a single week of primroses, bluebells, foliage and young birds attempting first flight on the edge of tall green corn.

Traquhair groaned in his bed.

For there was never any escaping Meldrum's bird. Even in London, suspended in an oubliette of a kitchenette where grime and medieval plumbing were glossed over with plastic coverings and gadgets it had chirruped, shrilled and piccoloed away as though life were not long enough to record the joy of merely living. In certain moods Traquhair had eyed the bird with irritation tempered by wonder, at other times he had gloomily thought how something always went wrong with his own pets, something "happened" to them as to his wives. But Meldrum's pets, for whom people might think an early death would be the greatest kindness, prospered and sang in a cubic foot of steel.

Tweet-tweet, chip-chip-chip, crrrrrrr, pipipipipipi, tulee, chi-pupupu chipupupu chipupup, pupuchip pupuchip, chop-chop-chop, chippili tippit chipilitippit, tchp-tchp, cheeeeeeee...

And what world, forsooth, was it talking about?

Better if he had had no inkling. Sweet winds, sweet smells of long ago, sweet wondering sense of immortality in this life. Joy of the instincts to which all other joys were inferior. The

The Lifeline

exultation had come and gone, but always returned, sometimes in strange disguises. Almost every day started by promising it. Even to-day! But the promise now was unbearable for the ceiling he saw above him suited the song of Meldrum's bird about as much as an execution yard wall. No. To-day the promise promised to be broken for ever.

He belched astringently and drew in fresh, factual air!

Sunday! Helen's first day in harness. Yesterday evening on his return from the Tea Bank he had shown her where to find things and told her what she had to do "till we open."

He lay expecting to hear sounds of life below, knocking and scraping, poking and riddling, then clinking and rattling, all culminating in the pregnant wobbling of a loaded tray and a tap on his door.

Or if the tray failed then he would come down to a clean air, a dancing fire and a hot breakfast. . . . Ageing and lonely, he would have that, at least, for a brief spell.

He dozed off and woke again at nine-thirty. The bird was quiet and he thought he could hear through the open window the peaceful clinking of the Meldrum family at breakfast. Till to-day, he thought, Meldrum had cooked breakfast for him. From now on he would see less of him. Perhaps Helen would be company, provided of course that she had not already left.

He expected ingratitude. It was normal. He even welcomed it for it freed him from the person indebted to him. Yet now he felt a pang that the girl whom he had taken on—in spite of her condition—should do nothing for him in return. Had Creevie and MacFarlane got at her? Or Meldrum? It was not impossible that Meldrum himself might have told her she would be better off almost anywhere else under the sun.

He belched again in a morale-raising way and scratched himself peacefully. Then he stole a panoramic look round the room. There it all was: his eyes became furtive as they took in the untidiness, the motley assortment of objects, the stuffed peregrine and the gigantic picture of a Highlander drawing a bow—a rare piece of evidence which he had found in Paris.

Any moment now he would get out of bed.

The Lifeline

Perhaps the world in the shape of the Tea Bank, MacFarlane, Creevie, Dewars, Meldrum and Helen combined to make him linger in hot dark and vacancy; perhaps the recurring patterns of the buried but inescapable past anchored him with apathy.

He lay several more minutes before a smile began to grow in his little eyes, a smile which at last reached the corners of his mouth disturbing his beard like the progress of a big animal under bushes. For the old stirring had come in his stomach, the frail harmonic, presumably, of that long ago feeling which had blended his father and mother when they struck a certain all-important spark long ago.... A feeling for life, an erection, as it were, of the spirit.

It was at this moment he put a leg out.

Soon the room was vibrating with his movements, and finally with his song: " The Nutbrown Maiden."

He put on his burnous and—still singing—he went to the window.

There his short-lived song died quietly.

At nine-thirty on a Sunday morning Fluach Main Street has something in common with those phantom ships which once disturbed the short hairs of ancient mariners. Sure enough there it is; but life is absent. Mere lying-in of inhabitants could scarcely account for such desertion. The single scurrying cat has the furtiveness of a sole survivor, the finality of a full stop.

Not a day this Fluach Sunday but the funeral of a day!

He groaned and went down into the living-room only to be confronted by the stale cold untidiness of the night before centred on an empty whisky bottle and a dirty glass.

Already he missed Meldrum and repressed an impulse to call.

Through the window the paralysed cement mixer stared at him with the central oscillating container stuck still as the magnified eye of a dead fish.

He went into the back and tapped on Helen's door. At the third tap there was a sound of life. At the fourth a groan as though she were being born all over again, this time without the satisfaction of yelling.

The Lifeline

"What about a little breakfast, my dear," he said, with a touch of sarcasm.

He went into the kitchen and started cooking some eggs and bacon. In a few minutes, still half-asleep, she appeared in a dressing-gown contriving to keep her back to him as though ashamed of a face that was neither washed nor powdered. Tactfully he withdrew but paid for it a few minutes later when she came through with an egg that seemed to be made of pale-yellow rubber and bacon cooked to tasteless shards.

After describing how he liked his egg he asked her to join him for breakfast. Why not? But she said she didn't take breakfast, and went through.

After eating half the egg his jaws came to a standstill. He got up and went back to the window. It was raining now—slowly and gently, and some boot marks round the cement mixer had turned into puddles. The road was still deserted and there was nothing to look at except the hearty optimistic poster "Are you good enough for the Army?" and the accompanying picture, a man wearing earphones under a bush. It was an extraordinary question from a man under a bush. He felt there must be some logical term for it like a syllogism or tautology. . . . He found himself staring at it for longer than he liked.

Loud clanks and rattles came from the kitchen. Was she offended by what he said about the egg? He wanted someone to talk to and debated whether to go and teach her how to fry an egg.

But to what end? She would fry as she chose.

He went into another room with the vague intention of seeing "where we stand" and found more debris and work half-finished.

What happened now? One day, a lorry would come and collect the cement mixer and the tools. That would be all, until the men came in bowler hats, the undertakers of his material possessions. He would have to go back to London and beg a job in advertising 'spots.'

The Lifeline

Meanwhile the Cullan camp was filling up daily.

" Just one Saturday night," he muttered. " Just one."

He opened the room Meldrum called "the junk room" as though such a name designated some obvious difference between it and other rooms. The first thing he saw was Helen's pram.

He closed the door.

Back in the living-room the one eye of the cement mixer began to develop a pupil, iris and lashes and when he moved it moved with him, keeping him in sight.

A tea chest of books still waiting to be unpacked was covered with newspapers and one of these, an old *Daily Telegraph* for 1950, yellowing with age, attracted his hand. Old newspapers had a dimension that was entirely lacking from new ones. Pathos. June the 5th, 1950. *Big Four Flop.* . . . *Gromyko walks out.* . . . To Mrs. Harrison-Smythe a daughter, Janet 7 lbs. 5 oz. Janet now would be seven stone.

He pored over it for a time and then played music in his head with names that had already acquired the faint, nostalgic quality of old tunes—Malenkov, Eden, Korea and so on. After a time his defeated eyes rose and took in the *Daily Express* where Helen must have left it. Now his hand strayed out as though with a vague sense of coming to terms executively with the present moment or with the world that he had intended to leave behind him down south. The main headline was bigger than usual. " THE PERFECT GRAB " and led into a story about the theft of £200,000 of jewels from a big West End jewellers. The grab, apparently, could not be faulted. No trace could be discovered of jewels, thieves or the thieves' transport, and the night watchman was still unconscious. " The perfect grab." He pondered the phrase and the implications, if any, for the ten million odd readers, excluding those who saw it in the distance in carriages, tubes or upside down under fish and chips. " The perfect grab "—it chimed with " The four-minute mile." A challenge to youth. He turned over the page and came to a whole-page advertisement which was three-quarters picture and one-quarter text in big print starting off with five

The Lifeline

words in capitals : WHAT MORE HAS LIFE TO OFFER ? ... They've got two Fords. A Ford Zodiac and Ford Anglia. ...

Spellbound as an archæologist, bending towards a unique find, he scrutinised the page which seemed to be part photograph of a *papier-maché* model, part photograph of live people and part drawing.

Father, in a bowler and carrying a brief-case was getting into the Zodiac and mother was getting into the Anglia with a shopping bag; behind came two children, a boy and a girl galloping down the crazy paving from a low-gabled Tudoresque detached house no bigger than its garage, and windowed incongruously beneath its traditional gables with huge rectangles of plate-glass like a shop. The face of the father was something between Anthony Eden and an ideal American executive whom Traquhair had often seen wanting stomach powder in *Men Only*. The mother's face was so lit up with joy for her Anglia that she might have been a queen who had just given birth to a boy after fourteen girls. Traquhair fell into a brown study. The satchelled boy and girl particularly attracted his attention for it was inconceivable they should have been two boys or two girls. One and no more of each was as suitable as the bowler and as the face in which the ex-officer of yesterday's Burberrys was losing out to something a shade coarser, squarer jawed.

The picture confronted Traquhair with the confidence of a mirror: staring into it, he began to feel himself sprout a bowler, a back-room job in Lime Grove or Shell, an adjusted wife and also adjusted hormones so that he had begotten one of each sex as easy as whistling or as getting two Fords. Last year when things had looked financially rosy Zoë Prin would probably have married him—perhaps because a picture such as the one by his feet would then have become feasible, a reality for her. They could have taken their holidays in Sweden and finally been cremated with smokeless fuel.

Oh, my God, he thought, I must stop; this way Meldrum lies.

Surrey spin wins the day. Sole Mio's great race.

The Lifeline

Soon Traquhair's eyelids drooped and his eyes went out of focus . . . closed. Then suddenly they opened wide.

He was alone. But to be alone without drinking, dreaming or reading was to invite a dreadful game of grandmother's steps with monsters of memory. A quick glance round and there they were—the monsters—all frozen, smiling, stationary and quite harmless ; then he looked away from them and pretended they weren't there, and the next moment he usually felt a chill in his spine ; for if they touched him he would cease to exist. Naturally a few minutes after such a sensation he would usually be striding somewhere down the street with his kilt swinging or talking to the postman about life on a windjammer, or to Solicitor McWilliam about mambas or to the little Meldrums out in the back about Afghan cattle thieves, always, of course, in a context of personal experience.

But this morning he did not move. Nor did he fetch a bottle or fall asleep. Nor did he daydream in the usual manner. He simply stayed staring over the fallen newspapers at a spot nowhere, feeling that now it was too late to change, supposing, for the sake of argument, that it was ever possible to change. A desire to look inwards for the first time seemed to be tugging somewhere inside him like a faint-hearted hand on the edge of a dressing over an enormous wound. The desire faltered. A sure picture of the exact location of the nearest whisky bottle broke into it instantly like the peep-peep-peep of " beam " guiding an aircraft. His eyes again half-closed momentarily. Then he opened them concentrating on the feeble, craven voice within of attempted self-recognition. Why could he not live without Meldrum and his bows and arrows, his instincts, and atmosphere of the Domesday Book, his medieval stare as historically recognisable as the narrowest streets in a cathedral town ? He found himself on the verge of asking those very questions which must have been asked all round him ever since his arrival at Fluach, questions which even the Wotherspoons and the Meldrums were unable to answer, such as, What had happened to his two wives ? . . . Where did he come from ? . . . Who were his people ? . . . Where did he go to school ? . . .

The Lifeline

Was he quite sure that he still knew the answers? Like heavy snow the years seemed to have covered his tracks as quickly as he made them. Convenient and misleading metaphor! Truer to say he had needed to cross out the past systematically. . . Lately the instalments due for erasure had shrunk to weeks, hours. Time past, personally speaking, scarcely existed for him. No good! He gave up, he was out of practice when it came to retracing steps. Whenever the past had thrust itself upon his notice he had waited in craven apprehension or increased portentous artificiality for the revelation to pass— like a storm. No, he had no personal past; instead he had Meldrum, and the bottle of Camp Coffee on the mantelpiece, and the other bottles each one full of feeling and sense of identity, vast identity, large as love, large as life.

The newspapers had so fallen that one, the *Daily Telegraph*, bulged upwards, pushing towards him that very agony column which had recently given him an emotion. He read:

CONSCIENCE MONEY.—*His Majesty's Inspector of Taxes wishes to acknowledge receipt of £500 from " Sorry," March 4th.*

One of Traquhair's fingers stole up to his beard and began to work on a curl, making it more of one. He blinked sleepily. Soon his closed eyes made him look as though he were asleep.

From the kitchen came sounds of Helen fiddling with the radio. A burst of hymn like a train coming out of a tunnel vanished instantly and gave place to routine sludge on the Light.

Should he go back to Lime Grove. " Hold it, Friar Tuck, don't jump the gun."

Conscience money!

A sudden suspicion that Meldrum might be watching him brought his eyes to the door. Nothing there. Not satisfied, he got up and moved through into the kitchen which had a window facing backwards at the annexe. He could see no sign of life. Sometimes Meldrum himself lay in on Sundays. Perhaps to-day he had gone for a walk on the hill. Or was he watching, standing well back, from a window? Traquhair

The Lifeline

folded the *Telegraph*, which he found he was carrying, so that the agony column was hidden.

" Are you beginning to find your way about ? " he said over his shoulder to Helen, wishing to divert her attention from his reconnaissance.

He was vaguely aware of a crump of crockery, like an elaboration of the reply he never heard. Then he went back to the living-room, and after standing for a moment with his back to it, he took down the key from above the picture of the dying stag.

Had Traquhair been merely taking snuff, the movement of his hand could not have been more fluent or practised. At the same instant he began humming in an every-day manner.

23

Enclosing the key in one of his big hands so that only one end of it stuck out and very little at that, he moved quickly through to the back whistling the " Nutbrown Maiden," the tune which had died on his lips an hour or two earlier. He had read so many thrillers and stories of crime that it came as no surprise at all when Helen waylaid him as he passed the kitchen door and wanted to know about lunch. A hitch of this kind was *de rigueur*. Not that it was really a hitch, but it felt like one, if not actually a trap, and when she went on to ask him to help her shift a sack of potatoes through to the larder he suspected her of wanting to see what he'd got in his hand. (*Miss MacDonald*, he heard as he broke his nails on two ears of hessian, *I want you to think very carefully: Did Mr. Traquhair have anything in his hand when you met him in the passage?*)

Finally, sweating, he reached the back door, and from there a view of the backyard and the distillery chimney from which there was very little smoke. Good ! Low fires ! Little activity. Did they work a Sunday shift ? . . . He did not know, but the authoritative chiming of church bells suggested not.

A strange elation suddenly possessed him as though never before had he been free, never till now. It was as though he were standing on the edge of a cliff convinced that he could fly and determined to put the matter to the test, possessing as he did quite exceptional equipment. No man, he thought to himself, is truly grown up until he has broken with conscience and made arrangements in that respect for himself.

As he passed the annexe, guilt or some presentiment, drew

The Lifeline

his eyes up to the Meldrums' window and there, below the bird cage, he saw a thing that was seldom stationary—the face and body of Olivia Meldrum.

So closely did she seem to be concerned with where he was going that for a moment impetus went out of his walk. The next moment he might have stopped, waved, or spoken—had she herself not drifted back out of sight with what looked like the barest hint of a smile.

Did he feel comforted? No. If he was a boat heading for the open sea then this sight, he knew, was not the last solid outcrop of land, not the friendly virginal lighthouse with its greensward and goats, but a wobbling flag far out above gnarled invisible rocks, if not an hallucination, a trick of the sea itself.

Reaching the door of the first outhouse, he found it unlocked. He peered in briefly as though looking for a tool.

Stephenson must have kept his hens here. White feathers still lay beneath the perches on top of a deep silt of droppings. He came out again and glanced towards the annexe where he imagined the window would by now have acquired another couple of forlorn, certain eyes—Meldrum's.

Two more sheds he visited before coming to one that was locked. The key fitted.

There was a table and under the table a trap door. After a long look he lifted the trap door. . . . Yes, there it was like the face of someone he knew very well. He sat, knelt, sat again, tried head first but finally reversing, very slowly he disappeared, wholly and magically, like a huge cork sinking through the neck of its own bottle.

The way was long, fœtid and dark. Several times the big man stopped and lay gasping. Supposing he was caught! The very idea gave him a melting sensation in the knee caps. In the past he had pictured himself as a being hedged in by moral reflexes, involuntary as the behaviour of Pavlov's dogs. For what had prevented him from saying good-bye to respectability long before now on a million occasions? Habit and fear. He now

The Lifeline

imagined he despised that fear and the majority which had the power to instil it in him. For that majority was itself a murderer when it suited itself—in time of war. That majority was an unmitigated self-seeker, and a devoted hypocrite. Compared to it he was a courageous individual; a free spirit who had hidden his light under a bushel for too long. Now he was bringing it out—taking the law into his own hands for an innocent, harmonious and beneficent end.

Two families would be supported, the hydro workers served and the Government repaid in instalments of "conscience money" all receipted in the *Daily Telegraph*. Such a system would merely make him a man like thousands of others who practised Hire Purchase on the grand scale. He would break the spirit of no law but the letter of many. Up to Pharisees and Pharisees only to blame him.

But, of course, all this ratiocination and giddy self-justification was quite incapable of calming the apparently independent judgment of his stomach. There all was chaos. Indeed, he might have just had not an idea but a dose—and a Turkish bath.

Sometimes in the hot dark he rested his greasy, pouring forehead on his hands, waited, bowed like a praying miner, waited for his heart to be reasonable. Then he wormed forward again, striking matches, feeling lost, lightheaded and with every passing yard more stranger to himself.

At last he came to solid earth ahead. Then, turning on one side, he felt upwards.

Earth rained in his ears . . . but he touched stone. After listening for what seemed an hour he got to his knees, put his back to the stone and heaved.

More dust and little particles rained down through his hair and over the tops of his ears. Then his eyes had the strange experience of rising like suns exactly level with the surface of a floor which stretched away some fifty feet, to a wall gapped at one point where a small companion way led up and through to another room.

There was a brewery smell and a ticking sound.

The Lifeline

Turning his head slightly, he peered up and saw what looked like two miniature domes of Moscow churches, two fifty-foot, pear-shaped, copper stills with corrugated pipes a yard thick leading from their thin upper ends. On one was written " New Wines," on the other " Second Take." Closer, in fact within reach, was a colossal circular container bearing the legend " Spirit reservoir. Capacity 6000 gallons."

So it was true, all true!

And the edge of the reservoir actually touched the hole from which Traquhair's head was peering.

He listened . . .

Not a sound except the ticking as of something vast and hot, cooling.

Then—no mouse ever emerged with more apprehension of cat—he climbed out, stood and felt different as though born again to another identity. The reason for this was perhaps the shape and size of the stills, the like of which he had never seen before. Such colossal alembics towering up in shadows, sweating as though alive, seemed the diabolic or angelic transmutors, the very dynamo of some heaven or hell which could only be visited by a human being at the cost of his previous identity. He was a burglar in God's laboratory.

Traquhair moved round the spirit receiver on tiptoe. The top was sealed by an iron cover heavily bolted to the sides, but out of it stuck a wooden dip-stick graduated in inches. He remembered Stephenson telling him that one tenth of an inch represented sixty gallons, in other words that amount could be removed before the dip-stick showed an alteration of one-tenth of an inch. So approximate was this method of measuring that three times he bobbed it and three times it returned a fractionally different reading.

At present it registered $41\frac{1}{2}$ to 42 inches, in other words the reservoir contained about 2520 gallons.

He could draw ten baths of whisky before anyone would notice. But what kind of whisky?

What was the stuff like?

He pulled the dip-stick up until it showed wet. Then he

The Lifeline

licked it. . . . Warmth instantly spread through his head as though he had blushed.

At that moment, in the distance, he heard a voice and footsteps. . . .

A few seconds later he was sweeping a few bits of earth and dust back into his tunnel and then following them, pulling the flagstone back into place above his head.

Then he lay back in the dark, breathing heavily and mopping the sweat from his brow and neck, listening till the footsteps petered out into silence.

"*Heugh heugh!*" he said softly.

But he was trembling and felt a little sick. Half of him longed to finish here and would have jumped at any opportunity to do so. The tunnel was as described but what about the pipeline? With luck it might have rotted away.

He struck one of his last two matches. The sulphurous spurt and roar deafened, the brilliance dazzled; then everything settled down and the sober flame revealed earth, a system of miniature pit-props, a dumbfounded beetle. . . .

Traquhair, who disliked insects, impulsively recoiled only to feel something touch his cheek. He jerked aside in panic and brushed his face with his spare hand. Then he held up the dwindling flame, burning his fingers.

There was a pink pipe hanging by his cheek—like an entrail come loose, and half-way up it a rusty bulldog paper-clip.

The match went out.

So it was all, all as Stephenson had said, down to the bulldog clip.

He lay then and stared up at the sky above him. The close, black sky. A mole's heaven. It was shot with childish visions. Cloaks of invisibility, magic carpets, enchanted purses, all-conquering swords. . . . Traquhair scattering gold in the streets.

Such fancies had come his way before, but this time there was a difference, the biggest difference that a man may imagine.

He struck his last match and looked more closely at the pipe,

The Lifeline

unclipped it, felt fast evaporating wet on his skin, put it to his lips—and tasted fire.

Yes, it was as though some nonexistent world of which he had always been the secretly ashamed, and yet none the less persevering devotee, had developed . . . a nipple. A tangible sustaining, alimentary nipple.

He could even do without Meldrum . . . now. For he had got the link on tap. He had a lifeline.

24

STRANGE LIVING-ROOM that he returned to! The newspapers still lay at the foot of the chair, the cement mixer still stared, paralysed, the bar, the bedrooms were still unfinished.

And yet it was all different, as different as he himself.

Exhausted, he slumped down in a chair with an orthodox drink and gave himself up to the solutions which galloped through his head like a confusion of cinema reels. He thought of running a shack " whisky bar," a Highland novelty, thought of bottling the spirit and running it to Glasgow where he knew an Italian head waiter who already earned five thousand a year and was broadminded; he thought of piping it into a tanker-lorry done up with Esso painted on the side and running it to London, but in the end all these ideas blew up and away like scraps of paper leaving him always face to face with the dead-fish eye of the cement mixer and a feeling of wonder that things should be so different and yet still economically the same, himself still dependent on Messrs. MacFarlane and Mackay....

What would Stephenson have done?

Cars and pedestrians were passing the window meaning the Wee Free were coming out. Some of them glanced furtively in the direction of the hotel as though a black mass might be in progress.

The sight of all these good people observing the Sabbath was so arresting that for a moment Traquhair's eyes kindled with selfless surmise as though at the spectacle of sheep streaming through a gate into a field where the exhausted pasture was still better than the weeds outside.

The Lifeline

Except ye be as one of these, he thought, for at that moment Mr. and Mrs. MacFarlane, both in dark-blue suits trimmed with white at cuffs and collar, one with a big handbag, the other with a paunch, both with complexions like scones and staring straight ahead, drove by in the largest, latest Humber Snipe, at twelve miles an hour.

When this shapely, self-propelled monument to the appreciation of two acres in Redditch had slid smoothly behind the paralysed cement mixer Traquhair felt a twinge of returning hopelessness. Some people's leaks were legal.

At that moment the telephone rang.

Nadia Wotherspoon?

He put out his hand and in the tone of a man disturbed too early on Sunday said, " Hallo. . . ."

A woman's voice replied with immediate tremulous diffidence: Could she speak with Mr. Traquhair?

" Speaking," Traquhair conceded.

The voice now prostrated itself, as it were, at the thought of what it was doing: disturbing his Sunday. " But," she said, " I said to myself, I must tell him, I must . . ."

What was this? Courtship? The Recogniser? Such urgency brought a fastidious frown to Traquhair's face. Reception was bad and it now appeared the woman was not only horrified at having rung Mr. Traquhair on a Sunday, but at ever having taken such a liberty at all. (Reception got worse.) But it had fallen to her to tell him he had been elected Chieftain if he could manage to stand again so soon after the Football Queen.

Traquhair cleared his throat whereupon, as though already half-denied, the voice, again with an access of emotion, said she well knew Fluach still needed certain amenities which cast the name of the body she belonged to into disrepute and made it difficult to ask for the services of a man such as Traquhair without a feeling of shortcoming on the part of the body to which she was attached.

" Chieftain?" There was momentary silence. The voice became clogged and tense with tears as it tried for the first time

The Lifeline

apparently to define activities which it had always taken for granted. The Amenities Committee was such and such, the games so and so—and the Chieftain was, if possible, a person notable for his appearance, traditional connections with the county and solid worth. This year, however, they had wanted more. In view of the Prime Minister they had wanted " Someone *very* special. . . ." Traquhair's face had gradually altered, become slightly stiffer about the mouth, sterner about the eyes. After the word "special" he drew in breath deeply, and from then on, perhaps for weeks, never entirely let it out. " I see," he said at last, and it seemed his voice also had changed, become slower. " I see. . . ."

The silence at the far end was complete. It suggested the voice had closed its eyes while waiting. " My dear lady," said Traquhair at last. " I should feel honoured, honoured. Thank you. . . ."

" Oh, Mr. Traquhair . . . thank *you*."

He replaced the receiver. A strange light had come into his eyes.

Oh, he could smile at the title " Chieftain," smile with the best of them ; and marvellous, wasn't it, how the whole thing went on in 1958 ? Marvellous.

But this contemptuous comment was just to camouflage a curious elation. I am in numerous company, he thought. I am one with all those dukes in the gossip columns and the millions who read about them and flock to see where they have dinner, where they sleep and what colour pyjamas they wear. Far from being ashamed he could feel of the very spirit of the age. Besides, you are as young as you feel, goes the saying. Why not, therefore, you are as chieftain as you feel ? Well, he felt very chieftain and always had. Such an emotion might have amounted to lunacy given his background had there not been a crying need for a chieftain. (Here he paused for a moment's amnesia.) Not just in Borneo, nor merely in the heart of one old Fluach maid, but in all the dukeless, backwatered people of Fluach. He did not go all the way with The Recogniser, but he did go some of the way.

The Lifeline

He found his eyes resting on the Camp Coffee bottle, on the picture of the officer being served by a noble black: the icon of his first understanding . . .

Less and less did he need Meldrum.

He stirred uneasily. For the first time in his life he experienced the boredom of achievement. Indeed, it finally came as a relief as well as a surprise to find the eye of the cement-mixer, still on him, still motionless, unrecognising.

25

IF there wasn't a motor rally John S. Mackay lay in on Sundays with the *Sunday Express* till midday. Then he found an excuse for using the car fast before lunch and after lunch he probably edited colour films of last year's garden openings, cutting out duplications, say, of the back view of the Princess Royal praising antirrhinums or the Spotes' azaleas. Sunday evenings were spent on business trunk calls. In between these events he turned a deaf ear to almost everything his wife said, for no matter what she said her voice got on his nerves. His occasional polite but imploring replies had the effect of making her speak more than ever, because who else was there to talk to if she didn't talk to him now the children were away to school?

On the evening of the Sunday in question he had settled himself by the telephone with a worried face. It had been an upsetting week. The whole business with Traquhair had left an unpleasant taste simply because it had taken place so close. Whenever he went out of the door he seemed to run slap into the man. But it was nothing compared to his concern for the Cullan dam subcontracts. By rights the County Council should have supported him, because of local unemployment, instead they had done the opposite because of personal jealousies. He had been underbid, someone had told him, by firms from the south. The last hope was the M.P.—or personal contact with the managing director of Wormalds.

After a few minutes' thought in the chair beside the telephone Mackay decided to ring Sir Duncan Fidge himself at his home and then one or two Conservative councillors.

The Lifeline

He raised the receiver and asked for Fidge's number in Gerrards Cross—Beechwood Hall.

Not only had it been a bad week, it had also been a bad Sunday. He had run into Brian Creevie who seemed to be enjoying the Strathire Arms fiasco, then he had quarrelled with his wife when she suggested asking the managing director of Wormalds to dinner. He said he wasn't going to suck up to any man alive. She had said he was "just pig-headed proud" —wanted the same as everyone else, but liked to pretend he didn't. He hadn't quite understood except she sounded as if she had been looking for an opportunity to go for him. They went round and round. Suddenly he seemed to be looking at her for the first time in twenty years and to his astonishment she had immediately congratulated him on doing just that very thing. But it hadn't made any difference. He still felt he couldn't ask the managing director of Wormalds "just like that without having met him."

"Hallo . . . Sir Duncan . . ." he could never quite say "Duncan."

Suddenly the door opened and there stood his wife flushed from the big fire beside the telly and already exasperated like a child taken from its toys. "There's a man at the door for goodness' sake, John. . . ."

"Well, what about it, can't you see—— ?"

"I'm in the middle of a play."

"Well, what d'you think I'm doing ?" he said. "For goodness' sake, Margaret, have a bit of sense."

Husband and wife stared at each other glassily, the one covering the mouthpiece with his hand and the other trying to catch at least the dialogue from the telly in the next room, neither prepared to yield an inch.

"Well, you can't do two things at once," she said.

"What—— ?" he said.

"It's business," she said, explaining. "I'm sure it is."

"Well, what d'you think this is ?"

"It isn't likely such big business. . . ."

"As what ?"

The Lifeline

He perceived she was hiding something.
Staring hard into her eyes, he said:
"Margaret—who is it?"
"It's that man."
"What man?"
"Oh, for goodness' sake—I can never say his name. The man with the big handle... I mean hotel."

John Mackay said: "Margaret. You're going to the door this minute and you're going to say I'm out."

At this moment there came a knock on the uncurtained window and there stood Traquhair making a coo-ee face, waggling the fingers of one immense hand as though amusing a child. His tam-o'-shanter was drawn down one side of his face and his other was supported high on the shaft of a shepherd's crook. Lower down he seemed to start all over again with another huge head, in the middle of his loins, this time the head of a snoozing beaver.

Margaret giggled as though tickled, blushed, smiled and whispered hectically: "Hurry," as though saying "Hallo."

John Mackay said: "Excuse me, Sir Duncan—hold on," into the receiver and went out of the room as though he had seen boys stealing apples. He opened the front door and with only minimal courtesy said: "Well, Mr. Traquhair, what can I do for you?"

Traquhair murmured: "Sir, could I have a word with you?"

"It's late enough, isn't it? Frankly, if it's about my letter——"

"Your mother advised me to come now."

"My mother!" Surprise quenched Mackay's voice.

"She lives opposite."

Mackay stepped back.

Traquhair's foot was inside the door and his tam-o'-shanter half off.

For thirty seconds John Mackay was silent then he said curtly: "Come in, Mr. Traquhair. It just happens I'm on a

The Lifeline

trunk call to the M.P. . . . But come in, come in. I should think you'll wait, won't you?"

Traquhair bowed very slightly at him, focusing him ironically.

Mackay always moved violently through his own house, much as though most things about a house were so much theatrical waste of time or—same thing—money.

" Sit down, will you? . . . I'll be right back." A moment later he was. " We'd better settle your business first," he explained.

" I interrupted you, I'm afraid," said Traquhair, turning from photographs. " Delightful children you have, Mr. Mackay."

Mackay kicked the logs on the fire and turned the nob-ventilator in the economy grate. " One of each," he said. " What'll you take, then?"

Traquhair paused fastidiously as though gauging whether Mackay's words were hospitality or insult.

" Er? Oh, I see. Whisky *if I may*." He seated himself, solid and amicable.

" Water or soda?"

" A splash of the former, if you please."

When the whisky was poured Traquhair said: " Mr. Mackay—I've come for advice. I've been appointed willy-nilly Chieftain of the Cullan Games. . . ."

Mackay moved his head in such a way as to convey polite, but faint interest. In fact he was staggered.

" At first I thought it was a mere formality, a dead letter, now I am told there are certain social functions involved which still have leverage and cannot be neglected by anyone who does the job properly. ' Ask John,' said your mother. ' There's nothing he doesn't know about that sort of thing . . .'"

" Then she's talking through her hat," said her son emotionally. And he stared into the fire as though about to go up and tell her so.

" Your modesty does not deter me, Mr. Mackay," said Traquhair, and began to relax, spread his legs, his kilt and took

The Lifeline

out a snuff box. " The truth is I don't know where to start. What, for instance, must I dress in ? What do I have to do when I get there ? How shall I entertain Hilldersley ? Am I bound to go down to Holyrood for a preliminary handshake (as I'm told I shall have to), and to whom should I introduce the Prime Minister ? I'm told the director of Wormalds is a 'must' . . . as he is in a position to help—or not to help—local unemployment, to say nothing of awarding or not awarding contracts to local firms. . . . *Heugh, heugh . . . touché?* Finally, believe it or not, there is the threat of royalty. In such matters, the truth is, I'm a babe in arms and without the advice of people like yourself I shall drop every kind of brick. *Heugh, heugh.* We don't want any more bricks, do we ? "

John Mackay remained still and silent after Traquhair had finished speaking. His round rather warm, dreamy yet obstinate eyes, expansive forehead and small childish mouth, all seemed given over to a problem which lay deep in the embers of the fire.

At last Mackay's head gave an almost imperceptible negative shake. " Well, for heaven's sake . . ." he murmured.

Pessimist by nature, Puritan by background he greeted difficulty with familiarity almost with pleasure ; relief from it with suspicion. Frivolity, a category this which almost included royalty—certainly chieftains—he greeted with distaste as though nothing but courtesy prevented him from reacting to it "frankly." But there were people in the world (he knew because he was married to one of them) who could lose sleep at the possibility of being invited to a Buckingham Palace garden party or being introduced to a Prime Minister. For all he knew the managing director of Wormalds was a man of similar tastes. Perhaps he was the kind of man who would think nothing of asking Mr. Hilldersley to dinner without ever having met him. . . . He didn't know. Since this afternoon's exchange with his wife he felt shaken. The words still buzzed in his head. Fond, yes, in a way he was fond of her ; she was part of him, a habit by now, but that she could be anything but daft had never occurred to him till she had suddenly said

The Lifeline

what he had been thinking: that he hadn't looked at her for twenty years. . . . " Blind as a bloody bat ! " Was he blind ? If Traquhair controlled something that his wife and the managing director of Wormalds wanted, then he must be careful to accept the fact that here before him was a new, relevant Traquhair.

But it was too much and John Mackay again whispered to the glowing vision in the fire : " Well, for goodness' sake ! " A moment later he raised his glass bleakly to his lips.

" I beg your pardon ? "

The eyes of the contractor returned purposefully to the fire. He knew the people who ran the Amenities Committee to which he had often refused to be co-opted. There was Major Murray, Miss Jimpson . . . and the others, half-daft and nothing better to do. The spectacle of them in a half-moon made out of embers made him shake his head until it was slowly borne in on him they might get him his fifteen hundred pounds back, as well as sub-contracts. The £1500 was not so important, but the sub-contracts represented the big leap from small time to big time ; perhaps from provincial to national status.

If they made Traquhair a publicised figurehead, an entertainer of celebrities, of the director of the Cullan Dam and royalty, anything might follow. . . .

This train of thought was so pungent that Mackay became more than ever oblivious of the questions he had been asked, about dress, Fluach protocol. . . .

Traquhair was happy not to disturb him, for he thought he heard in Mackay's silence far away, like the horns of Robin Hood's merry men coming to the rescue of a tortured widow, the sound of a cement mixer revolving rhythmically, with a slapping scraping sound, saws sawing, hammers tapping, a general chorus of tools at work. . . .

" Ach, for goodness' sake," Mackay began stickily. " There's nothing to it. . . ."

The difficulty of now at last concentrating on "Chieftainship" brought an astringent frown to his large forehead. Only by visualising the director of the Cullan Dam Works on one

The Lifeline

side of the "Chieftain" and Sir Duncan Fidge, M.P., on the other, could Mackay bring himself to go on.

"To be quite frank, Mr. Traquhair, I don't know the first thing about it. I never go near the games. But my impression is you need to look much as you look now and behave in a way which should come quite naturally."

And he smiled softly with a sort of sleepy appeasement at his frankness. So much, at least, he demanded in return for resuming work on the Strathire Arms. For he knew what was coming next.

But he was wrong. It did not come at once. Traquhair broached several subjects including Canadian light industries before saying: "By the way, reference your letter. Fifteen hundred on the button would be awkward. But supposing I pay you by instalments of two hundred pounds a month starting May first . . ."

Mackay agreed, almost impatiently—as though frankness for once were giving him pain.

Then his wife came in blushing and saying the play was over. Mackay suspected her of having listened at the door for she blushed and giggled every time Traquhair opened his mouth as though he were tickling her. She said she'd been watching a play, but was "sick of it" and was "just dee-lighted" to make the acquaintance of someone she'd heard so much about, and so often seen. Then she spoke with scorn of Fluach and the rarity of "getting someone like yourself now, Mr. Traquhair."

Mackay looked sad. Traquhair kissed her hand and she flushed more violently than ever.

"You must come again, Mr. Traquhair," she said. "It's kind of dead up here. We're obliged for the visit."

Mackay rattled change in his pocket briskly and cocked his head on one side, lowering his eyes. By then he was holding the front door open, unable to look at either his guest or his wife.

"That's it then," he said. "Go as you are."

26

ALL THAT WEEK and the next the cement mixer churned and the hammers hammered; and on the Saturday which fell fifteen days after the football dance the new bar at the Strathire Arms was finished. Traquhair nailed a horseshoe above the door and the following day went to church.

Fluach has three churches, the large stone Church of Scotland, the large corrugated iron Wee Free and the small rough pine-and-asbestos " Piskie." To the first go shopkeepers, factors and farmers' wives, to the second fishers and people of the poorer sort, and to the third, on every third Sunday during the sporting season (March-October) go people from the lodges, large people in new tweeds, such as April Gunter-Sykes and the Spotes.

All three churches are full on Sundays, so full that a latecomer may find himself stuck in an aisle searching vainly for a seat and confronted by rows of blank stares as though for some obscure, presumably religious reason he had become suddenly unrecognisable.

When Traquhair appeared in the Church of Scotland, the day after his bar was finished, bearing the two books he had been given at the door, every eye fastened on him.

He was in good time and there were still plenty of empty seats and pews, and it was one of these last, the centre one beneath the lofty eighteenth-century pulpit, that he occupied, shutting the door behind him and composing himself instantly to prayer in the Church of Scotland manner with one elbow on the little shelf in front of him and his eyes shielded by the fingers of one hand.

The Lifeline

For several generations this particular pew had belonged to the factors of the Marquess of Strathire and was still sat in every Sunday by Mr. Aldwich, the present factor, and his wife.

No one felt in a position to warn Traquhair that he was breaking an unwritten law. It was convenient to suppose that he must have had Mr. Aldwich's permission—a possibility instantly excluded by the expression on Mrs. Aldwich's face as she came in through the main door. By then the church was full. As the Aldwiches came into the aisle Miss Jimpson brought the congregation to its feet and the choir from the vestry with a passage from Verdi's *Samson*.

The Aldwiches paused at their gate with that look of moody stupefaction which may be seen in cows who, when left to go home by themselves, find the way blocked. After a vague glance round at other central positions, all tightly occupied, they pushed in and joined the big trespasser who was staring out of the window with the expression of one who is present in the flesh only.

Of his flesh there was no doubt. The Aldwiches fitted themselves in as best they could.

Those who looked furtively sideways may have imagined they had gauged the full extent of the newcomer's trespass but, as so often in tiny Fluach, they didn't know the half of it, any more than Traquhair did himself.

The Marquess of Strathire owns the *Trumpet* and his factor, Mr. Aldwich, supervises it to the small extent that it needs supervising. Our local editor, like his predecessors, has to be careful never to print anything which would offend the marquess or his friends or even any of the Socialist council in case they put even higher rates on the marquess's vast acreage of desert. Big and sometimes little editorial matters are therefore put before Mr. Aldwich for censorship, but, on the whole, the stationery and printing department of the business is left entirely to an ex-Italian P.O.W. called Rosso. As a result, last week, the *Trumpet* had printed a thousand paper napkins for Traquhair's hotel with the Strathire Arms—coat-of-arms, and

The Lifeline

motto, *Si je veulx*, on each. Rosso had thought it natural, probably traditional, that the Strathire Arms should use the Strathire Arms. Delivery had been made before Mr. Aldwich was informed. When he was informed the editor had almost been sacked and Mr. Aldwich, after cabling the marquess in Nassau, had been called a " fool " in the reply which passed through Fluach Post Office in clear. He was grey from sitting up all night with lawyers and wording a fifty-pound cable to Nassau. Beside him sat Traquhair.

" Oh, Lord . . ." intoned the minister, raising supplicating eyes to Heaven and beginning to improvise, " we who have sinned against thine immortal and holy ways, forgive us ; we who have not loved our neighbours as we should, forgive us ; we who grasped or grudged, forgive us ; we who have nourished evil designs in the depths of our hearts or practised contrary to the spirit of the law as laid down by the ministers of thy handmaiden Elizabeth the Queen and her holy churches, forgive us. . . ."

" Amen," said Traquhair and the Aldwiches in sober unison.

The pew seats are about four feet long and accommodate ideally two normal adults and a child. Mr. Aldwich is not exceptionally big but his wife is as broad if not as heavy as Traquhair. Together the three of them did not really fit at all. Only the adaptive attitude of each to his or her neighbour made the feat possible. Mr. Aldwich had to sit almost sideways on, and Traquhair folded his arms and sat a little forward, while Mrs. Aldwich sat round-shouldered and a little backward. Both the Aldwiches wore a curious expression throughout the service as though somewhere in the building, they would not say where, a man was present who had come in without his trousers. Normally Mr. Aldwich sings loudly and reinforces the choir's descant but to day Traquhair sang so lustily that he created a certain reluctance among those close to him to sing at all.

And yet on the whole, perhaps by his mere presence, he created a good impression and probably did much to reassure the feelings of those who had heard various highly coloured

The Lifeline

accounts of his behaviour at the dance. Surely a man who spent such a long time on his knees before his Maker, occasionally looking out from his hands with such a concerned face, could not be as bad as some had made out.

During the sermon, Traquhair's chin and beard remained sunk on his chest above his folded arms, and his brows knit in responsible reflection. From behind, through the high plain-glass window came such a beam of sunlight as turned much of him black. Then he looked like an etching from *In Memoriam*.

The service always ended with an anthem on which the choir had worked the preceding Tuesday and Friday evening under the instruction of Miss Jimpson. To-day it was marked by a curious incident.

Miss Jimpson had plunged her fingers into the harmonium and was staring up into the driving mirror above the stops, with radiant eyes, encouraging her pupils not only with a look of musical enthusiasm but also, from her mouth, with a soaring instantaneous volume, sometimes bass, sometimes treble and sometimes skipping from one to the other like a coloratura, when suddenly she turned right round on her stool, as might a pilot who has completed looping the loop, and smiled straight at Traquhair.

Apparently this woman both knew him and approved of him. Naturally he put it down to *Robin Hood* and felt no satisfaction.

As she reached the end of her music she again caught his eye and began to improvise a sort of concluding cadenza which somehow seemed to be connected with himself, if not actually in his honour, for she kept on looking at him in the driving mirror. What possessed her?

Finally with rigid arms and a last stampede on the pedals, she wound matters up with a tremendous prolonged chord during which she again turned and smiled at him openly as though welcoming—taking him to the heart of our little community.

Whoever she is, thought Traquhair, she likes me. Bewildered

The Lifeline

but pleased, he inclined his head very slightly from the neck. After the service, in the graveyard, he last saw her looking back at him—with tears in her eyes. He left amid a murmur of respectful greetings. All around there was a look of relief in people's faces as though he were an ally of the accepted order after all. And in fact his look of grave responsibility, of involvement was sincere. He had much on his plate.

27

BRIAN CREEVIE had been in bed with a cold since a few days after the football dance. It had gone to his chest where it persisted.

From his piled-up pillows he had a clear view of the Strathire Arms. At first he had been entertained if not positively gratified by the expected sight of work suspended.

His mother brought up the big German field-glasses he had got in the war and sat on the end of the bed using them. But for him they were not necessary. During long trunk calls to his stockbroker his soft eyes had rested peacefully on the stock-still cement mixer.

The restfulness of his expression during this period had been not unlike that of a mother after labour, for he had brought forth fact again after prophecy and never had he had more joy of a birth.

Ever since meeting Traquhair at the Wotherspoon party his head had hummed with dialogue in which he and Traquhair had argued about every subject under the sun—always with the same result: the complete defeat of Traquhair. In the arena of Brian's mind they had been brother officers in R.E.M.E., schoolboys in the same class or team and now finally rival hoteliers. Whatever the situation Brian had got the better of Traquhair simply by " knowing his man." People could think him jealous, fanciful—that was perfectly all right by him (he smiled and made a gesture of complete, genial indifference—a downward, oblique, smoothing motion, smiled really charmingly as he walked about his empty room in his Jaeger dressing-gown), and they could play the old gramophone record about him being under his mother's influence—

The Lifeline

that, too, was perfectly all right by him (again he did the long smoothing motion). The only point he would like to make was that he knew what sort of person Traquhair was and what would happen to people who put their trust in him. Hadn't he told Johnny Mackay that Helen would be the Beauty Queen? And that he would find difficulty in getting paid his second instalment? Hadn't he? He had. Helen had been the queen and now, there, not two hundred yards away stood a paralysed cement mixer and a lot of parked tools—meaning one thing only: that Johnny Mackay hadn't been paid.

For there were these unfortunate things called facts. If you stuck to them you could be sure of a wasp's nest round your ears in no time at all, but Brian, despite the stings, preferred to give his allegiance to facts and to nothing else.

When the mixer began to rotate—a fact—and be fed by men with spades he experienced only slight discomfiture. People like Traquhair always staged temporary comebacks. But they gradually, so to speak, made a fire with their clothes in order to keep warm. The moment came when the fire went out.

He took another rusk, opened *The Financial Times* and rang for his mother.

"Don't worry, Mother," he said after she had looked through the glasses. "Just wait. That's all you need do: wait."

Two days later the *Trumpet* came out with another picture of Traquhair. This time it was half the block which had originally appeared depicting him with "his assistant on the moors." It even included one of Meldrum's feet. Beside it were headlines.

CULLAN CHIEFTAIN CHOSEN
HONOUR FOR FLUACH HOTELIER

His mother, who had brought in the paper, agitated him with impossible insinuations and illegal remedies. She said the Amenities Committee should have been abolished after the war. They began quarrelling about where to put the inhaler, Brian insisting that one copy of *The Financial Times* was

The Lifeline

sufficient to protect the Sheraton table. Then, fairly calmly, he rang Johnny Mackay. Out. Then he rang Lionel Spote who might quite well have been chosen himself. But Lionel had flown to India unexpectedly for conversations with a friend about Tibet. Mrs. Spote was in Ireland. Finally, he put through a trunk call to Sir Duncan Fidge—a natural choice for the chieftainship, failing the marquess. But Sir Duncan was in committee.

He began to worry and his temperature went up. Cerebration started and he and Traquhair both received Mr. Hilldersley dressed as chieftains. Possibly owing to the aspirins and vague associations, they were both dressed first as Sioux chieftains with long bows, and then as businessmen in a position to persuade Mr. Hilldersley to bring light industries to the Highlands. His eyes shone. He started a thriller to try and calm his mind. But he kept hearing his mother rustling. Here she was again with the field-glasses, which made her look like some strange insect, one of those quirks of nature which the microscope and television have brought to general notice.

" Is it necessary to sit on the bed ? I'm so hot . . ." he said.

She had sat in such a way that his legs felt constricted if not positively swaddled, hence himself tethered.

" Please ! . . . *Mother!* "

Suddenly she sucked in her breath.

What had she spotted ? Reluctant that she should have succeeded in tantalising him so easily he asked irritably if he could have a look.

With a few twiddles he drew the image of the Strathire Arms from the optical fog which had apparently favoured her. A hoarding was being hoisted :

THE STRATHIRE ARMS
UNDER NEW MANAGEMENT
THE BAR AND DINING-ROOM WILL BE OPEN
ON FRIDAY, April 8th. ROOMS AVAILABLE
from May 24th. FISHING, STALKING,
PONY-TREKKING August-September

The Lifeline

Creevie's circular field of vision moved slowly along the façade. John Mackay's head electrician was staring up at one of the chimneys as though it were about to give birth to lightning or several jackdaws. Men were coming and going through the door of the new public bar which was in the modern farm-building style of quick architecture—a windowed hangar with a porch, the whole thing about as big as the War Memorial Hall opposite.

When the big glasses came away they exposed the face of an altered Brian Creevie. Facts were behaving eccentrically.

These were difficult days at the Bishop's Palace. The central heating was never right, the food bad, the maid left because of what Brian said to her when last week's *Financial Times* was used to light a fire. British Hydrogen went down seven and six in two days. Brian got up in his dressing-gown.

Then on the Sunday after the Strathire Arms Bar was finished he was sitting in his room reading the *Sunday Times* when his mother came in.

Knowing her knock, he had not said " Come in." Nevertheless, she had come in, so he refused to greet her.

She sat down close and leaning closer still, whispered : " He was in church. In the Aldwiches' pew ! "

Brian attempted complete indifference, but was unable to sustain it.

"Shirly not, I said when I saw him," murmured Mrs. Creevie. " You in church ! No, no, no ! "

" It's years since you've been, too," Brian said suspiciously.

He had no time for church, yet now, like his mother, he fell speculatively silent as though somewhere in the upper air he could hear a swift rustling sound—the finger of God descending to crush Tulloch Traquhair. Blasphemy on a certain scale created God.

28

"THE LORD WILL PROVIDE" Traquhair had told Meldrum as the empty shelves behind the bar were hammered into place. But day after day had gone by and nothing came either by lorry, rail or post except a few miserable samples of beer, mineral water and liquor from firms which, like themselves, were trying to make a start such as Cornish Wines, Ltd., and the like.

Traquhair seemed unconcerned and sang. Olivia Meldrum also greeted the preparations with nothing but enthusiasm. She came across, praised the empty shelves and the new bar mirror, lingered among the wood shavings as though perfectly confident that here in a few days, hundreds of hands would stretch for alcohol and be gratified.

Even Mackay's labourers and the women who came in from the village were infected with a genial spirit of creation and optimism. Only Meldrum avoided the place—and the subject.

Traquhair, accustomed as he was to Meldrum's moods, had to admit that this latest sulk, coming as it had, at the very moment when it was imperative they should all work in smoothly with each other, was something special. As far as he could see, it had started the day after the Football Dance and touched bottom the day he went to church. Since then Meldrum had worked almost entirely in the garden which by now he had redeemed from wilderness.

"Tell me, Olivia," he said one day in the lowered tone of an accomplice, "is our mutual friend blowing up for another crisis."

The Lifeline

(The first "crisis" had been in London just after Meldrum's dog Loki had been run over by a big American car. Meldrum had "gone mad" for several days, raved like an Old Testament prophet, about cars, advertisements, the Royal Family, the B.B.C., etc.)

" I don't really know what you mean," Olivia said.

The "really" was the operative word. It meant that she *did* know what he meant but refused to be jockeyed into committing herself for or against her husband.

" Well, is he ? . . . Because we've got a lot on our plate, and in a few nights I shall need his assistance to fill the bar."

" Moving bottles in ? "

" A barrel to be precise."

Her face momentarily betrayed interest but she turned away. For a few moments Tulloch waited for her to relent and offer her services as an intermediary between her employer and her husband. But nothing came. Clearly he must make his own arrangements.

" It weighs about two hundredweight," he said with a sudden touch of moody self-pity.

But she had nothing more to say.

Once before, in Spain, at a moment when death seemed to be approaching as certainly as a stranger walking towards him on a pavement, God had thrown up a barrel right in the path of his frenzied retreat. A moment later, upside down in the hot dark, his nose squashed into putrid lees he had listened to the terrible thuds and explosions of close hand-to-hand fighting —and survived. True, one of the exuberant victors had fired into the stoup for joy and given him a war wound. Still, he had survived. Was it surprising therefore that another stoup, swimming silverly into the headlights one night at Upper Kintullochy, had inspired him—first with the poignance of nostalgia—and then with the profound eureka of a man saved ? On the bar counter such a vessel would have what advertisers called I.C.I. (Immediate Consumer Impact); at the same time it would save the problem of proprietary brands,

The Lifeline

bottles, bottling and fraud. He had bought it on the spot. There remained the problem of transport.

One day, coming up behind Reoraidgh as he bent like a horseshoe, over strawberry plants, Traquhair said breezily, " Reoraidgh, you're quite a stranger. I was wondering if you could give me a hand to-night ? "

Straightening, Meldrum intimated by silence that his job was to obey.

" A small matter," Traquhair went on nervously, " and on the way we can have a talk ! "

Then Meldrum said quietly, " So this is it ! "

" *Heugh, heugh*—sleuth that you are, Reoraidgh ! Nine o'clock if you please, at the front door."

They set off punctually in the Rolls. After a mile Traquhair said : " Well, well, here we are ! "

" Yes, here we are ! " replied Meldrum.

The barrel was visible in the headlights.

" Lovely, isn't she ? " Traquhair said.

" What are you thinking of doing ? " Meldrum said.

When Traquhair had finished telling him there was complete silence.

" Come, Reoraidgh," Traquhair said at last, " see it this way : it's hire purchase. What I borrow, I'll pay back—in conscience money to the Inland Revenue. Have you never seen conscience money in the agony column of *The Times* ? Well, you soon will, believe me. Besides, tell me what harm I'm doing ? Depriving a few thousand shareholders of a fraction of a penny and some distiller directors of some shillings that were anyhow going to the Government to be spent on H-bombs and dentures. Listen, Reoraidgh, the other night I went for a drink and d'you know what I found in the cupboard ? Nothing. A lot of empty bottles. And I looked round to console myself with you. At least, I said, to myself, I've got that to fall back on. Then I remembered : you weren't there. You were living all the time away in another building. From

The Lifeline

now you were to be always in the annexe. How can I explain? It was as though a man kept two things he valued in a cupboard—one of them his soul, whatever that is, and the other the bottle. One day he feels the pinch and goes to the cupboard—only to find it bare—so bare, Reoraidgh, you've no idea. It would have been all right if just one had gone. But both! Ah, Rory-Pory, I had to have a lifeline, just a little one for now and then. I would never have needed it if you'd been living here—under the same roof. Honestly."

When at last Meldrum spoke he said quietly: "I'd go back if I were you, instead."

"Go back? . . . Where to?"

"Television."

"But you're joking. You'd hate that."

"*I?* What has that got to do with it? I could get a job up here . . . anywhere."

"You mean while I went down there?"

"Why not?"

After a few moments, devoted jointly to pain and astonishment, Traquhair said: "Well, that would put the lid on things."

Meldrum said nothing. Traquhair said: "And up here what employment would you obtain, pray? The imagination runs riot."

"Gamekeeper—or labourer."

"All the Lady Chatterleys up here go south in September. You've chosen a poor beat. My dear Reoraidgh, be serious. What about your book?"

"What book?"

"The one you're writing."

"How d'you know I'm writing a book?"

"I found it one day. Olivia and you were both out. There it was—lying under the nappies and the bird seed. I took it out and there on the flyleaf I saw exactly what I expected to see: Meldrum's Law: *The Environment is Master and must be destroyed.* Heugh, heugh! Forgive me. Then I read the first sentence: "Oh, my friends, my dear friends, listen, the

199

The Lifeline

moment is at hand..." Then, of course, I put it down. After singling turnips all day you won't feel really *en veine* when you get home. Not at your age. No, no, chum. Your only chance of survival to-day is in remaining as secretary to Tulloch Traquhair. That way you can finish your book."

It was Meldrum's turn to be silent.

"Besides, with this little dodge I've just suggested I'd have thought you could earn good money and still feel vocational. Be honest, Reoraidgh. The only priest to-day who has got any grip at all is not the priest proper, nor the ex-essential artist but the publican. He without any question, dishes out the contact which we all (except you and that sheep) so badly need —with each other and with It. Aha, Reoraidgh—*touché*. My Lifeline is the only one which can hold its own to-day. Take Orders, Reoraidgh, therefore; take the Collar with Uncle Tulloch."

The headlights picked out the emerald eyes of sheep and roofless cottages, weeds and tarmac. Mountains cut shapes from the starry sky. Had Meldrum sobbed? Traquhair heard a suspicious sound. He rocked his head back and forth from shoulder to shoulder and made a flatulent sound with his lips. "A joke, Reoraidgh, a joke—just me. I took a peep. Forget it. Give this thing a trial then, put it that way. I'm too fat for that tunnel, too weak for the barrel by myself. Just once or twice. Till we get started. Think of the things people do to get started. I mean, not only Al Capone: the Cecils also started as embezzling accountants."

A full moon had risen behind Ben Cullan and in its light they could see a small tiled cottage by the roadside. At one end of it, reaching almost to the lower edge of the tiles was a barrel twice as big as Traquhair.

"Possibly I noticed it because on one occasion I saved one of the gems of our culture in just such a receptacle," Traquhair said, switching off the engine and reaching for the ropes. "The old witch it belongs to is probably asleep inside. Five quid. Rather a lot, but she said she was leaving some luck in it for

The Lifeline

me. You ought to show her that wart on your hand while you're here, Reoraidgh . . . if nothing else."

They opened the dicky and prepared three sleepers which they had brought with them. Then they went for the barrel.

Only when quite close to the cottage did they perceive that one window was in fact lit by a candle, the material of the one-piece curtain being thin enough to reveal the outline of a single flame.

Traquhair tapped gently and said : " It's us, Granny. Don't bother to come out."

They worked for half an hour. Just when they were about to drive off the cottage door opened and they could see the old woman standing there with her stick like an illustration in a fairytale. She raised one crumpled hand in salutation as the headlights briefly caught her with magnesium brilliance. Then she and the cottage vanished and the Rolls purred homeward bearing on its back a colossal hump—the barrel—as ungainly as a dead bee in the grip of an ant.

" Just a juggie now and then," Traquhair said placatingly. He took Meldrum's silence for consent.

When they got home they scrubbed the barrel till two a.m. By four, after twenty relays of buckets, it was filled and they were worn out.

29

THEY CAME in anonymous-looking buses—buses without destination or origin or conductor, the mudguards caked with brick dust, cinders and mud, paint flaking, wipers jammed, radiator plugged with a rag. They sat shoulder to broad shoulder with their shirt-necks wide over bronzed throats, and their eyes somehow white, as though charged with light though this might have been an effect of the darkness of their weathered skins or of brows that hooded habitually into deep intensifying protections against too much brightness of sun or flame, dust, wind or blast. And when they filed into the public bar of the Strathire Arms they were at first ill at ease, clearly conscious of their motley clothing, big feet and of dirt ingrained beyond the reach of soap or scrubbing-brush. Something about them suggested a huge adult orphanage on a spree. Their origin, for all it concerned them, might have been tied round their necks on labels and their destination too. But the present moment lay under them like a prize galleon of old under pirates, and they prepared to loot it armed to the teeth with pound notes.

They had been going to the place they had been to last week, the Seaforth Arms, but before they got there the Strathire Arms parking place, crowned by a lit sign saying simply WHISKY, had opened its arms to them like a mother and the first Cullan bus went straight in without changing down, just using the brakes hard when a few yards short of the wall.

The rumble of their boots on the hollow floor, their cries to each other in Irish, Polish and broadest Glaswegian, their crude haste all suggested they were closing in towards the fulfilment

The Lifeline

of some specific need—hunger, thirst, lust. Yet they were not mainly hungry, thirsty or lusty. Many of them were very tired having worked seven days of ten hours a day ; a few—the tunnel borers, had stood fifty hours of the last week at the rock face, eighteen feet by eighteen, four above on a platform, four below. Each had held a borer, ten feet long, which made as much noise as a machine-gun. Four machine-guns above, four below enclosed by rock, firing continuously for three hours and every borer's face invisible to the face almost touching it, hidden in fog of compressed air, oil and particles. Some could stand it a day, some a year.

They had wallets like false bosoms.

An hour later Traquhair, Meldrum and Helen were working like film cowboys at the peak of a Red Indian attack. Sweat gleamed on their brows as they pulled, poured, side-stepped, accepted, counted, handed and listened. A steady hubbub in several dialects and two or three languages was mixing with the rattle of dice and the clack of dominoes. When the room was full the door continued to open. The new faces that appeared would recognise fellows and lose their tentative expression.

Traquhair was dissolving. Hours of stationary gluttony, of dozing fantasy, of wheeled transport had coated him with flesh which in the present conditions melted like wax held before a fire.

He was in a strange mood.

The spectacle of this advance guard of heavy industry, relaxing, drinking out of his barrel, drinking the Government's milk straight as it were from the hidden breast of the Government, half of it to go straight back into rockets and more power schemes gave him political and philosophical thoughts. He pictured the annual revenue from alcohol and tobacco, a figure which occupied two columns of *The Times* like a statistic in *Believe it or Not*. He listened to the close uproar as though it were one single phenomenon, a piece of music which haunted him with some familiar yet elusive message. Soon abortive bursts of song, drools of invective, protestations of sincerity,

The Lifeline

tones of yearning, of objectless love, jealousy and despair took periodic shape out of the amorphous roar like waves in a storm.

Meldrum did not look out of place. Often servers behind bars adopt an impersonal and fugitive expression as though they were confronted by a nudist colony of which they were not members. Not Meldrum. Without assistance from alcohol he could match the look in the eyes that came before him. Yet seemingly he disapproved.

Traquhair answered him in his heart: You have never broken a law, Meldrum, is that it?

How innocent you make yourself, how hard you work, how little you ask, how you efface yourself—is that it? I wonder why? Perhaps because a man would have to feel very good, very simple indeed in order to bear the burden you bear on your conscience. Fortunately you are weak enough for society to dismiss you as a bed-bug; but supposing you were strong, or in any sense typical—annihilation would be the only hygienic course. Your views need trouble no one, Meldrum, they'll wither where they fall, unnourished by a single sympathy, but what we may not so easily forgive you is the fact that you have married and had children. Either your expectations of the future are insincere or you have knowingly created victims for the crime you not only expect, but advocate. Meanwhile, you clutch at whatever straw will enable you to inhabit your extraordinary world, even straws you despise! You clutch at me. Very well—pour!

Traquhair dismissed Meldrum from his mind, slapped the big barrel as though it were getting towards the bottom, as though he would have to go out in a minute and come back with another on his back. He was drunk too—with prosperity, progress. He laughed resonantly and looked a very caricature of "mine hoste," of "old-fashioned hospitality," and good cheer. Many of the nips were rather larger than the men were accustomed to, measured as they were by eye, and soon there was a happy relationship between servers and served. Traquhair's little eyes gleamed with a sort of far-away pleasure. He often gave more change than was right or forgot to take money.

The Lifeline

He answered quips about his private still with grave hints at its whereabouts or—suddenly serious—gave a solemn lecture on the neglected opportunities of those who could buy raw spirit—"perfectly legally"—had their own oak (he touched the barrel) for years of maturing under special conditions which had been "faithfully observed—oh, yes, indeed, sir!—by the monks of Iona!" and above all, he raised an index finger, "your burn water"—*nach fior sin!* "Where did this come from? Why from Rum. My homeland." His listeners let their eyes fall to their drink with new respect though by then everything was confused. The big man and the barrel seemed to puzzle them, so much that some closed their eyes sleepily while he was talking and looked irritated and frustrated as though it was a pity to be getting like this so soon.

The door kept opening and shutting, now letting out faces corrugated with a single simple purpose, and letting them in smooth with relief.

Suddenly a group of incomers included a very old woman in black carrying a large handbag, and a tightly rolled umbrella. Had she been swept in by the crowd? Her heavily powdered pale face, black lace fichu, high-heeled patent leather shoes, black velvet neckband and dark purple cameo suggested she had strayed from a banker's funeral in Glasgow. Yet she came in here, even after seeing the kind of people who were already in.

There were many Catholics and superstitious men present, men who had passed their childhood in places that had not changed much since the Middle Ages.

Nothing could have been further from their anticipations than this old woman. Bloodshot eyes fixed on her with immense caution. Backs obstructing her progress to the bar slowly turned and then shifted clear sharply as though tapped on the shoulder by death.

"Thank you *so* much. If you please . . . thank you . . ." In this way she reached the counter quicker than the burliest man in the room.

Meldrum's eyes for the first time lost their look of gloomy

The Lifeline

prescience. Helen busied herself at the till, longer than was necessary. But Traquhair leaned forward and murmured with exaggerated gallantry as though the old lady could rely on him to hammer the lot into a proper deference to respectability.
" Madam, what can I get you ? "
" A double whisky, *if* you please. Ay feel a little faint."
There were some smiles round about, but Traquhair's face never flickered. With water-jug poised he questioned her with his eyes.

Having paid with much ceremony, she turned and went back through the crowd, spilling little and pausing only to search round for a seat which she found far away, near the door beside two tousled men who were arguing in broken Scots.

" She probably doesn't know the private bar's open too," said Traquhair.

Helen said grudgingly : " *Mrs. Creevie!* "

Traquhair said " What ? " and returned his eyes to where the old woman had taken a seat.

She was no longer there.

He peered round. She had vanished. By her empty seat stood her empty glass, proving she had been.

Near the door drinkers looked uneasily at the empty seat and soon the table by which it stood became deserted.

Traquhair leaned forward to the next customer. " Sir . . ." His prodigal manner was unchanged, but in his heart he felt as though he had seen a magpie, walked under a ladder and spilt salt.

" Some friend of yours, Meldrum," he said in a lull. " Some Messenger from Beyond."

" Mrs. Creevie," Meldrum said.

" And what would Mrs. Creevie want in here ? "

" I expect she heard about the barrel. It was the talk of the village this morning. I expect she wanted to see what you'd put in it."

Traquhair turned away as though Meldrum did not exist. There was plenty to do and by now no alternative but to continue doing it.

30

AT FIRST the village was reticent about the success of Traquhair's new bar. The whole thing had happened so quickly; there seemed to be an ephemeral, mushroom quality about the plaster-board construction with its cattle shed appearance and the big barrel inside. Where was all this yesterday? Where would it be to-morrow?

In Strathireshire recent years have seen the quick rise and even quicker fall of many light industries and miscellaneous projects. Some of these were inspired not by mere philanthropy to Highlanders, as were the Carnegie libraries and the Spote factory for Braille typewriters, but by solid desire for personal advantage. For instance, Sir Duncan Fidge's, the M.P.'s, Brackenator probably increased his majority at the very least by the number of people employed in the plant. But whatever their motives, innovators have not prospered in Strathireshire. It was therefore only natural that a week or two should pass before anyone in the village would allow that Traquhair's venture was even promising. In that time the Cullan camp had been filling up and on the third Saturday the Strathire Arms car park could not contain all the buses and second-hand cars which flocked in. Two policemen stationed themselves outside and several fighters were arrested. Extra week-end labour was recruited by Mr. Traquhair and the rumour grew that eight hundred pounds had been taken in cash in one day. From then on people like Harry Skene, the butcher, and Mr. MacFarlane, the banker, tended to lubricate their business small-talk with remarks—half-probes, half-comments—such as " Things getting quite busy out east,"

The Lifeline

or "Yes, yes—he's done it quite nice, though the drink's a bit rough, they say." People began talking about "the New Bar" as though there had never been a bar in that place before.

And indeed the Strathire Arms had changed enough to warrant such an epithet as "new."

Behind the scenes, of course, comment was outspoken and speculation about the barrel feverish. Mrs. MacFarlane in particular, who, on the alert for swift appreciation, was impatient of her husband's moral insinuations and suggested Traquhair might be trying out a new cheaper whisky which would soon have the backing of big grocers and stores. She was one of the first to begin talking of "the New Bar" as though it were established. In fact, she had words with Brian Creevie about this, told him he was just plain jealous and rang off. No one was more bewildered by her *volte-face* than her husband.

Soon Mackay's workmen were again busy up at the hotel, and when they left, there in the neat triangle of grass before the front porch stood some old whitewashed top-gallant mast with a gallows-like cross-tree bearing the escutcheon of the Strathire family with the words *Si je veulx* written in squirly writing over a boar's head and strawberry leaves. Indoors there was now an office, a rippled-glass guichet marked with the word "Reception" cut into a Formica panel and a bell marked "Ring" which when pushed sometimes elicited a rumbling and clattering from within and the sudden uplifting of the framed glass, as dramatic as the opening of a fire engine's garage, and the swift emergence of Traquhair's face and beard. "Sir?" or "Madam?" he would say with a deference which was tempered by the irritation of one who has been interrupted in mid-difficulty. Sometimes he had a quill in his teeth or his Japanese calligraphic brush behind one ear so that inquirers wondered whether they were meant to laugh. Doubt never lasted long, for whatever his get-up Traquhair's expression of hard-work-disturbed commanded businesslike reactions.

The Lifeline

Perhaps after all, people said, the place was going to be a success.

Girls were interviewed for jobs and two taken on. An advertisement appeared in the *Scotsman* calling attention to the hotel's existence. First bookings were made. Extra sheets and furniture arrived in vans. Cupboards were stocked up with crockery and cutlery and the thousand paper napkins embossed with the Strathire Arms and *Si je veulx* were stored in readiness for use. (Traquhair had replied to a communication from Mr. Aldwich simply saying that he, too, had put the matter in the hands of his solicitors.)

J. S. Mackay was paid the first instalment of his bill, two hundred pounds. Helen appeared in a new dress.

Four more barrels full of whisky had gone down the throats of the Cullan dam builders, and later, the empties had travelled conspicuously to the station. Refills had arrived conspicuously and after lying conspicuously for a few hours on the platform, heavily sealed, had been carried by MacLachlans Haulage to the front door of the Strathire Arms in the middle of the day. People waiting at the bus stop, and Brian Creevie on one occasion at his bedroom window, had marked the prodigious unloading operations. Helen and Meldrum guiding the monster barrel down ramps while MacLachlan and Traquhair steadied it with a rope, from above.

Undoubtedly the barrel on the counter itself became a "draw"; so, too, did Traquhair beside it.

During his spells on duty at the bar he regaled strangers with extraordinary stories about his life in various parts of the world. On one occasion it transpired he had been attacked by a mass of migrating weasels and only escaped with his life because of a close and climbable tree. And on another, when he was a deep-sea diver for pearls in the Solomons, he had saved himself by looking a shark straight in the eyes—"something a shark can't put up with."

And so on, while his great hand folded over the barrel's tiny spigot like a squid clasping a winkle and the noisy dribble of spirit was drowned by his deep imitation of the white hippopo-

The Lifeline

tamus's love call or his shrill take-off of two Chinese prostitutes quarrelling.

One day a parcel of writing-paper, embossed like the napkins with the Strathire coat-of-arms and *Si je veulx*, arrived from Bond Street. The helps saw it lying about and the following day the postman let it be known that Traquhair had written to the Prime Minister of Canada, Mr. Hilldersley.

Was it surprising that something more than mere confidence began to be noticeable in Traquhair's bearing? He walked down Main Street on air, punted himself along with his sevenfoot *crummach* and gave greetings in the tone of one who wishes to encourage *esprit de corps*.

Major Murray, in the back of the cobbler's shop, passing round his flask of official sample, began to suggest that the vote which had made the man chieftain had been unanimous. He even went so far as to mutter confidentially: " 'S big man, oh, yes, 's big man," as though referring to something more than Traquhair's physique, something he had done in the war which to this day was little known except among a few men "in a certain position," something above all which transcended the yardsticks of conventional (small man's) morality.

Lorries from southern breweries parked at the door. Orthodox bottles clattered in cases as they were carried in. John Mackay told Creevie he would get his fifteen hundred back and no bother. Creevie, up and about again but paler than usual, said he wasn't so sure.

Traquhair attended church regularly.

But what about the man himself? On nights when he "drew the rations" as he called it, Meldrum's face swam out of the stars and Traquhair sank down at his feet drowned in sweat. They never talked of what they were doing; but once, when Traquhair offered his secretary a glass of whisky, Meldrum refused contemptuously.

Recently Traquhair had quite given up those gloomy periods of introspection which had visited him when the glories of the football dance had left him face to face with the paralysed mixer. Memory then had come to his lonely door like another bill

210

The Lifeline

which he couldn't pay. Years since he had felt so lonely, so mortal. To make matters worse, the crisis had coincided with the arrival of Helen and the removal of Meldrum from the intimate kitchen relationship which they had enjoyed now for several months. Gone the jolly intellectual sparring over the omelet, the long digestive session talking to Meldrum's back while he washed-up or swept; gone the pleasures of teasing someone who cared. The relationship could still have continued despite Helen's presence had it not been for Meldrum's immediate reaction to the leak. Once the whisky was flowing the man had used Helen's presence as an excuse for never going near Traquhair except when he could not avoid him.

Traquhair tried every kind of reconciliation. They would both, he pointed out, be dead in a hundred years' time; the State, anyhow, owned everything so how could you steal when you never possessed? And so on, the advice usually being interrupted by gulps of whisky. In fact, gradually he drank Meldrum out of his system, put the man's shadow out of mind as though, in the modern context, the man was nothing, not even an impediment, a psychological dreg from the Stone Age.

It was about then the big man became a familiar figure on Strathireshire roads driving opened-up in his 1926 Rolls. He managed to go fairly fast but to look as though he were going very fast indeed, faster than the cars that passed him, partly because his beard was always plastered against his chest by the wind and partly because the flaps of his deerstalker seemed to be pulled down simply to keep his ears from being blown entirely off. All this and an expression of grim resolution and blinkered single-mindedness added thirty miles an hour to his real speed. People thought it a great car, but Fluach Motors, the garage where all Fluach cars get blended while being partially repaired, said the Rolls had a Jowett engine and was on its last legs, the battery in particular being so old it was no wonder the owner always parked on a rise.

Opinions varied as to where Traquhair went. To pubs

The Lifeline

probably, more and more, though no one ever saw him drunk. But where else ? Gradually it transpired that he had begun to frequent local landowners, people who just came up for the salmon fishing and grouse shooting. The Wotherspoons introduced him to Lord Seaforth, who bred tree-frogs in the deserted nurseries of his castle.

Soon the two men had breakfast together on Tuesdays.

At first Traquhair had tried to share his impressions of this new world with his secretary, use them as a bridge back to the mainland of his secretary's affection.

On his return from the Wotherspoons or the tree-frogs he would seek Meldrum out, swabbing the bar counter, say, and sit on the stool opposite and take pleasure in simply listing Spote's or Mrs. Gunther-Sykes's possessions, their acreage, rivers, moors, farms, servants, other houses, ancestors and finally with a deep ironic laugh their personalities as though these, after what had gone before, were mainly foregone conclusions, something the poor dears had no say in, did they but know it. For by then he had forgotten the tree-frogs and could only remember the sensation of leisure and effortless power which he enjoyed vicariously in their company.

In the past Traquhair had been much given to discussing the rich and powerful, the "upper classes," and so on, all in a near-Marxist vein. His assumption that they were deservedly doomed and could be abused in generalised terms never prevented him seeking their company or aping their dress. And as a topic of conversation they apparently now had no equal. He had always loved nothing better than to talk on and on to Meldrum's back about the characteristics of so and so—usually, even in B.B.C. days, a member of the upper classes. Other people apparently were simply not so interesting ; their scope for differentiation was inevitably less, even if they were worthier people. But never till now had Traquhair frequented his "upper classes" *en masse*. " Heugh heugh . . ." he luxuriated in recalling the sudden candours of Lord Seaforth, the jewel thefts, the arrogance, the wild outspokenness, mostly in words that were loaded with special *entre-nous*

The Lifeline

significance. But Meldrum was not interested, would not be wooed.

"You know, Reoraidgh, we should take a leaf out of their book. They stick together more than ever these days. Who can blame them. *Heugh heugh!* Like us, they all have a leak. People with leaks must stick together. Mrs. Gunter-Sykes's leak is from bacon-cutters in Sheffield. Spote's from shipping; the marquess's from oil and miscellaneous. Ours, whisky. That's all, Reoraidgh. All in the same boat. Don't make us feel ashamed, Reoraidgh. We ought to have a club tie—golden manna falling on a blue ground—what? Lovely grub. You know, Reoraidgh, you can't get capital nowadays unless you've already got it. The door's shut except to the wide boys."

But Meldrum would not accept his attitude any more than he would accept his whisky.

Seeing him with a bow one afternoon, Traquhair made a last attempt. "The dead season, Reoraidgh, the dead season! But we ought to keep our hand in. Weeks since we sped a shaft. How about a tussle at two score this afternoon?"

Meldrum said: "Are you giving me an order?"

Traquhair said: "I see. It's as bad as that, is it?"

Their eyes met and Meldrum turned away, taking the bow upstairs to the annexe where in the evenings he decorated the woodwork with a red-hot nail.

Traquhair then stood below the annexe window and having made convivial noises at the caged bird, engaged Olivia in conversation. This gradually came round to the advantages of the new gadgets and amenities, the result of their new, common prosperity. Olivia's great round, blue eyes and her husky low voice praised the progress mentioned. Believing Meldrum to be in earshot Traquhair prolonged the whole business and exercised his vocabulary on the "general improvement of our lot."

Then one day Traquhair hailed Meldrum, confidently, from afar, saying, "Reoraidgh . . . Reoraidgh, your troubles are over. Look what I have here, down in black and white, on the front page of your favourite avant-garde daily, look,

The Lifeline

read . . ." He put his finger on a slim paragraph in the agony column of the *Daily Telegraph*:

Conscience Money. His Majesty's Inspector of Taxes wishes to acknowledge " First instalment " £200 from " Longbow."

" Well ? . . . Doesn't that clear the air ? "
" What about next Thursday ? "
" Well, what about it ? "
" Have you got the bottled whisky yet ? "
Traquhair turned, saying : " You know that's impossible."
" Personal contact. Go to Inverurie. You're always going on about personal contact, about remembering the telephone girl's birthday and so on. Try it on the distillers."
" Personal contact ? Use myself ? It wouldn't be fair to my rivals. No, no, Reoraidgh ; conventional weapons, please, not the H-bomb even in business ! "
Meldrum turned away and picked up a crate of beer. Ever since the bar opened he had carried things as though hoping to collapse under their weight and be injured.
With the crate on his shoulders he said simply : " You had better draw the next lot by yourself. I'm through with it."
Traquhair experienced a qualm of fear, for in crime there is no neutrality : an accomplice remains an accomplice—or he becomes a threat.
" Reoraidgh . . . what does this mean ? "
" Don't worry," Meldrum said, lowering his eyes. " It only means what I've just said : That I'm not going on with it. What you do—that's your business."
For a moment they stood facing each other in silence.
" Once more . . ." Traquhair said at last.
He thought Meldrum was going to agree, but after a few seconds the man shook his head and began to turn.
Traquhair took his arm. " If I promise that it will be the last time ever—for me too ; then, will you do it once more ? How now, Reoraidgh ? A last leak ? "
Meldrum's eyes came up and held his. At last he said steadily: " Yes, if it really is the last ! "

The Lifeline

After this it might have been supposed the atmosphere in the hotel would have improved but it didn't. A shadow still hung over them, the shadow, Traquhair protested, simply of Meldrum. Even Helen seemed to be under his spell and was always going over to the annexe and even ate there occasionally —this after refusing to eat with him. Frightened sheep, he thought, and saw all humanity packed tight at a gate swaying and scuttering this way and that while the smoke-like dogs of conscience, accepted notions, hustled them in blind lunges first this way and then that. Weariness swept over him.

Never before had they been so prosperous and he was paying the money back now by instalments to the people from whom he had borrowed it. Yet, Meldrum's face, Helen's increasing idleness, the general apathy about everything except money made him long to escape as often as possible into the tiny limited world of the Spotes, Wotherspoons and the Marquess of Strathire. After all, it was where he belonged. The *Trumpet* had just published his picture yet again, under the headline: " Old People to hear Chieftain on Hallowe'en Panel." Olivia, Reoraidgh, Helen were all very well, but they had their station in the new order, not far from that of tramps. Loyalty must not obscure the fact that the same station had only been his by accident and for short periods. To-day, like water, he was finding his natural level which was elevated. The Wotherspoons, for instance, were being widely asked by friends if they could meet Mr. Traquhair. First candidates had admittedly been poor fish, but lately the queue had been joined by none other than Laura Spote, Lord Seaforth's heiress and the wife of Lionel Spote. He was to meet her on Wednesday. Here was his final acclimatisation to that other world where leaks are taken for granted and therefore forgotten, although they are in fact the *sine qua non* of membership and the premise of language. If Meldrum had become diffident in his presence, it made sense. Meldrum had no leak. Let him remember it.

Dressed in full Highland evening-dress, as lurid as a cock pheasant in spring, he happened to meet Meldrum on the

The Lifeline

Wednesday evening as he was going through to the garage to fetch the Rolls. They halted opposite each other. Rather theatrically but with pungence Traquhair said: " Good night, Reoraidgh." It was as though he were taking leave of him in more senses than one.

And in the same tone Meldrum replied: " Good night, Tulloch."

31

THE ROLLS went well to the Wotherspoons and Traquhair speeding through lanes of emerald sheep's eyes towards warmth, good food and company, gathered in his honour, felt uplift, even beginnings of that familiar amnesia which had so often obliterated the most recent chapter of his past in order to facilitate the one to come. He thought of the *Trumpet* headline: "Fluach Chieftain," and had faith he would shortly see it mirrored in the eyes of the other guests. Indeed, when he came booming into the Wotherspoons' drawing-room, his hand was placed encouragingly behind Henry's kidneys, to lubricate precedence at the door, as though he, Traquhair, were now the host, inevitably, wherever he went.

And then, there he stood—surely a picture of traditional elegance, aristocratic confidence and animal spontaneity. Only his small restless eyes suggested a different man within.

Lionel Spote he had met but not Laura.

Any woman who was attractive, aristocratic and very rich in her own right gave Traquhair a falling sensation below the navel: the same sort of feeling perhaps that many people get, in a small way, when they post their treble chance pools. For he became, immediately, her suitor with hope so vivid that it felt like a drop, or a precipice.

He bowed over her hand at the same time raising it to his lips and pressing it gently into the hairs round his mouth, keeping it there a moment as though challenging her wish to remove it and pressing it a little between finger and thumb as though it were a freshly caught trout that promised well for the pan.

The Lifeline

" *Ow!* " said Mrs. Spote. " How d'you do ! " She gave a little cooing giggle which brought a slight frown to the longish face of her husband who came forward and at once greeted Traquhair with a sort of urgent, responsible formality as though anxious to restore social relations to the disciplined reticence without which life soon became impossible.

But already Traquhair had felt encouraged by the barmaid familiarity of Laura Spote, and was taking her in with eyes that flattered as they looked : a dark-haired, pug-faced *belle-laide* with short teeth, fortunately well upholstered in generous lips, eyes large, black and long-lashed enough for a Balkan spy in a cartoon and a slack soft body which seemed to have been so cuddled by life as to give all-comers licence to continue the cuddling. He had expected stiffness, formality from this queen-to-be of Strathireshire.

Oh, how he loved her, what friends they could be now. For she, too, had a leak—a magic wand. If she felt like building a castle in Spain then that was just what she could do : build a castle in Spain. Looking at her he fell into a trance, briefing an architect in Seville. . . . A smile of almost mystical delight kindled in his eyes. " *Heugh heugh*," he said, quite as though summing her up in two sounds and appointing her as his accomplice, *vice* Meldrum.

" Tulloch—whisky ? "

" Half and half and plenty of water, please, Henry."

Laura tittered and Lionel said : " Henry, have you got myxy yet ? "

" Not yet, Lionel."

" Poor buns ! " said Traquhair. " Poor buns."

" They do an awful lot of damage," Lionel said reasonably, but Traquhair had turned to the ladies. He could never discuss myxomatosis. Those club-headed abscess-eyed monsters had nudged his ankle in the backyard and all but made him scream. Laura Spote on the other hand, a healthy thirty. . . . With kindled eyes he sat down beside her and put his colossal arm along the back of the sofa. " I wish politicians would get myxomatosis, don't you, Mrs. Spote ? "

The Lifeline

Spote, whose sole interest and occasional employment was a kind of sober, theoretical political journalism based on knowledge derived from much reading and occasional lunch with various M.P.s, abandoned his conversation with Wotherspoon in order to display on his face a clear reaction to Traquhair's presumptuous generalisation.

"I don't want anyone to get myxomatosis," said Laura Spote.

"Ah! Good woman . . ." Traquhair's voice tailed away as he took her in more closely. Her kind of leak was certainly something special: it emanated now from her depilated pores, her sacklike dress strictly adhering to the trend of the very latest collections, from the tone of her slightest utterance, from her scent which came to him with a faint backing of human female, from the extreme softness of her every position as though she had been trained up from one womb after another, wombs of flesh, of long clothes, nannies' laps, of cushions, eiderdowns, Jaeger combinations, silk linings, hot rooms, hot cars, carried here, assisted there, handed out, handed in, praised, cosseted and fawned on—by all presumably except the severe gentleman whose plebeian name she shared and who looked at Traquhair, even now, as though he had come in through the window.

But Mrs. Spote seemed to approve of him. She was a friend. . . .

Suddenly he thought of Meldrum, elbow-deep in washing-up, of the dust round his bed and bills with angry red overstamps; of the big barrel on the counter and the gleaming faces surging round like a Goya day of judgment, of Creevie watching from the Bishop's Palace, of grunts in the moonlight, of the telly sound in the backyard and Olivia's treadmill, and Helen bringing more precarious life into the world under his precarious roof. How far away it all seemed. How very far!

Laura Spote said: "You must really come up and see us some time, Mr. Traquhair. The boys are still longing for you to show them how to shoot a bow and arrow. They're tremendous fans of yours."

He bowed. "I await your command."

The Lifeline

Mrs. Spote looked at her husband. He looked away. She turned back, and said: "Are you going to the Perth races?"

Her tone suggested this event was at hand, also boring but a probability if not a "must" for *people like themselves*. He found himself plunged into a faint but curious emotion, even though horse racing left him cold.

"I haven't made up my mind," he said. "We're rather busy currently."

"Lionel thought we ought to," she said.

"Ought?" said Traquhair, and looked at Spote with a touch of mystification.

"Laura is getting an undesirable reputation for stand-offishness," said Spote addressing Wotherspoon.

"From whom do you stand off?" said Traquhair.

"Not from you, Mr. Traquhair! So relax," she giggled.

The suggestion that he, Traquhair, conducted himself in an unrelaxed way because he feared people were standing off from him, or because they actually *were* standing off, had the effect of fastening his eyes to her face. What did she know? Fears of all kinds schooled in his breast and he was unable to speak.

Spote frowned at his wife as though she were doing something very silly in being intimate with Traquhair. "Mimsy!" he said. "Shouldn't you put that glass down?"

"Why?" she said flatly, "I'm enjoying my drink."

"You sound as if you were."

"Don't be such a schoolmaster."

She seemed to say this for Traquhair's benefit, seemed purposely to be introducing Traquhair to the fact that she thought her husband a bore.

"I should have been a schoolmaster," Spote said apologetically to his hostess. "But sometimes Laura has to be reminded how much she's drinking or talking."

"Where were you at school, Tulloch," Nadia said dryly, coming to the rescue.

"A shed, a mere shed, in the first place, dear Nadia. You wouldn't have heard of it. No school bus in those days. Four

The Lifeline

miles there and four miles back, all weathers, along the loch's edge."

" Which loch ? " said Laura Spote.

Traquhair felt Spote's eyes on him.

" Loch Slean in Rum."

" And then Winchester ? " said Nadia.

" *Heugh heugh*, dear Nadia. She's teasing me," he said, turning to Laura Spote. " She knows what I think of Wykehamists. Poor Wykehamists. Mostly maimed. Spend their lives in splints, all kinds of splints, sexual splints, political splints. Manneres mummifieth man. Winchester ! I'd send the flame throwers in to-morrow if I were Minister of Education."

Spote had one shoulder which became noticeably higher than the other in moments of stress. It happened now and gave him the look of a man suddenly crimped into some sort of splint. Was it to hear opinions like these, his face seemed to say, that we motored fifteen miles ?

" I hope I offend no one present," said Traquhair.

Dinner was uneasy despite the usual excellence of the Wotherspoon food and wine. Traquhair began to suspect a satirical if not disapproving attitude behind Laura's ease. And suddenly she said:

" What goes on in that hotel of yours, Mr. Traquhair ? "

" Goes on ? " he managed at last. " How d'you mean ? "

" Who's that beautiful woman ? What d'you do to make her stay ? Or is she hiding ? I get it all from my grieve whose sister cleans for you. And who's the Beatnik who appears beside you in the *Trumpet* ? Is he your archer or your secretary, or both ? Don't tell me there isn't a price on his head ? How d'you think you're going to get girls there even if you get guests . . . what ? " she giggled confidently at the others and then fixing her black provocative eyes on him, she said: " Spill the beans, Mr. Traquhair, we're all on tenterhooks ? "

After the shock of the initial question, Traquhair was relieved that others followed. They gave him time to think and by their scope, speed, presumption and numbers provided

The Lifeline

an opening for irony. " You ask me so much," he said conscientiously, " that I hardly know where to start. . . ."

Spote here began a conversation with Nadia, commandingly, as though refusing to allow the rest of the table to encourage either his wife or Traquhair by listening to their indiscretions.

" The boys are longing to meet your archer," Laura flitted on, blushing for some reason.

" So are we all," said Henry broadmindedly. " But Tulloch won't let him out."

" Someone's got to do the work," Nadia said though she had seemingly been intent on Lionel—whereupon Lionel gave up.

Traquhair put out helpless arms like the legs of an upturned horse. " You don't know what you're saying. Meldrum is better left where he is."

Laura said : " Where did you find him ? Was he in Robin Hood with you ? I met him in McConnachies. He gave me quite a turn."

" Meldrum ! " said Traquhair. " Phew ! " He shook his head and sighed as though he had never known how he had come by such an assistant.

" Did you advertise ? " Laura pattered on, while Traquhair's little eyes flitted round. What were they thinking of Meldrum ? Did they hate the sight of him ?

Carefully he said : " I knew him long ago. Then I ran into him after the war. He was down on his luck." He paused. " I said, ' There but for the grace of God go I.' "

This curious and appealing version of what had happened took Traquhair himself by surprise so that he was late in suiting it with a humble and benevolent cast of countenance. He returned to his food and sawing through a bit of steak, consoled his conscience with second thoughts to the effect that it was partly true. But he could see Reoraidgh's face. . . .

" Poor cretin," he said. " A field day for the psychos, but then aren't we all ? " He dabbed his lips with his napkin and looked intelligently at Lionel Spote who, according to Nadia, had had experience of the couch.

The Lifeline

"What's the matter with him?" Laura said tetchily, as though sick of the whole psychological circus.

"*Heugh heugh!* That, madam, is the million-dollar question."

Spote looked round as though collecting votes for distaste. His expression suggested that it was cheap to discuss the intimate difficulties of others at all, except with a serious intention of assistance or compassion. . . . " Shall we talk about the Cullan Games," he said.

"I want to talk about the archer," Laura said in her clipped touchy voice. "What's the matter with him?"

Traquhair leant towards her and with one index finger raised he said in a stage whisper: "The world is mad but I, Meldrum, am sane; the world is sick but I, Meldrum, am healthy; the world is sad but I am happy . . ."

"Is he?"

Traquhair became sincerely speculative. At last he said: "Yes and no."

"Like most people," said Nadia.

"There are differences. He is waiting," said Traquhair.

"What for?"

"For the M.P.S."

"The *what*? . . ."

"The music-practising Socrates."

"Who's he?"

"*Heugh heugh.* Dear Mrs. Spote—do we really want to know? Besides, I might get it wrong and, anyhow, it's corn, pure corn."

"Let's have it."

"Well, we are to understand that the M.P.S. would combine the cerebral powers of a Socrates and the feeling powers of a Beethoven; on the one hand, the powers of ratio, am I right? And all that that implies in the modern world in the way of differentiation, specialism, extroversion and analysis and on the other, the synthetic powers of feeling (music par excellence) without which, of course, the development of ratio is useless in that it will only create a world that is further and further

The Lifeline

divorced from any felt meaning. Do I take you with me so far?"

"No," she laughed indifferently. "But go on."

"He himself leans heavily in the direction of feeling, as he claims, merely 'to balance the boat.' There is a catastrophic list to one side, he says; he feels science has become not man's slave but his master and at the very moment when nature seems to be harmoniously controlled it is becoming vindictively lopsidedly, as never before, the controller."

"What else?"

"There are frills with which I wouldn't like to frighten you."

Spote had fixed Traquhair with an odd look into which had crept surprise, doubt and finally faint, distasteful fascination.

"What did he do before he came to you?" said Laura briskly.

"He was secretary to the Bath Archers and he made fishing-rods by hand above a tobacconists'."

"Does he play the flute," said Henry whose scholarship had been in classics.

"He sings like a child sometimes when he's working. Monotonous, circular stuff. No more differentiation than a top as I've told him, but it makes him salivate all the same. A rum bird, our Reoraidgh. . . ."

"Is he from up here?"

"A few generations ago. Lately the Meldrums were in India, factors of some sort for a rajah, finally in Bath."

"And you took him on because you were sorry for him," said Nadia, disguising her narrowed eyes with a faint and agreeable smile.

He stared at her quizzically. "My dear Nadia—you wouldn't be insinuating, would you? . . . Certainly—certainly twenty years ago Reoraidgh was a dream. . . ."

No one was surprised when Spote, quite soon after dinner, suddenly rose from his chair and bending over his wife, said: "Mimsy—home, I think . . ."

"What on earth do you mean?" she said.

The Lifeline

"Home," he repeated laconically and yet somehow helplessly. He was staring at her with slightly distended eyeballs as though panic-stricken already by the impulse to which he had given way.

Quite simply she said: "No. If you want to go home, you can go."

The schoolmaster veneer crumbled and Spote seemed suddenly vulnerable and victim. "I see!" he said.

Then, obviously harrowed by his own bad manners, he turned to his hostess and bending towards her with one fist lightly clenched level with his chin, he said: "Nadia, you've got to forgive me. It's something I ate at lunch . . ." Whereupon the lightly clenched fist suddenly spouted an erect index finger which reached almost as high as his eye.

Nadia laughed and offered him medicine.

Spote said: "I'm afraid it's past that."

Having said good-bye all round he said formally from the door: "Then, Laura, I'll send Dermot for you."

"You needn't bother. Tulloch will take me home. It's on his way."

Spote was silent until the single word "Good!" escaped him like a sticky bubble bursting.

32

"TULLOCH will take me home?" . . . Simple words but they lifted Traquhair's heart. He got to his feet and just as he had taken leave of Meldrum in the darkened garage so now he bowed to the retiring Spote. Then he turned back to face the young woman who would soon be Lady Seaforth and the owner of nearly all Strathireshire—Laura, who wanted him to take her home. Emotion prevented him from sitting down. Life was taking the shape it had promised long ago.

He took off his tie and unbuttoned the top two buttons of his shirt, sighed, walked about and sought for words.

"Don't take anything else off," Laura said. "It's hot enough in here as it is."

Delightful pug, flirtatious tease. "Am I a stove?" he said, pausing beside her and looking down at her tenderly. She was always trying to avoid entertaining royalty and failing so Nadia had told him. She really had something. He suddenly saw himself spreading a scarlet cloak before her feet so as to save her from a puddle, yes, and discovering South America for her, bringing her potatoes, cinnamon and Spaniards' ears. His little eyes kindled into gimlet, horizon-searching jewels and his hand strayed up to his spade-beard.

Airborne now. Far, far away lay the Strathire Arms and that neurotic couple the Meldrums, far away dust, far away bills. Yes, the more successful admirals had been pirates and the Cecils cunning accountants. . . . A little consolation and the means were marvellously sublimated in the ends. "*Heugh heugh*, dear lady . . ." he began.

The monologue started.

The Lifeline

He sported in the boisterous waves of his own voice, walked about, conducted, as it were, the orchestra of his words with his massive hand, or glass when it was empty. He was a Swabian business man complaining of stomach pains to a Zurich psychologist, he was two Chinese tarts quarrelling over an unconscious petty officer, he was a *curé* with halitosis confessing a duchess; but after every departure he always returned to base, the bearded Highland giant whose cheese-coloured navel had now begun to wink through a chink where a button had been brutally parted from its hole.

Was it Laura Spote or escape that made life such a darling that night. Sometimes joy made him lose the thread and he was left in mid-gesture, lapped in their laughter, encouraged by their sympathy. He felt he was communicating the joy he felt.

Suddenly in a pause, which had merely been for breath, the clipped voice of Laura cut in: " I hear a lot about you from Brian Creevie."

Traquhair took time to understand what she had said, and then even longer to appreciate its relevance. What had Creevie got to do with their happiness? He parted his huge arms in a gesture that was as sad as bemused.

" Creevie . . ." he said blankly. " Brian Creevie ! "

" He's a friend of ours."

" And of Tulloch's," said Nadia.

" *Heugh heugh,*" laughed Traquhair. " Dear Brian Creevie ! "

The thought of the man, for some reason, was at the moment the most unwelcome thought that could possibly have occurred. Indeed, it was as though a frosty wind had suddenly started to blow on the mood that was blossoming within him.

" He talks an awful lot about you," said Mrs. Spote. " In fact, he hardly talks about anything else."

" He does run on rather, doesn't he ? " said Traquhair.

" Do you know his mother ? "

" I'm told I've seen her."

" Very old."

" So I understand."

The Lifeline

" He's done very well, hasn't he, Nadia, with that hotel ? "

In saying this Laura seemed to be genuinely seeking information about one of her people, her *subjects*. Traquhair affected interest and joined her in looking at Nadia, waiting for the verdict.

" Brian ? Brian has always been a worker in his own way. He ferrets about, studies prices, trends. All's grist to his mill. Between inhalations he's quite effective. After the war, he made a packet in lead and copper simply from buying up stuff which everyone else thought useless."

" A scrap dealer," said Traquhair.

" Well, he's got himself a new Bristol, Tulloch," Nadia laughed.

" We'd better get into your Rolls," Laura said encouragingly. " Are you sober, Mr. Traquhair ? "

" As a fish."

" And safe ? "

" As a pram."

She got her things and they all went out into the night, Traquhair and the Wotherspoons falling naturally into the pattern of a little court round the young woman who, short of a revolution, would soon be queen of this area. Even the sceptical and astringent Nadia seemed to be quelled into something like submission to this latter-day princess, whose body swayed erratically but confidently towards the car as though gates, doors and fences would miraculously open before her, which they did even here at the Wotherspoons'. Her armless pauses before obstacles produced immediate results and when she was giggling in the front seat of the Rolls as though on the brink of adventure, a rug was put round her knees and she was asked if she was all right not only by the car owner himself, but by her hostess who sounded responsible.

" At least you've got the hood down," Nadia consoled through the open window."

" Provided it stays down," Laura laughed.

The teasing added fuel to the flames of Traquhair's satisfaction.

The Lifeline

" *Heugh heugh*," he chuckled as he performed various archaic adjustments with the advance-retard switch on the steering-wheel.

Then he switched on and a red eye glowed and a petrol pump began ticking. He put on large leather gauntlets and then with finger poised on the starter, turned and speaking across Laura, said, " Bless you, dear Nadia, and Henry for a lovely evening, though the best is yet to be. Still, thank you for everything so far."

The commonplaces of Laura's milieu tripped from her tongue. She seemed to hurry through them as though the sooner they were over the better for everyone concerned. Nadia did not encourage them. Henry occasionally added a pleasant laugh when suitable. Now, thought Traquhair, now we glide away looking sideways with raised hands like the Queen and the Duke of Edinburgh from St. Dunstans.

He pressed the starter. " Tck . . ."

Or like two chieftains taking off to fly the Atlantic in a single-engined plane. " Tck . . ."

" Hell ! " he said.

" Tck . . ."

" Have you switched on ? " said Henry.

" *Tck, tck* . . ." The red circle still glowed hopefully in the dashboard but a long deathly silence came seeping up from the engine.

Traquhair scrambled out.

" A torch, Nadia ? . . ." he said. " This has happened before."

" Wouldn't you like to borrow a car ? "

Henry struck a match and between them they managed to get the handle in, but it could only be turned with more effort than came easily to either of them. Then Nadia came with a torch and all three looked under the bonnet. " Is that a Rolls engine ? " Henry said.

" Largely," said Traquhair.

" I don't want to be here all night," Laura called. The pitch of her voice had gone up already.

The Lifeline

" It hasn't seized up, has it ? " Henry said, stepping back and wiping his face.

" Oh, take them in our car, Henry," said Nadia.

" It'll have to be the van. The Buick's in for repair."

" What sort of van?" Laura said nervously, but Henry had gone.

Traquhair came to the open door. " What am I to say ? " he said.

" Nothing," Laura said. " It's not your fault. Next time, Nadia, you might ask Brian Creevie as well and then I can get a lift home." She giggled teasingly as though to show she was only joking—having first allowed herself the relief of not joking. It was cold and getting late. She was put out already. What would she be in ten minutes ?

A green tradesman's van appeared and stopped with a lurch beside them. Sacking covered circular openings in the back and more sacking was taken from inside. Traquhair in his fine kilt had to get in first on hands and knees. There were no seats in the back but they gave him a *Daily Express*. Crawling in, he smelt old sheep, dung and spilt creosote. Dust and moist cotton-waste met his hands. Then Laura got into the front talking fast and giggling. After all, it had been a sort of adventure : Traquhair and this van.

Fresh farewells. Jokes about Tulloch's car. " We'll keep it as a deep litter," Nadia called. Traquhair himself was silent in the back. Indeed, for once he was invisible and inaudible. It was as though he were not there for that was how they seemed to be behaving. A constriction of his lungs, owing to his head being pressed between his legs, made adequate protest impossible. But in his heart a new certainty was born, and a new resolution.

After a few miles the van stopped to put Laura down at her front door. Craning his neck, Traquhair caught sight of white walls in the moonlight, turrets, bow slits and tiny small square windows crossed by iron stanchions. Lawn rolled away

The Lifeline

mistily to right and left; there was a smell of earth and sleeping flowers.

More good nights and Laura stooped low to catch a glimpse of him as though he were under a table or something.

"I should get a new car," she said. "If I were you. Before the season starts."

When he got home he remembered his first homecoming to the hotel and how Reoraidgh had been there to open the door for him. To-night the building seemed deserted though presumably Helen was asleep in her room. Even if there was no Reoraidgh, even if he had made fun of his friend to strangers and come back like a pig from market, there was at least whisky.

He went into the deserted bar and filled a jug from the barrel and took it up to his room. While he undressed it stood beside the old Camp Coffee bottle on the mantelpiece.

Then he said his prayers. "Please, God," he prayed, "send me a suitable car."

33

BRIAN CREEVIE had never particularly wished to have the Prime Minister of Canada staying in his hotel. But so many people had spoken to him as though he did wish it, that he had come to doubt his own feelings. Finally, he had allowed himself to be persuaded by his mother to write a letter to Mr. Hilldersley inviting him to stay "with his own folk." The wording, hers, had made him sick, so sick that he could not avoid feeling a certain satisfaction at the reply which was not even signed by the Prime Minister.

Dear Mr. Creevie,—I am instructed by Mr. Hilldersley to thank you for your letter of May 11 and for your kind offer.

The Prime Minister regrets that he is already provided with accommodation.

In reply to your inquiries he says, yes, he thinks he does remember his grandmother speaking of Creevies in the old days. Apparently they were noted for their size. This would accord with the description you give of your father the late Ian Creevie.

Yours sincerely,
ANGUS GOODBODY
(*Private Secretary*)

" It was presumptuous," Brian said, " to write to a Prime Minister like that. If he's staying at Balmoral the Thursday he's unlikely to be staying with us the Friday ! "

Three days later the *Trumpet* published the usual block of Traquhair and one of Meldrum's feet across three columns, and beside it the headline :

The Lifeline

HONOUR FOR FLUACH HOTELIER
Canadian P.M. to lodge with Mr. Traquhair

and farther down a sub-head:

" A night wi' his ain folk."

" Well, dear," said Mrs. Creevie when Brian had read it, " what are you thinking ? "

He did not answer because no answer was possible. Had he mentioned one of the stray thoughts which whisked through his mind it would have given as little information about the main body of his attitude to Traquhair, as a stray shoe told of its owner. People thought his antagonism to the man had something to do with hotels. But then people hadn't a clue.

Several times a week in the past month Traquhair had passed him, sometimes quite close, in Fluach Main Street, without ever showing a trace of recognition.

There was, however, one place in which they met intimately, and often ; a place in which Brian remained closeted with the man for hours, oblivious of hotel, health and the stock market.

The scene of these meetings was inside his head, and the purpose an endless obsessing dialogue fed by memory of the few remarks that Traquhair had made either to him or in his hearing or to someone else who had reported them. Given these perpetual show-downs, Brian was able to prove that he was *right*, not about running a hotel and whisky for heaven's sake—facts in that direction spoke for themselves—but about everything, from Stephenson to Church.

Take the *Daily Express*. He had heard Traquhair abusing it in the distance at the Wotherspoons.

But the virtues of the *Express* were not to be sneered at. It was above all *Professional* ; it was "up to date," streamlined, imaginative, amusing, *efficient* ; it got things first (he cited instances) and often its "angles" which snobs might deplore, contained more than a grain of unpalatable truth. The *Daily Express* was the work of *technicians*. Now this was a vital point, the corner-stone, as it were, of his whole disagreement with

The Lifeline

Traquhair. Because what was required nowadays, in every department, were more and better technicians. Given the complexity of modern life this could only mean specialists. Already the achievements in every single department of human activity were to-day enough to make us feel we only came down from the trees *yesterday*: take packaging for instance. It was marvellous what they could do to-day. Lovely jobs. He had just got in some Palgraves' biscuits. The Cheddabix were a pleasure to handle. Well, that was specialism; and the same went for road-making. Yet you kept on bumping up against reactionaries, pessimists. He was quite sure the people who said we would double our standard of living by 1970 were right. (1984—ha, ha! That was a joke.) Good heavens, we *had* doubled it already, since 1945. What about the Asiatics and food? He might have guessed Traquhair would come up with that. Well, the future of fuel had already been solved. Why not that of food? We could probably eat the sea, given the necessary process. War? War was finished, dated—so obviously that he suspected the Aldermaston marchers of merely wanting blisters and attention or both. Good grief, who *on earth* would be fool enough to start a war? It would be *inefficient*, and to-day Americans and Russians, Communists and capitalists, were beginning to blend in the direction of a common future which would be dictated not by dictators, but *by what was efficient*.

Take hotel lunches for non-residents. There were no mysteries. You studied the nature of your local demand, during the season and out of it. You decided whether to plump for main dishes at fourteen shillings a portion, fairy toast, bamboo decoration, bottles in baskets and mobile spirit lamps on trolleys and aim at a prestige market, or you tried to get a name for a good seven and sixpence worth, in which case it was wise to boil the meat first, cut it while still inflated with moisture, reheat it sliced and finally arrange it on the plate yourself so that no plate showed. In this way you could calculate the number of portions from any given weight of beef and hence your profit margin. In time, perhaps quite a short time, every

The Lifeline

branch of life would be brought in line with the simple dictates of efficiency. Take education : he could not imagine a subject in which there was more dead wood awaiting removal. Knowledge to-day was so intricate that a lifetime was scarcely adequate to cover one subject. Yet, how did we respond to this situation ? By letting the people with the more favourable genetic backgrounds spend seven years on Latin, Greek and other irrelevance, up to the age of eighteen—stuff that largely had no direct bearing on their eventual special subject and profession for which a lifetime of study might be inadequate. This at a moment when we were in the middle of a technological race with Russia and Asia! If we lost that race he, Brian Creevie, wouldn't shed a tear personally. Why ? Because it would serve us right. Anyway, he was confident he would always be able to get a job in a world where people valued efficiency ; yes, even a job with Chinese or Russians.

Most of the trouble in the world to-day was due to words. Words meant different things to different people. Well, it was high time this sort of nonsense stopped. Words meant what they meant. Hence dictionaries. Occasionally, of course, dictionaries, out of habit, included words which didn't mean anything at all like "soul," but then, at least the dictionaries told you it meant nothing. That is to say, they put "immaterial" after it which was merely adding a noise to a noise. No, words could be defined and in the course of definition many of them might drop out of use altogether ; others, with help of the applied sciences, would be recast. Instead of people saying, " Oh, my God," they could start saying, " Oh, my Father-Figure "—if they must—and so on. For even the trivial silt of the past must be removed. One day, in the name of efficient communications, there would be, not a basic English, but a basic Esperanto, and if, to the romantic, this seemed merely a regression in the direction of original grunting, he, Creevie, could think of countless people whose conversation would suffer no reduction in content if they were limited to basic grunting.

True, the grunting would be confined almost entirely to

The Lifeline

private life. Professional life, on the other hand, would enjoy an ever-increasing vocabulary of fabulous complexity simply because the final demands of efficiency in each specialism would demand nothing less if full justice were to be done to the subtleties and sub-subtleties of the objective world. But here language would be no problem. An Esperanto would come automatically, indeed, it already was coming. Attempts were being made, when new technological terms were coined, to keep them the same for all nations. In this way a Jap might soon be able to talk to an Iroquois Indian about an isotope, but a Scottish youth find it hard to communicate with his own grandfather about religion. All this was a matter of fact. People could take it or leave it for the moment, but in the end they would have to lump it.

Obviously, soon life would be created. Then—just wait—for the Traquhairs of this world, writing to *The Times*: Dear Sir, It is with consternation... A new emergency? Of course. Good. New conditions were creating new emergencies all the time and being met by new solutions. Even Traquhair might be justified in despairing at the idea of a thirty-hour week for industrial masses in a bad climate—*were it not for television*. But, in fact, there *was* television. And there need be no limit to it. Any more than there need be a limit to hobbies. So why be afraid of unlimited leisure? Even if people's imaginations were already hard taxed to fill the various TV bills there would always be more and more experts who could tell more and more about their various lines—in an entertaining fashion of course, and so society could be entertained by itself inexhaustibly as it in fact always had been. The problem of boredom, like the problem of nutrition, would be thus solved. We could eat the sea and look at ourselves.

Culture? A "living" culture? He would submit two exhibits for the defence. Marks and Spencer cottons and Penguin books. Even culture had never been healthier or more widespread.

To sum up, Mr. Tulloch Traquhair: we shall neither be starved, poor, ill, bored or killed. Finally, and this he agreed

The Lifeline

might pose problems, we may so extend the normal expectation of human life as to make immortality a term that will have a certain meaning relative to the complete lack of meaning which it has enjoyed ever since it was first used. For let us finally admit, Mr. Traquhair in your church pew, immortality, to date, has been a completely meaningless term; the guggling sound of a child, Mr. Traquhair, a basic, disingenuous grunt concealing a desire for consolation.

It was at the end of this mental fugue, that Brian, excited and brilliant-eyed, heard his mother's question as it were, retro-aurally.

"Nothing," he said.

Mrs. Creevie said: "You looked funny, dear. I wondered what you were thinking—about Mr. Traquhair?"

"I couldn't care less about Mr. Traquhair," Brian suddenly said petulantly. He had opened the new *Field*.

His mother considered him.

"As I've often told you, I'm interested in *facts*," he said.

"Shurly ... shurly ... Brian," she murmured. "Yur not going to lie down under it, Chieftain ... host to a Prime Minister ..."

He said nothing.

"How like your dear father! Ah, how like him!"

In the subsequent seconds the fate which had overtaken his father seemed to be implicit in the ticking of the grandfather clock, the close faded air, the long tabouret needle and in the *Trumpet* lying open at the page which must have once recorded the sudden death of that legendary Highlander. Long ago Brian had suffered from a recurrent nightmare in which he had known that his father was not dead at all, but shut away from him still in some room of this house and fed through a hatch by his mother. A momentary memory of that possibility (it had felt truer than any fact) weakened him with sudden fear and a faint trace of nausea. The hotel! What did he care about the hotel? Next year he would really get a manager and go away for the winter.... South Africa, Canada, Australia—even if it meant losing his mother's capital to some fourth cousin

The Lifeline

she had never met. Fluach was dead. There was no one here, except Lionel Spote . . . for one fortnight a year. Mrs. MacFarlane, Fidge, Nadia . . . Would he mind if he never saw any of them again? John Mackay—him perhaps. The last shudder of his recent cerebral battle and demolition of Traquhair, passed through him and again he said:

"I couldn't care less."

"How like him!" cooed his mother.

"Like who?" he said irritably.

"Your father . . ."

"In what way?"

"In shrinking, dear; shrinking from his responsibilities."

"Well, what would you like me to do? Write to Mr. Hilldersley and tell him he's staying with a man who is the laughing stock of Fluach, a man who chose a boy as Beauty Queen, and a tart as barmaid, a phoney in a kilt who was probably born in Newcastle and has lived ever since in a studio, a friend of a criminal and a Communist. Well, Mother, is that what you would like me to do?"

His sarcasm was apparently misunderstood for she murmured in a tone of admiration: "Now, dear, you're turking. Yes, now you're turking!"

"And become a laughing stock ourselves—if not prosecuted for slander?"

"Like you, dear, I'm fond of *facts* . . ." she said, and with these words she opened her bag and from it took a small bottle full of liquid as pale as water.

"You see, we have this, Brian, and *we intend to use it*."

"What's that?" he said, his voice gone numb. It looked like a specimen of someone's water. Traquhair's? . . . The thought gave him a shiver. (There is still a witch in Upper Kintullochy.)

"A sample which I obtained of the whisky on sale at the Strathire Arms. You see, dear, I heard it was being served from a very big barrel! . . . And I had Chessman in Edinburgh make certain checks for us."

Brian stared at his mother, stared and stared, as though seeing her for the first time.

The Lifeline

Old age had been unkind to Mildred Creevie. It seemed to have taken a grotesque delight in ripping off the demure pussy-sweet face of Miss Caley, 1900, as in the miniature on the piano, and putting in its stead a sort of Ordnance Survey map, with myriad contour lines, of all she had said and done in Fluach ever since. It seemed possible that someone, given a certain almost divine skill, might have read those lines as though they were hieroglyphics, not one of them the result of chance. Terrible to think the old woman might have had emotions which corresponded to such grooves and gashes. Pale purply grey bags underslung eyes which seemed inoculated against further dying by being already dead, those mottled hands like tired, tenacious claws, that small smell of fusty isolation and limp black chiffon. She wanted no friends, no visits, no company. She ate by herself.

Surprised in a graveyard at night, Mildred Creevie would surely have taken off with a mere rustle and floated away over the steeple, faded till she was no more than a smut on the face of the moon.

She leaned towards her son. " I'm sending it to Stevenage," she whispered.

" Why Stevenage ? " Brian said, speaking much louder than usual.

" To Analco, the analytical chemists. And with it ai shall send a seemilar quantity of Fluach eighty per cent proof which ai've obtained from *kind* Major Murray."

Brian was silent . . . until he burst out : " Well, for goodness' sake, Mother, do what you like. But I don't understand. You can buy ' Fluach ' perfectly legally."

" *But not sell it profitably when it has been bought legally.*"

Brian left for his hotel office and did not come back for lunch, tea or dinner. It was a fine evening and Major Murray, driving home from the distillery, saw him with a putter and seventeen balls on the deserted ninth green. He was putting —alone, with a shadow of himself that sloped away, tenuous and long, to the east as though part of him were already stretching out towards Australia.

34

MELDRUM was sitting in Helen's room decorating a bow. The finished stave, unstrung, stood between his legs and with the help of a red-hot nail and some dyes he was making a sort of trellis pattern on the wood.

She had grown used to his occasional visits which had started with his doing odd jobs for her, making her room more comfortable and generally pleasant.

It would have been strange if Helen had not accepted him. There was no one else.

On the wall were cuttings from newspapers, signed photographs of Scottish broadcast singers, " To Helen with love," though she'd never met them, and one of Elvis Presley.

To-day she had brought tea into her room, hoping Meldrum would see the preparations and follow, which he had.

He carved almost as though asleep, lost in a kind of impersonal concentration. There was a slow daintiness in his fingers like that of a chimp when it's given something unfamiliar. If he wasn't full of reverence she once thought, even for a broom.

He spent hours embellishing the woodwork of his bows with minute and scrupulously executed patterns of arabesques, loops and circles, crosses and dots. The passionate attention which he lavished on the thousandth repetition was something like the devoted perseverance of his blackbird for whom, too, there seemed to be some special aesthetic in sheer repetition. His eyes bent close to the stylus gleamed with fanatical concentration as though he were a thief with limited time exploring the combinations of a safe : every completed design endowing

The Lifeline

its successor with that much more possibility. But the activity, as perhaps with thieves and locks, was to a large extent an end in itself, or if purposeful then only purposeful as breathing or sleeping are purposeful—tending towards instinctive satisfaction, of which the highest manifestation is joy.

But could such a word as "joy" be compatible with this sad-looking man whose "awful secret" gave his employer so many opportunities for badinage? Meldrum often sang and while singing, as while working, his mouth would appear to salivate (as Traquhair was fond of describing) like that of a dog before its dinner; and his eyes, lost in the decoration of bows, often looked as though they had opened in the middle of deep sleep, the thin margin of consciousness being—joy.

Traquhair accused him of being "an internal Sisyphus " and yet when he leaned back with stylus poised from his "doodles" (as Traquhair called them) was there any gaze in all Strathire-shire which dwelt more contentedly on the material, the object? Work for Meldrum, whether swabbing his counter or carving his bows, seemed to be an act of love, a perpetual love-making without climax. And the simpler, the more manual it was the better it seemed to suit him.

But lately his visits had become rarer and his work more and more subject to interruptions—periods when the life would seem to go out of his hands and his eyes would brood with mournful certainty on some point in space.

" What does he say to you ? " Cathy had asked Helen.

" You'd be surprised ! " Helen said uncertainly.

For it was days since he had said anything much. He used to tell her about bows and arrows and old customs, about Christmas and Easter, how they had started and what they had meant, about human sacrifice, animal sacrifice and Communion, about prayer and breathing and rhythms, about patterns in things so small you couldn't see and the part that eluded pattern which in matter, he said, was life, and in the mind imagination, and so on till you were dizzy like you got when you kept the telly on for too long. Still, it was peaceful, spooky, almost as though you were hearing about yourself

The Lifeline

long, long after you were dead from the voice of someone who had loved you. But since the back-end of last week he had given up talking. Yes, Cathy could laugh till she split, but she liked him around; she even got a glimmer of why Mrs. Meldrum had stuck it.

Suddenly Helen said: " Where does all that whisky come from ? From Mull, is it ? I heard it was from Mull."

Meldrum made several small digs with his knife before he said slowly:

". . . Whisky ? What whisky ? "

Helen said: " What is it you do at night out at the back ? It's lucky I'm the love-thy-neighbour sort. I never heard such a noise. Mr. Traquhair's there too, isn't he ? "

" What d'you think we do ? " he said at last.

" Well, frankly, I thought you filled the barrels at the back till that one came from the station. But even that one was sort of odd, because when it was lying outside after the lorry went I turned the tap to fill a flask for a customer before lunch and it was water came out."

Meldrum said nothing.

Helen said: " I won't say any more. I just wondered, see. . . . And then your face always as though you were going to have an illegitimate child. . . . You won't go to gaol, will you, Mr. Meldrum, like the other feller did ? "

" Why d'you say that ? "

" Because. That's why. I don't want to be left on my own suddenly. I'm bright, you see. I don't expect you to believe it. But I am. Desertion by all and sundry wasn't in my contract."

After a few minutes she said: " You been his secretary long ? "

" Not too long . . ."

" In the war, like ? "

" No.

" You was with him in Robin Hood, weren't you ? "

" No."

" He said he first met you in an Airtex temple, at midnight in Peru, hundreds of years ago."

The Lifeline

" I met him in Marks and Spencers, Bath."
" Was he ever in that bayonet charge, really ? "
" What charge ? "
" With the Jerries."
" I don't know."
" He said he was in a bayonet charge. By golly, I'd run a mile if I saw a man like that coming with a bayonet! Or I'd climb a tree."
" You'd be safer on the ground."
" I thought you were friends. . . . I mean, special. By gum, he's maad, that mun. I could laugh—when he calls himself a pregnant sow and a stuffed overcoat. Said he'd sold the car to Mrs. Wotherspoon for a deep-litter. The other morning one of his eyes wouldn't open. You should have heard him bawl. Wouldn't touch it himself. I had to open it for him. Just got gummed up in the night. He's a turn. Said he'd dance naked down Main Street with Bardot for the Wee Free: charge a bob a look and they'd still take the money 'cos that's all the Wee Free thought of. What'll he do at the games? Is it right a Prime Minister's to come here? He was making up a song about it."
" Yes." Meldrum gouged away at his wood. Then Helen said :
" Well, I don't know. Search me." Then : " Remember Mrs. Creevie, do you ? " she said suddenly. " The old bird in the palace. The one that came into the bar, remember—the first day we opened ? "
" I remember."
Helen was silent for a moment debating whether to tell. Then she said : " Well, you want to watch out."
" Why ? What d'you mean ? "
" I mean, that's what. She took that whisky away with her."
Meldrum was silent.
" She did so. In a flask. You don't know Fluach. She's been wanting this hotel all her life, Cathy says. She wanted her husband to get it. Now she wants her son to get it. You want

243

The Lifeline

to look out. If you're making your own whisky she'll be on to it. And if Brian Creevie gets anything on Mr. Traquhair, take it from me, you can order flowers."

"How d'you know she took the whisky with her?" Meldrum said.

"I saw."

"Why didn't you say anything?"

"None of my business, was it?"

Meldrum sat still, his hand suspended from his work. At last he said in a grudging tone: "Well, don't worry, Helen. There won't be any more noises in the back. It's to be bottled whisky, known brands from now on. Did you see that portfolio he had this morning? Money. Hydro wages. He's gone to Inverness. We'll have White Horse to-morrow. Finish now with that barrel. We can get on with what we have to do—you can have your child in peace...."

"And you?" she said suddenly. He said nothing.

"I don't get it. Bows and arrows with all that education! What makes you want to swab a bar and hand out nips and stand listening to all them soaks night after night. Didn't you ever want to do something different?"

"Yes, perhaps I did."

"Well, I don't know.... Bows and arrows and handing out nips for ten quid a week. I don't get it. D'you know what? He picked up one of your bows in the kitchen once, and looked at them black lines you're making. Know what he said?"

"What?"

"*Daft!*" The cruel brief monosyllable fell on the air like the sound of a slap.

Meldrum's face lifted and turned.

"You don't want to worry," she said hastily, penitently. "He's in no position to talk."

"Daft!" Meldrum said in a speculative tone.

"People in glass-houses..." she said. "Isn't that right?"

The shattering roar of an aeroplane broke in on them suddenly—and as suddenly ceased; but ceased outside the building; on the ground. Then they heard the muffled bang

The Lifeline

of a car door and Traquhair's voice boom: "Ho la. . . . Is anyone within?"

Meldrum put down his bow, got up and went to the window. Helen followed him.

Below, parked in front under the hotel's porch light was a long, low dazzling car. It shone all over and was streamlined as a projectile; it crouched sleekly and yet massively with compressed potential like a rocket in position, and yet had something about it which also suggested softness, *haute couture*, high politics, an heiress-starlet with gold leaf on her nipples. . . . Laura Spote.

"Ho la," said Traquhair, and then making a gesture towards the vehicle. "Let me introduce—the Donizetti, seven and a half litre."

If Traquhair could have seen his secretary's face his arms could not have remained affably outstretched in the direction of the gleaming powerful car, his body could not have stayed in the winning posture of a serenader beneath his lady's window.

"Oh, my!" Helen gasped. "What a beautiful car—what a lovely thing!"

With hand still outstretched, like a circus ringmaster introducing his lions, Traquhair slowly bowed lower till the nape of his neck gleamed up under the outside light.

35

TRAQUHAIR'S NEW CAR soon became a common sight in Fluach. He must have done something to the silencer for he could be heard like a diving aeroplane far away. When seen as well as heard, his big face, wind-clamped beard and bow-topped deerstalker, his elbow lolling calmly over the whizzing road surface, gave an impression of earned wealth, courage, skill, power and imperturbability. A rumour grew that he had once been friendly with Brigitte Bardot. But he never looked to right or left, never showed the slightest signs of having secured that which his enemies most grudged him—people's attention.

By now the last repairs and modifications to the Strathire Arms had been completed and the *Trumpet* had published a description of the comforts which awaited the Canadian Prime Minister. On another page of the same edition there was an announcement that both Sir Duncan Fidge, M.P., and Mr. Tulloch Traquhair had accepted the Fire Brigade's invitation to sit on their October Brains Trust in aid of Old People's Homes. And " Correspondence " was headed by a letter from Traquhair about litter.

Demonstrably the man was beginning to occupy what Major Murray called "a certain position." Even the old original rumours of his friendship with Johnny Stephenson were attributed to Mrs. Creevie or her son Brian, both of whom were known to have good reasons for resenting any proprietor of the Strathire Arms. And yet there still hovered certain uncomfortable question marks, and these in the weeks that followed were somehow brought home by Traquhair's

The Lifeline

lack of a silencer and by the background noise of a frequently diving aeroplane which he had added to everyone's life.

These misgivings about the chieftain were not entirely eradicated until the "visitors" came.

Every year "visitors" or "tooreests" in scores come from the South; and every year they give us fresh eyes with which to notice what has happened in our little backwater during the last months : this man has died, that house has been knocked down, this schoolgirl was "dux." . . . Last October concrete lights had sprouted at intervals down Main Street, seven times higher than the houses, each suspending a vast brick, as it were, of jaundiced light above the heads of passers-by.

When the visitors came Fluach looked in the mirror and noticed, as though for the first time—its Traquhair, and its new lights. But chiefly Traquhair.

There they stood, the visitors, when he passed. Scores of them all down Main Street. White-collar fathers looking conspicuously washed, pink and collarless with toy bucket in one hand and raincoat over the other arm as though in readiness for some testing alfresco experience; mothers made up for a wedding and dressed for the sands; adolescents like spies in a cold waiting-room—all on holiday, all or nearly all suffering from that touch of family claustrophobia which even in normal years turned many of them hungrily towards the lives of Fluach residents in the hope of being diverted from faces that were all too familiar and from time unmitigated by work.

They fairly fed on Traquhair.

That's Tulloch Traquhair. . . . He's getting the Queen to stay with him. . . . And the Prime Minister. . . . He shoots stags with a bow and arrow. . . . He can bend a back axle with his two hands. . . . His car goes a hundred and thirty miles an hour. He got stuck in a lift with Diana Dors.

Some of course already knew him from television and were fascinated by the spectacle of his three-dimensional flesh walking Main Street in a kilt, or streaking along the golf course road in a car which looked and sounded like an aeroplane

The Lifeline

without wings. Many regretted they would not be present at the games when, presumably, he would stand a little behind the Queen Mother.

She was coming, wasn't she?

In the Scottish Church the "visitors" saw Traquhair regularly (nowadays in a cubicle by himself) next to the Aldwiches and immediately in front of the pulpit. During the sermon he folded one arm over his stomach, and used this as a rest for the other which propped his chin. Sitting thus he received the words of Mr. Megginch with an expression of humble discrimination.

We residents were questioned about him respectfully. Of course we knew all sorts of things. Yet somehow his selection of a Teddy boy in the last ten of the Beauty Queens, his membership of the Communist Party and friendship with a criminal, and his patronage of every bar in the county tended to get deleted from the picture we painted, or, if not deleted, then perhaps allowed a discreet, almost invisible place like a French M.M. in a marshal's buttonhole. Indeed, the fact that he enjoyed warm feelings for people of the same sex, for Communists and people in prison discreetly underlined him as the fine contemporary ideal of the modern British citizen and helped him to become the object of a certain snobbery.

At the same time people went to drink from his barrel as though it was the last receptacle for the genuine, the old, the native Scotch; and if he happened to be briefly on duty at the bar, they would remember whatever it was he said to them with a feeling of responsibility as though they owed it to their friends to get the wording exactly right.

No, we had not really appreciated him. And as was only right, our headmaster was the first native to make the point clear.

There is still a lingering reverence for education in Fluach, the reverence which in the last century made Scottish education so good. Now it suddenly transpired from a visitor staying at the Strathire Arms that Traquhair spoke German, French and Italian as well as he spoke English. A cultivated man, the head-

The Lifeline

master decreed, and in saying this he and some others had vague feelings which they could not really put into words : that Traquhair was a small sample of a dying species, of "great men"—above all, of *general* men like Winston Churchill—soldier, scholar, athlete, historian, artist, a rebel-traditionalist who shakes the accepted order only to strengthen it, assigning God a fatter cloud of mystery, the Queen a more solid throne, aristocracy a parachute of capital gains and the Fluach Women's Rural Institute a feeling of security ; but not a good democrat, not a good committee man ; a man, in short, who simply could not help his *size* which was, for all its virtues, inescapably dated.

Of course, we said, you had to admit circumstances helped him. His birth (the visitors understood him to be a relation of the duke), his money . . . and then the contempt in which we hold our corrupt County Council, its convener and other dignitaries, the absenteeism of the marquess and his prominence in the *News of the World*, the psychological isolation of Lionel Spote with his *New Statesman* and *Encounter*—all this we had to admit, probably played into Traquhair's hands. He was acceding to a vacant throne.

All the same, on 24th June when he opened the Women's Guild cake competition he made a speech (again about litter), and there can be little doubt that the subsequent applause was for more than merely the speech. It was for what he *was*. People—and they were not merely visitors—clapped themselves silly. Fluach was gradually crowning him.

36

SHORTLY BEFORE the first guests arrived at the Strathire Arms, Traquhair visited Olivia in the annexe. She was ironing and apparently not surprised to see him. She wiped her hand on her skirt and gave it to him to kiss. Having done so, he dabbed his lips with his big coloured handkerchief and composed himself in a chair from which he first lifted two nappies, one rough, one smooth, still moistly moulded together by the shape of small limbs.

"Throw them anywhere," she said.

Having laid them at his feet and lit a cigar, he blew a long, calm executive plume of smoke straight up into the air. "Dear Olivia," he said, "I wanted a word with you. . . . How shall I start ? . . . You will probably have noticed that expansion has made new demands on the existing organisation."

The ironing position showed off Olivia's long back, and when she straightened, her bosom too. Now she did a plunging rotating motion pressing heavily on some recalcitrant pleats. The result was a vigorous jollification of her bottom which seemed pleasantly free of corsets. . . . His concentration drifted.

"Would you like me to stop ?" she said, in her husky voice and turning round, putting her hair back in that characteristic gesture, so innocent, so amenable, framing a slow smile.

"Please do no such thing. We can talk perfectly well like this."

Whenever he looked into her beautiful blue eyes, he remembered the story of a certain minor poet whom he had once met in a pub. This man told how, years ago, before the war,

The Lifeline

he'd had an affair with Olivia and, because she was driving him mad, broken it off. He had got out, got right away. Then it started: a letter from her, of such intricate filth and obscenity that even to hold it in the hand gave a feeling " like a small electric shock." Could it have been true? Was it possible this dutiful mother, martyred wife, immolated and wasted beauty, all this low sweetness of voice and strenuous readiness to help others could have really done such a thing? Such a possibility, naturally sometimes made him lose the thread of what he was saying to her face.

Yes, it could be true. For epithets, in her presence, could lose their momentum, scarcely pass the lips as though disconcerted by some ghostly voice urging the truth of their exact opposites. " Thank you " could become " Damn you."

She averted her eyes. Of course, he thought, she has known all along about the key and then about the barrel ... the "leak"; and has consented.

" Perhaps I do wrong, Olivia, to approach you without first approaching your husband but the truth is whenever I have approached him in the last two weeks he has walked the other way. . . . What can it bode? "

She immediately frowned as though pained, for Traquhair's sake, at such ingratitude. Yet with the same frown she managed to suggest he was invading a subject where gravity, not facetiousness, would be more to the point.

" He's not himself," Traquhair said, suiting his tone with difficulty to her face. " I know, I know . . ."

" No, indeed he isn't," she said passionately and managed a token short laugh before clumping the iron down on a vest the size of a lady's handkerchief, and shaking her head mutely, yet somehow theatrically. What pain, of labour almost, she must experience before she could *mean* anything.

" Then all the more reason for me to come to the point," he said. " Dear Olivia, looking around me, what do I see? . . ."

He looked round but she, after one glance, did not need to. " Coming down from the altar, as it were, that is to say from the goggle box, I see . . ."

The Lifeline

His inventory became silent, sparing her. The phlegmy stare of the empty television screen faced him. On its four spindly legs it looked like a vast insect, all eye. Round it stood a collection of H.P. furniture ; wallpaper bright with pennyfarthing bicycles in ink silhouette superimposed off-centre on silvery diving jets, the intervening space dotted with black leaves, all on a cherry background. At the height of the youngest Meldrum's face this paper was gashed and scribbled all round the room. An electric kettle lay drunkenly in the grate with its spout pointing up like the bows of a torpedoed ship. One knotted nappy still circled the table leg where it had lately contained the youngest on his pot. Crushed plastic toys looked like hen food. Papier mâché Stetsons, tommy-guns, the *Daily Mirror*, Meltis Week-end Fruits, all with a charcoal portrait by Augustus John of Olivia herself. Finally, Meldrum's bird.

" Olivia, dear. Two kids, well spaced, is the national ration for your bracket. Disregard this and the penalty is severe, an anachronism like the oubliette. I have a little suggestion to make to you : something which might be to our mutual advantage. The first living-in guests will soon be arriving...." For a moment his eyes rested on her face, but getting giddy at once, they flitted off into the distance and he continued in his calm deep voice : " Reoraidgh once told me you did two years at Nottingham University. Well, it occurred to me it must be painful to train a faculty such as the mind with much effort and expense, and then forfeit the joy of using it.... Rather like shutting up an athlete before the race. Don't I know it! Well I remember Hodgeson at Christ Church begging me to take the gown. *Heugh heugh!* Give me life, I said, not theory. You read history before your physiotherapy, didn't you ? "

" Yes."

" Well, don't tell me you never feel deprived, wasted ..." he said quietly, sparing even the room his eyes. " Speak your mind. I shan't tell on you for slighting 'the sacred role of motherhood ' ... ' the feminine principle.' ..."

The Lifeline

Olivia said nothing.

"It isn't as if, when you abandoned the joys of the mind, you were compensated with swansdown beds and Dior dresses. Even an ugly old man like me has more scope for dressing. Olivia! Don't let's mince words . . . you . . . *you* . . . are living here, *under a stone*."

"I don't quite see the point . . ." she said.

"Oh, Olivia. I know you have your jaunts south. A weekend at Sidgewick Castle with Ponto Suffolk, another at Merton with Dame Woodrich, a dinner with an Indian psychoanalyst . . . a Brahmin follower of Freud, the whole top potpourri. But the point is simply this: that you should become in fact what your husband is in name: my secretary. That is to say, the hotel's secretary—and thereby earn enough money to pay for a substitute squaw to . . ." He waved his hand eloquently at the room around her.

"A substitute squaw!" she said.

"No offence. In the last resort drudgery, if sufficiently absolute, can make our unique individuality seem a bit of a hallucination. Before a firing squad there are only a few common denominators of behaviour, and after the explosion, provided the aim is good, none. In a sense you're against the wall, anonymous. I'm offering you a place in a little bit of sun in our modern world, a place for you to throw out a petal or two, the place which was your rights until . . ."

"What about Reoraidgh?" She frowned as though keeping back tears.

"*Heugh heugh!* Reoraidgh! . . . The doubt is mutual. . . ." He looked bleakly out of the window.

"There is no time for a Poor-Rory, but this we can ask, quite simply: What hope has a Romantic to-day. None. At best he can be carried, for old time's sake, by people like you and me. The Reoraidghs of this world like the Iroquois Indians, need a Reserve. Together we can give him one. Take the job—and make his Agony as comfortable as possible."

The sound of the iron moving up and down was all the answer he got.

The Lifeline

"Earn more," he went on. "Lachlan is past the age of infantile dependence. He could still cling to your skirts if you came over to the office for a few hours. You would be earning fresh wallpaper, perhaps a holiday. Have you ever had a holiday? . . . I thought not. Better clothes for the children. Above all, you would be happier. All that training which must be festering in your mind would get some fulfilment. You'd see . . . new faces. And my dear Olivia (was this what you wanted to compel me to say?) you would be doing me a service. The truth is, I don't want strangers . . . messing about with my papers."

"I see," she said as though he had at last said something sensible. Was it his imagination that she was raising him?

"*Heugh heugh*," he laughed. "All my love letters, my dirty little secrets; my fans. No, thank you. I like to be sure of the person who's going to open my post. . . . Such a position of confidence would be suitably paid. . . ."

"You couldn't get a manager, I suppose," she said at last.

He looked at her intently to probe her meaning. Raising him again? Sarcasm? Insinuation that really he was inviting her to manage the hotel—*do everything*. . . .

"*Heugh heugh!*" he said in his deepest, most conspiratorial manner. But that was all.

He blinked.

Olivia looked out of the window—at the distillery. Her face clouded with doubt and anxiety. She said: "Reoraidgh's been strange enough as it is lately."

"I would go farther!"

"He needs me here."

"While he's in there? You can get dailies from the village."

"He thinks a woman's place is the home."

"You don't say! And where is his place?"

"Working hard. And you know it," she said with sudden contempt. "Look at the garden!"

"Some days I do little else." He smiled at her with a sort of sleepy relish.

"Come, Olivia. Skip it. With Uncle Tulloch you must

The Lifeline

skip it. We know Reoraidgh is longing to lose his life in order to save it, but to-day he can't. That particular cheque has begun to bounce, has it not? But I oblige. I am his cross. I give him a barrel to carry. Yes, he is reduced to that! Now it so happens that Father Traquhair needs you too—in the office. You are practical. Of course I appreciate your . . . role as a mother married to an unrecognised pauper genius just as I'm sure you appreciate my responsibilities as—well—*heugh heugh*. . . . Need I say more? I think not! In a short time Mr. Hilldersley will be here. The eye of the world " (he waved at the phlegmy stare of the TV set), " that thing, there—will be upon us. Are you waiting for some rich uncle to die? If not, I suggest you start saving up for that ruined windmill in North Wales where, if all goes well, you will end your days keeping Rhode Island Reds with Reoraidgh."

" You don't know what you're asking."

" I do. Exactly."

" I'm talking about Reoraidgh."

" That was what I divined."

" Women going out to work is . . . one of his things."

" What about men going out to work? That, too, seems to be one of his things."

Her silence scorned him.

" I see. You mean . . . he would throw a punch or two . . . if you moved into the office."

" Just one punch," she laughed with a sort of rueful snort. " It's always just one . . ."

Traquhair stared at her with strange surmise. Did he really hit her? Gentle Reoraidgh!

" Oh, for God's sake! " he muttered, and his little eyes drowned in certain vision of Reoraidgh beating her up.

" With a fist . . . or a stick? . . ." He was away now, quite lost in it.

" With anything."

After a minute or two he made a face and rocked his head back and forth.

" But I'll come," she said. " All the same."

The Lifeline

" I no longer ask it."

" But I will."

He made a face signifying reluctance, responsibility. But inwardly he felt neither; if anything, a certain exultation. Reoraidgh had been rude to him lately; worse—disregarded him. He suddenly wondered whether this might not be the reason for his presence here, asking what he was asking.

" To be a manageress is not in itself a definition of wearing the pants," he said.

" No."

" Besides you will be under me."

She paused this time before again saying " Yes."

" Anyhow, plenty of women who have centred their lives on *Kinder Küche Kirche* have reduced their husbands to the role of a mere appendage. Therefore the whole thing's all cock ... a mere game; at worst a defence for feeble men."

" Yes . . ."

" You don't sound convinced. . . . The trouble is Reoraidgh is for ever leaping to apocalyptic generalisations. Most husbands when their wives go out to work welcome the extra cash and a more interesting companion; they don't go into mourning for the feminine principle."

She said: " Well, I've said I'll come," as though unwilling to hear him discuss her husband any more. He stopped, but soon the picture of Reoraidgh's sad, disapproving face came before his eyes, and goaded him on. " Poor old Memento Mori," he said speculatively. " Homesickness . . . in the largest sense. I blame his childhood on the North-West Frontier. Mowgli would never have prospered in I.C.I. I suspect he resents his dependence on me . . . probably sees it as the last straw."

After a moment she said: " And what's going to happen when he resents feeling dependent on me as well ? "

" Well, what ? " said Traquhair with a touch of aggression. " Are we to be mesmerised into idleness, down tools just to spend our lives having a Poor Rory ? "

Taking her silence as closure and agreement, too, he rose

The Lifeline

and lifted her hand and kissed its damp callosities, then catching her eye and its expression he said: "*Heugh heugh!* Dear Olivia. Spare me. I know I'm not worthy to undo his plastic sandals. And this..." (He had kissed her hand again.) "... I know what you think of it. But there! You must allow a gesture or two ... I wave to your sex from a very far shore. Look kindly on my Continental contortions, see them, merely, as an apology to one of your extremities—from one of mine. We must look to our Reoraidgh to knock your sex both up and about, must we not?"

That night when Traquhair came home from the Wotherspoons, Helen met him in her dressing-gown. She was pale and shaken. "It's Mrs. Meldrum," she said. "She's in my room.... You'd better come."

"Why?" said Traquhair faintly.

"They were scrapping. She's got an eye like a rotten potato."

He could not be persuaded to go through to her, but went upstairs and was soon motionless with his head under the bedclothes pretending to be asleep. But pretending to whom? No one came to knock at his door. Across the yard a light from the Meldrums' living-room shone out across the yard throwing the bird cage into elongated shadow. Had Meldrum gone away? There was no sound of life.

Play, play, play, Tulloch reproached himself. Why did he have to *play* with things which he knew, in his heart of hearts, mattered to others. Retaliation? And why shouldn't he retaliate? Reoraidgh disapproved of him even though he, Tulloch, gave him more than he had a right to expect of any man—love. A craven sense of revenge crept into his heart and wanted to sit down in peace with that love. He knew he might have estranged Reoraidgh's wife by getting her to take a job, more perhaps than if he had become her lover. He was buying Reoraidgh out of his last stronghold.

Under the bedclothes satisfaction and remorse struggled for mastery of Traquhair's confused feelings.

Despite her black eye, Olivia started work in the hotel the

The Lifeline

following week and worked so wholeheartedly she made an immediate difference. She was energetic and practical.

Meldrum passed her without speaking and spent less time in the hotel. By day he was a lot with his younger children and in the evenings with Helen.

37

FAR ABOVE the deep blue of inlets and firths the golden purse-like flowers of gorse and broom were turning the braes of Strathireshire into seething yellow foam and filling the air with fragrance. More and more cars came streaming along the narrow roads, lone outriders of the vast congested herds to the south. The Unionist fête had been held at the castle and Mrs. Spote's little girl had presented Sir Duncan Fidge, M.P., with a bouquet of lupins. The game, fruit and fish stall, headed by April Gunter-Sykes, had broken all records. Not since 1910 had as many carcasses been gifted by the gentry. Among the kilted throng Tulloch Traquhair wandered in perfect ease and his voice, without straining, was quite as loud as April's except when she compared takings with Lady Boyne's bottle stall fifty yards away. There was something jubilant and emphatic in the ladies' clear-cut King's English as though such a scene could never have been envisaged ten years ago. Yes, all was well and would continue well. That very evening fifty miles to the north, Sir Duncan Fidge said he would again "tell Strathireshire" that his difference of opinion with its Socialist Director of Education, about the dumb child of Skelly Island, struck at the roots of democracy. Dumb the child may have been and resident of Skelly Island it certainly was, but Fidge was going to see that two such initial handicaps were not going to put it at the summary mercy of a "bureaucratic Big Brother." Even while April Gunter-Sykes and Lady Boyne compared takings, Fidge went on to promise the crowded lawn another rocket site by 1964—which would make jobs for ten thousand —or graves for ten million, muttered Traquhair, his little eyes

The Lifeline

gleaming as he bent smiling over Laura Spote's scented, white-gloved hand. April clapped methodically like a Vickers M.M.G. All was outwardly very well. Even Lionel Spote, whose shoulders underwent a desperate lopsidedness, matched by half his face shrivelling as though from a stroke, while listening to Sir Duncan's speech on the dumb child of Skelly Island, soon allowed Creevie to persuade him that things had never been better, except of course in the hotel trade.

But away from the babble of prosperous voices, far away behind the grimy distillery wall, within a hundred yards of Meldrum cleaning the bar, there stood a man who, like Meldrum, was not prominent in Fluach, but who was still to have a say in things to come. That man was Peter " Misty " MacDonald, Helen's legal—but not her natural—father.

People lost in the desert, wandering with swollen tongues, are said suddenly to see cool fountains and lakes. Hollywood tells us they pitch forward on their knees and creep reverently towards the nearest fringe of liquid and plunge their cracked lips and purple tongue . . . into scorching sand.

Misty MacDonald got a bottle of whisky a week from the National Health Service and bought two more with his wages, but he was left with the craving of a man lost certainly in some sort of desert, one of those deserts which have rivers flowing close beneath the surface, for there beside Misty, stood the " Spirit Reservoir "—capacity 6000 gallons.

Suddenly while Tulloch Traquhair was holding the hand of Sir Duncan Fidge, the two men having just been introduced by Laura Spote, Misty saw fresh earth on the flagstone at the base of the spirit reservoir. Was it a mirage?

Misty stooped . . .

Tulloch laughed.

A certain caution affected the two prominent figures. Fidge tried to walk Traquhair the way he was going by keeping hold of his hand and placing his free hand behind Traquhair's engaged elbow, a position somewhat suggestive of a quadrille. But Traquhair had no difficulty in remaining stationary. Fidge

The Lifeline

covered the repulse with a chassé which preserved his balance and a rotation to Laura Spote and a continuation of what he was saying . . . "that he had been so extremely sorry that he would be unable to be present when Joe—nice fellow, first class—Joe Hilldersley—comes to Upper Kintullochy. The last time I was over there I told him to come and stay with me at Inverurie Hydro, unless, Joe, you come in 1961, I said—for Pete's sake don't come in 1961, I've got rockets galore in 1961 and my own Ball Bearings in Detroit immediately afterwards. But with Mrs. Spote . . . Laura and you. Mr. Traquhair—Tulloch—here. And Lionel . . . Brian . . . I needn't worry; Joe's going to get a big hand. The sort of welcome he gave me. We paused at Niagara Falls. Tremendous wheat harvest they have there. Moose in the north . . ." Here Fidge's eyes flitted between Mrs. Spote and Traquhair and he began to go through them like a sleep-walker still sustaining their wrists and elbows. " Age-old connections with Strathireshire, Joe. I had the honour of attending the St. Andrew's Day dance of the Mackay Shoe . . ." His voice tailed off into warm expression of a stranger's Christian name which he seemed to intuit for his eyes momentarily crystallised into one gleaming split second of attempted extra-sensory perception.

Misty MacDonald stooped closer and put out a finger. . . .

Traquhair let the M.P. drift past him into the crowd. Beside him stood Laura Spote, the richest and prettiest woman present. Lord Seaforth's heiress, the Queen of the North. And in the distance a little knot of people had gathered round his Donizetti. The sun was shining, striking fire from the windscreen.

" Dear Laura . . ." Traquhair began.

Positioning his eyes like a bomb-aimer above sights and remote railway lines, Misty now saw that near the earth particles was a line, between two flagstones, deeper and darker than any of the other lines.

Lovers notice the smallest irregularity in the behaviour of the loved one ; and discover meanings where others would see

The Lifeline

none. Misty examined first the one and then the other three sides of that particular flagstone from the perpendicular. Then he started all over again. Then he looked over his shoulder and confirmed that the rasping of his mate's shovel and the whistling of improvised pipe music meant absorption in stoking; then he dropped clumsily to one knee, undid his shoelace and began slowly tying it, looking up as he did so at the open door, the companionway to the yard, the other door through to the furnaces. Then—he became momentarily still suddenly stooping low, took out a powerful pocket-knife and inserted a thick tin-opener attachment under the flange of the flag and levered.

It came up like a bit of exhausted sticking plaster, almost airily.

He was peering under when the whistling and shovelling stopped. Whereupon he let it down again while seeming to complete the bow on his shoe.

The interruption was of no account.

He could wait, now, an age, minutes at least.

38

TRAQUHAIR'S PROMISE to Meldrum that he had now "drawn the rations" for the last time was put to the test six days after the Conservative Fête, a Thursday. That afternoon a van from McConnachie's drove into the backyard and unloaded a hosepipe on a wheeled stand exactly in front of the door of the tunnel shed. For some time afterwards Traquhair could be seen standing with the driver and indicating various parts of the back premises which judging by his gestures were to be turned into flower-beds if not swimming-pools. A few phrases of Gaelic floated on the air; then the man got in and drove off.

During that night the lonely exertions of Traquhair, "drawing the rations" by himself assisted merely by the hose on a trolley, filled the air, not only in the backyard, but also down much of Main Street, with the fretful noise of a prolonged and complicated mechanical emergency. But no one heard, and even those who did hear were deaf and even blind, for on one occasion Helen crossed the backyard and ran into her employer carrying a bandolier of slack piping, the drum on the trolley having ceased to rotate. She said nothing—even when he addressed her. " Irrigation, all irrigation, my dear, irrigation of the roots, a drop of the Auld Kirk, a spot of Meldrum on tap."

She smelt whisky, but it might have been breath.

By the following day there had still been no delivery of proprietary whisky. The big barrel was found topped up with the usual beverage, and the enormous teapot, which in the past had always been found half-full of tea leaves by the kitchen sink

The Lifeline

on Friday mornings, was in its place and as usual heavy with a dark-brown swollen mush from which a few drops would seemingly have sufficed to make a whole bath of water look as if it had flowed off peat, or make a stoup of virginal rice spirit take on the hues of its Scottish cousin.

These days Olivia would already be at work in the office by the time Traquhair came down to breakfast. Sometimes while he ate he could hear her husky, urgent solicitous voice impregnating remote tradesmen with a sense of mutual advantage to be derived from all she suggested. Telephones rang, girls came for interview, a German student was taken on as cook and a Jamaican as "boots." When Traquhair went into the office he often found new equipment, files, trays and ready reckoners. He looked at her with thankfulness and relief. For this was what he had always wanted—a compliant but effective chief of staff. Sometimes he would sit down and toy with some new ideas in her presence as though she were some genie he had conjured out of a barrel, who could do his slightest bidding. "A casino..." he might say. "The Wee Free won't last long against telly, dear Olivia." He imagined lights with long, flickering beards trailing out down from the waterfront seen by lovely rich women from the sides of white yachts with squat little funnels; bonfires on the beach, carousal, or a Strathire Meeting—a ball which would take the place of the Oban or Inverness Meetings as the *clou* of the Highland season. "*Heugh heugh...*" And he would blow a little cigar smoke sideways and catch it in the act of taking shape as though here came the Marquess of Strathire and here came Lord Lovat, but here—and he voided the remaining nine-tenths of his lungs into a great elephantine formation of royal blue smoke which, with distended wings and veins, pulsed sleepily away, obedient to the slightest rhythm of the room's air—here came himself.

But sometimes these visions brought a frown to his face and an ebbing sensation in his heart, as though something were lacking without which it would all be sad, if not mere smoke. "How's the Last Hero, the Waiter, how's the M.P.S.?" he said one day. "Are we in the clear yet?..."

The Lifeline

Olivia chose this moment to be adding. Her lips sketched a smile while continuing to shape figures.

"I see him now and again in the distance," Traquhair went on. "He opened a door for me yesterday. He hasn't given you another shiner, has he? . . . Several times I've offered to have a Poor-Rory but he has declined. . . . *Heugh heugh.* . . . Is there anything we can do?"

Her refusal to stop adding at a moment when he was sure that adding mattered little, confirmed a feeling which he had had earlier—that she sympathised with her husband in everything, even in giving her a black eye. So he had better not take too much comfort from her co-operation nor from her simulated approval. She was doing it for her brats—*and even for Reoraidgh.* . . . He wondered what else she had done for them.

"Bless you, dear Olivia," he said ironically. "I'm told Reoraidgh calls me an 'old phoney' in the village. . . . Perhaps you agree with him. . . ." But her lips continued to move as though she were telling her beads.

An hour later he saw Reoraidgh go into the garage with a tin. He found himself following.

At first he could not see the man, could only hear clankings in the corner. "Reoraidgh . . ." he said.

"Yes." The voice was grudging.

"Quite a stranger, aren't you? Not long now, eh?"

"Not long? . . ."

"Before the games; before Mr. Hilldersley comes."

"I suppose not."

"There's no suppose about it. We'll have to be on our toes for him. But with this to transport him" (he patted the Donizetti), "and your Olivia to receive him he'll be a lucky duck, won't he?"

Meldrum's face became visible looming out of the darkness like the lid of a tin at the bottom of a pond.

"Olivia?"

"Yes, Olivia—and this."

Meldrum looked at the Donizetti.

The Lifeline

"A hundred and forty miles per hour, Reoraidgh!" Traquhair said winningly.

"Where in Strathireshire can you even go seventy miles per hour?"

"Oh, come, Reoraidgh, come. You give yourself away by never admiring. Here's beauty, modern beauty."

"But where can it be used? In all Strathireshire there's only three hundred yards where you can go more than sixty."

"Still, look at it. Think of the Prime Minister in it."

"You said you were going to buy whisky on the open market. Instead you spent the money on this car."

"I had to have a car."

"Like this one?"

"Money goes to money. I parked this car outside the Inverness branch of the Caledonian Tea Bank and got a loan, and with that loan shocked five years off the life of MacFarlane and paid a big instalment to the Inland Revenue: a double blessing for the community. Have you been watching Longbow in the *Daily Telegraph*? . . . My dear Reoraidgh, I'm only doing what everyone's doing. Shifting the stuff around: hire purchase. The only difference is that I am making my own arrangements. Therefore, I differ by a margin not of vice but of virtue, of courage. . . ."

"You've been filling up the barrel."

"Yes. I need never have troubled you in the first place. All I needed was a hose."

The suggestion that Meldrum was interchangeable with a hose full of whisky struck a curious chord, brought an academic smile to Traquhair's face. To conceal it he lowered his eyes to Meldrum's faded blue sneakers.

He made an effort, tried to combat countless inclinations to stray from what he knew to be the subject of Meldrum's thoughts. "Yes, Reoraidgh, I know I promised."

There was an uneasy silence until Traquhair said: "But what about my position? Surely I had to put that first—before consideration of personal convenience."

"I'm leaving," Meldrum muttered.

The Lifeline

There was silence.

Then Traquhair grunted as though he had been struck.

"Oh, no, no, no, Reoraidgh, you can stuff that one." He made an explosive noise with his lips. "Leave, indeed! Where for? The moon? Think of your wife and children. Also Helen; I wouldn't desert Helen!"

"*Helen?*"

"I'm not blind, Reoraidgh. We have more in common than you suspect. I've even feared you might get run in for bigamy. This while we're on the subject of morality. Fair do's. Give and take."

"What are you talking about?"

"About you and Helen."

"What about me and Helen?"

"Well, I've been thinking lately that you can't expect people to have such a nice sense of where charity ends and something else begins as you have yourself."

"We have her up quite often, is that what you mean?"

"I was thinking more of when she has you down."

Meldrum seemed to ponder this for some time. At last in the faint light Traquhair saw him smile.

"As though I should care," said Traquhair, sniffing once, sharply. "It has taken the slackening pressure and increasing wisdom of middle age to teach me that I have always really had some sympathy with the Sikhs: a boy for romance, a melon for pleasure and women—for children. . . ."

Meldrum smiled again—without a trace of amusement.

"No, no, good sir, don't run away with the idea that I covet your Helen or even your Olivia. I just wanted to jog your elbow. It would be a pity if our hotel were to be baptised with scandal."

"Oh . . . for God's sake . . ." Meldrum muttered

The contempt had the effect of pinning Traquhair to where he stood; and making him speak faster. "I don't wish to play the heavy headmaster, Reoraidgh, but I cannot escape the feeling that you have not respected her vulnerable position."

Meldrum said: "Do you ever *hear yourself?* . . ."

The Lifeline

"You know, Reoraidgh, perhaps we might be happier apart."

"Yes. We might. Oh, for heaven's sake! Don't think I blame you. You're no worse than the others."

"The 'others'? Who are the others, pray?"

Meldrum was silent for a moment, then raised his face so that the light from the open doors shone in his eyes.

"The people who are against life."

"Steady, Reoraidgh! 'They'? Who are 'they'? Hitherto your paranoia has had a certain size—almost its only redeeming feature. If you're going to have a neurosis I'm sure it's a good thing to have a proper one. But now you say 'they' like that, I fear your paranoia is no bigger than the common one which frequents so many books and plays lately. Now I suppose you'll be blaming the Americans, the Tories, the mock Socialists or even the Communists or Yellow Perils, oily seas or atomic weather, or even just the apathetic English. This is parochial after *Meldrum's Law*! *Heugh heugh!* Forgive me, Reoraidgh—do tell me—about the people who are 'against life'; and above all, how is it that you, the author of *Meldrum's Law*, feel in a position to make such an accusation against anyone?"

Meldrum was gloomily silent, staring at the floor.

"Ah, that secret of yours, Reoraidgh. What shall we do about it?"

After a whole minute's silence Meldrum's speechlessness sounded almost like curiosity.

"You should get around, Reoraidgh, you should get out more. There are daisies growing in the asphalt jungle, orchids even, did you but know where to look for them; and above there is the same sun, the same moon as there ever was; the gipsyness, the impermanent nature of the houses and the skiffle and the attitudes is merely in deference to the speed things are changing. Only a fool starts building in a flood. A boat is more suitable for the moment. These are mechanical facts which we would do well to face cheerfully. Float, it is a mobile, plastic, gipsy moment; cultivate a little gipsy joy, jazz celebrates the

The Lifeline

liquidation, it is the vast *recule* before the *mieux sauter*, anonymous, global, takes refuge in the diastolic beat which is the very pulse of life, even of invertebrates. *Weltschmerz* is *passé*. To-day the young, of whom I know several, have no *Weltschmerz*."

"No *Weltschmerz!*" Meldrum spat. "You mean they have so much they can't begin to face it. If it comes out at all it comes out like projectile vomiting; they regurgitate life, turn in hate against everything and then give the wrong reasons for why. Ach, you fool. . . . And all this from you. *From you!* But of course! That's who it should come from. Nothing is safe from your urbane chi-chi!"

The low passionate contempt in Meldrum's voice made Traquhair blink and raise his chin slightly.

Then Meldrum murmured: "And now you're all for changing women. Turning them into men. That's your last triumph! It wanted only that." And he whispered: "Why did you get Olivia to work in the office?"

"Don't you thank me? Isn't it possible, Reoraidgh, that I did it for you?"

Meldrum's mouth closed and pain showed in his face. At last he turned and went slowly out of the garage.

That evening Traquhair went through into the public bar to see if his secretary had turned up to do his stint. He had; he was there cleaning glasses. He did not look up.

"Ah, me! Ah, me!" said Traquhair in a conciliatory tone, moving conversationally close and then turning away coming to a halt, all this to spare the man his eyes.

Meldrum said nothing.

Olivia, thought Traquhair, must have told him to stay.

After a minute's silence Traquhair said quietly: "Thank you, Reoraidgh, thank you for staying," and with these words he went through to where Helen was serving a farmer, from the big barrel.

Traquhair leant on it and soon his voice was reverberating round the room answering questions about the Donizetti. "A poem, sir; a divine little sextet of cylinders. . . ."

The Lifeline

But Traquhair could not eat his lonely dinner. The Wotherspoons' telephone wire was down. He went and talked to Helen while she washed up. Then when she went out, he went up to the passage which overlooked the back.

The Meldrums' window was open and lit vividly by the last rays of the setting sun. (It was about the longest day of the year—towards the end of June.) Just as he was wondering what was being said in that room Meldrum himself came into sight behind the bird cage and after a moment put his hand through the little wire door and took out the white blackbird. His face, sunlit as though by a spotlight, was barred by the shadow of the cage and his hand flickered through the particoloured light before it closed gently round the tame bird. Then Traquhair saw him stand the frail legs on one forefinger and with the other scratch the top of its head with tiny movements.

Suddenly an effect, yes, surely it was an effect of light, struck fire from Meldrum's eyes. They began to glow like small holes in a white-hot furnace. And now the last, colossal shadows of daylight seemed to sweep towards this illuminated face like the bars of a bigger, all encompassing cage.

39

THE SUCCESS of the new Strathire Arms public bar had soon affected the bar trade of the Seaforth Arms. Mrs. Creevie pointed this out to Brian one morning, just as he was about to leave for the hotel.

" I never said it hadn't," he said tetchily.

She had the hotel books beside her and with them a recently opened parcel containing two medicine bottles.

" Well, it seems a little hard, dear, that you should suffer becurze of a creeminal." And she handed up a letter which she had ready in her hand.

It was headed ANALCO OF STEVENAGE and contained a report on two liquids submitted for analysis. Summed up it stated simply that Specimen A differed from Specimen B (raw whisky spirit), only by the addition of ten per cent weak tea, which gave it the same alcoholic content and colour as most commercial blends of whisky without appreciably altering the taste.

" Well ? " he said, handing it back.

" That's all we needed, shurly. Now we can put the matter in the hands of the police."

Brian exploded. Hadn't he made it clear that it was no crime to buy and resell " Fluach "? But, said Mrs. Creevie, was it not impossible to resell " Fluach " *at a profit* if you bought it at the official price ? And, anyhow, what about the addition of the tea—a milkman would lose his licence.

" Well, for goodness' sake, Mother, this isn't milk. If Traquhair can't get a quota he has to buy on the open market or from Fluach and sell at no profit until he can. He doesn't want his hotel to get a reputation for having no whisky. Use a little sense sometimes."

The Lifeline

She looked at him as though amazed by his attitude.

Then why, she said, didn't Traquhair call his whisky what it was: " Fluach " and sell it as such ?

" Because the local people don't like Fluach. You know that perfectly well. Anyhow, he wants to increase his quantity by a tenth to make it the normal strength and to make a small profit—otherwise he'd merely break even after all his work. Good heavens, we've blended whisky ourselves on occasion and put it in reputable bottles upside down. People never know the difference."

But how did Brian know the man *was* " buying on the open market," said his mother.

Well, there had been barrels coming from the station, hadn't there ? Did she think Traquhair had a private still ?

At the end of the argument Mrs. Creevie gazed at Brian as though he were slowly taking leave of his senses, or as she expressed it : " getting moeur and moeur like your poeur father every day." Finally she said he had spoken to her "very roughly" and with great formality she proceeded to leave the room. For the next seven days they communicated with each other through the daily help, and by notes left in the hall.

One day Mrs. Creevie "suddenly made it up" and was all smiles. Brian immediately became alarmed and wondered, with a feeling of mingled exhilaration and guilt, if the sample might not already be in the hands of the police. But, no. He found out from his barman just what had happened. His mother had been up twice to the distillery to see Major Murray. (Creevie's barman's house overlooks the west wall and rear entrance to the distillery office.)

" Well, Mother, was Major Murray interested ? " Brian said from behind the *Telegraph* that evening.

She feigned innocence and finally protested : " You forget that I have known Major Murray url my life. His sister was a very dear friend of mine. . . ."

Brian threw down the paper and made a breathy speech while roaming about the room. " I don't see why you can't leave it alone. A man like Traquhair doesn't *need* catching out.

The Lifeline

He'll catch himself out. He'll drop off like a rotten fruit. *A man like that is finally beaten by facts.* I don't see *why you can't wait* . . . without sticking your neck out," he added in a much lower tone.

And his face at that moment revealed what it cost himself to wait.

For he seemed to spend his life waiting for "rotten fruit" to fall into his hands. Why should his mother, for instance, ever die if she never moved, never ate anything but small quantities of milky foods and vegetables, protected herself even from the friction of air and never risked a change in room temperature? Supposing she lived to a hundred; he would be standing as now in this room aged sixty holding *The Financial Times* in one hand, three bills in the other, and wondering whether or not he would go away this winter to South Africa or Canada. But if he did go, now or when he was sixty, he knew that she would not forgive him any more than she had ever forgiven any other departure from her wishes. She would leave the hotel to the cat which she would acquire the day he left.

Besides was he capable of going?

What would happen when his mother *did* die?

He felt a sticky, panicky feeling. He couldn't just kiss his hand to all that stock. To do so would be unrealistic and lacking in respect for facts.

"Where would you be to-day," she suddenly murmured in her ventriloquist voice, " if I had always 'waited' ! "

He immediately launched into a speech about his career to date as a hotelier, the difficulties he had overcome, the state of the Seaforth Arms compared to what it had been when he had taken it over and the complete lack of capital assistance which he had had from his mother. She interrupted to say he had always had his lodging; fuel and " frequently food if we were to make a reckoning, dear." " In return," he interrupted her, " for what ? " Didn't she remember? Then let him remind her: he who owned a third of the hotel got a third of the hotel's profits, but that was all. She, who owned two parts, got a manager free, who did not embezzle (i.e. himself) and . . .

The Lifeline

" *Free?* " she said. " Just food and lodging and more than his fair share of the drink." " I pay six-sevenths of the drink bill ! " " And drink eight-ninths of it ! " He did not know how they had got on to this, he said ; what he had been going to say was that he felt no spirit of competition with Traquhair which apparently she *did*. He would like to see the man get his deserts, but that was all. He didn't understand her, he said : " Anyone would think the man had done something to you." Some curious change in her face and position when he said this goaded him to stick to the same line, saying : " Yes, Mother, I really begin to wonder why it is that you go on so, at your age. I know you wanted my father to get that hotel and then you wanted me to get it. But what's Traquhair done ? He's just a paper bag full of hot air. A man like that is soon punctured by *facts*, just as a soap bubble disappears as soon as it touches ground. Good heavens—*he's a child*. . . . Of course if I had any proof that the man was committing some crime I might take a different view. But personally I really don't understand how anyone—you or Johnny Mackay or the Amenities Committee—can take him seriously. I never give the man a thought. . . ."

A few days later Brian came back from the office with an attack of the migraine from which he frequently suffered and noticed the unusual sight of a letter waiting for him on the old oak chest under the barometer. " Unusual " because he took pains to have his mail sent to the Seaforth Arms for the same reason that he had locks on all the drawers in his bedroom. Living as he did close to his mother, he paradoxically devoted much energy to devising means of privacy from her. He often teased her with silence about his destination in the car and in the same way was loath to part with the information which a postmark might hint at, even supposing she would shrink from steaming a letter open, which, of course, she wouldn't.

As soon as he touched it he experienced an unpleasant twinge.

White envelope, ink handwriting and threepenny stamp. There was a girl who now kept a roadhouse in Surrey whom

The Lifeline

he had nearly married for seven years, but it wasn't from her. Nor was it one of those agreeable communiqués from Lionel Spote which assumed a certain importance, local or even national, in both writer and recipient. No, it was an altogether strange handwriting and on closer inspection appeared to have been written in block capitals, but at such speed that the result was like handwriting.

Anonymous ? Brian felt a thrilling fear in his loins.

Anonymous letters are a speciality of the Highlands; few people who are in a position to hire or fire or, say, levy taxes go long without receiving one. Sometimes such letters annoy the police by obliging them to do extra or even normal work, but sometimes they earn them commendations or even decorations from Edinburgh for intuition.

The idea that such a letter had lain within reach of his mother for several hours caused him to turn it over and examine the seal.

" Bri-an," she called.

He did not answer, but went straight past the drawing-room door into the gentleman's cloak-room. There he had another look. Something ragged and torrential about the block capitals added considerably to his malaise, so that his frail hands trembled as he tore at the paper.

Then he read:

> A certain hotel keeper is getting raw whisky direct from the distillery—by a small pipe let into the base of one of the stills. (No signature.)

In the distance his mother called, " Brian."

The purpose of Creevie's curious but intense world apart, often so much more real than any real world, had often been to get the better of Traquhair. Why then, when he held in his hand means of actually realising one of his fantasies, did he feel a flood of emotion akin to guilt, fear and revulsion, an emotion not unlike that when the girl in Surrey had proposed to him in a leap year.

Surely Brian Creevie should have danced, not blenched.

The Lifeline

" Bri-an. . . . Bri-an. . . ."

The silvery voice, coming now, untypically, for the second time suggested she must have seen the letter and wondered what was inside. What was he to do ? Show her ? The responsibility, the threatened prominence, the things people would say . . . all frightened him.

At eye-level were the groups of Fettes 1930, 1931, 1932 and 1933. Above hung the gilt-framed picture of his father which his mother had said, " did Ian no justice at örl," this being her avowed reason—which deceived nobody—for relegating the man's image to a central position among decaying putters, waders, shallow flower baskets and an arquebus.

Brian had seldom examined this picture. Why should he do so now ? Was it perhaps because the overall appearance of that dead Highlander was not unlike that of Traquhair ? There were the "togs" as his mother had always called them—which sat the man like a rough pelt. He was all in autumnal shades— his face, his beard, his kilt, his crook, the very skin of his hands —all autumnal like a silt of fallen leaves. The picture had been done for the old marquess and then presented to the Creevie family by the present marquess's first wife when she was modernising the castle. It had been put out, along with a lot of Indian brass, minor antlers, antimacassars and so on, when Maples had been called in. Creevie stared at the massive relaxed figure. Only the eyes seemed to peer, as it were, from a jungle of brow, beard, hair, weapons and hill mist with a look of dawning doubt, even of defencelessness as though for the moment at least the man had need of as much cover as possible.

A wave of self-pity came over Brian. That man there was a Victorian. Nothing had been right from the start. His father was his grandfather. And then why should he, Brian, have taken physically almost entirely after his mother ? What a greedy and unilateral mould she must have had inside her to have let the visiting seed have so little say.

Brian imagined his father having his portrait painted at the marquess's request in the old back parlour of the Seaforth Arms. It would probably have been in the first year of his

The Lifeline

marriage. While the painter cocked his eye at the rocky, composed sitter, the young wife had probably sat in the front room imagining that the bid for the Strathire Arms was going through like a hot knife through butter, reinforced as it would be by "a word from the marquess" or his factor, who in those days controlled the council, the licensing of hotels, everything. First a word from Ian Creevie in His Grace's ear, out stalking, and then a word from the marquess to his factor would have put the hotel in the bag. But what had happened ? Nothing. And now the Strathire Arms belonged to Tulloch Traquhair.

The resemblance between his father and Traquhair evoked a strange, abashed conflict of emotion in Brian's heart. He wondered if he had been aware of this likeness all along, wondered if it might not have lain at the root of his first reactions to the man that evening last February at the Wotherspoons. After all, some of his earliest impressions, feelings of mingled inferiority and superiority had been geared to just such an apparition in a kilt, friend of a marquess, of rough-spoken soldiers, gillies and sporting solicitors, but enemy of his mother, "education" and gentility.

" Bri-an . . ."

He could imagine that silvery call on two notes coming down the echoing corridor of the years, at first "I-an, I-an," and then with a certain dawning satisfaction a small anglifying change : " Bri-an, Bri-an."

He looked down at the letter. His fingers were trembling. What should he do ? had he really never had any choice, any power at all till now ? What did he want to happen ? Impossible to forget the months of contempt to which Traquhair had treated him ; impossible now not to feel that contempt an echo of the stare (to take one example) which his father had given him outside the beer tent at the Cullan Games—the day the big man had steadied himself on the pipe-major and asked heaven to witness who was ashamed " him or me," the father or the son. Impossible, too, to avoid memory of endless "encounters," hours of fantasy in which he, Brian Creevie, had humbled the man who had patronised him physically, mentally,

The Lifeline

and made him look a prig in front of all those people at the Wotherspoons in February.

Supposing he put this letter in the fire . . . Traquhair might go from strength to strength, for it was not really true that people "got their deserts." Too often those who had merely done their best along the lines taught them at home and at school, people who had tried to be good, not grasping, came off second best. If he did nothing Traquhair would prosper and Traquhairy in general would appear to be the best, the admired "point of view."

On the other hand, he knew what people were like; he knew something of the nature of anonymous letter-writers and had doubtless been the subject of some himself. The whole thing might be jealousy (this word came stickily into his mind).

More and more considerations flocked upon him, some cancelling each other out, some leading him, on different levels into mazes of irrelevance and emotion: back to the resemblance to his father, the dance in aid of Creevie Park. . . . Then suddenly there was a little explosion which wiped clear the whole screen of his mind and there he was walking down the passage saying: ". . . what I've said all along: (*a*) it's none of my business; (*b*) Traquhair will be strangled by facts without anyone lifting a finger against him; (*c*) if my mother wants to play at detectives then let her get her own clues."

He went through to where she was stitching at a tabouret, sitting very upright on the edge of the sofa and inclining the surface of her work to the light. Alert.

"I see you had a letter from Cousin Margaret," she said. "Have they got their new house?"

He let it pass, did not even answer but instead made two tours of the room eating salted peanuts.

"Can I see, dear?" she purred, dipping the needle point down into the stitches focused, as in a telescope sight, in the last remaining window of her cataract.

Perhaps it was boredom, the terrible familiarity of to-morrow before it came, rather than customary capitulation to his

The Lifeline

mother's will, which made him do it—fling the letter down beside her. Or perhaps it was some sudden feeling of resentment against anyone who looked "like that," anyone from God in old masters to Tulloch Traquhair. At any rate, he suddenly felt amazed at his recent concern for a man who meant nothing to him, a man moreover who, to the extent that he was typical, was the enemy of everything he, Brian, stood for.

"An anonymous letter, Mother..." he said contemptuously, and he dropped it beside her. Then he went for more peanuts and walked round the room gesticulating and talking breathily, his voice rising all the time as he reverted to his original theme: how silly they had been to bother with samples and all that carry on. Hadn't he said all along they had only to wait? Well, here perhaps was the proof—that they *still* need do nothing but wait (therefore showing the letter to his mother had made no difference).

His voice had got shriller, more hostile, fastidious and girlish.

Mrs. Creevie heard none of this. Her face, as she read the letter, had assumed the lifeless, weird fixity of a tree-lizard waiting for dinner. Individual words must have swum about in her webby cataract like unwilling flies. But she got them. One by one.

"Brian!" she exclaimed softly, and then in a different tone: "How very shocking!" To his surprise she put the letter away as though it were filthy and went back to her work.

He walked about and watched her.

"I expect you'll be going up soon to your room, dear. Will you take your tea here or up there. Will I tell Mary?..."

He lingered, on the move. The certainty that his mother was acting, that her head was already seething with plans, long-term plans which completely overlooked the fact it was high time she was tucked up for good and all, made his sensitive eyes shine with apprehension. Did she suppose she deceived him? "Well..." he said aggressively.

Politely, as though in deference merely to the difficulties of

The Lifeline

one who was near and dear to her, she said: " Very troublesome for you, I do see. Still, I think they'll make it quite easy for you."

" Who is they ? "

" The police of course."

" *The police?* Mother—think of some of the anonymous letters we've had in our time. . . ."

He had always suspected her of having written some herself, certainly one to the girl to whom he had been engaged.

She said nothing.

" Not tell the police ? With the Prime Meenister coming ! No, Brian—you're joking."

A few moments passed in silence while Brian swallowed aspirin at the drink tray, his adam's apple, prominent, anyhow, thrown into relief like a knee bone by the gargling position which he found necessary for the swallowing of pills.

His mother's voice insinuated itself softly into his ears: " Brian, dear, our interest is one thing, our duty another. The mere fact that our interest might seem to some to coincide with our duty, makes our duty that much harder to execute. But we must not be deterred. That would be too selfish. In fact, not right, dear, at url. Why don't you go up and get rid of that old headache ? "

She avoided looking at him or the letter, perhaps successfully, for a moment later he left the room without it.

That night he slept poorly and soon after one o'clock he rose and himself wrote a letter in block capitals—to Traquhair— telling him that if he was procuring whisky by an illegal "pipeline" then he had better stop for it was discovered. He posted this letter next morning but retrieved it from the back door of the post office an hour later. From then on it remained in his pocket, because he might still send it.

And yet he didn't. It felt like some part of his life—the thing he dare not spend.

40

LOCAL ORGANISATIONS from the Sheep Dog Club to the W.R.I. pick on the games as an opportunity to stage their annual, main, money-making event—whether this is dance, sale of work, amateur theatricals, motor rally, gala or exhibition of cage birds. For the Cullan Games are the *clou* as the French would say of Fluach's " Season."

McCann's annual circus lagers behind the children's playground on 1st August and, from then till 10th August, keeps people awake till midnight with churning machine-music—a noise like the combination of gigantic finger-nails scraping enamel and the trumpeting of lost elephants. On the actual day of the games McCann side-shows form the matrix for the central sporting arena. Indeed, for many, the games would be nothing without McCann's. The blue light from neon and the seed-pearl coronet of naked bulbs round the Wall of Death gives remote Fluach a tantalising whiff of unfamiliar big city wickedness, garish delights, forbidden thrills and fascinating women as exemplified by the Labrador blonde, Chloe McCann, whose shape in tight jeans and sweater, either walking upright or upside down on the handlebars of a bike roaring round the Wall of Death stirs guts already stimulated by bedlam. Even the old folk take an interest in McCann's, though they like to say Chloe is not so good as her mother Betsy, who in the old days had come in on a bronco and even while gripping her mount as a buzzard grips a convulsive, dying rabbit, had popped off balloons with a six-shooter in a way which made present-day westerns pale. Chloe might be a bit more streamlined than her mother, and she certainly gave a greater exultant,

The Lifeline

throat-clawing sense of speed, but the smack of Betsy's bottom on bucking saddle-leather, the dour crack of her weapon and the smell of dung had appealed to the instincts both more broadly and more deeply too. In addition there was a delicate aesthetic in Betsy's marksmanship. Nobody now ever rose and cheered Chloe to the roof, and when her unpleasant looking husband switched off in the pit and appealed for contributions to a fund for those who met injury riding on the Wall of Death, the pennies and sixpences clattered down rather reluctantly and usually from the hands of young people who enjoyed throwing anything into an unusual place just to see what would happen, and certainly the coins did look odd down there, and some of them gave a miniature Wall of Death display on their way down. The old folk fairly spat: " Ye'd no see Betsy begging." Of course as Chloe now picked the pennies up she looked a treat, several treats, and one or two attended the whole performance for just this moment and defended Chloe, saying it wasn't begging at all but well earned, every coin of it. What with the tightness of her clothes she might just as well have been naked. Her brown skin gleamed with sweat and occasionally she looked up under her gamine fringe with a smile for more, which went straight to men's trouser pockets. MacPherson Poltally, who has spent many years in South America, was reminded of women he had met up the Amazon. " By God," he used to say, " I wouldna like to be meeting *her* on a dark night if she was hungry."

In other words Chloe was carrying on the McCann traditions very well. Old and young alike still looked out eagerly for the first McCann bills.

But what was this? . . .

BETSY RIDES AGAIN. The poster burst on the village one morning from all the usual vantage points.

Betsy! Surely Betsy must be dead!

In small print there followed a galloping blurb about the NATIONAL COME-BACK OF BETSY, the pistol-packing grand-momma who could put out a candle at fifty paces firing back-wards between her legs, and who EVERY DAY FOR A WEEK,

The Lifeline

at six p.m. and again at eight, would SHOOT IT OUT with SOLEMN BULL, one of the last remaining genuine Blackfoot Indians still out of trousers.

The appeal to the under twenties, who spent so much time watching westerns was immediate; and to the older people the idea of Betsy McCann and her six-gun brought an indefinable bouquet of nostalgia as though a sudden breeze had blown from a far-away country, from youth, bringing a momentary belief they were all still there. Many of them, long ago, had courted down Quarry Road, which runs past the field where the circus stands, and heard the cracks of Betsy's guns mingle with the chittering of the oyster catchers overhead—and with the long, tail-chasing murmurs of courtship. They had thought Betsy and that time gone for ever, except in name only, and now here she was—riding again.

Chloe hardly got a mention on the bill.

A flutter of excitement passed through Fluach. If Betsy McCann and Mr. Hilldersley were coming back then why not so many others, all those able people who had once made the place such a going concern?

The straths would be inhabited again; smoke would spout cheerfully from the dotted tomb-like ruins along the lower hills, the dominions would give back legions of people, all brave, hopeful, young—and now rich.

A mood of quite irrational Highland revivalism set in. The poster BETSY RIDES AGAIN was plastered up all over the place and set the keynote of this mood.

Tills of shopkeepers creaked in expectation. Every hall was booked up; every room and every bed. The Amenities Committee had special audience of the Council's Public Works Committee, with the Water Engineer and County Architect in attendance. For an hour and forty minutes Miss Jimpson's old, old issue of a public convenience on the foreshore was hammered out again between those who thought it would not be bringing coals to Newcastle and others who looked forward to being shocked out of their wits come the crowds of July-August. Pipe-Major Hew McLeod, Miss Jimpson's opponent

The Lifeline

in council, whose purple civic nose had been badly put out of joint by the mere existence of Traquhair (a man who was often himself, McLeod, only more so and yet nothing of the sort, wasn't that right?) made a speech reckoned by the *Trumpet* to have been the most conspicuous of his career—for it used the convenience issue as a platform for the kind of rhetorical display which was normally the tedious preserve of the convener and a few other big shots like the Director of Education. Once on to Mr. Hilldersley's visit the pipe-major swung naturally into the question of Fluach's eternal shame—always having to borrow a pipe band from Rossiemurchat; sure, he didn't know where to look when he saw them coming. Given funds, he could guarantee a pipe band of his own (Miss Jimpson generously drummed her feet on the ground and the usual tears were plainly visible in her eyes. Ah! If they agreed about music, why not about conveniences?) So if funds were to be wasted on foreshore frivolities, where bairns would write a message on the seat no decent woman should be exposed to ("Shame," cried Miss Jimpson), he, for one, would think the Council had no intention of implementing the resolution passed on native arts and crafts at the time when the Parliament in England asked proof of enthusiasm before they would part with a penny.

He sat down to unusual applause—partly because councillors felt he had got the Rev. Abigail Skene in a cleft stick of obscurity, and therefore the Rev. Abigail, to-day at least, would not be able to spend an hour making them feel ignorant and wicked. But all this is another story—part of a concatenation as it were of minor explosions involving minor figures, mentioned only to illustrate the stimulus to local life derived from the idea of Mr. Hilldersley and Betsy McCann—of the "old days" coming back.

If the poster of Betsy McCann was the material trade mark of this mood then Traquhair was its personification. Like Nelson before Trafalgar his frequent full-dress appearance and ubiquitous spirit did almost, as he had boasted it had, after the football dance, "spread a sense of identity like the fiery

The Lifeline

cross." Bagpipes were heard in the evening down Shore Street above the din of wireless and television loudspeakers.

Scottish extremists began to seem normal.

Miss Jimpson was no longer alone in feeling a flutter when Traquhair came down the pavement like a battleship in full bunting; Æneas Mackay Skimbo had unknown sympathisers when he wrote to " Tulch Traquhair " to record yet another vision of a phantom funeral crossing a river. David Walker from the National Health was joined by other local intellectuals and modern foreigners, in thinking the kilted publican a logical manifestation of democratic, clan libido, an " archetype."

In the circumstances Traquhair might have been expected (after a few inquiries) to hail the resurrection of Betsy McCann with at least the same zeal as everyone else, or even hail her as another jewel in his own crown. One of the McCann posters had gone up opposite the Strathire Arms, beside the man under a bush asking Traquhair day after day if he was good enough for the army, so he had no excuse for ignorance. The words "Betsy McCann" were much larger than the words "Rides again," in fact, so large that they could be read quite easily from Traquhair's bedroom window. But for days he never noticed them.

Then one day when he was curling his beard and thinking of Meldrum the long hot tongs suddenly came to a standstill under his nether lip. . . . A moment later they clattered down with a curse.

He got his spy-glass. . . .

After the briefest examination he hurried out and strode across the public road in his pyjamas, in full view of the bus stop where two people were waiting, and of old Mrs. Mackay's window which had a face in it more often even than a TV set.

Halted in front of the poster his lips moved like a child reading to itself for the first time.

A short, sharp obscenity like a heel pulled sharply out of mud, escaped him. Then he said: " Oh, no, please, God, no," and turned away.

He came back walking oddly, paying no attention to a

The Lifeline

woman who was bicycling slowly up the slope right at him. She had every reason not to expect a giant in pyjamas. He never confirmed that his clothing was decent or made any adjustment to his course which took him uncomfortably close to her front wheel at a moment when she was all but stalling.

"Had she ever known when she was in the way I might not be here now," he said, and threw out an arm and went on out of earshot, still talking to himself. "Quite apart from my own feelings, which she never considered from the word go, she's making a big mistake. On the Continent, particularly in France, they like to see the idols of the previous century return to the boards if necessary in a bath chair or on crutches; they like a president of the Assembly who has to be propped up to speak like an invalid taking soup, an eighty-year-old artiste whose body has gradually become a plump miracle of taxidermy. But here no. Here people will ask why she isn't by her fireside in slippers. Anyhow . . . *Why* has she come? Why, why, why? As though I didn't know."

"Betsy McCann," said Meldrum.

It was the first time Meldrum had spoken to him for weeks.

Traquhair turned to face him. "Ah! You can speak, can you, Reoraidgh? Yes, Betsy McCann." He was about to add something but Meldrum's face put him off and he went back to his tongs muttering the name of the woman whose identity even now in his responsive mind remained fixed in much the same formal blurb as on the poster ". . . pistol-packing momma . . . the One and Only BETSY McCANN!"

41

IT WAS JUST AS WELL that those were busy days in the Strathire Arms. The first guests arrived, new staff were taken on and there was plenty for Traquhair to do despite Olivia's capacity for responsibility and work.

Meldrum had never referred again to his intention of leaving. Like Olivia's black eye the episode faded away. Traquhair behaved as though it had never happened, just as Olivia seemed to behave as though her husband had never protested with his fists. She lived so much at her work that she cannot often have seen him.

Nor in fact did Traquhair see much of Meldrum. For he drank much more and spent less and less time in the hotel, more and more time roaring about in the Donizetti visiting pubs, yarning with keepers and fishermen, drinking with the Wotherspoons till dawn. He spent a whole week-end with Lord Seaforth stuffing birds.

One night when he was drinking with the Wotherspoons, Nadia said that " Rizzio " had been saying that he had heard from his maid, who'd heard it from one of the dailies, that "Muck'n Meldrum" was going off his head—"grubbin' worms for his bird among empties in the dump."

Traquhair groaned and got up.

" Going ! . . ." The room was already trembling and muttering with his immense moving weight. " Gone long ago. Poor old death's head ! Why do I keep him on ? The other day I didn't. I said : ' Either you fit in with life at my hotel, or you go.' I also said : ' You're a sham. . . .' " Traquhair paused reflectively. " He said he would go. ' Then go,'

The Lifeline

I said. Later I took it back. He wept; thanked me on his knees. Said I saved him from himself—made it possible to believe in goodness, in life. Yes, those were his words. He crawled to me. Embarrassing really, when your foot goes through like that. Religiosity is harder to hit than dogmatic religion; but when you do connect—you almost wish you hadn't. The mess is too revolting. Dogmatic religion at least confers a certain toughness on its addicts; but religiosity . . . Indiarubber. Sludge. He crawled to me. . . ."

As though suddenly interested and anxious to remember more with exactly the same vividness he took a few turns about the room in silence, his eyes drifting here and there. " Poor devil," I told him, ". . . poor devil, you avoid me as though I were a murderer. Do you want the place to yourself ? Aha ! Not jealous, Reoraidgh, surely not jealous of Uncle Tulloch. I know you've been calling me an old phoney behind my back. An old windbag. Well, in future beware. Criticism when it is too harsh hardens the fault. You may make me proud of my . . . peccadilloes; you may drive me to flaunt them and feel I owe no one anything for what I take."

" Take ? " said Nadia, but immediately averted her eyes downwards.

". . . well, I take his wife's services." Traquhair lost the thread entirely and began walking up and down in silence. At last he began again, this time as though he were really trying to find something out. " What happened lately ? " he said. " Well, what ? I mean out with it. What ? What *did* happen ? " Candidly confronted with his own question, he crossed one hand over his heart and stared the question full in the face. " Nadia—dear Nadia, let me tell you in two words—*very little*."

" You make everything luminously clear," Nadia said.

" But he doesn't think so. Oh, no. *He* gives me his back. Whenever I come round a corner I see Meldrum's back. Ah, Rory-Pory, not jealous, are we ? Not secretly hating me, day in day out, because you told me your secret; or because your secret could find no worthier patron and protector than me ? Not choosing me as the first sacrifice on your terrible altar. . . ."

The Lifeline

Traquhair was startled by the thought which had almost escaped his lips and even come hand-in-hand with a frivolous laugh. Now it brought him up sharp like a man stopped at the Customs by a detective. For a full minute he walked about in silence. And then quite suddenly he sat down and said: "Merely because I'm adjusted!"

"Where's your glass?" Henry was saying, standing beside him with bottle ready.

Traquhair groaned and held up his empty glass.

"God help me, if he has grassed. Nadia... dear Nadia. I believe I'm fried! Supposing he has squealed? Judas Iscariot!"

Here Traquhair fell into a trance. Never had he adopted a more Messianic position.

They almost persuaded him to explain what he meant, and only with the greatest difficulty did he prevent himself. He even began a gesture, a sort of helpless eureka as of a drunk sighting a vat with a tap.

Then his arm fell and he said, "Merely because I'm *engagé*..."

When he went home he could not look at Meldrum, so the freeze was mutual.

By now events had their own momentum and he himself was a passenger. Whatever his suspicions he could not act on them. He could only persevere.

He summoned old Willie Mackay, the undertaker for the whole of Fluach and Rossiemurchat, to take measurements for the huge plywood maple leaf which was to be hung above the front entrance.

The old man had a vivid sense of the ugly. When it was activated he came all over bleak like a donkey in a blizzard, like now.

As he stared up at the empty space above the front door which Traquhair was indicating with airy and creative waves of his forefinger, his face intimated more and more clearly with every moment that passed, the likelihood of an impending run

The Lifeline

of deaths which would decently exonerate a Christian from the project under discussion.

"Ach..." he said wretchedly, and then stopped.

Traquhair said: "Well."

"It's not well at arl," he burst out. "Who's to design it? Ah canna draw a leaf."

In the depths of his shop there were remains of marvellous carriages and dog carts for duchesses long dead and gone. A "Valkyrie sledge" for Duchess Walpurga, who had built the two-hundred-foot green clock tower, fit for an asylum, on the new castle and put bow-slits in the new castle sculleries; gates with foliage relief work which had been the wonder of visitors and earned him inquiries from London. There was even the abandoned, countermanded beginning of a cradle for the present Mrs. Spote's aunt and this had pickable maple leaves all round it because her husband had been seconded to a Canadian regiment in the First World War.

"Ah cunna draw a maple leaf," he said, clapping his gums shut and then suddenly singing out a whole octave higher: "The wind'll tak it." This in an amateurish tone. "It'll waarp like a soup plate."

"Like a leaf, perhaps, Mr. Mackay!"

"Well, if it's a leaf you're wanting, put up a leaf."

"You refuse then..."

"Ach, I'll see."

Traquhair welcomed such distractions, for they were earnests of prosperity, the P.M.'s visit and the games. They provided him with topics of conversation for those hours he sat beside Olivia in the office; and saved him from thinking or talking of Meldrum. Reciprocally Meldrum himself helped by keeping more and more out of sight and therefore out of mind too. He served in the public bar and when not there he would be in Helen's room, or in his house carving, or on the hill. At week-ends when the hydro workers thronged, he earned his week's keep topping up their glasses, stoking them till their conversation roared, crashed, reared up into song, subsided in curses, became maudlin or confessional. The

The Lifeline

"Stoker" Traquhair began calling him, and when he heard the "hydros" going strong—"*heugh heugh*" (always from a distance—these days he had given up working himself in the public bar)—he imagined Meldrum very like a stoker, perhaps even wearing goggles to shield his eyes from the virulence of the glare he fed. The idea of the man at such moments gave Traquhair a curious exultation as though he were eavesdropping on the very innermost dynamo of life, a force so strong that all yardsticks of what was good or evil vanished before it like shavings in a furnace. Ah, Meldrum, I've sent you home. You should be happy. Dance, Meldrum! Thousands of millions of people may perish to effect a radical compensation in the name of your purring "harmony," and heaven, alas, will not be put in a rage. Isn't that it, Meldrum?

And yet how obviously Meldrum hated "stoking." He went through with it as though his last pleasure was to flaunt his complete defeat and total alienation from Traquhair.

Or was he secretly looking forward to victory?

During that busy, convivial last week did Traquhair really suspect Meldrum? Possibly. But possibly too, like a child that changes the subject, out of anxiety, he chose to concentrate more on that version of himself which he saw reflected in the eyes of Miss Jimpson . . . in further letters from "The Recogniser" and in the invitations to stuff birds now, every other evening with Lord Seaforth. The prospect of soon again being televised also helped to keep his mind turned outwards. In some ways he had missed the narcissistic glow of being a minor TV star and when a Canadian television company invited him to toss the caber at the games, in full Highland dress, he accepted with alacrity though subsequently (when his acceptance was published) felt it necessary to justify himself in a letter to the *Trumpet* in which he recalled the ancient origin of Highland Games—a chieftain's rally and tally of his fighting men in which all, including the chief, demonstrated and practised their strength. Happier would he and all his Scottish forebears have been, he wrote, had archery figured with as much importance as "brutal pitching of pine trunks and

The Lifeline

hammer swinging." History would have been kinder to Scotland and to-day Scottish M.P.s would be congregating in Edinburgh as opposed to Westminster. But the battle of Falkirk was over. What had been, had been, and though he personally would cut a better figure on 3rd August with " six feet of yew and ten deal arrows " he would try his hand at the caber and hoped " other fat, old amateurs " would follow him for the sake of tradition.

The day following publication of his letter he had seven closely written pages of Gaelic from " The Recogniser," and Miss Jimpson at last introduced herself in the street. She said it was going to be the best games Glen Cullan had ever known.

42

ONE NIGHT, in the distillery about two weeks after Misty MacDonald had found dirt on a flagstone, Major Murray was sitting alone in the Excise office listening through the open door to the last footsteps of workers receding towards the distillery gate. It was the heavy settled moment of summer when the birds seem to be rather silent as though resting from the business of breeding, and the green of trees is dulled as though made dusty by roads, and the crops are beginning to ripen and pale. It had been a hot day. A bee came booming in and after a few circuits over the hooded typewriter and the secretary's empty chair, went out and vanished into the pale-blue sky above the yard. Farm smells, sea smells came to him mixed with the malty stench from the long gallery where the grain fermented. For Major Murray they made up the dregs of another distillery summer's day. How many more would there be, how many more times would he lock up after a look round? The ancient window-panes of the cooper's shed, black and shinily opaque as spilt ink, and an archaic winch consoled him faintly with an intimation of other Excise officers sitting where he sat now on other summers' days one hundred . . . two hundred years ago. If there was any comfort in numbers the dead should be happy.

The pouches on his old face were flaccid and his eyes flecked; one side of his lower lip trailed and at meetings lately he had got the impression people were confusing him on purpose. All these new faces everywhere and new methods! The very street lighting in Fluach seemed to calibrate the road with tall pale symbols of his own senility. At home an empty house awaited him. And the fullness of some houses in the villages was a

The Lifeline

sort of emptiness. Hamish Gowan had gone in June; they had been at Passchendaele together and put down many a flask of official sample in the back of his drapery, now the Co-op.

From over the wall came the swarm-noise of Traquhair's new bar. Every now and again it doubled in volume as the back door opened and voices crashed gutturally on the quiet air. He thought fleetingly of Helen and then of Traquhair. . . . Chieftain! He pursed his lips and his face, even here, assumed an expression of stern, responsible respect. He even cocked his head a little as though in reproof of someone standing in Traquhair's way.

Seven o'clock. He went and unlocked the safe where he kept the keg of official sample for official visitors, filled his flask with trembling hands and at once raised it officially to his lips, took a sip—one for the road, then discovered, officially, the flask to be short of an adequate quantity, so filled it again and screwed on the silver top. Then he went round seeing the windows were bolted, the safe solid. After a good deal of official clatter, he reached the door which he locked noisily behind him. This crash was more or less a signal to the watchman and anyone else. It saved trouble if everyone knew where he was. Then he marched forward as though at the head of a company—on, through the yard casting an officer's eye at the coal that fringed the boiler room door, and at the spikes on the wall to make sure there were no ladders. Sometimes he gave a push to a door that was meant to be locked or looked into a black window to see there was no light. Fifty years had passed since a man spent the night inside and drowned himself in the big vat; but it could happen again. Preparedness, as he had often told his company both at Passchendaele and at Upper Kintullochy was half the battle.

It was still broad daylight. The noise of the hydro workers in Traquhair's bar came louder. Every now and again another bus drew up and for a brief moment voices would be harsh, articulate and almost comprehensible even at this distance. Then a crashing door would swallow them and the muffled swarm-noise seemed to grow louder.

The Lifeline

He thought again of Helen serving there ... thought of the letter her mother had written him—just before she died.

The sound of a door banging away on his left suddenly brought him to a halt, turned him in that direction. All doors should be closed by now.

He moved towards it.

There was a wind as usual and now the door banged again a bit more moderately as though having attracted his attention it were now merely concerned with luring him on. There it was: the door to the still-house. A cat came out fast, changing direction as though being shot at, and now as he advanced an old Highland instinct for the consequences of interfering, made him cough loudly.

In the doorway he stopped because it was from there he saw a pair of legs on the floor by the spirit container, just a pair of legs upside down, lolling a bit to one side. The air was heavy with the fumes of raw spirit.

He cleared his throat in a tactful and yet peremptory manner as though given half a chance the legs would leap to their feet and join up with all they lacked. But they never moved.

" Is anyone there ? " shouted Major Murray.

But his voice tailed away and he walked up to the legs and was then in a position to see how they went down into darkness through the square gap. This gap would have been exactly fitted by the loose flagstone which lay beside it like the last bit of a puzzle awaiting insertion.

Dimly lower down, he now saw a face watching him from a cushion of earth.

Never, not even after sleeping with Lily MacDonald had Major Murray received such an unswerving look from her husband.

" Come up out of that, Misty," he whispered. " This minute," and when the legs didn't move he gave them a push.

Nothing moved except what had been moved.

Major Murray got out the torch which he always carried, even during the day. The distillery was full of murky corners and once he had discovered gelignite simply because of his

The Lifeline

torch. (The gelignite was still in the office. Part of his museum.) He fixed the beam squarely on Misty's face.

No need to be the brother of Agnes Murray, Skelly Post Office, who told fortunes, to get an intimation of Misty's new condition. The enormous sobriety of death came across and invaded the major with the most unfeasible of all impulses—to speak to the man. "By God, Misty ! . . ." Then a moment later, catching sight of a leaking rubber pipe and smelling fumes stronger than ever : " That was one for the road. . . ."

And so it was. Spirit was still dripping out of it and the earth was shiny and saturated. Misty must have gone out on a great flood of fire. . . .

The sight of such a great passion had a disturbing effect on Major Murray ; all along Misty must have wanted something to take the place of life, must have pined for little sips, great gulps of the only alternative. But why should Misty reserve such a last stare for Major Murray ? Others had slept with his wife, others had given him uncongenial orders, others had patronised him. . . . Was it that he, Major Murray, had provided him with the deepest insult of all, the pretence of paternity to Helen ?

The beam of the torch strayed from the face which stood out livid and sparkling with moisture at the lips like a road sign in headlights and probed speculatively along the tunnel.

The dulled eyes of a pit pony and a string of tip-wagons would scarcely have surprised him, for this beat all.

Major Murray was an old seventy. After a few tugs at Misty's feet he went to the door.

The lodge where the watchman sat had no window facing this way. The only visible life was the cat which had paused for thought in the middle of the yard. Its sinewy body was crouched ready for further, total flight.

From the hotel came the swarm-noise.

After a moment's indecision Major Murray went back and again took hold of the dead legs and hauled and hauled. It was like Passchendaele mud. Inch by inch the body yielded, came away out of its dark hole. When it was laid out straight

The Lifeline

on the flags he climbed down shakily, muttering and examined all round with his torch, examined a bulldog clip on the earth and a streaming pipe. After a moment's thought he stopped the flow by restoring the bulldog clip. Then he shone his torch down the tunnel. It led straight towards the hotel.

He shook his head.

When Major Murray was out he took a rest to collect his thoughts, get his breath. He mopped his brow. It was getting dark. In a minute the night-watchman would be coming to look for him.

His eyes fell on the body, on the nose—the same colour as his own. He wondered if being upside down had done it, or just the final quantity.

He must think—hard enough at the best of times. For thoughts had a knack of bolting. He could never quite catch them, before they charged off summoned by some faded, faraway bugle, some social imperative.

He saw in his mind's eye the big barrel on Traquhair's counter, remembered hearing people say that Traquhair's whisky tasted strong, that it came from Mull. He remembered old Mrs. Creevie coming up and making insinuations that distillery employees were smuggling it out and selling it to Traquhair or that Misty was getting it out to his daughter—her face as she said, " his dörter, Hammish." Well, he had put a flea in her ear because it was only a few days after Traquhair's appointment as chieftain by the Amenities Committee and it had been just plain as a policeman that the woman was jealous for her son. Besides, a man like Traquhair, a man in a certain position . . .

Major Murray straightened and stirred as though in the chair of the Amenities Committee. The games, the Prime Minister of Canada already at Balmoral on his way here. The publicity!

His old eyes became sterner and sterner with indignation. And what proof in the wide world was there Tulloch Traquhair knew the first thing about the tunnel ? Smugglers' doing very probably. Wasn't the bulldog clip rusty as the German Fleet

The Lifeline

in Scapa? A man in Traquhair's position always earned insinuation. Nelson, Haig, Churchill... they had all gone through it.

His mind became confused as though he were falling asleep.

Hilldersley. The games. The Amenities Committee, Misty, Helen, the barn behind the railway in 1942 where he met Lily MacDonald after the Home Guard exercise—everything went round and round till he shut his eyes.

Again he mopped his face as though drying after a bath and kept muttering, "By God, by God," as though the balloon this time was certainly going to go up, if it hadn't already.

What should he do?

"... knowing what we both know," Lily had written, "and Misty being like he is, I should be obliged if you would help the child in any way you can when I'm gone. Hamish, she'll have little enough..."

There were several empty rooms in his comfortable house. Some had photographs of his children in their gowns when they took their degrees; shelves had school groups, school books. Trench mortars had pushed him up a bit in the world. The man there beside him had gone down a bit. "The daughter," he thought, "even further." But if he had ever taken Helen in, people would have suggested he had ulterior motives in sheltering a pretty girl who "didn't come from the same background"; or they would have regarded it as "proof." Second cousin, yes, but people didn't take their second cousins in. Finally, that letter from Lily could have been a mere device. So he had done nothing. But when he passed Helen in the street and she was cheery, he felt—connected. It was something about her. He couldn't say exactly what.

At last he rose clumsily to his feet and with great difficulty replaced the flagstone and dusted meticulously round it. Then he pulled out his huge, his almost vat-like flask and tilted it vertically above his lips. When it was empty he put it near the dead man's hand, closed the dead eyes, muttered something friendly, unintelligible and went to the door where feigning horror, he shouted:

"Hey—help—help. It's Misty."

43

THE FUNERAL of Misty MacDonald falling as it did two days before the arrival of the Canadian Prime Minister and on the Tuesday of the Ladies' Doubles, which was also market day at Inverurie, promised to be a quick, furtive almost shamefaced affair, a hasty shovelling of earth over someone who had in a sense been dead for many years.

And yet it was a good funeral.

Many blinds were down in Main Street, in the shops and houses. Looking at them you wouldn't have thought so many people would have known he was dead, let alone cared enough to make a gesture.

Blinds, however, are the small change of Fluach mourning. A man's popularity and/or importance is measured more by the number of men who follow him to the grave. Misty might achieve the screening of a few windows but no one expected more. The little knot in Galbraith Street, Mr. Megginch, the minister, Misty's landlady, Mackay the undertaker and the sexton, after conversing for a few minutes round the handcart, went inside as though they might as well get on with the short service since no one else would be coming. Helen, they decided, would have been there before now had she been coming. For all they knew she might have started her baby.

And if she, the next-of-kin, didn't come—would Major Murray? Not only was he Misty's employer but his cousin as well; and everyone, including Mr. Megginch knew what relation he was supposed to be to Helen. Casting last looks over their shoulders the officials filed in leaving a street that was empty except for a child's bicycle on the kerb and the handcart waiting for the coffin.

The Lifeline

And then suddenly Tulloch Traquhair appeared with a black band on one arm and Helen on the other, and behind him an American MacDonald who was staying at the Strathire Arms for the games.

Fluach windows have eyes and Traquhair at first created a most unfavourable impression. After all, he had never known Misty, and had only been Helen's employer for a short time. People thought that the less attention drawn to Misty's life and death, and to Helen's condition and relationship to the deceased the better. In any case, the man was unsuitably dressed for a funeral. This was no moment to look like a burning bush, talk loud, laugh and escort a girl like Helen as though she were his wife.

Then Mrs. Meldrum appeared driving the Donizetti. The back was full of fresh flowers which were soon recognised as coming from the gardens of Strathire Castle. Crabbe, the head gardener was known to be friendly with Mrs. Meldrum, even treating her as though she were a friend of the family.

"*Heugh heugh* . . ."

The deep, spoken laugh boomed down the street.

Laughing!

Shocked eyes faded back from windows.

Attracted by the noise the Rev. Megginch came out of the house and shook hands first with Helen and then with Traquhair.

Traquhair's drone and restrained jollity might have been merely anticipating and usurping by some fifty minutes, the minister's opinion that here was no cause for sorrow. Was that why Mr. Megginch looked so put out?

Now some workers from the distillery had begun to turn up all looking conspicuously black and white, washed, collared and be-suited. Traquhair was heard to express satisfaction at the mounting numbers as though Misty's funeral were some sort of carnival, an apéritif to the games.

Gradually shock wore off and the adverse opinions which had formed in some people's minds, when they first heard and saw him burst into Galbraith Street, began to be mollified.

The Lifeline

Perhaps the flowers helped, perhaps the general attention to Fluach's dirtiest street and most ignominious inhabitant. Only Willie Mackay's opinion of Traquhair, as of the maple leaf, never left his face a single moment and prevented him from looking as professionally funereal as he usually did. With one hand raised to steady his prehistorically tall top hat the old undertaker darted about with his black tails flying, looking like a joke about ghosts, apparently searching for some latecomer who should have been there even if Traquhair shouldn't. Who was he looking for ? At last a murmur, suitably subdued, went round : " Major Murray . . . Murray . . ." Where was he ?

" Well, men from the distillery are here . . ." said Willie Mackay. " And relatives ? "

A voice from the back said : " The major's ta'en a cauld in the heid."

" Is that right ! " said the undertaker and with these words, satirically spoken, he came near to expressing in public what for years had only been mentioned in private : Major Murray's true relationship to the chief mourner. In other words, Helen had no reason of any kind for being present and Traquhair less than none, but Major Murray, cousin and employer of the deceased, owed the deceased an apology and his own daughter, since she was here, a little of his overdue company.

" Well's he not coming then ? " said Willie Mackay. " He's keeping his bed, is that right ? "

There was a murmur of impatience from the mourners. Willie had no need to dot the i's.

" Perhaps we should proceed," murmured Traquhair.

They went into the poky little dwelling, into the living-room where an upright grand with squirly writing above the keyboard was covered like an altar with a tasselled cloth and flanked by two vases of the kind won at McCann's side-shows. Two photographs centred in oval mounts faced the old kitchen range with its little grilled rectangle of coals in the middle of a great expanse of gleaming battleship grey, kettles, hooks and knobs.

The Lifeline

The simple coffin lay on four chairs, its surface bare as a village-hall table.

Mr. Megginch was brief and workmanlike, a style which was matched by the expression of Misty's relieved landlady.

Traquhair mopped a tear. The passing of any one human life is as important as the passing of any other when measured by standards which fortunately do not intrude on daily affairs but which nevertheless do exist and at certain moments gleam, as they did now in this extreme case, like the light of an extinct star, or flicker over people's hearts almost imperceptibly like those dubious streaks of the northern lights on the sky above Rossiemurchat, in the back end of the year.

". . . thy survant Peter whom it has pleased Thee O Lord, to summon to Thine etarnall presence."

"Amen," said Traquhair and Willie Mackay in unison, no one else speaking.

Then they filed out.

It was only a hundred yards to the cemetery. Willie Mackay waved vaguely to the rest as much as to say, follow on as you like, it won't make much difference. As always, his furtive commands suggested impatience with death as though he were sick of finishing beautiful joints, inlays and handles just to give hard tack to beetles and postpone decay. Perhaps, too, the whole business was getting too near the bone.

The minister was again brief at the grave, asked the Lord to notice "the special quailing of Thy miserable survant, Peter MacDonald before Thine awful Throne" and so "grant him Thy mercy without which his life hereafter would quench the hopes of many like himself, still of this world, and so turn them even farther from *Thy* ways, O Lord."

Traquhair's hands remained folded in front of his sporran during this prayer. His little eyes rested on the sheer clammy sides of the deep rectangular slit. . . .

"Oh, death where is thy sting . . ."

He wept at this moment as always because there it was, the sting, two yards long. Huge tears drooled down his cheeks so that his face looked like a lettuce after a thunderstorm. He

The Lifeline

might have been burying a much-loved wife, companion of many years, burying his youth, not a stranger.

Then suddenly someone handed him a spade.

No one had told him that local custom required the chief mourners to fill the grave in.

The clay soil was heavy as lead and about as intractable. Soon he began to mutter and sweat. Finally, the stoker from the distillery relieved him. Then it was all over and someone heard him say: "Gentlemen, I think we owe ourselves a drink. . . ."

This remark quickly became general knowledge. In the opinion of some, the funeral procession became bigger on the way back. Certainly all who followed Misty to his last resting place ended up in Traquhair's public bar.

Drinking after a funeral, like the drawn blinds before, is a custom in Fluach.

It is performed as though it were a sort of purge—as though the dried earth on hands from spade handles and the mud on shoes were too much of an earnest of the common destination to be borne soberly.

Yes, when the male mourners of Fluach come out of the cemetery they'll take a dram with the same alacrity as a tom cat goes courting. Life! They smack their lips and open the fags, hand them round. . . . Life! The unspoken toast glows in even the oldest eyes. Spirit is knocked back as though it were a spot of evidence for the metaphysical sorely needed.

Fluach clay, up at the cemetery, does stick a bit too intimately, clings a little repulsively like some metaphysical excrement . . . some other kind of proof.

The spigot of Traquhair's barrel was scarcely turned off between glasses. Pipe-Major Hew MacLeod, whose salary as caretaker to the village hall, Company Commander and clerk to the cadets, Chairman of the Mod, etc., etc., wouldn't hardly wet a teaspoon, stood at the bar till tears fell of their own accord down his rough cheeks, and his eyes filled with a reddish misty requiem.

Voices came louder than usual and eyes were turned with

The Lifeline

unusual directness, for Fluach, on their host. By God, they had seen the man handle a spade for a few throws. . . . He must have an arm on him like a horse's leg—like big Ian Creevie. . . .

Looking at him, thinking of him there—host to a Prime Minister and yet barman to themselves and escort for the pregnant daughter of the deceased, had the effect of loosening their tongues, warming their hearts. Where had Major Murray been? they said roughly.

"He tak a cauld!"

"Is that right!"

A few smiles were eloquent.

Soon they began to approve "Mr. Traquhair's kind action" openly.

One old man suddenly speaking for all, made a speech to this effect, holding Traquhair's hand throughout, across the counter, and using it as a sort of massive punctuation. "Man!" he said. "You did right," as though Traquhair had done something extremely courageous.

"Mister Tulloch Traquhair," he went on and turning as though he were a herald sent from the Queen in London. "I hope you have a long life and a happy one, and when you come to the end of it, which I hope you won't a minute before you wish, I hope it's easy."

"As easy as Misty's?" said Traquhair. He had heard of the man's weakness.

"Misty's was that and all," said one man knowingly.

One or two near faces smiled reflectively and eyes showed knowledge of a rumour. Pipe-Major MacLeod turned away with the responsibility which became a councillor and with a dainty "Ach," added, "Child's storees. Non-sense."

"Well, I don't know. They do say Doctor Smiley saw Misty after he was found, and said the distillery must somewhere have a waste like a bath—wasn't it?—and Misty must have put his lips to it for he was just full of it—just full. Even his lungs."

Traquhair threw back his drink so that it vanished like slops out of a door.

The Lifeline

" Ai—drrooned, not drunk. Just drooned, he was," said another.

" Well, what d'you know ! " said Traquhair.

" That's right, Mr. Traquhair. Misty must have tapped a pipe. That's what they're saying."

Traquhair's little eyes flitted fast over the faces of his guests, but found nothing there; no vestige of suspicion, just speculation.

" *Heugh heugh*," he laughed. " Happy man ! "

" There was police up at Major Murray's," said a voice from behind.

Traquhair, staring down into his empty glass, gradually closed one eye as though aiming.

44

THUNDER THREATENED all that evening and by nightfall the storm still had not come.

Traquhair could not bring himself to go to bed and sat by the open window reading the *Daily Express*, with a large, dark-brown whisky in one hand. Misty's death and Meldrum's manner were far from his thoughts.

He sipped, read, and rebounded, in a small way, from what he read. Only occasionally he raised his eyes and looked up, with a fearful trace of self-consciousness at a sky which seemed to be getting no rest from light any more than it was getting eased of its water and electricity: for now the towering mountains of cloud, still vaguely whitened by a sun that had long since disappeared, gave birth to the moon low down in the south.

What vistas of silvered and shadowed immensity: Everest, Mont Blanc and Kilimanjaro, one on top of the other, would scarcely have reached the knee of this meteorological wart. Traquhair's little eyes were weaned from the print. The sky sent him, awed him with the thought that it had often looked exactly like it did now above a very different kind of man, a man dressed in skins carrying his home-made nets, a man like Reoraidgh.

By a curious coincidence the lowest part of the cloud hung just above the distillery chimney so that this immense boiling of vapour, which filled the whole heavens, looked as if it had come from the furnace which Misty MacDonald had recently polished. At that moment Fluach Distillery looked like a vent for the whole globe's internal combustion.

He went to the sill and sat without newsprint, without

The Lifeline

company and for the moment at least, without fantasy. Facts fastened his attention: three cats on the distillery walls, sorting things out; then a shadow towards the annexe door—the eldest Meldrum going home.

There was a light burning in the distillery office: a most unusual fact.

" Misty put his lips to it . . . drooned . . . just drooned."
" The police up at Major Murray's . . ."

Traquhair's eyes narrowed and then reopened reluctantly. He raised the glass to his lips.

By nine to-morrow, nothing would have happened. But by ten, by eleven . . . If by midday the police hadn't called then it would mean they intended to wait till Hilldersley had gone away; perhaps till he was back in Canada.

Thought of the Prime Minister made Traquhair smile. Was it the imminence of publicity, as a Chieftain of the Games? He saw himself at the head of everything like a drum-major twiddling his magic staff, the very cause and regulator of the whole exhilarating music. His beard stirred from the passage of that strange, persevering animal beneath it, the joy of Tulloch Traquhair.

Facts interrupted. He again raised his glass.

Meldrum's window gaped in the moonlight. It was like an open mouth possessing one last, front tooth—the gleaming bird cage, which for some reason had to-night been left unhooded.

" Cheer up, Reoraidgh," he thought. " They have found my leak. Even if you didn't tell them—they have found it."

Did he really believe it?

Soon he turned in.

Later, hours later, a muffled explosion shook Fluach. At last, most people thought, the storm is breaking. Others thought, " Blasting," and remembered where it said in the *Trumpet* they were a month ahead of schedule at Cullan. Still others judged the shudder to be the fleet practising off Inverurie; and yet others attributed the disturbance variously to a dog scratching, a wife turning over or their own imagination.

The Lifeline

But what was it?

Traquhair's bed had seemed to hop a foot sideways as though in preparation for a more serious leap. But nothing followed.

He had been half-dreaming of Meldrum and this sudden violent interruption consorted well with the pent-up face which had been swimming before his sleepy vision.

He looked sideways. It was 3.15.

In Glenview kneeling before his bed among the carved oak shields of his sons' Fettes house emblem and medical school rugby shields, Major Murray, who had prophesied for so long that the balloon would go up, received the sound with a sigh of consummation and bowed his hitherto expectant face to old hands as though here, in the privacy of his own bedroom, alone under this deserted roof, beside mementoes of a family grown up and gone away, alone with his old, old uneasy memories he had at last heard promise of ultimate peace.

"Oh, Lord . . ." he began in the hectic, earnest intervening tone of an improvising minister. " Thou hast looked upon the indiscretions of Thy servant with a forgiving eye; Thou hast erased the path of wickedness and evil fame; Thou hast measured Thy mercy to Thy sinning child Helen and vouchsafed security to her home; Thou hast spared Fluach, shortly to be the home of the Right Honourable Joseph Hilldersley, Prime Minister of the Dominion of Canada, guest of Fluach, guest of the Amenities Committee, guest of our most noble Sovereign Elizabeth the First . . . and of Tulloch Traquhair, Esquire, of the Strathire Arms . . ."

A few minutes later he lay asleep with the old creases in his face ironed out, his nether lip slightly agape revealing his bare gums. (On its upper partner, under his nose, there was no sign of the cold which had allegedly kept him from Misty's funeral.)

Unconscious though he now was, there still lingered about the corners of his mouth a trace of that facial discipline and hair-trigger indignation which had for so long publicly main-

The Lifeline

tained the honour of majors, managers and Puritans. And even now after the explosion the large brow and stubborn jaw seemed to affirm, as ever, that the balloon could be expected to go up yet again, and people "in a position" must hang therefore together.

His cat curled up in the crook of his knees and beside him on the bed-table his alarm clock and flask looked like a respectable bourgeois couple, himself and his late wife, in Princes' Street gardens, listening to the band on Sunday afternoon. But his breathing was regular: Fluach could sleep in peace.

Far, far away under a canopied four-poster in Balmoral, Mr. Hilldersley stretched sideways in the dark and took stomach powder. The Gillies' Ball had involved him in heavier drinking than he could manage and during a royal speech on litter he had taken another whisky after promising himself he would stop. To-morrow he would visit his grandpaternal croft. This morning he had been up in the new hovercraft with the Duke of Edinburgh and whether it was that or the piper after dinner, or Nehru in Cairo yesterday he didn't know, but there was a fluttering, as of a trapped butterfly, in his left eardrum. When he lay back he sighed as though retreating, for a few hours more, to the simplicities of nightmare and acidosis. The back of one wrist lay momentarily against his sweating forehead.

Before dawn Traquhair again appeared at his open window and looked askance at the distillery chimney which more than ever reminded him of a great gun pointing at God. Had it fired in the night? Was God hideously wounded? The possibility of seeing Meldrum himself also looking out and speculating on this stale event brought his eyes to the front of the annexe on which the moon was shining full and making it look more than ever like an open mouth. . . .

Something was missing; the single tooth . . . the bird cage had gone.

The Lifeline

Why should Traquhair think twice about the Meldrums moving their blessed bird cage ? No reason, yet he did think about it two or three times. The thing was such a fixture and Reoraidgh's approach to it several times a day such a ritual that to miss it was something like going into a familiar church and finding the altar had been removed. Besides, why had the curtains not been drawn ? ... They always drew their curtains.

Because of the hot night, he thought.

Here we go, he thought. I'm beginning to see fate in chance details ; the next stage is walking on the lines in the pavement and having lotteries on my own safety depending on odd or even stairs. Why bother with small omens. The writing is on the wall, everywhere, like advertisements. And now Meldrum has lost his bird.

Soon he went back to bed where he endured a number of superficial and unsatisfactory dreams.

45

WHEN Traquhair saw the dawn he closed his eyes. But there was no escape: the day of the Prime Minister's visit had come and he was drawing slowly into it as a train draws into a terminus.

He rose, dressed and went downstairs.

The hall clock said seven-thirty and Helen was on the move in the kitchen making tea. Lately the demands of guests, the example of colleagues, and perhaps the discomforts of late pregnancy had improved her punctuality.

"Well, the great day is here," he said.

"Ai!" she said.

"What a night," he said.

"It was kind of hot," she said.

"And what about the earthquake?"

"Was that what it was?"

Traquhair sat down by the stove and looked at the everyday objects with a glimmer of satisfaction.

"Well, what was it then?"

"Things blowing up inside and out," Helen said in a reflective, auto-biographical tone.

Traquhair said: "Cats with six legs on the dope factory wall playing Bartok and a black and silvery mountain beetling above me; then a crump which took me back to the war before you were born, an earthquake for good measure.... Coffee? That's the way..."

Pouring, she handed him a letter. "There's this came in the night. It was on the mat. One of your fans, isn't it, can't sleep without communicating? They're faithful, aren't they?"

The Lifeline

"No stamp," said Traquhair, slipping his finger in reluctantly. "It's my 'Recogniser.'"

"Your what? I expect it's unanimous like my mum used to get. From 'Shocked' or 'A Friend'—they're the worst. Turn you up sometimes, the ones from 'A Friend' did."

"Well," said Traquhair heavily. "It is—from a friend."

"Then frankly I'd put it in the fire unless you've got nothing to be ashamed of."

"Dear Mr. Traquhair," it read, "Your means of procuring whisky has been discovered and communicated to the police. A friend."

Traquhair was not one of those so foolish as to wish to "know the worst." Reality, when at last it banged on the door was always greeted as a stranger even though previously recognised from an upstair's window.

"That's it, then. *Heugh heugh!* Some misunderstanding. Now what..." But already his voice was beginning to change. "This is where your famous justice comes in. Now's the moment of Hallelujah for the MacFarlanes and Creevies, men I could have as my butlers, if I'd ever abused the shortness of life by imitating. No doubt Meldrum will now offer me the balm of his tears, Meldrum who, given a chance, would have done this to me anyway. Dear Reoraidgh. Tell me more about that marvellous conscience of yours, absolute, free from reflexes from all that was dinned into you, that conscience for which you offer a thousand million lives. *Heugh heugh!* Crap triumphant. Farty MacFarlane triumphant. Creevie triumphant. *In hoc signo....*"

Traquhair got up and lurched to the swing door which he blasted wide with one thrust. "MELDRUM," he shouted in the hall.

"For goodness' sake, Mr. Traquhair, the guests aren't called yet!"

"Well, where is he? Find him. Tell him he's in a very serious position...." Traquhair went to the window and looked out into the backyard. "Where's Olivia? Has she

The Lifeline

forgotten that it's to-day the Prime Minister comes? She said she'd be over early...."

He was talking faster and moving about holding the letter. At one moment his eyes rested on the pregnant girl and a sort of hopelessness stayed his tongue as though dimly, but only dimly, aware that he was talking to himself and had been all the time, ever since he first addressed her from his deck chair.

"Come, child, help. Find Meldrum. What...?"

"I never said anything, Mister Traquhair, there're the breakfasts to get." As though to prove her assertion and her indemnity from all his problems, the door opened and the girl from the Islands, the Jamaican from St. Andrews who was reading psychology, and the German chef all came in still greyish and closed-in by webs, mental and tangible, of sleep.

Traquhair made a strange noise as might a sorcerer surprised by his own effects. Certainly he had seen them all before but never so vividly.

"Oh, my God!" he muttered sincerely and reverently. "Where are we? This is chaos. Where's Meldrum?"

Just as he had depended on Meldrum to find the tunnel in the first place he now felt he needed him to "undiscover" it—make things as though it had never existed. In front of the Jamaican and the German he became conscious of the kilt round his loins as though it were a flimsy sail hoisted in a gale. He sat down. "Where's my coffee?"

The Jamaican brought it over to him, and then looking up what did he see, complete? Himself to be in the position of the officer on the Camp Coffee bottle, served by the black man.

"All you need is a turban," he said to the coloured psychologist who looked understandably mystified.

He gulped down the coffee and went through to his living-room where he kept the tunnel-shed key above the picture of the dying stag. Ever since managing the "leak" himself he had continued to keep the key there, partly out of habit, partly because in his heart of hearts he had preserved and enjoyed the illusion that Meldrum was still assisting him. It had been "for us" that he kept the key in its old place.

The Lifeline

His big hand went up with swift familiarity and clutched—nothing; groped—in dust and emptiness. Had Reoraidgh taken it?

At once he went back to Helen, called her out of the kitchen and questioned her about Meldrum. Had she seen him that morning? No, why should she? It wasn't eight yet. Had she seen him last night? Yes. When? At eleven.

Slightly reassured, he opened the back window and seeing one of the Meldrum children, shouted: "Where's your father?" Remembering the guests, he repeated the question in low, penetrating tones, which brought a face to an upstairs window.

But the child was the four-year-old. He filtered off sideways and disappeared without a word.

Olivia normally came through to the office at half-past eight, but they had arranged that to-day she would come at eight. It was now twenty to. He was debating whether to go across to the annexe when he was surprised by the sight of her crossing the yard towards him in her dressing-gown, eyes downcast and arm holding up her hair in the graceful gesture he knew so well.

He went to meet her at the back door. "Well? . . ."

She raised her stunned blue eyes to his and accepted his unusual presence there, at that hour, as though it were only natural.

"Is he there?" she said.

"No."

"Oh, God," she said, and closed her eyes.

"Are we speaking of the same person?" said Traquhair.

"Reoraidgh," she said.

"No. He is not here, I too . . ."

"Oh, God!" she repeated.

"Where is he?" said Traquhair coolly. "I don't understand your tone!"

"He went out—after his bird. . . . But it's not just that . . ."

"His bird . . ." said Traquhair coolly. Her sensational face had calmed him.

The Lifeline

She stopped a foot or so from him and they stared at each other. Traquhair made a half-cock gesture, half-plea but also, reluctantly, half-distress signal. " This is no time for a lark," he warned. " I'm looking for him too. He's in very serious trouble."

" What trouble ? " she said flatly, almost without interest. " Oh, God ! "

He looked into her misleading eyes. The way she kept saying " Oh, God " presumably about some other trouble gave him presentiments of hysteria, simulated or real. He became colder still. Her capacity for dramatising herself and all that had to do with her now, in their present plight, affected him with feelings of acute hostility and a desire to withhold every sensational crumb from her appetites. He was tempted to say Reoraidgh was in the kitchen drinking tea.

She still had a faint mark like a shadow round the eye which Meldrum had hit. But he refused to be misled. Her dazed expression was habitual, her atmosphere of crisis permanent—neither had anything to do with bruises or even disappearances.

" A little solidity, please, Olivia," he said. " There's no need to get hysterical. Just tell me which way they went."

" How on earth do I know where they went ? " she said with derision, and then in her husky warm-toned intimate voice she added : " And what's the matter *with you* ? "

" Dear Olivia ! " he said, this time braving her eyes, and for a moment it seemed as though he might come out with what had surely been implicit in many looks between them, many silences, many avoidances in the past months.

She was looking at him closely and suddenly he perceived she was inviting him to consider that whatever might be his trouble it was nothing compared to hers . . . or Meldrum's, and never had been. For his was unreal. Yes, tears were standing in her huge eyes which now fixed him as though he were and always had been an accomplice in her own personal crisis and should face his share of responsibility. " *He has* gone . . ." she said, with a break in her voice.

" Go on," said Traquhair after a pause.

The Lifeline

". . . The cage must have been blown off its hook. He got up in the night and found it empty. You know what that bird meant to him . . ."

"I'm afraid I don't," said Traquhair. "A bird!"

Olivia looked at him in silence to see if he was speaking the truth then turned away as though she might have expected it. He was being wilfully stupid or he really didn't know. "Never mind then," she said. "But one thing you do know: that's the state he was in—about . . ."

"You?"

"Yes."

"My dear Olivia. I should love to have a Poor-Rory. But this is not the moment. He has got something I must have at once. An object. . . ."

"What?"

Traquhair was silent. At last he said: "Did Reoraidgh and you communicate? . . ."

"He's my husband."

"No time for *non sequiturs*, Olivia, for God's sake! Did you or didn't you? . . ."

"Sometimes," she said.

"Well, then . . . well, then . . . did he leave a certain key?"

"A certain key? . . . What sort?"

"A big black one."

". . . a key?" Her eyes measured him. He turned from them. They put him off. To the extent they were practical they merely frightened him with extremism. In every other way they offered him such a charming blue fairy tale that he turned as though from the *reductio ad absurdum* of his own mirages. He licked his dry lips. "I must find him," he said. "He can't have gone far. . . ."

He was about to pass her and mount the first slopes of the hill, but she held him with her eyes, stared at him as though begging him to understand.

"Tulloch!" she suddenly blurted, and stopped.

For the first time she got through to him.

Suicide, he thought.

The Lifeline

The word pushed before his eyes a sudden vision of Meldrum's recent facial expression.

He touched Olivia's arm—she looked at him. He stared up instinctively at the hills—then down at the sheds.

"Oh, God!" he said.

"You see!" she said.

Torn between concern for the hypothetical intangible threat to his secretary and his own very real and immediate emergency his brain seemed to be splitting away from his heart. One moment seductive whispers lured him to believe that "flowing with the current" of events would be less painful than action and achieve as much; the next loud voices urgently exhorted him to take a pull and help himself, and his secretary....

For a few moments he stood in doubt and then suddenly hurried out towards the tunnel-shed in a manner that was somehow a caricature of his usual prompt and executive movement.

But the tunnel-shed was locked.

After a brief rattle he moved sideways to the tool-shed, whence he issued almost as soon as he had gone in with a spade. This he took to the door of the tunnel-shed. Then he turned and looked round, saw eyes at one bedroom window which receded even as he looked. Across the road Mrs. G. Mackay, mother of J. S., was also for some reason staring in his direction and there were four people at the bus stop, their heads just visible above a line of sloping wall. He took it all in at a glance, turned again and leaned his spade against the shed.

Then he fetched a barrow, placed it as though in readiness for the results of digging, outside the shed, and then because of the eyes, did not use the spade for prising open the door as intended but merely tried the handle again.

Nonchalantly he felt his pockets as though for the key, dived into his sporran—and finally retired leaving the barrow and spade in position.

Back in the house he began calling spontaneously and involuntarily for Meldrum while rummaging in the junk room

The Lifeline

for something with which to break down a door inconspicuously. But what if police came and found a broken down door? ...

"Meldrum," he suddenly yelled. He was crying inside. Then he got to his desk and began blundering through papers, receipts from brewers and Schweppes, invoices, refusals ... At last, he came to two or three snippets of newsprint pinned together—cuttings from the *Daily Telegraph* acknowledging "Conscience money" from "Longbow." His movements became slower as he separated them....

"Excuse me, Mr. Traquhair."

Helen was standing at the door holding an enormous maple leaf of painted plywood. "Willie Mackay left it. Will I put it up?"

Traquhair stared blindly, his little eyes far away.

"What's that?"

"The maple leaf for Mr. Hilldersley.... Is there something wrong?"

"Yes. There's something wrong."

He was on one knee with a hand deep in a drawer full of chaos.

"There's nothing happened to Reoraidgh, is there?" He met her eyes....

Seizing his deer-stalker and crook, he set off up the hill. After a hundred yards he felt conspicuous, came back and fetched his bow and quiver. Then, up again. Every now and again he stopped and shouted. His enormous voice echoed out over the village. Quieter next time. At all events, he must give an impression of business as usual!

A calm front. The thought came to him again and again as he raised his voice ever louder and more frantically over the village roofs.

Fluach's last lobster boat paused and the skipper shaded his eyes looking inland as though up there someone were drowning. And hinds rose out of gullies and walked gracefully away from the exceptional noise.

After two hundred yards Traquhair collapsed on a ledge of

The Lifeline

grey rock. Wearily, as though he had come ten miles, he dabbed at his face with a flamboyant scarlet and green silk handkerchief. Sometimes he rolled his head and put out one hand—addressing the jury. Shareholders take ten per cent, I took one. And not for myself. But for everyone. For the Cullan Games, for Mr. Hilldersley, for Miss Jimpson, Meldrum and Helen. It was for Strathireshire. . . . It was for the hydro workers, for Reoraidgh . . . a Whipsnade to preserve Reoraidgh. . . . For God's sake—a little leavening . . .

"Your Honour, we here have proof that Mr. Tulloch Traquhair was in the process of paying the Government back. Longbow had already refunded a thousand pounds to H.M. Inspector of Taxes. . . ." (*Applause.*) "Quiet, please!"

"How much had he stolen?"

"Your Honour, I protest!"

Now, Mr. Hilldersley was speaking: "This great friend of mine who put his all at my disposal."

Hilldersley! To-day!

Traquhair's little eyes slowly focused on the village below, on the long line of Main Street, the smoke rising from a few chimneys, the deserted pier and the symmetrical bulk of the Strathire Arms. Soon, outside the front porch, little knots of people would be hanging about for a sight of the Prime Minister.

Getting to his feet Traquhair gave a last shout to the surrounding hills. His big voice came back to him changed and dragging with it a great weight of silence—the very coffin, it seemed, of Reoraidgh Meldrum.

Then slowly the big man went sweating down the hill.

At the bottom he found Olivia waiting for him. The sight of her still figure gave him a shudder and he was reminded that the first time he had ever set eyes on her in Bath he had had an immediate *frisson* of dread such as comes from the sudden sight of a cormorant drying its wings on a rock, or the covered bundle beside a road accident.

A moment later and the close-up sight of her queenly concern made him feel a toad for having always misjudged her.

The Lifeline

What had he ever known of her love for Reoraidgh? And why should he always have found it so inexplicable when he himself had been victim of the same derangement.

What, after all these years, did he know of either of them?

"Olivia, Olivia," he said, trying to convey his feelings in this double utterance of her name, "what news?"

"He took the car."

"The Donizetti," Traquhair cried, and somehow knew at once that this was what had happened. "But he couldn't drive," he added weakly, knowing well this would have made no difference.

"You mean he wouldn't," Olivia said. "He could, perfectly well."

"Poor old shadow-boxer, hypnotised hypnotist."

"What d'you mean?"

"What, indeed, my dear? I speculate. This morning you told me about his bird—how much it meant to him. Now my car. He inhabited a world apart—full of holy grails, princesses and dragons...."

"I think he is the realist," she said simply. "But the point is..." She could not finish.

"God forgive me, I know, Olivia. We must find him." Traquhair began walking and she followed. "We must tell the police, I suppose. Have you asked questions in the village?"

"Yes."

He reached the garage and looked in. Nothing but a patch of oil and sawdust in the middle. He looked at his watch. It was ten o'clock. In six hours the Prime Minister would be here.

Traquhair went down the village and duplicated inquiries already made by Olivia while Olivia rang the A.A. and the police. The morning passed in a thousand futile inquiries. Olivia could never express to anyone the urgency she felt. Still less could Traquhair, whose concern for his secretary was qualified, to say the least, by the knowledge that the police, whom Olivia had called in, had already been called in by someone else and might arrive at any moment to take him away.

He rang the Wotherspoons and various other acquaintances.

The Lifeline

Did they happen to have seen his car? . . . No, it wasn't stolen. . . . A little misunderstanding, too complicated to bore them with. He just wanted to know if they happened to have seen it. But the pretence was no good. Soon the whole village knew that his barman had disappeared—on the eve of the Prime Minister's arrival—and his car too.

Then Creevie rang up. Could he lend Mr. Traquhair a barman—or a car? Not only was the offer almost incredible coming from Creevie but, above all, so was the voice. In fact, if it hadn't been for the extreme friendliness of the voice the offers might have been interpreted as taunts. Rizzio wanting to help! It was so confusing that, in a way, it was the last straw.

After that Traquhair gave up, slumped in his chair and waited for things to happen. His sense of impotence was so great that he experienced a sort of transcendental peace though this may have been partly due to the anaesthetic quantity of whisky he had drunk since breakfast. When Olivia came and told him that Helen had started her baby he stared at her with a look as mad as her own and said: "*Heugh heugh*; of course she has." And he raised his glass in a toasting fashion.

Olivia said she thought she would take Helen into the hospital; it would give her something to do and stop her thinking.

Traquhair made an effort. He got up and went through to where Helen was sitting uneasily by the kitchen table, a very picture of expectancy, her in-turned eyes recording events like stop-watches and her fists closed.

" Sacred moment . . ." he began, but his usual voice failed him. " *Tha na's fhearr agaibh* " (" You have what is better "), he muttered, and kissed her head.

He waved them off in a taxi urging Olivia through the open window to come back as soon as possible. She said she might take the taxi on to look for Reoraidgh. He began to protest, but Helen had a serious spasm and Olivia ordered the taxi forward leaving Traquhair on the doorstep with the Jamaican who had carried out Helen's bag.

The Lifeline

"Mr. Meldrum went that way," he said to Traquhair, and he pointed up the back road.

"How do you know?"

"I heard him."

"But why didn't you say?"

"I told Hans."

So the black man and the German had known, but had not told him. Traquhair looked up the steep road leading in to the hills. The man might be fifty miles away by now. Or dead. An enormous apathy closed down on him and he placed one hand on the shoulder of the Jamaican steering him first through the door while at the same placing the other in his fancy kilt-coat pocket. This hand then closed naturally on an object which lay like a backbone in a pulpy mass of bric-à-brac, sweets, small change, papers, arrow heads and what not. It was the shed door key!

He was in the hall then. Just as he was turning to go out at the back the Island girl came up and said Sergeant Murray was in the kitchen, wanting a word with him. Just as he was about to reply there came the noise of tyres on gravel and a strange car drew up at the front. Traquhair caught a glimpse of a woman's silhouette at the wheel. The back windows which had come to rest opposite the hall window appeared to be starred at two points by bullet holes.

"See who it is," he said, and went through to his living-room.

There he sat down at his desk and stayed perfectly motionless like a person at Madame Tussaud's in the electric chair. Hearing the girl come in again, he didn't move.

"It's Mrs. McCann, sir—and a gentleman."

"And where's Sergeant Murray?"

"I asked him through, sir, to wait in the hall."

"Thank you, Iona. I'm coming."

He went.

There seemed to be a lot of people in the hall, but one of them was his mother, a small woman like a barrel-organ monkey in boa, panama, veil and Edwardian skirt, eyelids

The Lifeline

green as mouldy orange peel below ringlet fringe and hands that were never still, co-operating as they did with eyes and tongue in securing the attention of all present, even strangers twenty feet away at Reception.

" Little Twinky ! " she said passionately, raising her arms to his neck and standing on tiptoe.

" Mother," he said, taking her in his arms. " What a delicious surprise."

" For me is there no surprise ? " she said. " But promise : I do not intrude ? Is he here yet ? Say one word and I vanish . . ."

Over her shoulder he could see the clock by the map of the village and lochs. It said three twenty-seven.

Without letting go of her bird-like hand he turned towards the seated policeman and still addressing his mother, said : " Sergeant Murray here, whom you have never met . . ." (he paused while his mother smiled engagingly at the sergeant and the sergeant himself rose awkwardly to his feet) " has come on a little matter which shouldn't take us long. If you'll forgive us, Mother, just a moment and go in there. I'll join you in a minute."

She effaced herself effusively. " Come, Pete," she said, and a man of about sixty with pointed shoulders, whom Traquhair had not noticed, trod out a cigarette with his heel and clearing his throat in an assertive manner trailed after her. " Your stepfather. Don't worry ! " she muttered as she passed. " *Celui-là, c'est un minus.*"

The two disappeared into the big room which was to be kept for golf club socials, wedding receptions and Unionist meetings.

Traquhair turned.

Sergeant Murray came close with a few heavy steps and said : " Sorry to bother you to-day, sir. . . . Meant to call earlier. Got held up." He cleared his throat stickily. " You'll appreciate we've certain obligations in the matter of security with regard to the Prime Minister : on holiday—yes, quite so, but he's still the Prime Minister, if you follow me, Mister Traquhair. Well, we've had a letter handed in at the station which while

The Lifeline

not envisaging reflections on your person or even entirely holding credit itself, any more than such letters ever do, yet involves the station in certain responsibilities with regard to the Prime Minister's person and formalities with which I'm sure you'll co-operate...."

Traquhair did his spoken laugh. "*Heugh heugh* ..." But how empty it sounded, like two slaps on an empty barrel. Never had it sounded quite so spoken. "Go on," he said. "An infernal machine on the premises! But, my dear sir! We must investigate..."

"Well, Mr. Traquhair, as I said, it's not casting insinuation. We'd simply be obliged if we could have a look round your back premises, seeing as it's come to our ears something might come out of them which would sully a man in the position of Mr. Hilldersley—or say, of yourself!"

"But, my dear sir! Of course!" And Traquhair escorted him into the backyard....

46

THE ROAD which winds uphill from Fluach and finally flattens out along Glen Cullan, leading inland towards Upper Kintullochy, is an archæologists' paradise. On the map the area is covered with tiny italic labels such as " Pictish remains," " Broch," and " Hermitage," and even without a map the eye can detect strange banks and contours that seem to be the work of man rather than natural forces. In prominent positions there are stones sticking up in silhouette, like so many colossal ironing-boards, or crouching in a family-like way over a number of smaller stones, all as conspicuously man-arranged as the chimney walls of the many derelict crofts, or as the relics of children's play.

In bad weather it is a desolate landscape. The giant fingers of the triangular, eroded walls point up at the low clouds like so many monuments to a race that left no posterity, which is more or less what they are. Startled sheep, sheltering in hollows and nooks, jerk up their heads and grass protrudes from their suddenly motionless jaws while their bright vacant eyes fix with petulant and apprehensive resentment on any human being that appears. Every lank, heavy fleece is beaded with moisture. Ravens voyage raucously overhead, grouse stutter from slope to slope and the Cullan burn tumbles noisily down towards the sea through shallows like long grey hair, and pools dark as night.

Apart from the shepherd, the only people who ever come up here are occasional hikers in the summer and the marquess's stalker with a guest from the castle. A whistle to a collie, holiday voices or a single shot—these are the few human sounds which occasionally disturb Glen Cullan.

The Lifeline

Birch fringes the burn and on the face above Fluach there are a few isolated rowans, and lower down patches of sycamore, oak, rhododendrons and thorn. It was near these that Meldrum first parked the Donizetti and began looking for his bird, calling it with a strange sibilant noise and holding out his hand with food in it as though from somewhere the bird was watching him. . . . But always in vain. Then he drove farther in and repeated his random invitations.

The school children who sang rhymes about "Muck'n Meldrum" and their elders who found him " odd " would have felt confirmed in their estimation by the sight of him hunting so confidently in such a place for a bird—a tame bird which was probably already inside a cat or a hawk. They would have noted his black broody probing stare turned slowly this way and that towards the darkest places of the undergrowth or towards the skies demanding with relentless determination the appearance of his pet as though without it he could never consider going back.

He pushed on, deeper into that long decaying fossilising valley of the past, pushed on as long as there was cover enough for a bird.

Whenever he saw a likely place (likely, that is, to him) he parked the Donizetti opposite one of the small white diamond-shaped signs which at regular intervals post the passing places on the minor roads of Strathireshire.

Sometimes he sat for a bit before getting out. A passer-by seeing his face would have been tempted to "sympathise" without knowing anything about why the man was there. But only tempted, nothing more. For sympathy involves sharing, if only by identification, and no one in their senses would have risked that.

It must have been about the time Traquhair was calling for him on the hillside far below, Meldrum, after a long stare in the direction of a cliff that fell sheer to some caves, heard a squabbling and twittering of small birds. Such a noise might have denoted the presence of a hawk or perhaps of a freak bird.

The Lifeline

His own pet might well have roused just such confused, mobbing reaction.

He went off uphill and soon stood at the mouth of a big cave—the cave which is well known in Fluach and figures prominently in various local legends, the chief of which is that it is connected with the sea by a tunnel. He stood staring up at the silvery wall of rock where, here and there, rowan trees and bracken sprouted even where there seemed to be no ledge of soil. A blackbird gibed at him briefly and flew off, leaving silence where there had been twittering. Meldrum held out his hand in the feeding gesture and repeated the sibilant noise which he had used earlier. Nothing came, though his eyes roved with such serious expectation that anyone who had been with him must soon have been affected by his improbable confidence and joined him in raising their eyes to see if they, too, could see this fugitive by which he set so much store.

Suddenly, in the black mouth of the cave there was a fluttering sound such as a bird caught in a house or garage makes when it stalls and turns from a window in mid-air. His eyes dropped. There was a glimmer of wings which against the background of darkness did seem briefly white. It could have been imagination, it could have been merely his desire to see what he was looking for—a desire which by now, faced as it was with the terminal blackness of the cave, must have leapt at any opportunity to find.

Meldrum stepped in and immediately felt the coldness and dankness. Of that at least, we may be sure. Stray patches of light to right and left and even higher up revealed that he was in a sort of gallery which had other openings at other levels. The place seems endless but it is an effect of light. He did not go far in. His pet was not a bat. Quite soon he stopped as though conscious of the proximity of what he was looking for. Here in final darkness would be his bird, not in the cage he had made for it, but in liberty, in its own right.

Happiness and expectation showed in his face, and as his eyes became used to the darkness he started to look about him.

The Lifeline

He might have been in a cathedral with some piazza bleached white under a southern sky behind him. But this could not be a Christian cathedral, with some Olivia-like Madonna, a rather garish albino lady in a side-chapel holding court alone among tinsel and candles to some lonely old women. Perhaps if it could have been that, this forlorn man might have looked no farther. But it was not that. And as far as containing an Olivia was concerned—even his own home did not now do that.

The vague stone shapes around him might also have been some old museum after closing time, full of fallen idols, dead investigated symbols—and he himself a down-at-heel curator who, unknown to visitors, had no home, but stayed on each night, without food, drink, sleep; without ageing, a living ghost, a soul in search of a bearable body.

A sudden movement caught his attention in one of the stray spots of light on the ground. He moved towards it, quickly, as though this place to which he had been guided, if not called, first by the sound of mobbing birds and then by the flutter of wings, must end in one of those extraordinary finds which almost everyone has, once in a lifetime and which they then relate, often in a tone of apology, as though it were some sort of miracle which, in the telling, can only invite everyone's doubt or even suspicion.

Yes, the movement came again. He moved closer, stooped . . . saw nothing but stones and blinding whiteness of sunlight. Certainly no bird. . . .

He bent close, for there *had* been movement. He must have been sure but could see only a pattern of earth, stones, light and shadow. . . . He put out his hand with fingers extended. . . .

It was a snake, with open mouth.

His body froze and then seemed to go slack and sleepy as though hypnotised by horror. The tiny head was raised and the mouth wide open showing curved fangs, slim and sharp and hollow-ended as hypodermic needles.

Now he could not move, could not, could not. . . . What dream was this, or cerebral confusion, what dream of living

The Lifeline

things for ever borrowing a value which never was and never could be theirs?

Meldrum was in the car. He opened his eyes. He could not dream any more for his dreams had become his thoughts.

He sat and sat without moving.

47

THE SUN was sloping gently down to Ben Cullan and the shadow of the distillery chimney lay across the annexe yard as though telling a late hour on the face of a vast worn sundial.

Meldrum's children had huddled by their back door, disturbed and awed by the sudden appearance of their gigantic playmate with a policeman. In the past they had heard him talk contemptuously of flatties, rozzers, coppers and bogeys, but now they heard him say " Sergeant Murray " in a tone of shared responsibility as though he, Al Tulloch Capone, had become a plain-clothes bogey himself and an officer bogey at that.

They watched him wave towards the various sheds, hen runs and garages against the distillery wall and then hand Sergeant Murray first a bunch of keys and then one large key by itself. They saw him bow, almost imperceptibly, from the neck and then turn leaving the policeman by himself. As he passed he winked and said, " Watcha ! " None of them answered though they stirred uneasily as though touched by a weak harmonic of all those vigorous games they had played together. It was no good. Something was missing even from his wink. Had he really killed a lion with an umbrella ? Roderick, the eldest, stared at Traquhair as though prey to painful inklings.

One of the daily helps came to the annexe window and then sank back into darkness as soon as Traquhair, looking up, caught her greedy, cop-conscious eye.

He winked to the children again.

" Hiyah ! " said the eldest weakly and dropped his eyes.

Traquhair walked on. He was tired out, tired through and

The Lifeline

through. This moment felt not so much like the evening of a day but the evening of a whole life. Years of whirling faces, countries, languages, and heterogeneous experiences seemed to be suddenly slowing and settling down into this one leisured walk across a quiet yard, away from a man with a key, watched by a few reluctant children.

Calm waters sucked towards the lip of a roaring torrent are often velvet smooth. If he looked as usual now, exactly as usual, it was for the last time.

"*Herzchen!*" murmured his mother as he came in and rushed towards him. "Tvinky. The kilt . . . Words miss me. *Der edel Mann ist nur ein Bild von Gott!*"

Bending uncomfortably low, he again kissed her tenderly on both cheeks.

"Welcome, little monkey," he said fastidiously. "I don't know that language any more. The associations disturb me too much. The words miss me."

"*Ja, ja,* of course. Little heart," she went on, "you don't know Mr. Vessuchi, do you?" She was fidgeting and speaking carefully as though to a bull that had somehow got into the house: one ill-considered word, it seemed, and he might throw her and her escort out. "He is a great help to me. You know me, Tvinky, I have to have a man. Yeah, yeah, sure, don't all speak at once. I know what you're going to say. But when you get to my age the birds don't hang on every bush; I should know! And where or when better than to-day of all days, here of all places, Fluach—my God, Tvinky, forty-five years to-morrow! You don't know what you did to me coming in like that with a kilt and your beard like a burst sofa, the room trembling. It might have been him all over again. . . . *Ach Gott.* . . . I feel faint."

"Shall we sit down," said Traquhair in a stranger's voice. "I don't know what you're talking about, but then I never did."

At any moment he expected to hear a telephone, ringing like the bell of an ambulance, with news of Meldrum; or the sound of police feet.

The Lifeline

He felt he had one small purpose left, one thing he would like to achieve in his remaining moments of liberty: keep things disguised. If his mother became involved she might try and behave responsibly and that, at last, would be more than he could bear.

Meanwhile she had stopped in mid-gesture and looked round as though amazed they should be staying in this deserted wedding-room.

"Tvinklein, you have a Prime Minister, so, so I know— do I not! But is there nowhere but this morgue. Give the kitchen, the boothole, your bedroom, Tvinky, but not this morgue. It makes me whisper . . ."

"I haven't noticed it. And if you don't mind, I'd sooner . . ."

Instantly she closed her eyes and raised a hand as though disowning her previous utterance. "Of course, how like to me to underestimate. I tell Mr. Vessuchi, *cavaliere errante*, we are lucky to be here at all. Then I go and forget so myself. Old-fashioned virtue, respectability has its place. For what is it that I have missed? I look at Mr. Vessuchi beside me—*plus ça change!* Ah, Tvinky, I make a particular effort to come when I see in Court Circles the Canadian Prime Minister leave Balmoral to stay with my Tvinky. And where? I ask you. *In Fluach.*" (She closed her eyes.) "You see, all these years I torment myself wondering was it for the best, pretending— sending you to *Realschule*, to Uncle Cornelius and *la vie bourgeoise* in Hamburg, while I . . . Ah, Tvinky, there are certain things I have never told you."

Traquhair blinked twice while his mother took in breath like a singer.

"For some pipple they say the past is a help in difficult times; it helps them to live. For me it has always been ferh confusing. And for you—what a hope! But how to tell him . . . above all when to tell him. Years ago I think soon because youth is toff. A year or two with Cousin Cornelius in Hamburg and at *Realschule*, then Gottingen, then Oxford; then I tell him. And so one day I am performing in Liverpool in 1937 and I say to-morrow Sunday I go to Oxford to meet my English

The Lifeline

gentleman for whom I have endured nineteen years with Isaac Gruber McCann and shot a million balloons from horseback, flirted with lions, lived and loved everywhere and nowhere. I go to old Oxford. Statues like sucked Edinburgh rock, bicycles. Where is Tvinky? He has gone to Spain with some poets. My *Gott* what a fool, I say. His dig smells like a bear's cage without a window and he has added an armchair to the end of his bed to hold his feet—but he has gone. I go back. I write letters, letters, letters. Already terrible things are happening in Germany. I get news from everywhere. What to believe ? Tvinky is in Major Attlee's battalion at Estremadura. He is slow, what else. There is no cover but empty wine casks. . . . *Ja, ja!* He find a barrel big enough for salvation. *Il n'est pas tellement bête, celui-là!* "

Here she looked appraisingly at her son. " You think I didn't know ! But I did. Tug McDougall . . . *ja*, now you know how I know ! One man shoot into the barrel for luck and Tvinky get a wound. He become *Grand blessé de guerre*." (Here the little woman clamped a hand on her thigh and laughed. A faint frown appeared on Traquhair's face.) " At that moment I was swinging by my teeth above two *hareng*-fed tigers so he should learn Latin and Greek and be a gentleman like his father, and not suffer for—for what ? Ah ! " (She smiled wistfully, blissfully.) " For the beginning, Tvinky ! "

Opening her eyes and fixing them liquidly upon him, she said in a low melting voice : " Tvinky ! You have never asked me who was your father. . . ."

He considered his reply. And she waited to hear it. At last he said : " I took it that it might be the man to whom you were married."

" Shame ! " murmured the tiny woman softly, looking at her son with a spark of real spleen.

" Forgive me," said Traquhair.

" And see ! You still do not ask me ! "

Traquhair remained silent.

" Still, will I not jump my horses before I come to them. Listen, Vessuchi, *pantolino*, Spain finish. Europe begin. And

The Lifeline

such things in Germany, such things! Of course I think to hear next of all Tvinky's friends and poets in forefront of general war against the Nazis. Many a hero was upside down in his first barrel, but did well in his second. So where are they? Russia? Where on God's earth . . . I get a postcard from Hampstead. He is fireman. My giant is putting out St. Paul's like a little boy pissing on a bonfire. Then he is in the navy. I get a picture like the man on Players cigarettes because whatever my Tvinky does he stands out and now with his naval beard he loses his father's mouth which stood in (my *Gott*, I tell him once: ' Jan, you could only kiss a woman if she had a beak ') and so I think perhaps after all, things will be well, and when he is settled down in Dover I will tell him. Suddenly war ends and he starts acting and I think, ach, he will never like women properly. Then he marries—Vera Prokokieff —I decorate her. *Ja*, Tvinky, you must allow me to decorate her memory and when you were divorced you gave one very one-sided picture. I haff an allegiance to my sex and so I haff to decorate her.

"She was *héroïque* . . ." cried Mrs. McCann in sudden parenthesis, clapping her palm to her forehead above closed eyes. " She tried!

" Then what? I never see him. He is here, he is there, he is this, he is that. I give him shares in the circus. He has four hundred pounds a year. Lives in Sussex windmill, then on a barge. His name is Mercedes, Furstenburg, Garibaldi; he comes to see me once, twice, tells nothing, returns to Tullio Garibaldi and then suddenly one night I see men in fancy dress on television and one bigger than the others, so I look closer and there shooting a bow and arrow is my Tvinky. Hola, Forward Men. (That voice! *Wunderschön*.) He cries, Tarry a moment longer, Robin, and I trough der bishop hath had it. *Ja, ja*, no doubt at all: it is Tvinky, my Ruben Amadeus Gruber. Like me—in show business. Am I pleased. I am killed. Is *he* pleased? Look at his face. *Mann kann Geld zu tever kaufen!*

" Well, so you marry again. You want to give the public

334

The Lifeline

the impression that you dig women. What happens? Divorce. At last you take up with Mouldrum: you grow a shadow as well as a beard. You have Mouldrum's wives and Mouldrum's children instead of your own. Tulloch Traquhair. On B.B.C. you are often, every night. I think he will never settle down and now what does it matter to him who his father was? What can a thing like that matter to an actor. So when we meet at Scotch Corner in '55 I say nothing. Then what! I open the *Daily Mirror* and I see the Prime Minister of Canada goes to stay with TV star Tulloch Traquhair and *where*? At Fluach... Court Circles in *The Times* confirm. So the moment has come to tell him."

She again closed her eyes in mid-floor like a Puccini heroine drawing in breath for the last attack.

"Fluach... my *Gott*, I say *Fluach*!... Ah! The breeze smells of seaweed and the waddlers twitter on the bitch. My skin is smooth, my muscles covered with the tender cushions of youth, I sing in the mornings—*ja, ja*, the circus is rough, raging male god and I, the renegade niece of Rabbi Josef Cornelius Gruber, am a priestess of the temple steps, and think I haff no love but him, the circus. But perhaps I have been merely waiting, waiting for something which neffer come for one day as I shoot the balloons from a bucking horse I see a man cheering in the audience and the world stops: *Mein Gott*, what a man! It is Moses!"

She took a little walk, a few steps this way and that before she could continue—now in low lyrical tones.

"Every day, Tvinklein, he comes to the same place... waves... cheers. He is in a kilt, a reddish kilt with a hairy purse at the bottom of his tummy like a sleeping fox. Bite me, I say, and I get roses in the dressing tent and a bottle of whisky like Pavlova. Divine Fluach whisky. One day he is missing. Where? I am out of my mind. Where has he gone? A message comes. 'I am taking the Prime Minister out duck shooting. Till to-morrow! Cheerio *chérie*' (He learn French in the war.) And to-morrow I catch sight of him in evening-dress. It was then I sent you the Camp Coffee to Hamburg

The Lifeline

because the officer on the outside was a little like. That was how your nurse started to drink it. Do you remember? ... Years later you wrote one of your first letters asking who the man was on the bottle, the Highland officer. And I said, ' Jan Creevie.' ... And then that joke we had for ever because I preserved it, with tender passion. ' Have seen a Creevie? ' ' Am going back to Creevieland.' It was how I talked to you about your father. ' A regiment of Creevies,' and in the war you wrote me, ' We transported a battalion of Creevies to Alexandria.' Well, there was a Creevie, indeed there was. Not for long. A few summers—three, four ... enough. He loved me. I realised I had never been loved. Not before, not since. So gentle, so fierce. One day he shoot like an angel; like me from horseback and without aiming. So—plop so, *Quand même*, he nearly fell. ' Drams ! ' Ah, those drams. ...

" That summer I went away and he died. Perhaps would I have died too, Tvinky, if it hadn't been for you, already four years old. And to think I had got on a bucking horse to have a miscarriage and get rid of you ! When he was dead I had you put in cotton-wool, yeah, in a glass case."

She surveyed her son with eyes that congratulated.

" In a way so like him—you are ..."

" Like ... Ian Creevie ..." said Traquhair in a toneless voice.

" Like Jan Creevie," she said.

" I never saw him," he said.

There was a long silence during which Mrs. McCann stayed with her eyes fixed tearfully on her son.

" In other words," Traquhair said gingerly, " he was my father."

" That is so, Tvinky. Accept it ! "

" To do anything else would be ... unreal," said the big man quietly.

Vessuchi at this moment took out a packet of black cigars and after some preparation lit one for longer than was necessary to get it going. Then he put the match back in the box, dusted himself and trimmed his trouser turn-ups. His face reflected

The Lifeline

not the slightest concern. Nor, on the other hand, did he seem impatient.

Mrs. McCann went on: "I am getting old. Perhaps I do wrong to make a piece of my life, knit it"—she made a precise gripping gesture in the air—" all into one. Perhaps I should not have told you. . . ." She raised her eyes to examine his face. " But I think too, sometimes, that perhaps all these years Tvinky avoids me because he feels at the back of his mind something was always missing. So when I read you entertain a Prime Minister—*ja*, also a Prime Minister like Jan —and are in Fluach—like Jan—then I feel *frissons*: all things knit together like in a poem and I, *die ewige Jude*, have not wandered in vain. Nor you either. So I say one more gallop. Saddle Cello, I say, load my gun! For Betsy rides again . . . in honour of the Creevies."

She had approached him timidly and for the last few words had stretched out her arms with perfect theatrical timing.

Traquhair sat still, his eyes fixed at the floor by her feet. Vessuchi coughed like a man in a waiting room and suddenly extended one pointed shoe so that it came within the line of his momentarily appreciative vision.

Steps sounded outside, and the Island girl put her head in.

" Mr. Traquhair, sir! Please."

" *Ja, ja*, he kom he kom."

Traquhair's eye flitted up at his mother's face. He rose.

" Who is it?" she said. " The Prime Minister?"

" Perhaps," he said.

He was about to turn and move towards the door when he stopped, came back and kissed her.

" Little mite," she said. " How they love you!"

" We all imagine such strange things, don't we. All kinds of things. You that you ought to have been born with a revolver. . . ." He threw out a hand unable to finish the sentence. " Me that my revolver was in proportion to . . ." He shook his big head mutely and lowered his lips to the thinning hair which lay beneath him. " Thank you for telling me. I'm glad you came. In the years that lie ahead there will be

The Lifeline

moments when all this knowledge will provide food for thought, perhaps help things fall into place—if only like the balloons you used to shoot," he added in a mutter.

" Ah, Tvinky, what is wrong ? Your voice is funny. What have I said ? I should never have come . . . Tvinky, *you are weeping* . . ."

" On the contrary," he said, turned and with hands on the top of his sporran he made for the door, behind which he could imagine the face of Sergeant Murray doing its best to conceal triumph. He knew that particular expression, having been arrested before.

48

But there was no Sergeant Murray, no policeman of any kind in the front hall.

"Where?" said Traquhair, turning to the girl from the Islands. At this moment the hall window was filled briefly with the slow-moving silhouette of a big black car and the profiles first of a chauffeur and then of a small man in the back.

The Prime Minister!

After a moment of blank acceptance Traquhair's little eyes suddenly reflected a vestige of responsibility.

"Let him in, Iona," he said calmly.

So, Strathireshire police were going to behave tactfully. Not for nothing had Chief Constable Scroll won the O.B.E.

Or had Sergeant Murray found nothing?

Traquhair had time to take a look out on the back. The door of the shed that mattered was swinging and slamming in the breeze. Three Meldrum children had gathered in a group as though for security a few yards away and in such a position as to be able to see in, when the door swung wide, see in without having to go close. Their manner suggested a corpse lying just out of sight inside. Well, now he knew.

He turned at last wholly towards the front, a mountain of massive, formally informal hospitality, a man hurrying from affairs almost but not quite as important as those of a Prime Minister. A strange elation possessed him as though—yes, as though he had risen to stand on the back of a galloping horse.

Joseph Hilldersley was a small man in his middle fifties. High office and the business of getting there had resulted in a

The Lifeline

certain taxidermy of, at any rate, his face. Anyone could have deduced from a careful perusal of several daily papers that in the last hundred and sixty hours he had eaten with General de Gaulle, the Sultan of Kuwait, Nehru, Nasser, a Belgian uranium group, and the Queen of England. He had seen a dam, unveiled a memorial at Dieppe, addressed two thousand blind ex-servicemen, flown ten thousand miles, been up in a hovercraft with the Duke of Edinburgh, and endured temperatures varying from a hundred and twenty to forty degrees Fahrenheit (possibly swallowed eight different kinds of pills designed to effect various kinds of physical or psychological adjustment), conversed through several interpreters and read several hundred thousand words of condensed background information. He had worshipped in precincts dedicated to Allah, Buddah and to Catholic and Presbyterian Gods. And now finally he had visited the lost, crumbling patch where his ancestors had eked out a meagre living in a desolate strath.

At the end of it all he had come to rest face to face with Tulloch Traquhair.

For a few minutes conversation was stilted and twice when Mr. Hilldersley asked his host a question there was no answer, simply silence. On each occasion Traquhair subsequently started a new subject as though the last had been cleanly finished. Once or twice the larger man, in coloured dress, permitted himself a long stare at the smaller dun-coloured man as though the events of the last few months and in particular the last few hours had deprived him of confidence in the material solidity even of a Prime Minister. The simple truth, which would have been plain to the meanest and least informed observer was that both men had a lot on their plates.

Hilldersley, in fact, was under more strain than was implicit in his itinerary and agenda. That very morning, at Upper Kintuliochy, at the moment when he had been trying, as at Dieppe, to achieve a degree of concentration sufficient to fit his face for the cameras, and was raising his eyes solemnly, commemoratively and nostalgically from the blackened hearth

The Lifeline

of his ancestors, he had seen above the cameramen a curious golden whizzing object in the sky.

Mr. Hilldersley's eyes had narrowed like those of a man striving to recover focus through tears. Several people had spoken to him and got no reply. Flash bulb popping redoubled, the photographers almost shouted for joy, almost called to him to " Hold it," but he had not heard or seen them; he had had eyes, narrowed, visionary eyes, only for that shimmering circular apparition in the sky above the blackened scar of the ancestral hearth.

A Prime Minister who confessed to having seen a flying saucer would be a sitting pigeon for his opponents. It would help his party less than if he appeared in a strip-tease in Quebec.

And so, having unwittingly provided every Canadian newspaper with a splash photograph to suit headlines about the ancestral home, confirming thousands of Scottish votes, he made himself look away and his grey urbane face, after a period of partial dislocation, had been able, more than ever before, to resume the plasticity of an endlessly travelling salesman. By now his eyes were again passively but perpetually alert to the smallest demand of his multilateral function, though for a moment, the spectacle of Traquhair had momentarily struck a harmonic, as it were, of the flying saucer.

They took tea alone in Traquhair's living-room. The subjects at first were light industries for the Highlands, and Highland field sports. Seaweed, bracken, sheep, soft wood, atomic piles, a Canada-Strathire Association, hotel services by helicopter and Traquhair's projected "moon terminus" all came under the sweep of their responsible speculation. Meanwhile each, unknown to the other, was recuperating. As time passed Traquhair's voice resumed at least part of its normal impressive brio. His gestures came back to him and towards the end he was telling funny Highland stories and touching on his experiences in Spain, Cuba, America and the veldt.

His ironic remarks about various established institutions such as the White House, British landowners, trade unions, Sundays in Ottawa and Fluach submitted Mr. Hilldersley's

The Lifeline

capacity for tactful adaptation to the greatest possible strain. The P.M.'s qualified agreements of one moment were soon running counter to the qualified agreements of the moment before. While escaping into smiles of gentle tolerance he tried to reassure himself, with careful probes, that Traquhair was joking. But Traquhair was on the rebound and he was drinking. The tact of Strathireshire police, he began to think, might extend to a lifetime. People who had the ear of a Prime Minister (he began to feed with his eyes on that very organ) were *never* arrested. Rightly—for they had an opportunity to affect the destiny of nations . . . of the world. (It was coming to him now, his true position, like a rush of blood to the head.) If at any time their peccadilloes were revealed then they were very properly hushed up. Did anyone ever worry Winston Churchill in the war with a questionnaire about his tobacco ration? No. Well—*mutatis mutandis*—he could see Sergeant Murray, a man who himself, anyhow, survived only by the profoundest tact—simply recoiling from the task of accusing the friend of a Prime Minister just as might the United Nations recoil from the task of evicting everyone but Red Indians from America. He was established: finish! Slips-up there might have been. But they were buried under the imposing edifice of the present moment, solidly grounded, on the *fait accompli*. Even the Cecils, as he was fond of remembering, had started as embezzling accountants, Bulganin as a murderer.

Traquhair inhaled deeply, drank, laughed. His cigar smoke mingled with that of Mr. Hilldersley and at six-thirty he took him upstairs to rest, conscious of eyes peeping from behind door edges, guichets and passage ends, eyes assessing, among other things, the cordiality of their relationship.

The terrors of the morning had suddenly shrunk to their proper dimensions—become very small. By now, Rooraidgh was on his way home. . . . Coming to heel. Growing up. Facing up. Cutting the cackle.

He came downstairs turning his feet well out so they should fit on the space available and walking right in the middle of the way.

49

THE SPOTES' SHEPHERD saw Meldrum sitting in the Donizetti at the foot of Ben Niall at about eight o'clock that evening. It was nearly dark—and he was sitting so still the shepherd walked out of his way down, past the car, to see if there was something wrong. " If I didn't think he was dead ! " he said afterwards.

But Meldrum was not dead, though his chin was sunk on his chest and his hands hung between his legs with wrists and fingers like the rest of his limbs, stiffly slack as though life had moved out of them not wishing to share existence in the same body with the alien, autonomous life that now glowed in his eyes.

The dashboard clock and dials of the Donizetti, deeply set in imitation polished mahogany, stared up at him like the face of something asleep. As night came on the figures faded until they shone green and fixed like his own eyes. He switched on and things quivered as though suddenly alive.

He drove off slowly down the main Fluach-Inverurie road; there he turned home and began to speed.

The engine of the Donizetti made a rough noise at anything under eighty miles an hour. After that it moved towards peace, achieving it at a hundred and ten and only beginning to pine at a hundred and thirty. At a hundred and twenty its noise was no noise at all, but a sort of music in which every part of the car achieved its fullest and yet most individually harmonious expression. Then it was a harp touched perpetually on its sweetest note. At night wayside objects seemed to divide mysteriously before it like flak coming up at an aeroplane.

The Lifeline

Objects lit by the main beams seemed momentarily to freeze—road signs, human beings, cattle even, other cars were for ever being caught in a fleeting "still"—before rushing forward and vanishing for ever. An illusion grew that this was not a question of solids, but an idea passing through ideas. The purr was feathery, as quiet almost as thought, the windstream a whisper of which not the smallest draught penetrated; a pothole on the road was a velvet nudge at the base of the spine. As the purr entered the head there sprouted a curious sensation of omnipotence and the feeling that to turn the wheel to right or left would be to cleave a smooth lane at a hundred and twenty miles an hour through fence, fields, buildings, always without shock. No limit to power. This treacherous fairy-tale was somehow encouraged rather than corrected by a sudden inkling of the true consequences of such a course. A thrill started to live in the stomach and while it lasted, seemed capable of belittling troubles—perhaps troubles at home, in the business, in the digestion, or perhaps all troubles, even the deepest, most ineradicable griefs—the grief of ever having been born at all, of life unassuaged by the smallest spiritual comfort.

The music that Meldrum at last found was the high quiet song of an engine going 120 m.p.h. Then it existed for him as a person—the personification of the environment. He was face to face at last, not with the "music-practising Socrates," but with the music-aping machine. Then, alone and unwatched he made the gesture of the last hero: he destroyed the environment by depriving it of his ever more feeble co-operation . . . let his hands fall from the wheel, succumbed like a sleep-walker to the smallest whim imaginable, but the only whim, of any kind, that was left.

50

THE GIRL from the Islands who called Traquhair on the morning of the games went three times to his room—at eight, nine and nine-thirty. On the first occasion the sound of the curtains being drawn elicited a mumbled inquiry as to whether Meldrum were back. No, said the girl, and Mrs. Meldrum had been on to the police. By nine o'clock Traquhair still had not come down. The girl went up again to tell him he was "on the News," but he said nothing and when she came down she told the throng in the kitchen he hadn't moved, but was lying just where she had first found him like a washed-up whale waiting for the gulls. They told her that if Helen had been here she would have made Mr. Traquhair get up sharp, if he was to go to the games as Chief; so the Island girl went and reminded him of the date and the Prime Minister under his roof. But all she got was a groan and something that sounded like, " Reoraidgh. Reoraidgh ! "

She said it was right, wasn't it, that he was due to open the games at eleven ? Still no answer.

At a quarter past ten he gave the girl a fright because she went into his room to take the breakfast back for reheating and had gone through the door with scarcely a knock only to see him a yard away standing up, dressed in full Highland regalia, talking to himself and looking like nothing on earth.

" Is Meldrum back ? "

" No, sir, but his bird is."

" His bird ! What d'you expect me to say ? What about my car ? Please get a taxi from Inverurie—the biggest and the best. Say it's for the Prime Minister."

The Lifeline

He turned from her. He felt ten years older since midnight. He had been swimming against a current with Meldrum round his neck; had been rescuing or trying to drown him—did not know which. All he knew was that he had struggled and suddenly found himself free. But his new freedom had resulted in a curious nightmare of impotence: the water ceased to respond to his strokes, it gave no resistance, had in fact become air. He made vigorous efforts but did not move. Later he felt Meldrum to be somewhere vaguely above him, forcing him down farther away from where he could get a grip. He looked up and saw the man's face and deep-set eyes. The face would have seemed mad had it not been characterised by one last lucidity—a desire for vengeance. But he was almost awake by then and soon had a vivid picture of Reoraidgh writing to the police; and then of the man lying dead.

The door of the shed which he could see from his window was still swinging and banging in the wind. By now all the Meldrum children must have made a visit or two to the distillery " leak " and soon all Fluach would know if it didn't already. Gone now was yesterday's optimism and brief euphoria. He would be arrested. Given sufficient audience and prominence he would behave well—a little snuff, a gesture or two, a kindly word with the chaplain about prison and the purely relative nature of all morality and he would accept the rope like a . . .

Like a . . .?

He suddenly whistled a bar or two. There was time yet. Chief Constable Scroll, O.B.E., would let him go through with the opening and let the Prime Minister get well away, back to Canada, before sending a couple of plain-clothes men to pick him up one cold morning in a week's time. He could picture the face of the preposterous MacFarlane hearing the news; Spote's shoulder going up like the back of a frightened cat when he read it in the paper; Henry Wotherspoon's worldly smile and sudden high laugh like a child from upstairs before he said: " Jolly bad luck," and he imagined the joy of Chief Constable Scroll whose sins of omission in Strathireshire had

The Lifeline

helped his O.B.E., like soap suits the nozzle of a rectal pump. Only Meldrum's face came before him sadly (like that of Judas, he thought).

Brixton would be bare. Even so, he might have enjoyed this last day. If—if what? Without Meldrum, impossible Meldrum, all savour had gone. So, too, had his car. " Fool that you are, Reoraidgh," he said, fiddling with the other cuff. " You sponge on me like a louse on a sow's teat, but muck in till the day comes when there's a need for me. Then you sell me to Scroll, O.B.E., the hair-cream rozzer with a crown and star, a Jaguar and a blind eye for the maiming of deer with machine-guns by spotlight, assault and cruelty to children, but the nose of a bloodhound for parking wrong in deserted Main Street. Without the lifebelt of a little light company you would have gone mad months ago yet you puncture the last float you had. *Vive* Creevie ! "

At this moment the telephone beside the stuffed peregrine rang and Traquhair said : " Hallo . . ."

" Mr. Creevie on the line, sir. He says it's urgent. Will you speak with him ? "

" Talk of the devil ! Plug him in. Creevie ? . . . A strange moment——"

" That's just it, Mr. Traquhair ! "

The voice of his half-brother was again strikingly pleasant. Indeed, it was almost fulsome as though quite unknown to Traquhair they had been getting to know and like each other better and better ever since their last meeting at the Unionist fête.

" I thought you'd like to know I've found your barman—and your car."

" My barman ? " said Traquhair, sitting down weakly. " And my car . . . you mean Meldrum ? . . ."

" Yes. He's all right, quite all right. A miracle. He ought to be dead by rights."

" Possibly," said Traquhair. Tears pricked his eyes and he closed them. " What happened to him ? "

" Happened ! I'm afraid you'll have to write your car off.

The Lifeline

I never saw such a mess." Creevie's voice crowed with exultant squeamishness. " Really, I don't know how the man's alive. D'you want to speak to him ? He's just beside me."

" Wait ! " said Traquhair instantly. " There's no hurry ..." But curiosity got the better of him. " How did he accept survival ? "

" I beg your pardon ? "

" How was he when you found him ? "

" Sitting by the wreck with his head in his hands." (" Disappointment," interposed Traquhair.) ". . . What ? . . . In a rubbish dump. Went clean over a bank, and somersaulted twenty yards. A tinker found him and came on to the road to stop me. I went down and there he was amongst a lot of empty tins and bottomless buckets. . . . What ? "

" I didn't speak. Did he say anything ? "

" No."

Reoraidgh alive, Creevie friendly, and a Prime Minister under his roof ! How happy he might have been in other circumstances.

" Well, thank you," he said, at last. " Thank you."

" By the way," came Creevie's voice, breathier than ever. " I was wondering, could I give you a lift to the games ? "

" Why not ? " said Traquhair after a moment's silence.

" Or will you be travelling with Mr. Hilldersley ? "

" He's going later."

" Then we'll come and fetch you."

" We—— ? "

" Your barman wishes to come too . . ." Traquhair heard a sibilant aside and an affirmative grunt. " Yes, that's right. We'll come straight away."

When Traquhair told Olivia, she said : " Oh, thank God ! I thought he was dead." After staring at a spot in the table she began to weep, interrupting herself to say : " His bird is back."

Traquhair opened his hands helplessly as though words failed him. At last he said : " Good ! "

" I'll give up working in here," she blurted out.

The Lifeline

"Yes, yes," said Traquhair wearily. He never believed a word she said. "We'll all turn over a new leaf. Reoraidgh, our loyal friend and exemplar, is come back. . . . We must be ready to sacrifice the whole world to make him smile. We must be conscientious." His tone surpassed sarcasm. "We must learn to feel." He began to move away, then he stopped. "He wishes to come to the games. Will you bring the children later or will you watch it at home?"

"We'll come later."

"Order a taxi then for yourself," he said. "Reoraidgh, Brother Creevie and I will have to leave almost at once."

She muttered an affirmative. Her head was in her hands and she was staring into space as though someone was telling her fortune.

51

BRIAN CREEVIE brought Meldrum round to the Strathire Arms at once. On arrival he immediately revelled in further description of what had happened, while Meldrum stood about uneasily suffering Olivia's dramatic embrace and his employer's handshake. Conversation was not easy. Those subjects which lay nearest to everyone's thoughts, including the man's very survival, were clearly taboo. For it was not clear whether he had attempted suicide or merely the destruction of Traquhair's property. Everyone tried to please everyone else and to go out of his or her way not to question even the flimsiest façade. Normally Meldrum's wish to go to the games might have drawn an amazed speech from Traquhair on the subject of his secretary's ceaseless search for frivolous adventure. But now the decision was accepted without comment.

Traquhair broke off to "attend to Hilderkin"—as he had christened him. He went upstairs to the Prime Minister's private sitting-room and there briefed him on the day's activities. Then he came down and waited with a good grace while Meldrum changed out of his torn dusty clothes, visited his bird and children and in general prepared for another day, however far it might fall short of his exacting standards.

Traquhair had thought it best that Reoraidgh should discover the return of his bird for himself—or from Olivia. Such news, from his own lips, on the doorstep, however humbly phrased could never have escaped the suspicion of irony, if not outright mockery, resurrected as the creature was, so to speak, phœnix-like from the smouldering carcass of his own four-

The Lifeline

thousand-pound car—from skid marks, no doubt of solid burnt rubber, which should have led as surely to Meldrum's grave as a flowered hearse.

So Meldrum, hero and homecomer, went off with Olivia followed by the eyes of the Jamaican, the girl from the Islands and the German medical student, in fact surrounded, Traquhair noticed, by respectful silence. Yes! The return of the hero. Numbed as he was by recent events, Traquhair still experienced a pang of virgin astonishment at his secretary's capacity to involve his wife in a Poor-Rory at a moment when so much else was in the air. For by now, knowing Fluach, he was sure that the tunnel to the distillery had become common knowledge, likewise his blood relationship to Brian Creevie with whom he now found himself alone in front of Reception.

"I think the sun might come through later," Traquhair said with a knowing look at the clouds.

Creevie glanced up but failed to make contact with the weather. He was so pleased, he said candidly, to have been some use.

What was this friendliness? It seemed to have something to do with Meldrum, for he went on and on in his agitated breathy voice saying how ("I can tell *you*, Mr. Traquhair"), he hadn't given tuppence for Meldrum's chances when he saw the Donizetti; and then how pleased he had been to see the man alive, how in the past months he had come to meet the man here and there and found him "an unusual sort of person but not what people might think." (Traquhair had not the energy to inquire what people might have thought), and now he had come to like him. "Frankly, Mr. Traquhair, I've often dreamed of your barman."

Traquhair's little eyes slipped up fast sideways.

He had never wanted to have anything in common with Brian Creevie and now within twenty-four hours he found they shared dreams and a father. Words failed him; he groped for some adequate courtesy but ended in opening his mouth—shutting it, and sniffing, all with averted eyes. Perhaps he could have managed if Creevie's voice hadn't sung with a sort of

The Lifeline

glee that was both fawning and critical at the same time. He suddenly considered telling him they had a common father.

"Thank you, thank you. . . . How can I thank you?" Traquhair murmured. "Reoraidgh means a lot to me . . . this way and that. I thought we had lost him. Hum ! . . . And you like him too. . . . We have more in common then, Mr. Creevie, than either of us might suppose. . . . And we do ! "

These few introductory words designed to switch the conversation into other channels had the opposite effect for they acted as fuel to the flames of Creevie's friendliness. " For heaven's sake," Brian interrupted so brusquely as to elevate one of Traquhair's eyebrows. " And do call me Brian. I—I— I'd have offered my car earlier if I'd known how you were stuck." He went on to explain that during the last months he would have been glad to have given Traquhair any assistance he could with his hotel in the way of advice. People thought you could start up a hotel just like that, without ever having done it before, but he was sure Traquhair would now agree this was not the case. Even a bar trade wasn't all that straightforward. How many people outside had any idea that hotels could still only get whisky on a quota system ? . . . (Brian's hands were both extended putting the problem, asserting the intolerable strains on a hotelier's morality); and in the same breath he said : " For goodness' sake there's room for all three of us in front " (of the Bristol), for at this moment Meldrum had appeared, walking slowly towards them with lowered eyes.

Again Traquhair was in two minds whether to mention the bird. But in the end he said nothing.

Creevie persisted in claiming how easily they could all, despite their sizes and shapes, fit harmoniously in the front seat of the Bristol. But he was wrong. Only with the greatest difficulty could they implement his well-meaning idea. Traquhair, confronted with this simple practical exercise in adjustment, became clumsy and slow as a winter fly. The imminence of arrest shone bleakly in his little eyes and gave him the air of a child in disgrace. It seemed sad, even morally

The Lifeline

wrong that one so talkative should have so little to say for himself, and once as though conscious of his responsibilities as *homo sapiens*, in the presence of Creevie and Meldrum, he absolved himself from answering some question with a muttered, " I'm sorry. What ? " meaning all that had happened in the last forty-eight hours.

Like dough he swelled at the base when seated and obliged Meldrum to sit a little forward. Even so, the two men were in contact throughout the length of their bodies.

Scarcely a word had passed between them. Getting in, Traquhair had squeezed his secretary's arm. After that they had even avoided looking at each other. Creevie, on the other hand, was garrulous. The extreme friendliness which he had shown on the telephone had increased and now they were in his car he fairly sang at them. It was as though he were saying, " People say I wanted your hotel and couldn't bear the sight of you. But look at this : quite apart from the thing I did for you which you don't yet know about, I rescue your barman and take you to the games in my car. Without me you wouldn't have got there at all. It's true I'm a man who likes facts and haven't got much time for the Church and dressing up, and that sort of thing, but frankly—I can't explain why—I'm pleased to be doing this."

Traquhair did not like this pleasure of Creevie's, but he was glad of the way he ran on, describing the state of the smashed-up Donizetti and how miraculous it was that Meldrum had lived to tell the tale. For when Creevie ran out of information and opinions, the silence was immediately oppressive.

Traquhair could not bear it and soon mumbled : " Who would have supposed we would all have gone to the games together ! "

These words were as near as he could get to bracketing the countless confused feelings in his breast. He felt it signified a measure of acceptance, which was about all that could be expected of him in present circumstances.

" You know, Mr. Traquhair," Creevie burst out, " although we've only met once or twice I've often thought about you."

The Lifeline

The possibility that any answer whatever might encourage Creevie to say *what* he had thought, froze Traquhair's vision far ahead down the road and locked his lips. Meldrum, too, was pointedly silent.

" I have, you know," sang Creevie.

Traquhair bowed vestigially in the direction of his stepbrother. " Sir," he said. " Blood is thicker than water."

" What's that ? "

Traquhair paused before replying crisply : " Nothing."

They drove on.

Creevie was Creevie and that was that. Meldrum's silence began to gnaw at Traquhair's nerves. Tact and reticence was all very well. But why had the man opted for the games after such an experience, and why, having come, did he say not a single word about the car even though he, Traquhair, had squeezed his arm expressively, celebrating his survival. Apologies can be veiled between people of sensitivity. Why hadn't Meldrum at least squeezed his, Traquhair's arm in return or, say, looked at him, just once, not only in regret for the car but also . . . for other things. (For by now Traquhair was sure that even if Meldrum had not actually informed the police he must still have been responsible for Misty MacDonald learning of the leak via Helen.)

After a mile of silence, Traquhair said encouragingly : " I'm glad your bird was found, Reoraidgh. I'm glad."

A hundred yards of hedgerow passed—hawthorn, cow parsley, buttercups and grass.

Then as though answering, Meldrum said : " It's going to be O.K. about the police, isn't it ? "

After a few moments' bewilderment Traquhair said : " The police—— ? "

Creevie said brightly : " Yes, I'm sure it is," and half-smiled as though he knew exactly what Meldrum meant, as though in fact he and Meldrum had been having "a good talk" about the tunnel and everything else, too, over breakfast. Yet, now in the ensuing silence neither of the two men made any attempt to elucidate their meaning.

The Lifeline

"Well, Reoraidgh," said Traquhair at last, "*what* about the police?"

The old sinking feeling had returned.

Meldrum did not reply but Creevie's smile increased and sure enough he finally could not restrain himself. "I don't know anything—not a thing about it," he said, making a sweeping motion crosswise with his hand but almost laughing as he spoke. "All I can say is that I heard the most ludicrous rumours going the rounds and therefore some time ago I did what I've never done before, Mr. Traquhair—I wrote an anonymous letter. Yes, I did. I wrote an anonymous letter *to you*. Laugh. Go on. I'll tell you why. Because I received one myself about you. Well, I thought: at least he's got the right to know what people are saying. . . ." (Creevie paused. He needed to—for everyone's sake.) "Even now I wouldn't mention it if I hadn't heard just the last word in the whole fairytale—that the police went to your backyard and began looking for a tunnel. Oh, yes, they did thank you very much, had the floor up and found one leading nowhere—six feet— and now everyone is saying there was an explosion the night before last which was a certain person, a man in a certain position, thank you very much, blowing the tunnel in. You can't *beat* Fluach for fairytales. I'm telling you, and I know." (He was almost dancing in his seat.) "People here would believe *anything*. The taller the story the better." (Traquhair looked at him warily.) "The only reason why I wrote to you, Mr. Traquhair, was to let you know what *somebody* was saying and what somebody had almost certainly told the police— quite enough to bring them nosing round which I'm sure you wouldn't want any more than I would. An Englishman's home is his business, I say. Well, they did come, didn't they?"

"Yes," said Traquhair.

"There! What did I say?"

All three men stared hard down the road in front as the Bristol purred lazily towards the games. Creevie's elbow was resting outside the door in a confident leisurely fashion.

The Lifeline

There was silence for half a mile while Creevie smiled all the way.

Then Traquhair said in a faint unrecognisable voice: " These rumours . . . about the police finding nothing at the distillery and . . . at our place, and the blowing up of the tunnel. . . . I did hear an explosion Tuesday night. . . . What about them, Mr. Creevie. Facts, hard facts ? Or Fluach fantasy ? "

" Well, frankly your guess is as good as mine, Mr. Traquhair. I never heard an explosion Tuesday night."

" Did you ? " said Traquhair, looking uneasily at his secretary. " Olivia said it was what finally . . . browned your bird off. . . ."

" Yes," said Meldrum. " I heard an explosion."

" Would it "—Traquhair could hardly bring the words out —" be true about someone blowing up some . . . tunnel ? "

Creevie's delicate smile increased. He began to go even slower. " Mr. Traquhair. Look at it this way. The Amenities Committee has a certain responsibility to-day. What with all these bank rate inquiries, and what not, people's faith in established authority and morality is a bit leaky at the seams. No one wants a further deterioration. We've all got a certain responsibility. Personally, if I may give my opinion, I think you can forget about the whole thing. I like facts as you know, and I am drawing my conclusions from facts." Having delivered himself of these words with many gestures and a good deal of vehemence he followed them up with a statement which, spoken as he spoke it, sounded like the explanation of all that had gone before. " You know," he said. " Things are pretty dead really. I mean, you could get sympathy for anything, provided it took people out of themselves. . . . Going all the way to London on your hands and knees. I mean almost anything."

But Traquhair had not heard this surprising opinion from Fluach's great optimist and amateur stockbroker. He was lost in the man's previous words—about the destruction of the tunnel. Something inside him seemed to be inflating with oxygen, hope, life—imagination. Wings were spreading.

The Lifeline

There was a disturbance in his beard in the neighbourhood of his mouth. "*Heugh heugh*," he said, like two muffled noises from a cellar. " Lovely grub ! " His tone was meditative.

" You know, Mr. Traquhair, I think you and I have quite a lot in common."

" You mean Father."

" Farther than what ? "

" Our father."

" No," said Creevie, smiling. " There I'm afraid we must agree to differ. It's twenty years since I went inside a church and I'm not going back on it."

" I meant a personal father."

" What about a personal father ? "

" In common—you and me."

" Well, really. You're beginning to qualify as a native. That's the best yet. If you and I are stepbrothers, I'm a Dutchman."

" My dear van der Creevie. Devotees of 'fact' should above all be open-minded. I find they so seldom are. Almost always they are merely devotees of their own particular highly exclusive pattern of facts. You are my step-brother. Our father was Ian Creevie, my mother—still is—Mrs. Betsy McCann née Heidi Gruber. Take it or leave it."

Colour had slowly ebbed from Creevie's face while Traquhair was speaking. For it was as though the picture in the hall at the Bishop's Palace had suddenly stepped from its frame and sat down beside him, as though the old drunk outside the beer tent at the Cullan Games had at last put an arm round his shoulders (where Traquhair's arm now lay having nowhere else to lie).

" Well, really. . . . *How do you know ?* " Creevie said faintly.

" My mother—Mrs. McCann " (he dotted this i uneasily) " told me last night. I gather our father illustrated his feelings by performing in public on a nag with a pistol. Having begot me he died as men will after their crowning achievement."

The flags of the games came in sight, but the car was hardly moving because Creevie had suddenly launched into a long

The Lifeline

breathy monologue full of explanations of why there was room for doubt. " Good heavens, I'm not one of your old stick in the muds. I *do* like facts, Mr. Traquhair, and if the facts concern something my father did on a dark night fifty years ago " (Traquhair raised an eyebrow) " then that doesn't worry me ; I accept it. But, honestly, you know, I don't think anyone looking at you and me side by side would believe it. Of course I've never met your mother, I don't know what she looks like, but I imagine ' she's bigger than a kettle ' as they say in Fluach—which Mrs. McCann isn't."

" Well, that only goes to show," said Traquhair.

" What ? " said Creevie.

" How surprising facts can be. For instance, that my mother should be about the same size as yours, if I may be personal ! Anyhow, what about our big father and you ? "

Creevie's tongue seized up as though facts had gone off like Gadarene swine.

" Time marches on," Traquhair said politely, looking at the speedometer. " I have scheduled duties. . . ."

The Bristol picked up a little speed. Brian still said nothing.

" What a lot of surprises," said Traquhair after a moment. " We have all had some shocks. In the past months we haven't seen much of each other, but I see that we have been in touch if only enough to emphasise the dimensions of our increasing disassociation. It was Reoraidgh here who brought us together this happy morn—poor Reoraidgh who went away looking like Judas Iscariot. . . . Hm ? . . . No doubt the spectacle of his smashed car impressed you, Creevie. A pulp of strawberry jam and chunks of whitish stuff like sodden bread might so easily have greeted your eyes when you looked into the cab. Instead there he sat like Rodin's ' Penseur ' on an empty bucket. Forgive me. I see it all so clearly. How could you not have been impressed" (Traquhair turned to his secretary), "by his determination on behalf of life . . . eh, Reoraidgh . . . life wasn't that it or was it the other . . . fellow ? . . ."

" Yes, we've all had some surprises," said Creevie.

" All except Reoraidgh," said Traquhair with an increasing

The Lifeline

touch of satire. A sense of well-being was building up inside him. Ever since Creevie's explanation of the explosion he had been imagining Miss Jimpson and The Recogniser working all night with gelignite, pick and shovel to destroy every trace of his tunnel, cleaning it right away as though it had been merely something necessary that had become unnecessary. He looked at his secretary. " Reoraidgh is never surprised," said Traquhair. " Any more than is Bradshaw's guide to the railways. Frightening man ! "

Creevie said : " I should have thought he had the biggest surprise of us all."

Meldrum said : " I had a surprise."

" You did not expect your bird to come back at this juncture? Was that the surprise ? . . ."

Creevie said : " What bird is this ? I heard you mention it before."

" *Heugh heugh!* " said Traquhair. " Answer him, Reoraidgh, but remember he likes facts. My dear Creevie—Brother mine —he had a bird. . . . It's a fact ! "

Traquhair turned while talking towards Meldrum and looked at his face, whereupon he stopped, converted the beginnings of the next word into a flatulence which sounded like penitence. Now his silence was chastened, confused. " God forgive me, Reoraidgh ! Here we are," he said. " We shall never know what Reoraidgh's surprise was. Take it, Creevie, that his bird came back with a branch in its mouth. Or a leaf, Reoraidgh ? Was that it ? A reprieve, at any rate. Continuity is not to be entrusted after all to one mutated parsnip and half an Eskimo in the trough of the Great Atomic Sigh. Perhaps we should sing something together. . . ."

The car had halted by a little table on which a money box was acting as weight to retain its skirt—a poster of the Cullan Games and car entrance fees. A policeman stepped forward. It was Sergeant Murray. Catching sight of Traquhair his rather pedagogic signal to slow down changed instantly to an almost parade ground salute with the flattened fingers against the edge of his diced cap, and a smile.

The Lifeline

He stepped back at the same time shouting to some youths to get out of the way.

"*Heugh heugh* . . ." said Traquhair. His little eyes were shining and he had forgotten everything, everything. . . . Ahead was a swarming crowd.

52

THE ANNUAL SITE for the Cullan Games is scarcely exaggerated by the pictures in the holiday brochures. Granted even reasonable weather the surroundings are a natural vehicle for the literal gaudiness of colour photography. Heather the colour of black currant fool stretches out of sight along the round back of the Silver Rock while the face itself gleams as though dripping with mercury or veined with quartz. The ruins of Pictish *brocks* peer through storm-stunted trees, crooked burns, dramatically brown and white when in spate or blue as a Capri cove in fine weather, tumble down towards a wide view of sea : Loch Cullan, which will soon be graced with the austere, pale beauty of a dam, stretches far back between hills so steep that the loch's unplumbed bottom can be guessed by theoretically producing the slant of the slopes till they meet. Rows of huts, narrow-gauge rail networks for tips : cranes and scarred hill-faces mark the site of the Cullan camp; nearer, on either side of the Cullan burn and on the hills fronting the sea, stand crofts above long narrow fields, like unrolled carpets, of hay, seedy turnips, undernourished potatoes, all reached by bedstead gates where implements have begun to merge with the ground on which they stand.

For travel agents visually at least the country round here has everything to offer. The very dilapidation of the crofts is an asset, and the variety of geological shapes and the desertion must make a strong appeal to those many who are said to want to "get away from it all." Accordingly British Railways, even on Fluach platform three miles away had posters with Bonnie Prince Charlie on them saying simply, " Come to Glen Cullan."

The Lifeline

This advice had been widely reinforced by publicity in the national dailies. Yesterday Mr. Hilldersley was shown standing in the ruined shell of his grand-maternal croft. "Tomorrow," the *Daily Express* had said, " he will watch local lads toss the caber and dance reels at games presided over by Tulloch " Little John " Traquhair, who means to give the games a new look. Others present will include Mrs. Lionel Spote of Rossiemurchat whose Darksward Swanker fetched a record fifty thousand pounds at Perth bullring. The buyer? Her cousin by marriage, multi-millionaire Bran Phillbury of Texas."

This sort of thing must have been the reason why the space round the arena was packed, not only with the usual " tourists " and natives who always use the occasion as a chance to see each other, but also with hundreds of people who had come by charabanc from the caravan suburbs which in August double the population of Nairn and Inverurie, and some of the other coastal towns to the south.

A small space in the canvas grandstand, insulated from the other seats by a silver rope, had as usual been set aside for the chieftain, his distinguished guest, Mr. Hilldersley, the Lord Lieutenant, his deputy and other notables. Near it television cameras had been set up.

At five to eleven the space enclosed by the silver rope was more thickly populated than is usual so early. Brigadier Hobson, the Lord Lieutenant, Lord Seafield, Sir Duncan and Lady Fidge, the director of the Cullan dam; Major Mackay Halpick, in a kilt with an usher's rosette in his lapel making him look rather like one of his own prize bulls, and Margaret Mackay, wife of the contractor, J. S., who would not waste his time sitting there "just for plain gaping at other folks," were all present.

In normal years few or none of these people would have turned up for the opening which is a mere formality enabling a start to be made with the countless heats of Highland dancing, piping, competitions and races. Both the Lord Lieutenant and Spote had tried to find out, on the telephone, whether the Prime

The Lifeline

Minister would be turning up at the start. In vain. Yesterday no straight answer could be got from the Strathire Arms. Spote, who had rung seven times, had been told that Mr. Traquhair was not to be disturbed, a rebuff (to a Deputy Lord Lieutenant at that) which still had some bearing on that conscientious but reluctant official's present warped position and facial expression. For finally all the notables, after consulting each other on the telephone, had decided they had no choice but to turn up *in case* the Prime Minister attended the opening. If he did not, they were well aware they could look forward to three heats of the ten-mile bicycle race round the four hundred yard perimeter of the arena, ninety-six minutes of eleven youths going round and round and round with cheese coloured thighs pumping slowly up and down like something in the window of a watchmaker.

The possibility of having come simply to see this and hear Traquhair make a speech had wrought havoc with Spote's temper. Laura had been obliged to go and sit some way away from him.

Outside the silver rope, but still beneath the long grandstand awning, there was Major Murray from the distillery, Mr. and Mrs. MacFarlane from the bank, Factor Aldwich and his portly wife and far away in a corner Betsy McCann in a brilliant green boa, heavy beads and a sort of velvet Stetson decorated with ostrich plumes and a cairngorm plaque. Her act was not till four o'clock. Beside her Vessuchi, except for the overwide brim of his hat, looked comparatively inconspicuous.

Spote's malaise was increased by his expectation of "some really embarrassing gaffe on the part of Traquhair." Such fears, said Mrs. Spote, were priggish. " Only you," replied Lionel, " could fail to realise what a man like this could let us in for." An hour ago he had learnt from Creevie that Traquhair's barman had escaped death by a miracle in that fantastic car. Personally, he had always thought Traquhair a complete bounder and a snob as well; it spoke much for the tolerance of everyone round about that they had been prepared to receive him in their homes after he had admitted friendship

The Lifeline

with his predecessor Stephenson. Personally, he had felt under no obligations whatsoever to have anything to do with the man and now (there was no smoke without a fire), he was inclined to think he had been right. " Prime Minister or no Prime Minister, I half-regretted coming." If the Prime Minister should in any way suffer embarrassment (Spote said) there were five people solidly to blame—the Amenities Committee, headed, he understood, by Miss Jimpson who taught his children music extremely badly and Major Murray whom he could see out of the corner of his eyes, looking official and casting unctuous glances inside the rope at Fidge, himself, and others. Spote deplored Murray's irresponsibility. For people like his wife who had come *because* of Traquhair—he had no words. (It was shortly after this that Laura had gone away and sat somewhere else.)

Yet Lionel Spote was not alone in resentment of the chieftain. Imagine the thoughts of Mildred Creevie as she scanned the internees of the silver rope through her lorgnette. And Chief Constable Scroll with his choir-boy's complexion and Clark Gable moustache, what was he thinking? Miss Jimpson, on the other hand, wore a perpetual calm smile which might have befitted a model for the angel of the Annunciation. It said simply : Soon He will appear.

Perhaps Major Murray's expression came nearest to being typical of all the faces—it was even very like Spote's, who despite his thoughts, wore a mask of judicious calm, a refusal to be stampeded by old wives' tales ; above all, a proper regard for appearances. Everyone "in any position", thought the Major, "would take the man as he found him" and the rumours for what they were worth. Major Murray's moderation went further. Tunnels ! he thought. People had nothing better to think of. To be frank, the atmosphere was getting very like 1939 just before the balloon went up.

Thin cheering suddenly broke out and a car could be seen bumping across the field. Were the cheers for Hilldersley or Traquhair, both or neither ? . . .

The Lifeline

Mrs. Creevie's lorgnettes dwelt incredulously on her son's Bristol. (She had come by taxi.)

Mr. MacFarlane whispered to his wife who was having her first afternoon out of doors for a year: " Creevie's car ! "

" I know that," she said irritably.

Mr. MacFarlane, hearing of Traquhair's loans from the Inverness branch had recently recommended a further loan of five thousand pounds to the Strathire Arms. Then came this week and the rumours. Naturally, he had refused to consider them. His eyes, set glassily on the Bristol, brimmed over with desperate respect, not only for a Prime Minister of Canada but also for "a Prime Minister's host."

At this moment Mrs. McCann started a clap and was followed by Vessuchi.

Whereupon many others—including Lionel Spote, Major Murray and Mr. MacFarlane—people who for different reasons were all determined the possible shortcomings of the elected chieftain should be covered by a proper and dignified reaction on the part of the Strathireshire community as a whole, at once began clapping too. Naturally, they imagined the hospitable applause must have been begun by the Lord Lieutenant or some other member, so to speak, of themselves. None of them noticed that the first clap had come from Betsy McCann.

Spote looked round nervously but drew comfort from the increasing volume of noise. Brigadier Hobson raised field glasses and examined the approaching car.

The notables clapped and clapped. Spote, prone to negative reactions on occasions like this, sublimated all in prodigious clapping much as though avoiding the whole cat's cradle of his many private dilemmas in a public act of Commonwealth enthusiasm. The methodical and resonant battering of his hollowed palms rang eloquently in the ears of his wife who had returned to her seat beside him.

" It looks like Brian Creevie's car," she said dryly. " Why don't you wait to see who's inside." (His answer was continued clapping for by now the whole crowd round the arena had taken up the applause.) Spote, a martyr to political guilt,

The Lifeline

suffered acutely from a feeling of total alienation from popular taste in everything, from fish and chips to the latest skiffle star. He went on and on clapping—as did Major Murray and Mr. MacFarlane. . . .

The Bristol stopped; its door opened and a dark stranger appeared (presumably a private detective, Spote thought), with a beard and made way—for Traquhair in a red kilt and plaid.

A number of hydro workers who had gathered on the fringe of the arena at once gave a rousing cheer, no doubt associating the distant sight of Traquhair with the redeeming sensations of many happy Saturdays. These beginnings of ovation were soon reinforced. For clearly Mr. Hilldersley would step out, if he had not already done so. There was an impressive, heart-warming uproar.

Few people had a really clear view of what was happening and fewer still were in a position to be sure that neither Creevie nor Meldrum was the Prime Minister. So the applause continued while the three men were moving towards the middle seat of the segregated island of seats where Spote and Brigadier Hobson, the Lord Lieutenant, and some others, all except Spote in kilts, rose to meet them and be introduced.

However, before the trio reached the silver rope, the notables realised that the Prime Minister was not present and some sat down again. But not all. Not Spote.

It was none the less a conspicuous moment for Tulloch Traquhair and a rewarding one for members of the Amenities Committee. Not even the marquess could have looked the part better. When he took his seat even Spote inclined awkwardly towards him in acknowledgment of the smile which the big man bestowed all round.

A few minutes later, brilliant and conspicuous as a dragonfly on a white page, Traquhair mounted the dancing stage in front and opened the games. He spoke without notes, relishing the long, confident pauses of a trained comedian, judging laughs, letting them have space but not too much space. His courtesies to the people of Strathireshire who had done him the honour of appointing him as their representative were not skimped.

The Lifeline

He spoke a little about litter : it being really so simple, he said, to keep a place clean. You keep your houses clean, why not the fields, the woods, the whole world ?

Spote's eyebrows rose in gratified surprise, but only momentarily. He had moved in the very highest circles and had often noticed royalty's frequent obsession with litter and anal jokes. Now he realised he was listening to phrases which sounded like a replica of those he had once heard from the lips of Princess Georgina of Battenberg. His brow clouded in futile surmise? Was it possible that Traquhair had once heard a royal speech ? A sort of participation mystique, you could hardly call it snobbery, he thought, might make such a man as Traquhair grow wings if he met an angel, or speak about litter after meeting royalty.

By this time Traquhair had finished and everyone was again clapping, and several people, not only Spote, felt sure that the postponement of the Prime Minister's appearance had been carefully contrived by the chieftain. For comfort they now had ninety minutes of the first and second heats of the ten-mile bicycle race, first heats of piping and Highland dancing, the competitors being mainly people with English or even foreign names and complete strangers to everyone present.

From inside the silver rope cold eyes rested on Traquhair as he walked back towards his seat. But at least there had been no gaffe—except the substitution of himself for the Prime Minister.

Just as he reached the gateway to the grandstand a man in a check shirt and bow-tie came up to him and said something. Traquhair halted with one massive hand resting paternally on the man's shoulder, his face a picture of open-minded attention to the pleas of no matter who. As he listened a smile of dawning memory illuminated his face. He nodded, at last, with amused condescension, helpless obedience. . . .

53

OUR GAMES are a pretty dull affair these days. The children enjoy the swings and a few shepherds and crofters from remote areas inland quite enjoy the company. It makes a change. But the caber-tossing must rank as the saddest athletic entertainment in the world. How well, how very well we know the faces of the two or three semi-professionals who travel from games to games in vast hand-knitted sweaters which hang loosely from their big bronzed throats to their sporrans. One of them is nearly seventy, but can still hold at least one of his ends up; and another is a giant, not a giant like Traquhair, three-quarters fat, but a lean muscular giant with a genial daft face and tousled hair. He has a croft somewhere near Oban but has become almost professionally Scots and has appeared in a film of Robert the Bruce, without speaking, in America. By now he knows to an inch the moment when the judge in the mackintosh will decide the caber is too long and the first piece must be sawn off. Then he and the other three characters gather round and discuss how much. There is no hurry. There are three heats of the ten-mile bicycle race and the final, to circle round them and round them while they take turns tossing or sawing bits off the caber, or pitching the hammer, all of them achieving about the same results in exactly the same order as they did the year before. When the caber is short enough the giant, who is able to hold it higher off the ground than the others, both for the run up and at the moment of hoisting, manages at last to make it turn turtle after spending a dramatic second on its other end. Few people are ever looking at the right moment and most of these will have seen him do it for

The Lifeline

the last ten years. The applause is desultory and may be drowned by bigger applause for some pale, city youth with thin limbs who, coming up from behind in the bicycle marathon, momentarily takes the lead and enjoys brief prominence before burning himself out as certainly as a match.

The setting up of the television cameras in the centre had already added a glimmer of novelty to this year's caber event, but it was assumed that the same people would go through the same motions as ever and the cameras were there merely to give a background to Mr. Hilldersley's visit to the Highlands. Even when Traquhair went out into the middle with the man who had spoken to him, most people thought he was fulfilling the chieftain's usual roving role of conferring with the judges and various officials, perhaps taking one end of the two-handed saw for the benefit of a photographer from the *Scottish Field*, but in general mainly letting himself be seen.

Possibly Spote and one or two others watched the little group with a sudden twinge of apprehension. But the movement of television cameras in the wake of the chieftain had a reassuring effect. Traquhair was to be photographed as a typical Highland chieftain for a Canadian News film. In the heyday of the advertisement everyone, even people like Spote and the Lord Lieutenant, accepted this calmly, if not with boredom.

Suddenly the loudspeakers crackled; then unmistakably came the voice of Traquhair. "Ladies and gentlemen, the entries for the caber are not closed. May I remind you that the games are an opportunity for local talent. In attempting to compete with the three customary challengers from the south I hope merely to give a lead to the men of Strathire."

Some wolf whistles came from the hydro workers, and one strange cry from the far side, traceable by a few to the throat of Æneas Mackay Skimbo. Miss Jimpson, in the stand, was weeping.

Inside the silver cord several people conferred behind their programmes. Someone who had asked Meldrum told someone who told the Lord Lieutenant that Traquhair did really intend to compete. April Gunter-Sykes who had loudly arrived,

The Lifeline

laughed loud enough to drown the merry-go-round: she had wanted to know in the first place (she shouted) what those extraordinary little people on the Amenities Committee had thought they were up to—making a man "we none of us know anything about" Chieftain of the Games. Spote, who agreed with every word she said, nevertheless frowned as though receiving the dentist's drill. He avoided looking at her. Creevie, who was now sitting next to Spote, only on the other side of the silver rope, said defiantly that he could think of much worse chieftains. Spote whispered he couldn't. In the background an excited voice with a foreign accent had begun gabbling so strangely that everyone turned to see who it could be—the woman in the green boa and velvet Stetson.

Surrounding silence soon made her speech public.

"*Ach mein Gott*, Vessuchi. What is he going to do? Why does he have to show off *all* the time. Go out and tell him to stop and put his coat on. . . ." Aware of a certain interest in what she was saying she lowered her voice only to speak even faster in a mixture of English, German and Italian to the man beside her whose obvious fear both of her and of the thing she wanted him to do finally galvanised him to a reciprocal intensity. Soon their altercation was shrill and bitter and diverted general attention from the bicycles which were now going round for the fiftieth time and from the group in the middle which was still standing round the caber like policemen round an accident.

One old farmer sitting just in front of Mrs. McCann recognised her and could not control his curiosity. He turned. Seeing his close face smiling she suddenly interrupted her onslaught on Vessuchi and pinching her bunched fingers resentfully into her wasted bosom, she hissed at him: "Can I help you, sir?"

"Hallo, Betsy. Ye're just the same, dear!"

A huge sweet smile immediately lit her lined face. "Darling, whoever you are," she said, taking his shoulder and squeezing it, "don't interrupt." She was about to get back to Vessuchi when an idea struck her. "You, sir; perhaps you could help.

The Lifeline

Out there is my son Tvinky. He is going to do something silly. I want to send a message to him."

" *Who* is it you want the message to go to ? *Who*——— ? "

" Tvinky . . . ach." She struck her forehead with her hand. " What is his last name. My memory is water. Tvinky Gruber Garibaldi, Nielson, Tull—Tulloch Traquhair. *Ja, ja,* Tulloch Traquhair—the chieftain. The last time I saw him take his coat off he was six days unconscious. Vessuchi will not listen. . . . *Gut Gott,* look at that ! " The words died strangled in her throat.

Traquhair had raised one end of the caber, put it over his shoulder and was pushing it up into the air by walking along, bent double, towards the other end. When it was all but vertical he was all but in reach of the far end. A strange hush descended for he had reached down with his two hands and knit them under the base. Now he paused, then using his shoulder steepened the pole's position a final few degrees. Another pause—this time judicious, almost eerie for he seemed to be communing with the inanimate object as though asking it to come with him and help. Suddenly he hoisted.

A sigh rose from the crowd.

With the full weight of the pole pressing down through his stomach, carving a road in fact through his flesh which would have enabled him to see his groin direct for the first time in ten years, he began to totter like someone drunk. A tremendous ovation broke out. The leading bicyclist, thinking he was being overtaken again by a shrimp, avid for a moment's glory, stood on his pedals and did a crazy sprint ; a competing piper in midstrathspey, feeling himself singled out, turned puce with effort and his fingers moved at invisible speed on the chanter.

Only Mrs. McCann was unimpressed. She rose to her feet and said loudly : " *Mein Gott,* what a fool."

Mrs. Creevie examined her through lorgnettes.

The other caber tossers, who had hardly earned a cheer at all even though they had up-ended the tree before a yard had been cut off, stood sheepishly by.

Traquhair steadied himself and began to walk precariously

The Lifeline

towards the north. The television cameras came along behind. Mrs. McCann sat down and hid her eyes.

Somehow Traquhair managed to break into a trot, to increase the pole's height a little and at last heave it away. . . . At the same moment he seemed to follow it as though attached for he fell forwards heavily on to his knees.

The pole landed immediately, very close, on its lower end. Traquhair, looking up, let out a deep shout as he stared up at its swaying top. Which way would it go? Forward or back? He decided forward and was under the impression that it had already described a hundred and eighty degrees, as opposed to none at all. He rose and with a great cheer turned with open arms to the crowd who were shouting their heads off. At this moment the pole began to sway back. Warning shouts were lost in the uproar. The next moment he was lying flat on his face, unconscious.

Clowns, after years of training, could not have timed it better. In fact, many were under the impression that it was intentional, that even as chieftain he was prepared to fulfil his role as public entertainer. But Mrs. McCann knew better. She was in tears. The spectacle was all too familiar. It might have been forty-five years ago and Ian Creevie struggling to get both feet up and stand on the saddle. Hopeless people, prey to impracticable exuberance; always wanting to celebrate and play as though merely to be alive was something to boast of, an experience which overshadowed all the other experiences which it included.

Elderly St. John's Ambulance men half-petrified by decades of inactivity, were tottering out across the arena. They spent themselves on levering Traquhair on to the stretcher. Then, finished, they looked round for help. Lucky indeed that four caber tossers should be standing by.

They looked a brave sight coming in with their burden and the television cameras got a film which must have made many Scots in the dominions feel they stemmed from a tough stock. Four multi-coloured giants carrying a fifth. So must have ended Killiecrankie.

The Lifeline

The procession vanished. There was an anxious hush—until the loudspeakers gave out that the chieftain was all right: he had been only mildly concussed. (A wild cry was heard from the far side.) The caber tossing would continue and the crowd were reminded that the chieftain had expressed the hope that others would come forward to see if they could do any better than he.

Then a strange thing happened: people did come forward. At first a few hydro workers who had had a few drinks. And then others, local people.

A buzz gathered in volume. The sound was something like the swarm-noise which came from Traquhair's bar on Saturday nights. A mood of conviviality, a feeling of impersonal celebration and generosity seemed to be freeing the crowd from the inhibitions which till then had kept them moderately bored and powerless spectators, viewers of what had ceased to touch their feelings. Suddenly the caber turned turtle, and immediately from the far side again a shrill raucous cry broke the equality of the general murmur. Miss Jimpson rushing from the stand to get a glimpse of Traquhair's condition from close, had time to identify that distant yell as the heraldic satisfaction of Æneas Mackay Skimbo. Touched as he was on a very harmonic of the past, he must have been giving tongue hopefully for the future too. Old enough to be nothing but a shape of upright earth, he was yet fired by an inkling of that comforting fraction of himself which was also of them all and immortal. His death at that moment can have depressed no one lit as it obviously was by the glamour of a profound consummation. Anyhow, it was only noticed much later.

54

ROUND ABOUT THE SAME MOMENT that Helen MacDonald was delivered of a son, Tulloch Traquhair lay in the bicyclists' dressing-room with his head on folded blazers. A crowd cluttered the door and the ambulance men soon insisted there was a need for air. Miss Jimpson, after being almost forcibly removed, prevailed on the Lord Lieutenant to make a further announcement on the loudspeakers. Only Creevie, Meldrum and Mrs. McCann were allowed to stay with the unconscious chieftain.

" *Voilà!* " said Betsy McCann surveying her son with tears in her eyes.

His collar and tie had been loosened. The St. John's men said he was stunned, but she said he was asleep. He did certainly look as though he were dreaming of cabers bowling over and over like walking-sticks. She pinched his cheeks to prove her point. He winced but showed no signs of waking. The men in blue treated him for shock, and Mrs. McCann herself was heaping blankets on him when the circus manager came into the dressing-room and said she was needed. Almost at the same moment the sound of cheering came through the open door and Vessuchi put his head in to say the Prime Minister had arrived. Mrs. McCann said she would come back, then looking at the great hill of flesh and blankets she said : " *Mein Gott*, what a fool ! Just so lay his father forty years ago, covered with one horse blanket."

Creevie had watched her with keen interest. As soon as she had gone he said to Meldrum : " I didn't like to say anything not having been introduced." Then he went on, became

The Lifeline

garrulous about what Traquhair had told him in the car, and what since then had never left his mind—their common paternity. No wonder he had so often been struck, he said, by the resemblance between Traquhair and the portrait in the downstairs lavatory. Almost the last time he remembered meeting his father had been beside a booth something like this one, on the fringe of the Cullan Games—should he ever forget it ? . . . And now here he was again with a man like that, in a booth like that, at the games : life really was extraordinary.

Yet clearly, for Creevie, this occasion was absolutely different. His cheeks were quite pink, for him, and his lustrous eyes shone with happiness that he normally reserved for "facts," not people. Never before had he ever mentioned that scene with his father to a living soul.

Meldrum did not seem to understand what Creevie was talking about and paid little attention. He just remained near the unconscious figure of his employer as though kept there by some tenacious and mysterious obligation. Undiscouraged, Creevie, walking up and down behind his back, went on : "Good lord, what am I saying, I've really only known you ten minutes. And to think that when I first met your friend I couldn't stand him. In fact, the way I felt about him quite embarrassed me. I used to think about him, you know, at the strangest moments. Do you think many people do that ? . . . Spend a lot of time thinking about some one person ? It's such a waste of time really, isn't it ? When I got that letter which you say came from you, I don't know . . . I don't know what happened. I suddenly felt sorry for the man, even felt there was some kind of point to him. Of course I'm not blaming you for writing it. I can see how you felt. I'm sure I shouldn't wish to go to prison." (Meldrum frowned.) " Anyone's blind to-day who thinks that honesty and hard work pays. We've arranged things so that it doesn't. A fact. And yet when somebody like Mr. Traquhair comes along we spend a lot of time and energy condemning him. I motored past Leicester gaol the other day and someone had written across that vast brick wall by the main road, ' Come on in and join us.' It

The Lifeline

showed a certain perspicacity really. I see that now. Of course my mother doesn't, never could. To be frank, this whole business has had the most extraordinary effect on her. Do you know what I've been thinking—*that Traquhair reminded her all along of my father*. I wouldn't put it past her to have guessed that he was, in fact, a relation of my father's if not his son. You don't know my mother. Nor did I. Last night I moved to the hotel. I suddenly couldn't stand it another day. I think I'll go to Australia . . . or Canada. I can't face another winter in Fluach. The place is dead. I'm sure you don't want me to disturb you any longer. Is he coming round? It's nothing much, is it? Frankly, I hope you make a success of the hotel. I do . . . I do, really. Good heavens, I'd better be off. I've got no manager, you know, and unless I'm there something always goes wrong. You can't trust anyone. I might not see Mr. Traquhair again for some time. That's how things are: something like this suddenly happens, like an air-raid or a London fog, and everyone comes out of their shell, but the next day things go on outwardly at least just as usual. Yes, I'm thinking of getting a manager and leaving as soon as possible. I need a rest, a complete change. My doctor told me so. I've got a pain here." (He touched his groin.) "I've missed the boat a bit. Still, I can face facts. The day before yesterday I thought I'd started seeing things; in fact, I had—a liver spot in front of my eyes—as big as—well, frankly, a flying saucer, up above the hills, towards Upper Kintullochy. I like facts so I'll call it a liver spot, thank you very much, till I see it seven times more; then I'll write to the *Trumpet*, but not before. I don't drink. You know, you look pretty grey if you don't mind my saying so. If I were you I'd get a doctor to check you over. It's a miracle you're still with us, frankly. Well, good-bye, and give my regards to Mr. Traquhair when he comes round."

Meldrum thanked Creevie for his material assistance and efficiency without which, he said in his low colourless voice, they could not have been where they now were.

Creevie read no *double entendre* into this but with undiminished

The Lifeline

euphoria said good-bye, and took a last almost affectionate look at the big casualty.

As he opened the door a foreign bicyclist came in. Creevie tried to dissuade this entry, but the man said it was the changing room, wasn't it, and he'd been invited and his clothes were inside. He had been double lapped in the ten-mile race, wanted to change and go home. But he came in and sat down on the floor with his head in his hands.

A few minutes after Creevie had gone, Traquhair's eyelids twitched as though struggling against a sticky substance. They opened at last, revealing eyes fixed in visionary peace on the far wall. Then, shifting slightly, they focused on Meldrum—and continued to reflect paradise. Then they moved round a bit, but seemed to have difficulty in taking anything—except paradise—in.

This was not surprising for he seemed to be looking through a microscope or a telescope and all he saw was a pulsating pattern whenever he moved his field of vision. But paradise faded slowly as he became conscious of his head which was apparently grafted on to something infinitely large, throbbing and painful. Now he began to associate the skittish dots and this throbbing extension to his head, just as one might associate a loud band and distant dancers. There was a rhythm common to both.

But where was he? Why was he? Who was he?

Never had these difficult questions seemed so nebulous or more pressing for never had the world offered less in the way of concrete exterior evidence. Round him were no one and no object. Nor was there darkness or light, but a sort of grey emptiness; and except for his extended head, where the band was playing to the dancing dots, there was nothing to look at or listen to. His very limbs seemed subject to that "weightlessness" which was being studied in case it sent space travellers mad.

Was he dead? Or in solitary confinement?

Into this vacuum, thoughts and attempts at memory crept

The Lifeline

with enormous diffidence like tourists without money, friends or passports.

The impact and severity of events, in the last few days, had paved the way, as it were, for brain-washing with a long preliminary soak. He felt he was no one, never had been and never would be anyone. Sounds certainly there were knocking about and echoes of speech for ever prompted disingenuously by feelings, the whole posing as thoughts—these were now the crestfallen travellers who began to creep out like mice in a house full of cats.

Could he move? It seemed as if he did not know how to make a start.

Well, was he dead?

At this moment, haloed by dancing dots, nebulae and nuclei, stars and bacteria, the face of Meldrum swam into definition far above so that for a moment he felt like the captain of a small tug looking, up, through mist, at the Statue of Liberty.

"Reoraidgh?" he said tentatively, uncertain of their relationship in the old let alone the new environment. "Is that you, Reoraidgh?"

He stared questioningly at that familiar face as though seeking many answers. At last he said tentatively: "*Heugh heugh* . . ." for the one feeling that broke through with any confidence was the irony of having 'passed over' only to be confronted by the face of his secretary. How often that face had swum out of the dark, of the living-room, the garage, the backyard at night, the tunnel and disturbed him with presentiments which eluded expression. *Plus ça change.*

"Well . . . where are we?" he said, his voice gaining in strength.

"Where we always were."

"No junket now, Reoraidgh. No point in dying if you go back to Square One. That would be cheap. . . ."

"You're not dead."

Traquhair quizzed his secretary's face in silence.

"So it would appear," he said at last, but with a certain reluctance. Then: "So they got us, did they? Sneaked up

The Lifeline

behind, then blop, with a blackjack. Scroll will get a C.B. for this, I suppose."

"Scroll never touched you."

"Something touched me."

As he spoke a memory of the caber poised for its final fall came back to him. And the whole scene. . . . That was it! Out there . . . they had been throwing the hammer at the same time. One of those gigantic advertisements for Fair Isle knitwear had caught him with the hammer. The mere idea of it made him feel worse. He closed his eyes and felt he mustn't move. His skull must be bonemeal, the sort of thing you gave roses in poor soil.

"Oh, God, Reoraidgh," he said quietly, for he remembered phrases like "he did regain consciousness briefly and was able to recognise his secretary." "Oh, God!"

"You're all right," Meldrum said quietly. "A bit of concussion perhaps. Nothing more."

"All right. Am I?" He pondered this opinion for a moment. The tone it was spoken in compelled him, against his every inclination, to relate his condition to that of others—no doubt to that of Reoraidgh. Reluctantly he returned his gaze to the face of his secretary.

For a few moments neither man said anything, but in that time the events of the last few days seemed to take shape in their eyes.

Then Traquhair looked away. "Uneasy with me, aren't you? Always have been. I suppose you feel the whole thing would have been O.K. if one of us had been a woman. . . . Yes, I suppose there should be a woman sitting there where you are now. . . . It was you that told the police, then, Reoraidgh?"

"I told Creevie."

"Creevie . . . why Creevie?"

Meldrum did not answer.

"Creevie of all people—I don't understand. Not a soul mate of yours, Reoraidgh, surely. Contributing to his store of facts were you? Going over to Creevie and then eloping with the

The Lifeline

machine! Down with me the foul, sham compromise, eh? And at heart all the time the old secret: *Meldrum's Law*."

Meldrum's face remained invisible because his head was hanging. The position made him look whacked as usual.

"You had a narrow shave, Reoraidgh, and nobody else did. Doesn't that make you think?

Meldrum said, "There's no point in going into all that. I don't know why I did it. It wasn't so much a question of minding what was being done right or wrong perhaps—as the talk."

"The talk?" said Traquhair a little nervously.

"Nothing ever felt, nothing . . ."

Traquhair raised one of his large pudgy hands and let it fall again. "I see," he said at last. "But are you quite sure? After all, I had *you*; I kept *you* on. Most people would have sacked you long ago. But we mustn't 'start' as they say. I thought the matter was closed. You came here to-day so I took it that . . ." Tulloch waved a tactful hand. He did not wish to corner his secretary's pride.

"Yes," Meldrum said. "I came with you to-day."

"And . . ." Traquhair again waved his hand, this time towards the door from beyond which now came an extraordinary burst of cheering. "It hasn't gone too badly, has it?"

After a moment Meldrum who did not seem to have heard Traquhair muttered: "I should like to make it up to you. But if you wish, I'll go."

Tulloch sighed theatrically.

"Have I asked you to go? Do you want to go? Isn't it possible, that after . . . all this, you know perfectly well what I mean? Things can't go on as before. In a sense we were all justified, even you and Creevie—in a small, small way. Others had more solid grounds. Hm! All the same, we have been lucky. We do not know who to thank, but it would be wise to do some thanking since the impulse is there. I could even thank a table. (That's where I differ from you and Creevie.) Therefore, I say thank God, Reoraidgh, d'you hear, thank God. . . .

The Lifeline

You weren't snuffed out last night and we aren't in gaol now. So stay. The fact is . . ." Traquhair paused. " I'm ashamed to say I need you. *Heugh heugh.* Poor old Appendix! How can we live with you; how can we live without you. Between these two rapidly colliding questions and the safety of the world stands nothing but Tulloch Traquhair, *homme pas serieux*. But believe me, Reoraidgh," he said his voice rising again, " you need me! Despise me if you like. Think me a Jewish hermaphrodite sow in a kilt, a wandering snob who would push sheep-dropping up Ben Cullan with his nose just to get an invite from Laura Spote ; think of me as a man so bereft of feeling, so frightened of death and reality that he made a contract with you and the distillery, and so obsessed with his own lack of identity that he tried to get behind the label of Camp Coffee when he was five and kept trying till he was forty-five. Think of me as old, drunk, lonely and sad or so unreal as to be past suffering and therefore past pity ; think of me as one who never made much progress in loving others more than himself except in theory ; but don't leave me, Reoraidgh, that I do beg."

Meldrum was about to reply or not reply when a knock came on the door. Traquhair raised himself on an elbow and while wincing from a terrible twinge down his neck, sighted the defeated bicyclist on the floor.

" Who's that ? " he said carefully.

But Meldrum was already at the door—admitting Mr. Hilldersley.

Mr. Hilldersley was such a late addition to the events of the last months and so quickly had his appearance been followed by concussion, that Traquhair stared at him for a moment before taking him in. Then he lay back on his blazers.

Hilldersley approached the bier with the cautious movements which often characterise approach to the seriously ill. Speaking level and low he said : " I certainly am sorry to find you like this, Mr. Traquhair."

Traquhair's powers of speech, which had lately been agile and even accompanied by gesture, seemed to have had a

The Lifeline

relapse. His eyes, too, had lost their animation. He meekly put out a hand which was taken by Mr. Hilldersley.

" How goes it out there," he said slowly.

" Very well indeed."

Traquhair's eyelids came closer together as though he died thankful. Then they opened a bit wider.

" What's happening ? " he said with a glimmer of genuine curiosity.

" There's a great spirit abroad. You gave a fine lead to them. I can tell you, Mr. Traquhair, it's done me good to come back to old Fluach. But now I must be getting along to catch that train." He put forward his other hand to join its mate which was already clasping Traquhair's. He said that when he got back to Canada he would have much to tell people about the Highland personalities he had met, and how the old traditions were still going strong. Finally, after thanking Traquhair for his hospitality he said he looked forward to his visiting Government House.

No suspicion of what he had witnessed in the sky above Upper Kintullochy marred his expressions of gratitude for all he had seen. He even seemed somewhat weaned from his V.I.P. manner, and said he didn't like to leave Traquhair like this. " Are you staying with him, Mr. Meldrum ? "

" Yes," said Meldrum.

" Then I leave you in good hands, Mr. Traquhair."

When the door was shut Traquhair said : " They can't help it. They have to adapt."

Meldrum sat down on a bench against the wall. He was staying.

After a moment Traquhair said peacefully : " How are we getting home ? Creevie ? "

" The ambulance."

There was silence until the defeated bicyclist began to whistle through a cleft tooth.

Suddenly a muffled cheer from the arena reached them through the badly joined planks and under the door.

Hearing it, Traquhair's beard was disturbed by a smile.

The Lifeline

Such a cheer had been the last thing he heard before being struck by the hammer. He could imagine how naturally it had sprung from a thousand throats—at the sight of him trundling across the arena with a thing like the distillery chimney sprouting from his loins, a satyr fit to get the heavens with child, and then the miracle: himself pitching it, without practice, so it went over and over cheerfully till it measured its motionless length on the cold, secret earth.

THE END